HOMEWRECKER

JILL WESTWOOD

This book is a work of fiction. Names, characters and places are either the invention of the author or are used in a fictional context. Any resemblance to actual events or persons, living or dead, are coincidental.

ISBN: 978-1-948516-03-7

Cover design by James at Goonwrite.com

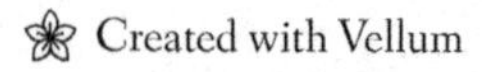

ONE

The repercussions of a drunken hook-up last way longer than the hangover. As I shuttle down a North Carolina highway, images of my bad behavior two nights ago flash through my mind. My chest pressed up against Dan's in the poorly lit hallway of a downtown bar. His stale beer breath, rapid breathing and muttered words of lust. He kept pulling me closer with his married-man hands, his tongue exploring my mouth like he was counting my fillings. How could someone so good at flirting be that bad at kissing? It was like going through a carwash where those rubber mats flap around and water sprays out of jets. Wet and flappy—that is how I'd describe his kisses.

I'm an asshole for thinking about his kissing technique when I should be contemplating how I became someone who would hook up with a married co-worker. Something I thought I would never do, even after four gin and tonics and a shot called a Purple Hooter Shooter. With a name like that, I should have known the evening would end with trouble and regret.

I also should have eaten more for dinner than a few

handfuls of tortilla chips and M&Ms. Several drinks into the evening, I was regaling my co-workers with a hilarious story about my ex-boyfriend who answered his phone during sex. That alone was inappropriate, and then I took it one step further and let Dan grope me in a dark hallway. I might have been drunk, but my thinking sharpened right up when one of our co-workers rounded the corner and spotted us.

The memories of that night combined with the stench of the vanilla air fresher in my rental car threatens to make me vomit. I open my window to let the midday air rush in, and I can almost hear my hair gasp in response to the change in humidity levels. By the time I arrive at the farm, my platinum blond bob will resemble a dandelion gone to seed, but that can't be helped. I am resolved to arrive at the goat farm looking as wild as I feel.

This is what I get for drinking enough to forget that my father has abandoned his life in New York and, in effect, me, as well. He was only supposed to be gone for the summer to visit his new girlfriend on her goat farm. Two days ago, he called to inform me that his plans had changed, and he was now a permanent resident of Joyful Goat Farm in Foster's Creek, North Carolina. He had already called the human resources department of the New York City Public School System to tell them that after thirty-three years as a math teacher, he was retiring. When he delivered this news to me, the only words I could get out of my mouth were, "You told the school system before you told me?"

As I draw closer to my destination, the watery coffee I purchased at a gas station in Virginia isn't the only thing getting cold. The anger raging inside me when I rented this car in Brooklyn is starting to dim now that I have 350 miles of road behind me. Somewhere on the New Jersey Turnpike I began questioning my decision, but it seemed too late to turn around. I would have ended up lost somewhere in Jersey, and there's no worse fate for a New Yorker than that.

My father will be shocked to see me, if he's even there when I arrive. He might be off herding goats or whatever it is you do on a goat farm. What if Renata is the only one there? Arriving on their doorstep at sixteen years old might be acceptable, but at twenty-eight it's borderline hot mess behavior.

My phone rings for the second time since crossing the border from Virginia into North Carolina, and I glance down to check the caller, even though I know who it is. My best friend Hugh. Again. It must be killing him that I'm not answering when there is so much for him to harass me about. He lectured me yesterday when I told him about hooking up with Dan. I ignore his call and turn on the radio, hoping to find some inspirational music that will cement my resolve, but the only two stations I can tune in are playing Bon Jovi's "You Give Love a Bad Name" and Dolly Parton's "Jolene." Even the DJs are throwing shade. I snap it off and grip the wheel tighter. Only twenty minutes before my arrival at Joyful Goat Farm, and yes, the irony of that name is not lost on me.

Of course, I want Dad to be happy. Married-man-make-out session aside, I'm not a monster. But there's a solid amount of evidence suggesting Dad's recent behavior has not been well considered.

1. He only reconnected with his old flame Renata six months ago, and for most of that time, they were dating long distance.

2. He loved his job, and when I say "love," I mean that he actually treasured the mugs that students gave him for Christmas, yet he walked away without even a goodbye

party at the school where he'd taught for the last thirty-three years.

3. Dad is white and Renata is black, and I just passed a pick-up truck flying a Confederate flag the size of a twin bedsheet. Why the hell wouldn't they choose New York City as a place to unite as an interracial couple?

I swing onto an undulating country road flanked by green pastures. There's no going back now. At the very least, I'm in for an awkward evening, and I can always hit the road in the morning. Maybe Dad will be glad I came. I am his only offspring, after all, and he usually thinks everything I do is pretty freaking awesome. If I'm lucky, he already realizes the insanity of his decision to move here and will be grateful for the rescue. I stop short of hoping that Renata has already grown tired of farm life and would be up for living in New York. It would be much easier to get him back to the city if she agreed to come with him.

My phone rings yet again, and this time I'm prepared to answer it and yell at Hugh to stop calling me, but the name that flashes up isn't his. It's a New York number, one that doesn't trigger a name in my contact list, so I send the call to voicemail then play it back.

Hey Andie, it's me, Dan. We need to talk...about the other night. About what happened. Call me okay? But don't leave a message if I don't pick up. Just call me. Soon. Like tonight if you can. Okay? We need to talk. Okay. Bye.

I unconsciously lean harder on the gas pedal, accelerating down this highway to hell. Now that would be an appropriate song. Dan's regular number is definitely in my phone so where is he calling me from? He probably bought a burner so his wife won't find out he's been contacting me. One illicit kiss and suddenly he's Omar from *The Wire*.

Dan and I taught the first session of summer school

together, and the only thing to be grateful for is that I didn't sign up to teach the next two sessions with him. This weekend was supposed to be the start of my summer break chill-out time. Based on the signs I'm passing, I'm trading the David Bowie film series for a Shriner's fish fry.

As I enter the town limits, I cruise by a dilapidated trailer. Alongside it are several cars on blocks, and a sign that says "Thank you, Jesus" in bright colors and comic sans font. Screw the pastoral vibe and the gentle cows. I need more of this poverty and decay to get me in the mood to destroy a burgeoning relationship.

AT THE START of the long dirt driveway, a white sign announces my arrival at Joyful Goat Dairy. My rental car, a two-door Hyundai, keeps bottoming out as it bumps along the ruts in the road, rattling both my teeth and my nerves. Finally, I see the farmhouse ahead. It's a two-story Greek Revival style house with a wraparound porch situated next to the grandest oak tree I've ever seen. It's the kind of tree you find on the pages of old-fashioned children's books. The oak's knobbed trunk is impossibly wide, and its branches provide a canopy for days, perfect for sitting with a book or napping on a blanket. With the sun setting behind the house, I have to admit that this place is loaded with charm.

From all the summers I spent working for my friend LaTonya's catering outfit, I can spot the perfect location for special events. Set up some chairs under that oak tree and a tent nearby, host cocktail hour on the porch at sunset, and you've got the ideal wedding venue. I'm already picturing dining tables with mason jars full of wildflowers and a rustic trellis made of saplings for the ceremony. If Renata plans to use this farm for weddings and other events, Dad hasn't said anything about it. All I've heard about is making goat's milk into cheese, which sounds tasty but not very lucrative.

Four cars are parked in the unpaved, dusty lot: a four-door gray Ford pickup truck, a smaller red pickup with Joyful Goat stenciled on the tailgate, a sleek black Lexus SUV, and Dad's tiny white Honda Fit. I pull in next to the looming gray pickup and notice the U.S. Marines decal on the back window. My father, the man who attended anti-war marches in Washington and wouldn't even allow me to own a Nerf gun as a child, is living in a house with military personnel. No wonder I feel like my world is upside down. I leave my bag in the trunk for now to avoid being classified as a long-term freeloader.

The warble of birds is the only sound in the air, and I have to admit, they do sound joyful. This is a lovely place to live, if you enjoy humidity as thick as a sweat sock and the whiff of what is presumably goat excrement in the air. The minute they hit the ground, my sandals kick up a small cloud of dust that will settle onto my toes. Note to self, lace-up sandals might not be farm footwear. My agricultural experience is limited to a fifth grade field trip to a berry farm on Long Island where I discovered I'm allergic to raspberries.

The porch's gray floorboards need a paint job, but the white rocking chairs are admittedly quaint and welcoming. I gently knock on the screen door and wait. When no one responds, I rap on the door again, louder this time. The sound of pounding feet across hardwood floor grows in volume until a little girl appears on the other side of the door.

"She's here!" she hollers over her shoulder, then swings the door toward her. Her dark hair is braided tightly against her head and finished in purple and white beads that clack together when she moves.

"Hey, I'm Andie," I say, wondering why she seems to be expecting me.

I wouldn't put it past Hugh to send my father a warning text that I was on my way. No one has answered her from inside the house, and we both stand there, listening to the silence. Renata has a six-year-old granddaughter, and I'm guessing this is her. She's pretty adorable, but I'm not great with little kids. Fortunately, she's more socially confident with adults than I am with small children.

"I forgot, they're in the barn." She waves me into the house. "I'll take you there."

"Are you Harmony?"

"Uh huh."

When I don't move fast enough for her liking, she grabs my hand and pulls me along with her. We careen through a sitting room, into a spacious kitchen and outside again into another porch on the back of the house, this one screened. She's small but mighty, this child, and before I know it, she's pulled me out the door leading to the backyard and we're sprinting down the steps.

We nearly collide with what can best be described as a wall of manliness coming up the steps toward us. He moves aside at the last second, and we glide safely past him.

"Watch out, Uncle Seth!" Harmony shouts, as if he's the one moving too quickly for his own good.

From my brief glimpse, I can tell he's a tall white guy, around my age and solidly built. Maybe I'm accustomed to scrawny Brooklyn hipster boys because he seemed Grizzly bear sized. I turn and glance over my shoulder as we scurry along through the grass. Yep. My impression was correct, but not in the "I do CrossFit and eat strictly Paleo" kind of way. He looks like he works outside and builds things with his hands, maybe tosses a ladder over one shoulder and a goat over the other as he goes about his day. Plus, he has a pair of seriously intense brown eyes. I know this because he's turned to get another look at me. Or us. He could be checking me out in an admiring way or making sure the loony woman with dandelion hair isn't kidnapping his niece. His expression is impossible to read.

I try to remember who Seth is in Renata's family. She has two sons, Michael and Trey. Seth is a family friend that she and her husband James adopted at some point, but I can't remember the exact situation. There's no time to consider it now. If I continue looking back at him, I'll take a dive on a stone or gopher hole and bust my ass.

"Barn is this way," she says. "You can meet my baby goat. I named her Tiana, like the princess. When she was born, she wasn't pretty, but then she got hair, and she's much cuter now."

She's preternaturally strong for someone her size and quite the chatterbox. I'm not sure who she thinks I am, but she's on her goat monologue now, and it seems rude to stop her. I learn about Tiana's eating habits, daily routine and family of origin. If I ever need to raise a goat, I'll probably be able to do it based on the education I've received from this kid.

The barn needs work, its red paint faded and peeled away from years of weather. The large front doors are open wide, and my stomach tightens, wondering what Dad will say when he sees me. It was foolish not to call him and say that I was on my way here. What did I hope to accomplish with a surprise attack?

Right up front, I need to say that Renata is a fine person, and under different circumstances, I would have no problem with her dating my father. She's actually the kind of woman I'd want him to meet: a former nurse, intelligent and kind, who had a good marriage to her first husband (now deceased). And let's be real, he's not going to attract a gold digger with his teacher pension. What I do have a problem with is him jettisoning his whole life to be with her down here in middle-of-nowhere North Cackalacky. If she'd relocated to New York, I still would have been concerned about the fast pace of their romance, but I could have embraced it.

Hay crunches softly under our feet as we enter the barn, and my eyes adjust to the change from bright sunshine to dim overhead lights. The ripe scent of goats is so strong now that I can almost taste it. I wish I could say it isn't an unpleasant smell, but it is. Very. I don't think I've ever used the word fetid before, but this situation calls it to mind. Stalls made of metal line one side of the barn, and Dad and Renata are inside one of them, crouched down next to a goat.

"Grandma, the cheese lady is here!" Harmony calls out.

Although I love cheese and consider it a food group, I'm not thrilled about this new identity. Cheese is too closely associated with stink and cellulite to feel like "cheese lady" is a compliment.

Dad and Renata both look over at us and gape when they see who's actually walking toward them. My heart lurches, and I don't know if it's because I haven't seen Dad in a month or if I'm seeing him in the context of his new life for the first time. Shit is getting real.

"Hey, hey!" he calls out to me, rising to his feet. "What are you doing here?"

He walks out of the stall and pulls me into a giant hug, while Harmony looks on in confusion, wondering why

Cheese Lady is getting such a warm welcome. I let him hold me for a long minute, his bushy mustache tickling my cheek as he pulls away.

"Apparently, I'm here to make cheese," I say.

Renata approaches, and I can tell she's wondering if I'm open to a hug from her. A handshake feels weirdly formal, but I'm only a hugger with people I know really well, so I give her a quick squeeze with a back pat and leave it at that. She's got a fit body for a woman her age and skin that practically glows even though she doesn't wear any makeup that I can detect. She's the opposite of my mother who's always trying desperately to look younger by plumping herself up with fillers and Botox.

After our initial greetings, everyone looks at me expectantly, waiting to hear why I'm here, which makes sense. No one travels 350 miles just to enjoy a glass of iced tea on the porch. I've already practiced what I'm going to say, which is why it comes out sounding robotic and rehearsed.

"I had some free time after summer school ended, and I thought it would be fun to surprise you."

"Wow," Dad says, looking over at Renata, then back at me. "Well, we're thrilled you did."

Renata and Dad explain who I am to Harmony, and I give her my best kid-friendly smile. She insists on introducing me to the goats, whose bleating I interpret as an enthusiastic welcome. Tiana, a fawn colored alpine goat, is cute, as promised. Harmony gives me some pellets to feed her by hand, and although I'm a little wary that Tiana might bite me, it turns out goats don't have upper front teeth. Her ears are like velvet, and she wants to cuddle on my lap, which I allow, until Harmony wants her back. She asks Renata for a brush and begins to groom her pet with a tenderness that seems surprising for someone her age.

"Did you drive down here?" Renata asks when I'm finished meeting the herd.

"Yes, I did." My back crackles when I stretch my arms in the air. "It took about ten hours, but I stopped a few times."

"We've got to hang out here in the barn until Lois gets here," Dad says, referring to the actual cheese lady.

"And Moana has an infection." Renata gestures to the goat they were tending to when I arrived. "We need to give her a hoof bath."

My city brain conjures up an image of a goat in a manicurist's chair, hooves soaking in water while she reads a magazine and sips Prosecco. Probably not accurate.

"Not a problem. I'm kind of tired anyway."

Renata looks down at Harmony. "Can you show Andie to the blue room, sweetie."

"We'll get you when it's time for dinner," Dad says. "Harmony, and Renata's sons Michael and Seth are joining us tonight so it's perfect that you're here."

We. The word is a knife. He means his new family, a group that doesn't include me. Dad and I have been a two-person unit since I was in middle school. Now I've suddenly been replaced by a new cast of characters, and Dad's teaching career has been exchanged for infected goat hooves and cheesemaking.

WHEN WE GET BACK to the house, I grab my bag from the car and Harmony leads me to the "blue bedroom." I expect everything inside the room to be blue, like some weird Alice in Wonderland meets Avatar design. I'm almost disappointed to find out that the walls are painted a soft white, and the color blue is mostly relegated to accessories, like toile curtains, blue and white ginger jars and seascape paintings. The four-poster bed has a white quilt that looks handmade and is high enough off the floor that there's a step stool with a needlepoint cover sitting next to it. From the window there's a bucolic view of the back field with the goat barn in the distance. It's the kind of room you'd get at a bed and breakfast, another business they could easily start here.

I'm grateful when Harmony goes back downstairs because I've been up since five this morning and crammed into a compact car all day long. The beginning of a headache is creeping up my neck, and the bed is calling me for a nap, but I can't seem to close my eyes without seeing images of my hook-up with Dan. Huge mistake. My biggest ever. And there's nothing I can do that will truly make it right.

In hindsight, we were on a collision course for the better part of a school year. He was already a member of the Howard Worley English department when I started working there six years ago, and I always thought he was funny and good looking, in a sleep-deprived young father kind of way. This past fall, he moved into the classroom next to mine, and we started eating lunch together during our shared planning period. At the time, I didn't think our behavior was inappropriate because I never considered screwing him, but looking back on it I wouldn't be happy if my husband got a beer with his female colleague every Friday at four o'clock. What seemed harmless at the time now felt thoughtless and shameful because it led to that fateful moment at the bar.

Ronnie had to be the one who caught us. The others might have woken up in a puddle of drool the next morning, wearing their pajamas inside out, and doubted what they'd seen, but not Ronnie. He was fairly sober and, according to his pinched expression, completely disgusted with us. Hell, I was disgusted with us, too. I motored out of that bar like my reputation was on fire. The cab ride home was a blur of nausea and humiliation as the cabbie navigated through stop-and-go traffic. I kept hoping I was having a nightmare, but no, I wasn't that lucky.

My phone chimes to signal an incoming text, and I dig through my purse to find it. Shit. My department chair Barb.

Dear Andie, How are you? Please call me when you are free. I need to discuss some work matters with you. Thank you, Barb.

Barb is sixty-two and composes text messages like she's writing them with a quill pen. My stomach cramps when I think about what work matters Barb wants to discuss. I doubt it's the new curriculum. Ronnie probably blabbed and word got 'round to Barb that two of her underlings were screwing around. Is hooking up with a married co-worker a fireable offense or would they just strongly suggest one of us transfer to another school?

There's no way we can work next door to each other anymore. If one of us gets moved to a windowless room in the school's dank basement, it will definitely be me. Our principal strictly enforces the dress code on female students because, in his words, "It's unfair to expect male teachers to remain professional when they're looking at girls in revealing clothing." As if grown men have no control over what their dicks might do. I'll be crucified for kissing a married man, and I hate Dan for it.

I need to talk to someone about the Barb situation, and obviously I can't call Dan. That leaves Hugh to pick up the pieces of my shattered psyche. Again.

"Hey, homewrecker," Hugh says.

I'm not sure if he's referring to the fact that I kissed Dan or that I'm planning to break up my dad's relationship. It's damning that there are multiple ways to interpret my new nickname.

"I'm here, I'm alive," I say, pretending I'm calling for my daily check-in.

When Hugh moved out of our apartment a year ago, I made him promise that we would still talk every day. Considering we're best friends who have lived together since we graduated from Columbia, it felt like a divorce when he moved in with his partner Raymond. He even took our cat with him. Honestly, I didn't want to keep Norman, who had a habit of upchucking nasty furballs in places like my shoes, but I made Hugh feel a little guilty about it anyway.

"How's the farm?" Hugh asks.

The sound of running water and clanging pots in the background means he's fixing dinner while we talk. Before Hugh moved in with Raymond, he was a five-night-a-week Thai take-out addict. Now he whips up things like marinated pork tenderloin and salmon baked in foil and sends me food porn pics of his plated meals, which seems cruel and unnecessary.

"It's positively pastoral here," I say sarcastically. "It's all so surreal, seeing my dad living on a farm. What are you cooking?"

"I bet." His spoon clinks against a pot. "I'm making chicken noodle soup. Raymond has a vicious cold, and I'm nursing him back to health like the saint that I am. How is Herb?"

"Attending to an infected goat hoof, I think."

"Well, that sounds...rank. But, hey, if Herb is happy, I'm happy."

That's a dig at me. He thinks I should be happy for Dad, too. His own father is a titan of industry, the kind who snorted coke off of models' asses in the eighties, before he settled down and married Hugh's mother. When Hugh came out in college, his dad took it as an indictment of his own masculinity, and their already strained relationship ended with a bang: the sound of a door slamming in Hugh's astonished face. The following summer, Dad invited Hugh to live in our apartment, and that's when Hugh found his surrogate dad, one who truly loved him just the way he is.

"I can't imagine he'd be happy here long term. There's nothing to do. We're in the middle of nowhere."

"He's doing Renata," Hugh says.

"Stop. That's my father you're talking about, and I'm going to puke."

If it's possible to sigh in a patronizing tone, that's what Hugh does.

"When you finally find the person you want to spend your life with, you're willing to make some compromises. That's how love works."

"Hugh, you complained bitterly when Raymond wanted to cancel HBO to save money."

"That was during *Big Little Lies*! And that argument nearly broke us."

"I can only imagine."

"Have you talked to Dan yet?"

I'm proud of him for waiting so long to ask this question and more than ready to unload my feelings on the topic.

"He left me a voicemail, but I didn't call him back. And I got a text from Barb, my department chair."

I appreciate that Hugh gasps at this news. "Wow. What did she say? You think she knows about Dan already?"

"She said she wanted to talk about work matters," I say,

imitating Barb's Upper West Side tone. "I'm terrified she knows, and I can't handle talking to Barb about what happened. She's buttoned-up so tightly, I'm pretty sure she gets dressed in the closet so even her husband won't see her naked."

"You know what they say. It's always the quiet, conservative ones who have the wild sex lives. Barb probably has a red room." Hugh laughs at his own joke before getting parental on me again. "I always warned you about workplace romances. Never shit where you eat."

"Dan doesn't qualify as a romance. He was a friendly coworker who became an error in judgment when I was at a low point."

"Hold on a sec. I have to put the veggies in."

I wish I were in Hugh's apartment, cuddled up on his couch eating chicken soup and watching *The Great Cupcake Competition* on TV. He always has quality dark chocolate on hand, and I really need some right now.

"I'm back," he says. "And I'm putting you on speaker so I can stretch and fold my dough. Did I mention I'm making my own sourdough bread?"

"Dammit, Hugh, what are you, Amish now?"

"I'll mail you a loaf." There's a pause while he sets down the phone and presumably grabs his dough. "You have to call Barb and find out what she knows. Maybe she really was calling about book lists or something."

"I know, you're right."

This was the problem with avoiding the unknown. You couldn't be sure if something truly terrible was about to happen or you were wasting hours worrying pointlessly. I could grind my teeth down to stubs tonight, then find out she really did want to discuss curriculum crap. I wasn't ready to call Barb yet though. I needed time to work up the courage.

"I wish you were here to eat some of this soup. I made way too much. I don't think it would ship well, otherwise I'd send you some of that, too. What's your plan to get Herb home?"

"Kidnapping?" I say.

"Seriously? You went all the way down there without a plan, didn't you?"

I don't want to admit that he's right.

"I'm going to sleep on it."

"Just talk to him. Maybe he'll convince you that he's happy and this is the right thing for him."

"I doubt that."

"Well, you know I couldn't live down there," Hugh says. "Small Southern towns aren't friendly to the gays, I imagine. I'm not even sure I could visit. They might shoot me on sight."

I rub the tight muscles in my neck because the headache is getting worse.

"You won't have to find out. I'll get him home."

TWO

The bed in the blue room has soporific powers and induces me to take my first afternoon nap in a long time. I wake up to voices and music coming from downstairs and throw my legs over the side of the bed, my toes landing on the foot-stool like the princess in a fairy tale. The mirror across the room, however, tells me I'm more unwashed Bonnaroo attendee than royalty. Right. A shower needs to happen immediately.

Once I've showered and put on a clean t-shirt and jean shorts, I head downstairs. Dad and Renata are in the kitchen making salad while Harmony steals bites from their cutting boards.

"Hey, everyone!" I call out loudly enough to be heard over the Sharon Jones music playing in the background.

Dad pours me a glass of red wine and tells me to take a seat on one of the stools at the island. As I watch him work, I'm struck by how quickly he has become a part of this family. He and Renata have a solid kitchen rhythm, and at one point I catch him pinching her butt as he moves by her.

"Pop, can I have a glass of lemonade?" Harmony asks.

As Dad gets down a glass from the cabinet, I raise my eyebrows and say, "Pop?"

"Harmony decided that's what she wants to call me."

I nod and gulp my wine, not wanting to think about the impact my father's departure would have on this sweet girl.

"We've got salad, corn and steak for dinner," Renata says. "I know you don't eat meat, Andie, and I've cut out red meat, myself. I've got a container of marinated baked tofu in the fridge. Would that work for you?"

Everyone here is being so kind. I have to harden my heart and remember that I'm doing this for Dad's own good. It will be much less painful for Renata and Harmony if he realizes now that he belongs in New York.

"Tofu sounds great. Can I help with dinner?"

Renata smiles warmly. "Sure. There's a bag of corn right here. You could take it outside and shuck it. Michael and Seth are outside, they'll help you."

"No problem," I say, carrying the lumpy bag out to the porch.

I shoot my dad a look because this damn bag of corn has stirred up a painful memory for me. He and I always celebrate the end of the school year by making ourselves a lobster dinner, complete with corn on the cob and baked potatoes, that we eat on his tiny patio overlooking the street. We buy a bottle of champagne and clink glasses, toasting the students who drove us the craziest that year. But this past June, Dad was anxious to see Renata again. He left for North Carolina the day after school ended without even mentioning our special dinner tradition. I know I'm being self-centered and childish, but I resent the hell out of this bag of corn.

Michael and Seth are indeed sitting on the porch, and there's a yellow dog asleep in a corner.

"Hey, guys, I'm Andie." I hold up the vilified bag of produce. "Who wants to help shuck corn?"

Both men stand and walk over to me.

Michael greets me first, saying, "Hey, I'm Renata's son, Michael. It's great to finally meet you. We've heard a lot about you."

"Likewise. Renata loves bragging on her sons."

Michael has a cute face and his mother's easy grin. "She really does."

Now that I'm standing up close to Seth, I can attest to the fact that he's at least three inches taller than Michael who's around six feet. At five feet nine inches, I'm not used to being around men who make me feel petite. He only says one word when his hand envelopes mine.

"Seth."

His voice is a rich tenor that rumbles from his chest. I give him only one word back because that seems fair.

"Andie."

His skin is rough and calloused, like someone who works with his hands every day, and his smile is more reserved than his brother's. Both of them are good-looking men, but only one seems approachable. I find myself holding onto Seth's hand a little longer than necessary, trying to decipher what's behind that detached gaze. When I realize what I'm doing, I jerk my hand away, and his lips turn up at the edges, like he's fighting a smile. He mistook my curiosity about him for attraction, which it most definitely is not.

"Maybe we should take the corn outside," I say. "I don't want to make a mess on the porch."

"You'll get eaten by mosquitoes," Seth warns.

"Stay here." Michael pats the seat of the porch glider.

"We can help you with the corn. The grill is lit, and we don't need to start the steaks yet."

I sit down with Michael, and Seth takes a seat opposite us in a wicker chair. Michael and I keep the conversation going as we rock gently and shuck corn. We discuss his older brother Trey, who is a hand surgeon in Manhattan, and what Michael likes to do when visiting New York City. We agree that there's no point in eating pizza anywhere else in the country and that the Times Square area is a tourist trap nightmare.

Seth listens to us silently, and finally I ask him, "How about you? What's your favorite spot in New York?"

"I haven't gotten up there yet."

Michael sighs as though he takes this lack of interest in the greatest city on earth quite personally.

"You always have an excuse for why you can't come with me," he says to Seth, sounding genuinely hurt.

"They aren't excuses," Seth says calmly. "I work all week and then I work on my cabin on weekends. Once I get my place finished and save up some money, I'll go to New York with you."

"My brother is all work and no play," Michael tells me, chucking a piece of shucked corn at Seth, who catches it deftly.

It's endearing that they talk about each other as brothers, considering Seth was adopted as a teenager, if I remember correctly, and I imagine it confuses people who don't know their backstory. Despite Seth's summer tan, there's no way he's passing for a biological member of this family.

"What do you do for work?" I ask, expecting Seth to say something construction related.

"I'm a paramedic."

I remember the bumper sticker on the pickup truck.

"Who's in the Marines?"

"I was." Seth stops his work to look up at me, then goes back to it without further explanation.

"We have a huge Marine base here in North Carolina at Camp Lejeune," Michael says, "but Seth asked to be stationed in California."

Seth corrects him, "I asked for Hawaii. California was my second choice. No point in joining the military and ending up a couple hours from home."

I try to imagine Seth in Hawaii, shirtless with a surfboard tucked under his arm. It's a pleasant image, considering the muscles that are visible on him already, but feels incongruent to the person sitting in front of me. He's as uptight as Keanu Reeves at the beginning of *Point Break.*

"Were you in California the whole time you were in the Marines?" I ask.

Seth sets down the corncob he's been working on, and it's completely clean, not a single silk caught in the kernels. He picks up another cob and gets to work, slowly and precisely.

"No," he says. "I was deployed to Afghanistan eventually."

"Wow. That must have been..." I can't find the right words to complete the sentence, and Seth doesn't rush to help me.

A full minute later, he says, "I was ready to go. You do all that training, and it feels pointless not to use it."

Being a teacher, I know that the kids who enlist are usually the ones who have few other options. I wonder about Seth and why he joined up, but it's too personal a question to ask someone I just met.

I watch as he peels down another strip of the husk. It's

kind of zen, the way he carefully removes each stiff leaf and drops it into the paper bag.

"I've never seen anyone shuck corn so meticulously," I say.

He doesn't crack a smile when he responds, "I take my work very seriously."

Michael chuckles. "Wait until you see how long it takes him to eat that piece of corn."

I've torn through my three ears of corn by now, and Seth catches me assessing his progress.

"Are we racing?"

"If we are, I guess I won."

"Congratulations," he says dryly, but his eyes light up a little.

Michael finishes his last corncob, places it on the table, then slaps his thighs.

"Time to put on the steaks."

Michael steps outside, and I'm curious to see what happens when Seth and I are left alone. I'm someone who can carry on a conversation with almost anyone, but I'm also good with silence. Seth's taciturnity isn't going to bother me. In fact, it will be fun to see how long we go before one of us speaks.

There's something weirdly sexual about watching his hands strip away the husks, then gently remove the silks, first taking them off in bunches, then removing the last ones thread by thread. Michael's comment about Seth lingering on each bite of food, makes me wonder if he takes his time with every activity. A man who moves slowly in the bedroom would be a nice change. My ex-boyfriend Kirk used to act like someone was timing us with a stop-watch. Foreplay accomplished in under five minutes and the crowd goes wild! From all appearances, Seth seems like he would take his time with everything he does. I'll never find out though. Even if I weren't here on serious family business, I can't imagine dating an ex-Marine whose commitment to silence is unnerving. Also, there's the fact that he seems more interested in that ear of corn than he is in me.

The dog in the corner snorts himself awake and wanders over to Seth. When he realizes there's a new girl in town, his brand of welcome is to jet over to me, wagging his tail furiously, and bury his nose in my crotchal region.

"Mutt, no," Seth barks at him.

Mutt pulls back to a more respectful distance, but continues to pester me for attention. He acts like he'll sit at my feet and worship me forever if I just keep petting his ears.

"Sorry," Seth says. "We're working on his manners."

"Is he a lab?"

"He's a mix, probably lab and collie. Wandered onto the property and kept showing up on my doorstep, kind of adopted me, I guess."

"And you named him Mutt because..."

"That's what I always called him. Like, 'Hey, Mutt, you back for more scraps?'"

He leans over to tousle his dog's fur, and I get my first glimpse of Seth's smile. When he sees me watching him, he clears his throat and resumes shucking corn.

"He's kind of an attention whore," I say, reaching down to pet the dog again.

"Is he bothering you?"

"Nah, I'm just kidding."

I give Mutt a belly rub to prove that I like him. He responds by rolling on his back, legs up in the air, in a completely undignified pose. I want to make a joke about the position his dog is in, but I'm not sure Seth will appreciate my humor.

We lapse into silence again, and I reach for other topics of potential conversation, not because I need to talk, but because I want to hear what Seth will say.

"Do you watch sports?" I ask.

"Not much anymore." He finishes the second cob and studies it for that one elusive strand of silk he might have missed. "I don't have a TV in my cabin. Sometimes I go to a bar to watch college basketball."

"I don't know much about basketball," I admit. "My dad and I are baseball fans."

He looks up and raises his eyebrows, as if this might interest him. I'm surprised Dad hasn't mentioned it before. Maybe he has, and Seth is yanking my chain. It's difficult to tell because this guy has a serious poker face.

"Please say the Mets."

I make a gagging sound because I'm very mature. "No, the Yankees, of course."

He lets out a long breath and frowns, like I've just confirmed that I come from a family of war criminals.

"That's a shame," he says, shaking his head. "We could have been friends."

SETH TAKES a huge piece of meat from the platter using his fork, then passes it to me. The steaks are sitting in a pool of blood—okay, maybe it's technically not blood, but it's some kind of animal juice and the sight of it makes my stomach churn. He watches me pass the plate to Michael without taking any, and I know he's going to make a comment.

The others are having a conversation about Harmony's desire to take horseback riding lessons, and they don't hear him when he says, "Is the steak too rare for you?"

"I'm a vegetarian." I reach for the plate of baked tofu Renata heated up for us.

"Why?" Seth asks.

I have to admit that his tone is as non-judgmental as it can be, for a person with a caveman-sized portion of beef in front of him. He sounds curious, not critical.

"I really don't like talking about why I'm a vegetarian in front of people who are eating meat." I gesture to the plates on the table that are full of dead cow. "It feels rude."

I've had this conversation many times before, usually at Thanksgiving with relatives Dad and I don't see often. Everyone worries that I'm going to be hungry (even though my plate is heaping with side dishes) and wants to know my reasons for rejecting the turkey that they're whispering is dry and overcooked again. My aunt Janice always pipes up to say that she thought I ate chicken and turkey, as if birds aren't animals. Yes, I tell her every time, birds are part of the animal kingdom.

Seth's eyes widen, like he wants to say something more, but instead he puts a forkful of steak into his mouth. I can imagine what he's thinking: it's also pretty rude to show up at someone's house unannounced and expect them to take you in as a houseguest. But this is my dad's home now, too, and as a daughter, I have a right to come see him. Kids show up at their parents' houses all the time, and the door is always open, right?

Dad overhears me and adds, "Andie has been a vegetarian since she was a kid. When she read *Charlotte's Web* in third grade, she bawled her eyes out and refused to eat meat ever again. She started a vegetarian lunch group at her school, and she tried to win me to her side. Pretty soon I was introduced to things I'd never heard of before: tempeh, quinoa, fakin bacon. I learned a lot from her."

"Yeah, but you wouldn't stop eating burgers," I remind him.

Now that I'm grown, Dad loves telling people how I came to be a vegetarian. He paints me as a bold young champion of animal rights. At the time, he wasn't impressed when I taped signs up around the house that said "Meat is Murder" and talked about slaughterhouses while he ate tacos for dinner. I definitely remember him threatening to take away my TV time if I didn't cool it.

"I was in 4H in elementary school," Seth says. "Raised a calf. I named him Stanley."

I try to imagine Seth as a kid. The features that are striking on a man—prominent nose and full mouth—must have looked awkward on someone pint-sized.

"I remember going to the State Fair to see you show him," Michael says, "You won a blue ribbon, and I asked Mom if I could get a goat or a pig or something. Anything, just so I could win a ribbon at the State Fair, too. That was a hard no."

Renata laughs. "You had a dog you never walked or fed. I wasn't convinced you could keep an animal alive. Plus, we didn't live on a bunch of land like Seth and his mom."

"What happened to him?" I ask, afraid of the answer. "Stanley."

"We sold him for slaughter," Seth says mildly, like he's talking about the weather and not killing his pet. "I made enough money to buy a BMX bike, and Mom made me put the rest in the bank." He takes another bite of meat and chews it thoughtfully.

I must be staring at him like he's a monster because Michael says, "You just freaked Andie out."

"Didn't you feel sad and guilty?" I ask. "Your pet was turned into someone's dinner."

"Yeah, that's awful, Uncle Seth," Harmony chimes in.

Seth swallows, then takes a gulp of water before saying, "He wasn't a pet. He was a farm animal. It's different. You're acting like I'm going to put your cat through a meat grinder."

I scowl. "What makes you think I have a cat?"

"You don't?" he says, as if it's a rule that every single woman living in a New York apartment has a cat.

The facts stand as such:

1. Hugh and I were co-parents to an oversized orange tabby named Norman, after Norman Bates, because he was a weird dude. He liked to sleep in the bathroom sink and eat non-edible things like cardboard (not at the same time, although had that been possible, it would have been Norman's idea of heaven).

2. Hugh took Norman with him when he moved out because he said Norman loved him more, which is insulting, to say the least. It's just as well because Norman would have eaten Marly's plants and been poisoned, and Hugh would have blamed me for lack of supervision.

"No, I don't," I say, glad I can shatter his stereotypes. "I don't have any pets, actually."

Seth picks up his ear of corn and begins buttering it tenderly, like he and this ear of corn are in a long-term relationship.

"This great love of animals and no pets," he says in a flat voice.

Anger tightens my jaw, and I can barely get out the words, "So you read *Charlotte's Web* as a kid, and it made you crave bacon?"

"We just grew up differently," he says, not at all offended. "I didn't have much time for reading as a kid. I was playing in the creek or helping my mom around the house. In high school, I was in Future Farmers of America. You..." He looks down at my t-shirt which is screen printed with the words *liberated woman* in huge black letters. "You were in future feminists of America, I guess?"

"Seth," Renata says in a warning tone. "Don't listen to him, Andie. Seth is a feminist, and no one here cares if you eat meat or don't eat meat. Let's talk about something else."

"What's a feminist?" Harmony asks.

"Someone who believes men and women are equal," Renata says. "And that girls can do anything boys can do, and just as well as boys can do it. And Seth believes that. His mother was one of the strongest women I've ever known."

Harmony rolls her eyes. "Of course girls can do anything boys can do. Girls rule, boys drool."

"Watch it now," Michael says. "We said girls and boys are equal. And Daddy is a boy, and I don't drool."

"You're not a boy," Harmony explains to him. "You're a daddy."

I should definitely let the conversation thread about animal cruelty die, like poor Stanley did. But one of my faults is not letting things go, which explains how I got to this dinner table in the first place.

"I would think being raised on a farm would make you more sensitive to the fact that animals are living creatures," I say. "Harmony clearly loves her goat."

Harmony nods. "I do. I would never let anyone eat Tiana."

"You're wearing leather sandals," Seth points out.

"How do you know these aren't vegan sandals made of faux leather?" I ask him.

We're locked into a showdown, and I'm not sure how we even got here. I lower my fork, which I've been holding in a manner that might be construed as aggressive.

"Are they?" he asks.

I pause and consider my answer, wishing these damn sandals were fake leather. The truth is, I can't afford the fancy Brooklyn stores that sell vegan clothing. These sandals are from Macy's clearance rack, and it's highly possible (though not certain) that they're proof of my hypocrisy. All eyes are on me, and there's way too much pressure on me to tell the truth. Besides, how pathetic am I that I'm going to lie about the origin of my shoes just to win an argument with a Neanderthal?

"Probably not," I admit.

"I rest my case." Seth spins the corncob in his fingers.

"At least I don't kill my pets," I say, quickly adding, "or I wouldn't if I had any."

Seth shrugs. "Maybe those shoes were someone's Stanley. You could be wearing someone's pet right now."

I push my chair back from the table and stand up to leave. "See, this is why I don't discuss my vegetarianism at dinner tables. Please excuse me."

Renata stretches her hand across the table, but I'm too far away for her to reach.

"Don't go, please, honey. Seth, apologize to Andie." She has her mom voice on now. "She didn't want to talk about being a vegetarian in the first place, I heard her say so. You don't know when to stop picking."

He stands up next to me like a contrite child and places his warm hand on my upper arm.

"I'm sorry, Andie. I thought we were just joking around."

I must be an emotional basket case right now because his gentle touch and worried expression bring tears to my eyes that I have to blink away.

"It's okay." I sit down again, mostly because I don't want to look like a drama queen.

Dinner is quiet until Michael, who I have tagged as the people-pleaser of the group, starts talking about how great it will be when he and Harmony move out to the farm someday.

"I thought you lived in Chapel Hill," I say.

Before dinner, Michael told me he and Harmony lived in the college town where he works at a lab that makes pharmaceuticals. He's a chemist who does something with quality control. It's one of those jobs that someone explains to you and you don't quite understand, but you nod to avoid looking stupid.

"We do," he says, taking the salt shaker away from Harmony before she dumps the entire thing on her corn. "But we're going to move out here next year. Seth's built a cabin for himself on the property, and this fall he's going to help me build a place where Harmony and I can live."

It's judgmental, I know, but I can't help thinking that Harmony might be better off in Chapel Hill, a college town and one of the more progressive places in North Carolina. My friend Amina got her doctorate at the University of North Carolina, and she loved it. I asked her about Foster's Creek when Dad started his long-distance relationship with Renata, but she'd never heard of it. She didn't travel much outside the Chapel Hill bubble and after meeting Seth, I can see why. Then again, Michael probably needs his mother's help, now that he's a single parent.

"Are you excited to live in the country?" I ask Harmony.

"Yes! Then I can see Tiana every day, and brush her and

feed her carrots. I can even learn how to milk her. Maybe I could put her in a goat show someday, like Uncle Seth did with Stanley. Only I'm not going to let anyone eat her afterwards."

"No one would do that," Michael assures her.

She eyes Uncle Seth, as if she isn't so sure that he's on board with this statement.

"I'm so lucky that two of my boys will be living near me," Renata says. "Now if only we could get Trey down here, but he'll never leave the city."

She beams at Seth and Michael, and I have to choke down the lump forming in my throat.

"Sounds like you've got your own family compound forming down here." Even though I try to hide it, the bitterness slides into my voice. Renata hears it, too.

"It's nice to have your family close," she says gingerly. "I'm sure you've missed your dad this summer."

I spear a piece of lettuce and shove it into my mouth, demanding that those unshed tears building in my eyes sink back from whence they came. I will not let these people see me cry. Especially the inscrutable Seth, who is watching my every movement.

Without Dad, I haven't been to a single game at Yankee stadium this summer. It wouldn't be the same without him, and Hugh and Raymond aren't sports fans. I watched all the games on television by myself with no one to help me swear at the umpires and chastise the pitchers. It's more than just ball games though. I like knowing Dad is nearby so that when I need him, when I need to go home, I'm just a short distance away.

My father must see my pain because he says in an overly jolly voice, "Andie's very independent. I'm sure she's glad not to have me looking over her shoulder anymore."

"Not really," I say, trying to match his lighthearted tone. "You're the only family I had there, so it was kind of a big deal when you said you weren't coming back."

The looks on the faces around me say I've missed the mark on sounding lighthearted, and I don't care. I've regressed from twenty-eight to thirteen on the drive down here. Maybe there's some time portal you travel through when you reach the Mason Dixon line. Or maybe my rental car is actually the Tardis.

"Isn't your mom still in New York?" Renata asks.

I'm kind of impressed by Renata calling me on my bull-shit. She's not going to let me get away with the sulky step-daughter act.

"She's not too far away. She stayed on Long Island after her most recent divorce. I don't really consider Mom family though, so much as the person who gave birth to me."

Again, my humor falls flat. Dad's expression is both irri-tated and pained, which is how I'm feeling, too. My pity party isn't going to get him home any quicker.

"My mom died," Harmony says matter-of-factly.

The room falls silent and my chest squeezes until there's no air left. If I'm dying of a heart attack, I deserve it. I'm a terrible person.

"I'm so sorry," I say quietly, unable to meet anyone's eyes.

Harmony goes back to eating her corn, and Michael puts an arm around her and squeezes her narrow little girl shoulders.

"I think I will excuse myself now," I say, and no one stops me this time.

I carry my dishes to the sink and brace myself on the counter for a few seconds before turning around.

"Thank you for dinner," I say, so that the last thing they hear from me tonight will at least be civil.

The longest walk I've ever taken is the one out of that dining room, everyone's eyes trained on my back. I've never felt so small or alone before in my life. I wonder if the blue room has ever seen a grown woman curl into a ball and cry so hard she's spasming soundlessly because she doesn't want anyone to know.

YEARS AGO, my therapist suggested I take up running to cure my sleep issues. She was right. I'm laughably slow and my max distance is three miles, but I'm no longer a jittery insomniac. My fifty-year-old neighbor who participates in marathons stopped me outside our apartment building once to tell me what was wrong with my form. After about fifteen minutes of attempting to coach me, he sighed and said, "Just do whatever is comfortable for you."

Thanks to the intensity of tonight's dinner conversation, my legs are practically levitating off the bed. There's no way I can go for a run now though. It's getting dark, and I don't know my way around the farm. Even so, I'm tempted go outside, do a few laps around the house and risk twisting an ankle. The alternative is a sleepless night and a bad mood tomorrow.

I know I should return Dan's phone call, but I don't have the emotional energy for that conversation tonight. What is there to say anyway? We took things too far and need to dial back to being work acquaintances. One of us will request a room change, and over time we will forget about what happened at the bar that night. It's better to wait until I speak with Barb and find out why she called me before I contact Dan. Then I'll have a better idea how bad the damage is and whether or not it can be contained. The fallout for him could be much greater. I push away thoughts of his wife Nicky, whom I met at the staff Christmas party last winter. She was perky and sweet, but her smile tightened any time I joined her conversation circle, and Dan spent the evening acting like I was someone he barely knew. My stomach sours when I think back to that night, seeing it for the first time with clarity and honesty. She suspected our mutual crushes even then.

When my father knocks on the door to my room, I'm releasing energy by doing sets of squats and push-ups. They're the girly kind of push-up, but it's working. When I stand up to let him in, my legs and arms are shaking from exhaustion. I'm much calmer than I was an hour ago, which is a relief. I don't want Dad to know how upset I was earlier.

"Hey, come on in." I step aside so he can enter the room.

He looks around at the furniture like he hasn't been in here in a while. Maybe he's noticing how I've already got clothing exploding from my bag and a bunch of crap strewn all over the dresser and floor. Organization has never been my strong suit. I thought Dad and I were both messy, but after I moved out of the house, I realized it was just me. His place was tidy and clean after I left home, and Renata's house is the same way. A place for everything, and everything in its place, as they say.

"Can we talk for a minute?" he asks.

"Sure," I say, climbing up on my bed.

He takes a seat next to me and kicks his shoes off before pulling his legs up on the bed. He leans back on the headboard and lets out a groan.

"Are you okay?" I say.

"Oh, yeah. Just tired. We usually go to bed early so this is late for me."

Late? It's nine fifteen. Even when he was teaching, he stayed up until ten. Farm life is supposed to make you healthy and hale, but he looks worn out.

"I'm so glad you're here, honey." He pats my leg. "I know you were upset when I called, and I feel terrible about giving you a shock."

"It was definitely a shock." I pick at the seam in my pajama pants and wondering if Renata is still glad I'm there. After my behavior at dinner, I doubt it.

I'm not going to launch into a talk about his relationship the first night. Not only am I physically and emotionally exhausted, I don't want to upset both of us right before we go to bed. There will be plenty of time for deep discussions tomorrow, when I have a better grip on what I need to say.

"I should have been more aware of how upsetting this would be for you. I feel like you've been going through a rough patch lately, and I haven't been there. I feel really guilty about that."

I narrow my eyes. "A rough patch?"

"You haven't seemed happy for a long time. I know you've been at loose ends since Hugh moved out, and you got that weird new roommate."

I'd learned a hard lesson, advertising for a roommate on Craigslist. Marly is indeed a freak and not of the "cool and eccentric" variety. She's a plant hoarder who feels more comfortable interacting with succulents than with humans. But once a roommate is in, it's nearly impossible to get them out.

"And frankly, I've been worried that maybe you're feeling unfulfilled with your job, too," he says.

"Teaching is exhausting, that's all. You know how it is."

"Yes, of course, it's tiring, but I loved it. It was my calling. I'm afraid that you feel like you have to continue with it, even though maybe it's not your passion. I don't want you to think you'll let me down if you decide to do something else. I just want you to be happy."

So much for leaving the heavy talk for tomorrow. His comments about my job are so out of the blue, it takes me a moment to process what he's saying. Dad always acted thrilled that I followed him into the teaching profession. He encouraged me to get an education degree in college and apply for jobs in the public school system. It was my mother who thought I was throwing my life away by becoming a low-wage state employee.

"What other job would I do?" I ask, feeling betrayed.

If he wanted me to prepare for other options, it was a little late to tell me now. I couldn't just snap my fingers and become an attorney or a journalist, two careers I'd considered back in the day.

"There are a million other things you could do," he says. "You're so smart. And I could help if you wanted to go back to school, get your masters in something."

I wasn't sure how this conversation became about me. He was the one who'd gone off the rails. Surely, he must see that. He was the unstable one who'd quit his job and moved in with a woman he'd known for only a few months. I hadn't done anything wild recently, other than the Dan incident and driving down here without giving him notice. Okay, maybe I did seem a little unstable.

"Don't you think I'm a good teacher?" I ask.

"Yes! Oh, honey, you're an amazing teacher. I'm not worried about what you're giving your students. I'm worried about whether the job is feeding your soul."

Feeding my soul. At what point in history did jobs

become more than a paycheck? I can't imagine anyone in a mill or factory questioning whether the job "fed their soul." It put food on the table, that was the purpose of working. Now we're supposed to find jobs that fulfill us emotionally, leave a positive impact on the world, pay enough to cover our college debt, and make us sound cool at our high school reunions. It's too much pressure.

"Okay."

I'm wary of continuing this chat and having flashbacks to my last doomed conversation with my mother. She actually asked me my age (normal mothers know these things), then proceeded to tell me how I should consider freezing my eggs, since it appeared there were no marriage prospects in sight. Marriage is my mother's cure all. Things not going well? Why not get married (again)? When I said I didn't plan on having kids, she said that was probably a good idea, since I was a lot like her, and we just weren't maternal types. She suggested that I still get married to someone with good earning potential because, god knows, I'd never make a decent living as a teacher. Always a joy, those talks with Mom.

"We have plenty of time to talk about it," he says. "You'll stay for a few days at least, right? I'd like you to get to know Renata and her family. It will be great. I can show you around the farm, introduce you to the chickens."

"Fantastic," I say unenthusiastically.

He laughs and kisses my head. Dad is well aware of my fear of birds.

"Everyone is so glad you're here." He climbs down from my raft-like bed. "Oh, and I hope Seth didn't upset you. Renata lit into him after dinner. I don't know what bug got up his ass tonight. He's actually a really good guy. You'll like him once you get to know him better."

"Sure, Dad," I say. "Don't worry about it."

"Goodnight, sweetheart."

Dad isn't lying. He truly believes that they're all thrilled about my arrival. Renata, once she got over the shock, did seem pleased that I was here, until the dinner incident. She was responding to how happy it made Dad to see me, and I assume that will be enough for us to find common ground. Michael was friendly, and I know he has bigger fish to fry than worrying about me, what with being a single parent. Seth is another story altogether. We didn't click from the moment we met. After our face-off this evening, I can't imagine things will get better. I didn't come here to make friends with these people anyway. I'm here to convince my father to come home.

Shortly after my mom left my father for a dermatologist named Phil, I began having anxiety attacks. Someone recommended that Dad send me to a therapist, and I was finally able to voice the fear that I couldn't tell my father: he was going to leave me, too. My therapist reassured me back then, and over the many years that I saw her, that no one could ever separate my father and me. He wasn't like my mom, and he'd proved that to me every damn day. Well, it took him twenty-three years, but here I was, in a small Southern town, watching Dad build a new life without me. He had a fiancée, stepsons, and even a beautiful step-granddaughter. He probably never thought he'd be a grandparent, considering I'm single and apparently don't have the maternal gene.

I would cry again, if there were any tears left. Instead I crawl under the covers and listen to the settling noises of the house until I fall asleep.

THREE

The birds. The fucking birds. Why in god's name are there so many of them singing outside my apartment?

I roll over and pry my eyelids apart, taking in the fact that the windows have toile curtains instead of crappy roller shades. Not my bedroom. Goat farm. Right. Close eyes and return to sleep. Except those fancy curtains aren't shutting out the morning sun, and there's still the mother-loving birds tweeting merrily.

The shower starts running in the bathroom attached to my bedroom, and I'm curious who's inside. I didn't know I was sharing with anyone, but after all, a freeloader can't expect a private suite.

I poke at the sore spot on my chin, which promises to be an impressive zit by the end of the day. I'm pre-menstrual, which explains both my skin eruption and headache. Maybe I can also use PMS to excuse my sorry behavior last night. At least I only have to face Dad and Renata this morning. Michael, Harmony and Seth will have gone home, which doesn't explain why my shower is running. Dad and Renata have the master bedroom down the hall with their own bathroom. Maybe their shower is busted. The plumbing in this place must be ancient.

Minutes later the shower shuts off—someone is serious about water conservation—and I wait for the sound of a hairdryer or electric razor. Silence again except for those maniacal birds. There's no clock in my room so I reach for my phone and see it's only a little after seven. I'm never up this early on days when I don't have to work, but between the light and noise, I won't be getting more sleep today.

This magical mattress, slightly lumpy and surprisingly cozy, helped me sleep through the night. I should get up and go for a run, but instead I lie under the quilt, staring at the ceiling. There's a water stain above my bed that suggests a roof leak. An old house like this has got to be a money pit.

Dad never wanted to buy a place in Red Hook, our neighborhood in Brooklyn, even though it would have been a great investment. He loved that a super would come and fix whatever was broken in our place and didn't want the responsibility for leaking pipes and busted radiators. Now look at him. This place has to be at least a hundred years old.

I consider staying in bed a bit longer, but I'm fully awake and desperately need caffeine. The scent of fresh coffee wafts through the air ducts and up the stairs, beckoning me to the kitchen. I slept in my underwear and a tank top so I pull on my favorite pajama shorts with R2D2 on them and head downstairs. Thankfully, the kitchen is empty because, as a rule, I refuse to make conversation before caffeination. It's better for everyone that way. I locate the coffee pot, fill up a pretty blue ceramic mug and inhale deeply. Someone has good taste in beans.

Dad and Renata are probably in the barn doing the morning milking. They mentioned yesterday that the goats get milked twice a day--once in the early morning and once in the late afternoon. Dad was always an early riser, too, conditioned by his years of teaching. When I was old enough to stay in the house alone, he took up running and would wake up at four forty-five every morning and put in a couple miles before showering for work. When he turned fifty, he slowed it down to speed walking to save his knees. I wonder if he still exercises here or if his entire daily routine has changed.

The kitchen is snug and peaceful, and if I were a normal person I'd sit by the window, take in the view of the pasture and contemplate life. Maybe I'd do a morning meditation or read one of the magazines artfully stacked on a kitchen stool. I certainly wouldn't contemplate rooting through the drawers and cabinets in Renata's kitchen to find out more about her and this farm.

I pick up a copy of *Mother Earth* and flip through the pages, but it's no use. I'm not a normal person, and the pull to snoop is too strong. I can't help it. I want to know about the woman who has my father's heart in her hands.

The cookbooks stored on a shelf in the kitchen island are supremely healthy: macrobiotic, paleo, vegan. Dad isn't in danger of cardiac issues here, but he might starve. The man has never eaten tofu or beans voluntarily, and, believe me, I've tried. The pantry is lined with glass jars containing grains, nuts, beans and flours of varying shades and textures. It's the most artistic food storage I've ever seen. I'd bet money that Renata does yoga and drinks kombucha tea. She'd fit right in with Brooklyn life.

I'm about to wrap up what has been an unfulfilling search when I come upon a notebook in the last drawer I open. It's spiral bound with a flowered cover, just the place someone of Renata's generation would write down notes. To snoop on millennials, you wouldn't get far without stealing their devices. Just as I'm deciding whether it's a major violation to look inside the notebook (who would keep a private journal in a kitchen drawer?), I hear someone clear his throat.

"Looking for something?"

Seth is towering behind me with damp hair and a suspicious look on his face that makes me feel ashamed. I couldn't appear more guilty if my hand was literally inside a cookie jar.

"Sugar?" I retract my hand from the drawer and close it softly.

He moves toward me until he's about an inch away, and I hope he doesn't hear my breath catch. For a second, I'm not sure what he's about to do to me, and, even more confusing, I'm not sure what I want him to do. He smells like soap and something spicier, perhaps deodorant or shampoo. Although they're pleasant, clean scents, they don't explain the reaction I'm having to his proximity. Because his blistering gaze is peering into my dark soul, I avert my eyes downward to his chest. The heather gray t-shirt he has on is worn thin and clinging to his pectoral muscles because he's probably still steamy from the shower and happens to be built like a brick wall. Crap. Looking down was a terrible mistake.

Before I can do something horrifying, like press myself against his broad chest and moan with pleasure, he reaches around my back and opens a cabinet door. The soft sleeve of his t-shirt brushes my cheek, and I let myself inhale more of him. This is what happens when you're a raging heterosexual woman who has put herself on a humping hiatus. When his arm snakes back around, he's holding out a ceramic sugar bowl dotted with delicate pink flowers.

"Thanks."

My voice sounds weirdly loud and cheerful. I absent-mindedly touch the place where his shirt met my skin, as if it has left a mark there.

It's too much, this kind of masculinity—the tendons in his forearms, the callouses and nicks on his hands, that scruffy facial hair that's not quite a beard or a goatee, but something in-between. When he backs away, I sigh in both relief and disappointment.

I usually drink my coffee black and unsweetened, but, having been caught in a lie, I'm forced to add sugar. I sprinkle in as little as possible under his watchful eye. Having to defile my coffee makes me resent Seth, even if it's unfair of me. Coffee is sacred.

"Don't be shy, take as much as you want."

There's a gleam in his eye that tells me he knows. He knows that coffee is meant to be bitter, like my heart.

I stir the coffee, my spoon clinking against the side of the mug.

"I just like it a tiny bit sweet."

"You're up early," he says, as if to hint that I got up before everyone else to snoop around.

How offensive. My kitchen investigation was purely spontaneous.

"So are you."

I'm determined to keep eye contact with him and not blink. Excessive blinking is a tell for liars, and he suspects me already. Those dark brown eyes though. It's like they're drilling down into my brain, dredging up every bad deed I've ever done. Seth should consider a career as an interrogator. I squirm under his gaze, trying desperately to hide how much he's rattled me.

Seth gives up our staring game first with a little shake of

his head like either he's seen enough or can't sort me out—which I take as a small victory—and grabs a mug to pour himself some coffee. I'm jealous of the fact that he gets to drink his without sugar. He does add milk from a pitcher in the fridge and stirs it in gently with a spoon, somehow managing not to clink the sides.

"I didn't figure you for a morning person," he says.

By "not a morning person" he means lazy and spoiled. Farm boy thinks he's cornered the market on work ethic, which is annoying to say the least. My friends did Outward Bound and SAT prep classes during the summers of high school, while I was scooping ice cream, babysitting and selling homemade jewelry on Etsy. Just because I've never shoveled cow shit doesn't mean I'm not a hard worker.

"You've known me less than twenty-four hours," I say, sipping my spoiled coffee.

"Fair point." He sets down his cup and begins rummaging through the refrigerator. "Want something to eat?"

He pulls out a glass storage container that's full of chicken parts and proceeds to fill a plate with two cold drumsticks and a wing. My stomach churns as I watch him. Based on our conversation at dinner last night, I'm convinced he's chosen this particular breakfast to annoy me.

"No, thanks."

Watching him consume the carnage on his plate banishes my appetite completely.

"Did you find anything interesting when you were looking in Renata's kitchen drawers?" he asks, in between gnawing on a leg bone.

Speaking of legs, I notice his eyes travel from my bare feet up to my thighs, and they don't stop there. It's a slow slide over my torso all the way to my face. Suddenly, my clothing feels see-through instead of solid. When I got up this morning, I figured the bra built into my tank top was enough coverage, but now I'm not so sure. Reflexively, I cross my arms over my chest.

"Why are you here? I thought you lived in a little cabin or something."

"I'm still building my place." He wipes his fingers on a napkin. "I haven't finished tiling the bathroom yet so Renata lets me shower here."

So that was him, showering in my bathroom this morning. All six foot three of him, naked and wet, about fifteen feet away from my bed. I bite my bottom lip until pain replaces the fantasy. He doesn't deserve my lust.

"That's kind of her. I'll be sure to knock then."

Seth gives me a confused look.

"Before entering the bathroom that we're sharing," I explain.

"Sharing?" He narrows his eyes. "How long are you planning to stay?"

I let my hands drop down to my sides and lean back on the counter because if he wants to get a good look at me, then let him. It's the most of me that he'll ever get. His eyes flicker to my chest then back to my face again, and I feel a little victorious. I take a long sip of coffee, making him wait for my answer.

"Not sure yet. I don't have to work until the school year begins, so I'm a free woman. And I really do want to get to know you guys."

For someone who doesn't like sugar, I sound like a one-pound bag of it right now.

"You do?"

He doesn't look irritated now. Instead, it seems like he gives a shit about whether or not I'm interested in him.

That's a surprise. And strike interrogator off the job list, he's terrible at reading tone of voice.

"Of course," I say, crossing a foot over the opposite ankle. "I think you and I really hit it off. Don't you?"

Seth's face closes like a window. He hasn't missed my sarcasm this time.

"Definitely."

He dumps the carcass on his plate into the trashcan and slides the empty dish into the dishwasher. Then he washes his hands in a water, soap, lather, rinse process that's as tedious as everything else he does. Half the time I don't even bother to dry my hands, I just flap them in the air. Seth? He makes drying his hands into an event, flipping them back and forth inside the towel hanging from the stove door handle.

"I have to get dressed for work," he says, carefully straightening the towel before walking away. "Have a nice day."

I smile at him sweetly over the rim of my coffee cup, enjoying the rear view of him as he stalks out of the kitchen, the screen door to the porch slamming behind him.

DAD HANDS me an egg that's still warm from the underside of a chicken. It's grayish blue and fits neatly into the palm of my hand.

"Aren't they beautiful?" he asks.

The eggs, in their various shades and textures, are lovely, but there's something about being this close to the spawning of my food that makes me queasy. I place the blue egg into his basket, next to one that's speckled brown.

"Yeah, lovely."

They've milked the goats, collected eggs, and taken their morning power walk, and it's only ten o'clock. Apparently, Dad is still exercising regularly, which is a relief. I can't complain that farm life won't keep him healthy. All I've accomplished is drinking coffee and scrolling through Instagram on my phone. Maybe Seth is right to think I'm spoiled and lazy. Then again, I work sixty hours a week during the school year, so I deserve a little down time in the summer.

Renata offers to make me an omelet with the eggs they've collected, and I don't want to offend her so I accept. I'm glad I do because once she starts cooking, delicious smells pervade the air. After the eggs set, she adds chopped tomatoes, spinach and red pepper to the pan.

"How do you like your omelets?" she asks. "Hard or runny?"

"I like them hard."

I smile to myself. If Hugh were here, I'd add "like my men," but Renata and Dad aren't the right audience for that joke.

Renata flips the omelet and catches it in the pan, making it look effortless, but I know it's not that easy. Add great cook to her resume.

"Renata makes the best omelets, the best everything," Dad says, giving her shoulders a quick squeeze as he peers into the pan.

"Oh, stop," she says, pretending to smack him away.

The pleased smile on her face tells a different story, and I can't blame her. Who wouldn't want to be adored this way?

She's barefoot and wearing cute cuffed shorts and a tank top. She and Dad met during their senior year of high school in Brooklyn, which means she's around fifty-five years old, but she could pass for ten years younger. I don't know much about their story, except that they dated for a while, then broke up because of their parents' opposition to interracial relationships. That was almost forty years ago, and I have no doubt my grandparents freaked out completely when they heard Dad was dating a black girl.

"Can I get drinks for everyone?" I ask.

"I'll take an orange juice," Dad says.

"Just water for me," Renata says. "Thanks."

I consider pretending to look for the glasses, as if I haven't been snooping around the kitchen earlier, but decide not to get that devious. After pouring drinks, I set the table with the silverware and plates. Renata directs me to the drawer of cloth napkins, which apparently get used at every meal. She really is that classy. I pick a colorful set that look like they were handwoven in Guatemala and place them on the table.

Dad is waiting for the toaster to pop and watching Renata with a pathetic schmoopie face. I can almost see cartoon hearts spiraling out of his eyes. It's astonishing that he's all in like this, considering they reconnected less than a year ago. Despite his friends' attempts to set him up on dates, he hasn't had many relationships since Mom left. The few that he had never became serious, at least on his part.

"You go ahead and start, Andie." Renata deposits an omelet on the plate in front of me. "I have to do one at a time, and if you wait for us, yours will get cold."

"Thank you." My mouth waters at the smell of my food.

"I hope you like it," she says. "Fresh eggs and goat cheese, and veggies from the garden."

The omelet is buttery, savory and moist, without a doubt the best I've eaten in my life. Dad's omelet is ready a couple of minutes later, and he joins me at the table. By the time Renata brings her breakfast to the table, I'm taking my last bite. She sits down and spreads the napkin on her lap before bowing her head and closing her eyes. It takes me a second to realize she's praying. I've never been around people who pray before meals, and suddenly I feel like I've spent my whole life being ungrateful. Even if I don't believe in God, it would be nice to say a little thanks to the universe for being given what many people lack.

"I want to show you around the farm after we eat," Dad says, wiping off his mouth. "I'm going to shower, and then I'll give you a tour. Leave the dishes for us to do, Renata."

"Thanks," she says. "I do need to go to the bank today."

He gets up from the table and bends to give her a kiss on the cheek before taking his plate to the sink.

After he leaves the room, Renata says, "Your dad spoils me. He does almost all of the cleaning up."

"That sounds fair to me. He should clean up if you cook."

Renata smiles. "To your generation, it sounds fair. To mine, it's a revelation."

"I'll be the one doing dishes if I get married. I can't cook to save my life."

Renata's expression turns serious. "I feel bad about what happened at dinner last night. I have no idea why Seth was being so salty. Sometimes I think he spends too much time alone, working on that cabin. He forgets his social graces."

"It's fine," I say with a smile, wondering if Seth ever cared about social graces to begin with. "No harm done."

Despite my reassurances, she still looks distressed. "If we're going to be a blended family, at the very least, I want all of us to get along."

A blended family. I'm part of one of those already, although I never gave it such a pretty label. My mother's second and third husbands have adult children, but I'm not even sure I remember their names. I certainly never thought of them as family.

I picture Seth's face in my mind and tell Renata what she wants to hear. "I'm sure we'll all get along just fine."

DAD STARTS the farm tour with a visit to the goat pasture. Once again, their smell precedes them. After milking them this morning, Dad and Renata put the goats out to graze, and I have to admit they're cute from a distance. When I tell him this, he assumes that I want to walk among them, and heads straight for the gate.

"They're such great animals," he says. "You're going to want to take one home."

I step around a fresh pile of goat shit. "Pretty sure I'd be breaking my lease, but okay."

Thank goodness Renata loaned me a pair of her old "mucking boots" to walk around the farm.

Dad wants to personally introduce me to all of his furry friends. The goats seem about as interested as I am at making these connections, but that's fine. At least none of them are sniffing my crotch. I pet a few of their heads, noting the softness of their fur, before something about their eyes begins to creep me out. It's their pupils. They're shaped like elongated rectangles instead of circles, and once I see it, I can't unsee it.

"There's something zombie-like about their eyes."

Dad laughs. "Only you would say that about the sweetest, gentlest creatures."

A goat named Rapunzel wanders over, which prompts me to ask Dad if Harmony named all of them.

"She named them until she ran out of Disney princesses," Dad says. "Then we started to go for real royalty. That one is Kate and there's Meghan." He points to two goats who are indistinguishable to me.

Princess Kate is napping in the sun, and I find myself envying her easy life. She isn't worrying about global warming, terrorism or the rising price of the avocado. I bend down to pet her soft fur and whisper, "Things are pretty desperate when you're jealous of a goat."

Dad wants to show me the chicken run, which requires a trek to the other side of the farm. High summer in the country is different from the city, and not only because I'm smelling goats instead of exhaust fumes and roasting garbage cans. The sun feels more direct somehow, like it might burn right through the top of my skull. I push a few strands of sweaty hair out of my face, thinking that Dad's floppy, wide-brimmed hat, although ridiculous looking, was a wise idea. There's no shade to be had in these fields, and no breeze either. And the *humidity*. It's not completely oppressive yet, but I'm guessing that in a few hours we'll be moving through liquid air.

"That's Seth's cabin."

Dad points to a white cottage with screened porch on the front and a red tin roof. I've read about the noise rain makes when it hits a metal roof, and I can imagine Seth lying in bed, listening to a summer thunderstorm with Mutt cuddled up at his feet. He's shirtless in this mental image because, hell, why not.

"I was expecting the cabin to be constructed of actual logs."

Dad laughs. "What, like Abe Lincoln's log cabin?"

"I think Tinker Toys are my frame of reference for log cabins. This place is really nice though."

Based on New York City real estate, I'd guess there is

about a thousand square feet of living space inside, which is double my apartment. He's got a chimney so there must be a fireplace or wood burning stove to keep him warm in the winter.

"He built this himself?" I ask, walking closer to the house.

Dad nods and follows me. "He did most of the work. Renata said he spent summers as a teenager working at a cabinetmaker's shop. I guess he got good at building things. He's also one of those people who's not afraid to try anything. He'll watch a YouTube video about installing windows and then go do it. I could never do that."

"That's admirable," I admit, thinking how I'm that way when it comes to certain things, like creating my own website or traveling to foreign countries. I'd never attempt to build anything like this though.

There are two wooden rocking chairs on the front porch and a little table between them with a book resting on it. I can't see the title from where I'm standing.

Dad bends over at the waist and examines his legs. "Don't let me forget, we need to do a tick check when we get home. They head for the warm, moist areas so check everywhere, if you know what I mean."

The thought of ticks burrowing into my armpits and genitals fills me with horror. Immediately, I start scanning the visible areas of my skin, stopping at every freckle and mole to make sure it isn't a bloodsucker.

"Ticks, here? We're not even in the woods right now."

"Tis the season," Dad says, grimacing. "They're everywhere, unfortunately."

Lyme disease. Another reason I have to get my father out of here and back to the city. We may have insidious bed bug issues in Brooklyn, but at least they don't cause scary long-term health problems.

"How is Seth related to everyone here?" I ask.

"He was Michael's best friend when they were growing up. His mom got cancer when he was in high school—cervical, I think—and he took care of her while she went through treatment. She didn't make it, unfortunately."

"That's awful. Where was his dad?"

"He died when Seth was very young. There wasn't anyone in the family to take Seth after his mom died so he went to live with Renata and James. He's really like another son to her."

"Renata's a special person."

There aren't many people who would take a teenager into their house and make him a part of their family. My heart hurts for Seth, having to go through that with his mother. Maybe I need to be more understanding of his abrasive personality. He's been through hell, losing both his parents at a young age.

Dad gives me his lovesick smile. "She really is amazing."

One thing is becoming crystal clear. There's no way Dad is going to leave Renata behind. If I want to get him home, I'm going to have to convince both of them that the goat farm is an overwhelming amount of work and a bad investment. They can cut their losses, move back to New York and enjoy their retirement together. Hell, maybe Seth would want to take over the farm for them. If I can work this angle, I'll get what I want without having to harm their relationship and everyone will end up happy.

"Hey, I noticed a stain on the ceiling above my bed. You might want to check the roof for leaks."

Dad sighs. "I hope not. Thanks for telling me though, I'll check it out."

"Where's Mutt?" I ask, wondering why Seth's dog isn't whining at us from behind the windows of the house.

"He goes to work with Seth." Dad chuckles. "Renata worries that dog has replaced Seth's need for a female companion. Dogs are easier to deal with than a lot of women, I guess."

"Hey!" I slap his arm. "That's not cool, comparing women to dogs."

"Sorry," he says. "You're right. I just meant that a lot of women are kind of high-maintenance. That's one thing I love about Renata. She's easy to be with and appreciates the little things in life."

"There are just as many high-maintenance men as women, believe me," I say. "You haven't dated as much as I have."

"That's probably true."

"My ex-boyfriend, Kirk? He needed music to fall asleep, only it had to be instrumental music. For a full year, I went to sleep to the sound of the pan flute. The guy I dated before him refused to wear any pants with zippers."

Dad holds up his hands. "Okay, stop there. I don't want to hear any more about your boyfriend's zipper-less pants. I believe you. And you need to date better guys."

"Agreed. Speaking of better men, we're playing the Sox tonight. Want to watch together?"

Dad cringes and gives me a guilty look.

"You're going to kill me, but we don't have cable out here yet. I've been listening to some of the games on the radio when they aren't televised on the channels we get."

"You don't have cable?" I say in disbelief.

Dad shakes his head. "Renata isn't a TV watcher, and I wasn't going to ask her to get it for me, just for the summer. When we decided that I'd stay, I started looking around for the cable company with the best deal. I've got a guy coming this week to set it up." He gauges my reaction. "Sorry about that. I know you like watching those big games."

He loves watching those games, too, or he used to. I don't want my dad becoming one of those people who changes completely for the person they love. I'm not blaming Renata; it's this place. Dad's a city guy trying to go country, and it's not going to work for him.

My heart rate picks up the moment I spot the chickens. They're running around in what Dad appropriately calls a chicken run, a huge patch of dirt surrounded by a mesh fence. In the center is a small wooden house with a ramp leading up to its door.

"I thought you fed them this morning." I cower next to him. "We don't need to go in there, right?"

"We put out their pellet food this morning, but we also bring them composted food." He picks up a metal can I've seen in the kitchen. "These are all our table scraps. They love it, and it's really good for them. I think it's the secret to why their eggs taste so good."

He walks toward the door of the chicken run, and I hang back.

"I'll watch from out here."

"Are you sure?"

"Definitely."

He sighs and opens the door, closing it quickly so none of the chickens escape. I watch through the mesh, happy that they can't peck at me from in there. I have to admit the chickens are kind of beautiful. They come in a range of colors from shiny, jet black to white with dark speckles to deep rusty red. There's a heightened excitement when Dad enters, and several of them start following him to the trough where he deposits the food scraps.

Chickens might not be as bad as other birds, particularly because they don't fly high enough to shit on your head or poke your eyes out. They also seem more concerned about pecking the ground than bothering Dad.

"See? They're harmless," he calls out.

I certainly don't want Seth hearing I'm afraid of the chickens. He'd enjoy that information way too much. Maybe it's time I face my fears. I swing open the door of the pen and right at that moment, two of the birds get into a squabble and start squawking and fluttering about. It's like they know I've let my guard down and want to remind me that they're not docile creatures after all.

"They're not going to hurt you," Dad says, oblivious to the danger he is in right now.

"No, thanks!" I call out, slamming the door shut again.

"Do you like their coop? Seth built it for us."

"Lovely," I say. "It's bigger than the apartment Hugh and I shared after college."

Dad laughs. "It's probably nicer inside, too. That place was a shithole. Remember your third roommate, Terrence the mouse?"

"Sometimes I miss Terrence. He was a better roommate than Marly." I think back to that first apartment Hugh and I rented in the East Village in our early twenties. "

We had fun living in that place, even though it should have been condemned. We were so happy to be out on our own that we overlooked all the bad stuff."

"I can't believe you guys slept in bunk beds."

"There was one tiny bedroom so we didn't have much choice."

It's funny how I look back on those times as some of the happiest in my life. Hugh and I would talk late into the night, sharing secrets that probably would not have been told if we hadn't been sharing a room.

"You've got to get over this crazy fear of birds." Dad exits the chicken run and heads to the barn. "I have an idea."

"That's okay, Dad. I'm fine with avoiding birds for the rest of my life."

Whatever magic he thinks he's going to find in there isn't going to work.

He returns with his hands full of a brown, grainy substance.

"Mealworm," he says. "They love it. Come on in and sprinkle some on the ground. You guys will be friends for life."

I look more closely at what he's holding and, yes, those are indeed dried worms. Not only am I not going into the chicken death match arena, I'm not doing it while holding dead bugs.

"Nope," I say. "I'm good."

"They're not going to hurt you. They're really gentle creatures."

Gentle creatures with talons and beaks who lunge at you when you're least expecting it.

"It's day one. Let me work up to it."

Dad looks disappointed, but he doesn't press. He makes one last visit to the chickens to drop the mealworm for them. As expected, they rush over and begin pecking at the dirt to consume their treats. One of them spots me outside the mesh and struts over to me. She regards me with curiosity, tilting her head to the side, and I'm sure she's wondering what I'm doing here if I'm not going to feed them. I have no good answer to that question.

My phone buzzes, and I'm not surprised to see it's another text from Dan.

Why didn't you call me last night? We need to talk.

"Everything okay?" Dad asks, closing the coop door behind him.

"Work drama," I say, shoving my phone in my pocket. "Nothing interesting."

We begin walking back to the house, and Dad taps my arm gently.

"Hey, I didn't mean to upset you last night by talking about your job. I might have been out of line there. If teaching makes you happy, that's great."

"It's okay. It's something I should give more thought."

Dad has no idea that this truly is the best time to consider whether I want to continue teaching. If I do stay at my job, it's going to be painful and hella complicated. There's another, more devious reason I'm glad Dad brought up my career. If I need to leave my school because of the Dan situation, at least Dad will think it's because I've had an epiphany about the direction of my life. Considering my mother cheated on him, he's the last person I want to find out about Dan.

DAD AND RENATA retire to bed early, but I'm not sleepy yet. After a long shower that includes a thorough tick check, I sit on the back porch and make a list on my phone of the things I'm going to need to get at the store, now that I'll be staying for a while: tampons, chocolate, a few more pairs of underwear. It's a beautiful night now that the humidity has finally dropped. The cicadas are humming, and I'm rocking on the porch glider in a peaceful rhythm. If Dad were only staying here for a few more weeks, like he'd originally planned, I might actually enjoy myself.

People Dad's age aren't supposed make rash decisions like this. He's supposed to be volunteering as a docent in a museum and playing pickleball. If I'm floundering at age twenty-eight, it's only natural. Can't I have my quarter-life crisis without worrying about Dad's life, too?

At ten o'clock I decide to call Hugh because I know he'll still be awake.

"This is going to be harder than I thought. Dad's got an adorable new family down here. I'm going to have to stay at least a week." I think about Dad's cute interaction with Harmony and Renata's good cooking. "Maybe two."

"Wait, who's living there besides Renata and Herb?"

I explain how Michael and Harmony live in Chapel Hill, but plan to move here soon. My voice tightens when I tell him about Seth and his cabin.

"Wait, she has two good looking sons living nearby?"

"Who said they're good looking?"

"I'm just guessing from the way you've described them," he says. "Are they?"

I push the floor with my feet to make the glider rock. Michael is objectively handsome, and there's a kindness and openness about him that enhance his good looks. He's a lot like his mom that way. Seth is a big hunk of sexy, but emotionally he's closed tighter than an oyster.

"They're both attractive. And she has a third son I haven't met yet, but I've seen pictures. He's pretty cute, too. He's a doctor in Manhattan, actually."

"Your life was so dull a month ago, and now you hook up with a married co-worker and then—"

I shiver and cut him off, "Please. Let's just refer to that lapse in judgment as 'the thing about which we never speak.' Like Voldemort."

Hugh ignores me and keeps listing, "...you jet south to

bring back your dad and there's not one hot son in town but two! And one in New York for later! You'd better be careful. Someone's going to offer you a reality TV show."

"Yeah, well, the one in New York is engaged, and Michael is a recent widower."

"Well, at least the wife is dead this time."

"Hugh!" I hiss.

"Okay, okay. Sorry." He sounds genuinely contrite. "That was in bad taste."

"And Seth isn't a biological son. He's a family friend who was orphaned, and Renata kind of adopted him as a teenager. I don't know the full story."

"Wow, this really is melodrama. And he's single?" Hugh asks.

"It would appear so. And based on his personality, I can see why."

"Let's move on to his looks. I need details."

Hugh is unabashedly shallow sometimes. Hell, all the time. I can almost hear him rest his chin in his palm as he waits for me to dish. I decide to be honest and appraise Seth as someone who doesn't intensely dislike him.

"He's about six-three and built like an oak. He was a Marine–stop moaning, Hugh–brown eyes that bore into your soul and dark hair, kind of long like it has grown out of a haircut. Interesting nose, sort of big and, I don't know, it works on his face. Oh, and full lips." How could I forget his lips. Women would pay hard cash to get lips like that.

"He's fucking Heathcliff meets Wolverine! I'm swooning over here. Now, if there is the opportunity to get him out of his clothes, like swimming in a lagoon or something—"

"Do you even know what a lagoon is? And are you even going to pretend to listen to what is going on with my dad?"

"Right, right. How is he? Is it racist that every time I

think of Herb and Renata I hear 'Ebony and Ivory' playing in my head?"

"Yes.

And that song is an embarrassment to both McCartney and Jackson."

"Fair point. How is it going with the happy couple?"

I pause the rocking glider by planting my feet on the ground. Was there a sound in the house? I do a quick inventory of what I've said aloud, in case Dad or Renata overheard me on the phone. After waiting a few seconds to see if I hear any other noises behind me, I resume talking and gliding.

"He's acting thrilled that I'm here, and he wants me to get to know Renata better. He told me I should spend the rest of the summer on the farm. Apparently, he thinks I'm the one who needs some time to sort out my life. He says he's fine, never been happier. I'm the basket case, and he's worried about me. Can you believe that?"

"Is this a trick question?"

"What do you mean? You think I'm messed up? The man quit a job he loved, gave up a rent-controlled apartment, and raced down here to pursue a relationship with a woman he just met."

"In truth, he didn't quit. Herb retired after working tirelessly for over thirty years. And he didn't just meet her, right? They had a love affair in high school."

"They dated about forty years ago! Basically, they were strangers when they got back in touch."

There's a sizable silence, then Hugh says, "Stay down there. This is going to be good for you. Spend some time with your dad. And the hottie son. The one without the recently dead wife."

. . .

"THE LAST THING I need to do is get involved with someone down here. I forgot to tell you, Dan texted me again."

"Awkward. He's more attentive than your last boyfriend."

I cringe because it's the truth. Kirk never called, only texted, and he barely did that. It drove me crazy. Hugh used to say that I'm only attracted to men who ignore me. Now I have an attentive guy on the hook, and I just want him to leave me the hell alone.

"What are you gonna do about him?" Hugh asks.

"I don't know. I haven't figured it out yet."

"I suggest you nip it in the bud. Contact him and say it's over. Tell him not to text or call again. You could always threaten to tell his wife, if it comes to that."

I shudder at the thought of calling Nicky. "That would be an empty threat. I would never, in a million years, call her."

"The threat of it would probably be enough. Did you pack enough stuff to stay there for a couple weeks? I could go to your apartment and mail you some things. I'm guessing there isn't very good shopping down at the general store."

"That would be awesome. I'll text you a list."

"And warn Marly," he says. "I don't want her stabbing me with a spade. That one is a little skittish."

"Will do. Thanks, Hugh."

"No problem, sweetie. And if you happen to fall on the lumberjack, I want details. This man-drought of yours has to end eventually."

"Goodnight, Hugh." It's time to end the call because I don't want to admit that he's right.

After my break-up with Kirk last fall, I decided not to date anyone for a while, partly because I was disgusted with the New York dating pool and also because work consumed so much of my time. Between my job and my friends, I was never lonely, and being completely independent felt great. At first, I didn't miss dating at all. If I needed a plus-one for my co-worker's son's bar mitzvah, I invited Hugh. The entire weekend was mine to waste or fill up with activities, and the pan flute was out of my life forever. The only thing I couldn't replace was the physical connection of a relationship. Self-love is a wonderful thing, but I can't surprise myself sexually with a vibrator or hold myself afterwards, it just doesn't work that way.

As I walk upstairs to bed, I consider the possibility of having a fling down here in the dirty South. Seth would be the obvious choice. Personality aside, he's hot, appears to be single, and isn't a total rando, which is comforting. Maybe we could have some satisfying hate sex out there in the green pastures under the night stars. I giggle at the thought, knowing that I'm not serious about any of this. It's a fun fantasy, but not something I'd really consider. After all, I can't complicate my mission, and sleeping with the adopted son of my father's girlfriend would definitely make things complicated.

FOUR

In addition to the birds warbling their songs this morning, there's a banging noise like two blocks of hollow wood being tapped against each other at a rapid-fire pace. I wake up thinking a toddler is in my bedroom playing some kind of preschool instrument constructed by the devil. Turns out, I'm wrong. There's another form of avian torture taking place. A woodpecker is drilling into the house's siding, right outside my bedroom window. I've never heard a woodpecker before so it takes me a few minutes to decipher what is making the evil sound, and several more to decide what to do about it. On an interesting note, real woodpeckers do have red mohawks, like in cartoons, at least this one does. It looks better on him than it did on Rihanna. When I'm done appreciating his natural splendor, I stick my head outside the window and tell him to get the hell out of here.

Once again, I'm awake way too early. I open the bathroom door and have one foot inside before I notice Seth is already there. He's standing by the mirror and wearing what appears to be a very small towel around his hips, but my interpretation of the towel's size might be skewed by the fact that Seth is farmboy sized. He's got a waterfall of muscles from his strong shoulders all the way down to those flat abs. There's not any softness here—no beer gut or flabby pecs. I work my eyes back up to his face, stopping on my field trip across his body to notice that he doesn't have a lot of hair on his chest for a caveman, just a smattering that connects with a trail leading down to...

A moment too late, it occurs to me that I'm very closely inspecting the towel again.

"Sorry, I didn't know you were in here," I mumble, my hand still resting on the doorknob.

He doesn't appear surprised or upset by my hasty entrance. There's no embarrassment at being caught half-naked, nor does he preen for me. I have no idea what he's thinking, as usual.

"I'll be done in a couple of minutes." He moves toward the shower.

I try not to notice the pull of muscles in his bicep or the curve of his backside in that towel when he leans to reach the handles to turn on the water.

"Okay." I want to ask if I can just watch him do whatever he's in the middle of doing because, damn, it's about to smell like soap and shaving cream and all sorts of manliness in here, and I can't seem to bring myself to walk out. His arms are a sculptural delight and bracing my hands on his chest as I straddle those hips would feel—

He cuts his intense brown eyes toward me and says, "Nice shirt."

I look down at my oversized gray Yankees tee that covers me to about five inches above my knees. It's from their 2009 championship season and tiny holes are beginning to wear in the shoulders. The mention of what I'm wearing breaks me from my horny fixation on his body.

"Right, you hate the Yankees."

"No offense. You must be used to it. They're the most reviled team in baseball." He looks me up and down in a way that could be arousal or loathing. I check his towel. Hmmm, maybe a bit of both.

"People hate us because we win all the time. They're just jealous."

"I think you've summed it up nicely. Now can I get back to my..." He gestures toward the shower, but I'm not finished with him yet.

"What do you mean?"

"That attitude. That's the reason people hate the Yankees."

Hot anger spreads through my belly. No matter how fun it would be to slip and slide around a shower with this man, that type of disrespect will not be tolerated.

I take a step out the door and say, "Hard to be humble when you have twenty-seven World Series titles."

He takes a step toward me, and I feel my heart speed up.

"You're just proving my point."

I reach toward him, and his mouth falls open slightly, like he thinks I'm going to touch him. Instead I grab the door handle, and my exit from the bathroom is punctuated with a slam that rocks the house. Immediately, I regret doing it. There's no dignity in acting like a spoiled brat, but there's also no way to take it back.

"Please knock next time," he calls out calmly from behind the closed door.

"Lock the damn door." I'm screeching like some kind of hormonally charged teenager who's fighting with her parents, but I can't help myself.

"Sorry, I can't hear what you're saying," he calls back.

What, are we eight years olds now? In that case, I wish I could flush the toilet and send freezing water raining down on him.

While Seth is showering, I try to read my emails, but I can't focus. I'm seething with anger and coming up with the punishing one-liners I should have used on him. I hate that he got the last word. I hate that he hated on the Yankees. I hate Seth.

I'm kind of surprised he didn't have any tattoos on that expanse of skin I saw just now. No. Do not think about Seth's skin or any other part of him. Focus on the hate.

Promptly five minutes after he turned on the shower, he turns it off again. Hasn't he ever heard of the joys of a long hot shower? He's so predictable and rigid. No, dammit! Do not say rigid or stiff or any other words that suggest sex talk. Disgust must triumph over lust.

The bathroom door on my side swings open, and, before I even leave my bed, I hear the door on his side shut firmly. Perfect. It's better if we don't even speak. Still, it's hard to know if he and I are really in a battle or I've worked this whole situation up in my mind because of my sexual attraction to him. Either way, I need to get over it.

By the time I shower, wash and dry my hair, and get dressed, Seth appears to have left the house. All is silent as I make my coffee and eat a carton of Renata's Greek yogurt. I decide to head to the grocery store later and shop for them. It's the least I can do when I'm eating their food and trying to convince my father that his choice to stay here isn't a viable one.

SINCE I GOT HERE, I've been curious to see what constitutes downtown Foster's Creek. Plus, I need tampons and enough chocolate to drown my fears that Dad isn't coming back to New York anytime soon. Dad gives me directions to the municipal parking lot, which, he informs me, has all of twelve parking spaces, and explains where I can find the local shops.

On the drive to the parking lot, I figure out that the main streets of the downtown are laid out in a pretty straightforward grid. Even someone with my poor sense of direction would find it hard to get lost. Coming into town, I pass through a roundabout that surrounds a stately red brick courthouse. There are several interesting stores, including a clothing consignment store called Twice Nice, an eatery called Ye Olde Sodashop, and a movie theater showing the classic *One Flew Over the Cuckoo's Nest.* All they need is a random wandering troubadour, and this could be the Gilmore Girls' Stars Hollow.

The parking lot is on a residential street, and I have to slog through the heat to get back to the shopping area. The houses are all old, some in a stately way and others a few years past rundown and headed toward dilapidated. One house has a hand-drawn sign in the window that says "Readings by Rita (walk-ins welcome)." The sign isn't lit up or colorful, almost as if the person who hung it there doesn't need people to notice it. Or maybe everyone who lives here already knows about Rita. I've always believed that some people have a connection with the spirit world, and I've never been in greater need of a psychic's advice than I am now, but I can't imagine knocking on a stranger's door and asking what she sees in my future. Maybe I don't even want to know what's in my future because there are several areas of my life that are potentially going to hell in a handbasket.

I walk a little farther and ask a young woman sweeping

the sidewalk in front of a cafe where I can find the pharmacy. The rich smell of coffee coming from inside the shop is enticing, and I make up my mind to stop here for an iced latte on my walk back to the car. It will be my reward for slogging through my errands in this heat.

The shops that I'm passing now are less old-timey and more hipster. For example, there's a butcher's shop whose sign proclaims that it sells "Kind Organic Meat" and a fitness studio that invites me to do bungee yoga, which sounds painful. This town is clearly a mix of the old guard and the newcomers, and I like it more than I expected I would.

The Oak Street pharmacy—definitely old school—has been caught in a time warp. If you want to buy peppermint candies, postcards or compression socks, you're in luck. They don't, however, have my usual brand of shampoo and their chocolate game is seriously weak.

"Is this all the chocolate you have?" I ask the middle-aged guy behind the register as I gesture toward a rack of Nestle's and Hershey's finest.

"That's not enough? You must really be hungry."

I'm not in the mood for his hilarious comments so I grab a Twix and set off to find the feminine products, the selection of which also turns out to be inferior. I could leave now, but instead I browse the aisles so I can freeload off their air conditioning a little longer. I've always wondered what *Gun and Garden* magazine was all about and now I have the opportunity to find out. It's right here on the magazine rack between *Southern Living* and a cooking magazine with Paula Deen on the cover. The store clerk keeps lurking through the aisles, keeping an eye on me, like he's afraid I'm about to pocket a bottle of nail polish. It makes me feel like I'm back in middle school again.

"Do you need help finding anything?" he finally calls out to me while I'm sifting through the greeting cards.

Apparently, there is no appropriate card to send your department chair to say "I'm sorry I'm slutty."

"No, thanks."

He appears at the end of the aisle with his hands on his hips. "Please put the cards back in the right spots."

I give him a smile sweet enough to rot his teeth and say, "That's what I'm doing."

The "dickhead" is implied at the end of that sentence.

After putting several envelopes in the wrong places, I add a couple of trashy celebrity magazines to my basket because I like reading about people whose lives are more screwed up than mine. Then I peruse the display of fuzzy socks because the hardwood floors of the farm house are cold in the morning. When I look down at the items I've collected—chocolate, tampons, lowbrow magazines and fuzzy socks—I feel like a single woman cliché. The cashier doesn't comment on my purchases, but I can tell he disapproves of me. Maybe all newcomers to town get his fish-eyed stare. I look around the store for cameras to see if he was watching me mess up his precious card aisle, but don't find any.

After our transaction is complete, I ask him how to get to Twice Nice, and he pretends not to know what it is. I tell him it's the consignment store with the bright purple and white sign, but he still claims not to know it, which seems fucking unlikely in a town this small.

"Are you new here, too?" I ask him, gripping my plastic bag tightly in my hand.

"Nope," he says, with a smirk. "I've lived in this town my whole life."

I try to stare him down, but it's impossible to look at

someone with that much visible nose hair for very long. In retaliation, I march over to the aisle with the nose hair trimmers, rip one off the rack and smack it down on the counter in front of him before leaving. It was petty, but I don't have time for passive aggressive Southern bullshit.

Fortunately, I pass a woman on the street who isn't an asshat, and she assures me that Twice Nice is only a block down the street, which is good news because I'm withering in the heat. I don't want to be too drained when I get to the consignment shop because I plan to be there a long time. Hugh and Dad tense up every time I spot one of these places because they know I'm going to sift through every rack, bin and box, looking for gems. Hugh says used clothing gives him the heebie jeebies and won't even shop with me anymore.

I'm so focused on my destination that I don't spot the EMS station until I'm directly across the street from it. There's an ambulance parked in the driveway outside, but no one seems to be around. This is probably where Seth is stationed as a paramedic, and I'd prefer to avoid him. I push my aviators up on my nose, like they're going to provide me with a disguise, then nearly trip on a Vespa parked outside the store.

Like every other consignment store, Twice Nice smells like tissues from my grandmother's handbag, which I find strangely comforting. Returning to air conditioning feels divine after the blistering heat outside, and I'm delighted to see that their inventory is a combination of vintage and thrift. There are rows and rows of clothing racks, wooden crates containing hundreds of vinyl records and a display counter full of jewelry. I'm in heaven.

The woman behind the counter looks to be in her early thirties, and she's wearing cat-eye glasses and a bowling shirt embroidered with the name Laverne. When I enter, she's picking through a stack of CDs, but she pauses when she sees me.

"Good morning!" she calls out.

"Is that your bike?" I point at the robin's egg blue Vespa outside.

"Yup, that's my baby. Her name is Stuart." She waves a CD in the air. "Are you up for some Morrissey or should we go with something more uplifting this morning?"

Her friendliness is refreshing and what I expected as far as Southern hospitality. Shopkeepers in Brooklyn might give patrons a head nod on a good day, but usually they ignore everyone. In the city, ignoring people is not considered rude; it's called giving everyone their space. It's the same reason we never make eye contact with each other on the subway. If someone looks directly at you for more than ten seconds, there's a good chance their next move will be aggressively weird.

I gesture down at my black t-shirt and tell her, "Black is what I wear on the outside because black is what I feel on the inside."

Her smile widens at my lyrical reference, and she bends down under the counter. A second later the first song on Morrissey's new album is blaring through the speakers on the wall. She knows every word, but thankfully she's singing at a low volume. The lyrics to this song are really speaking to my current mood: a big FU to society in general. The shopkeeper and I are bopping along to the music companionably while she straightens a display case, and I work my way through a row of dresses.

I'm already feeling high about what I'm going to score here. This is good stuff. Everything in Brooklyn thrift stores has been picked over or is priced beyond reason. The prices here are low and the quality is high.

"Whoa." I pull out a fifties-style yellow cotton dress. It's the color of daffodils, and has a flared skirt and pin-tucked bodice. I can tell from the zipper and label that this is real deal vintage. The waist looks too small for me, like most women's clothing made during this era, but it's worth trying on for size.

I continue shopping, finding a couple of t-shirts, a corduroy miniskirt that will have to wait until fall, and a pair of Levis 501s. There's also a pair of vintage overall shorts that are either the cutest things I've ever tried on or make me look like the Fresh Price of Bel-Air. The mirror in the dressing room tells me they're adorable, and I decide to believe it. When I head to the counter with a large pile of clothing in my arms, "Laverne" looks delighted.

"You found some great stuff," she says, folding each piece as she punches the prices into an adding machine. Apparently the vintage cash register is just for show. "That yellow dress is my favorite, but I haven't been that size since elementary school."

"It's snug, but I love it." I touch the butter colored material. "I'm probably too pale to wear it, but I don't care."

She dismisses that notion with the wave of a hand. "A little pink blush, and you'll be great. Everyone thinks they can't wear yellow, but it depends on the shade."

I wish I had somewhere to wear the dress. I'll have to ask if the Shriner's Fish Fry is a formal event.

She bags up my purchases and chats with me about New York and what brought me down to North Carolina. It turns out Laverne isn't her real name—the shirt is vintage, of course. Her real name is Catriona McBryde, and she's the store owner.

"Do you know Rita, the tarot card reader?" I keep my voice light because I don't want her to think I'm considering visiting a psychic.

"Of course," Catriona says. "Her name isn't really Rita though. That was her grandmother. Her name is Isabelle. She left the old sign out front when she took over the business. Ever been to a psychic before?"

"No." I smile like I'm not taking any of this too seriously. "I've always thought it would be fun though."

Catriona places both hands on the counter, palms down. My heart starts beating faster in anticipation of what she's going to say.

"I didn't believe in all that stuff until she read my cards last winter. She wanted a beautiful coat I had in the store—a sixties vintage wool from Saks Fifth Avenue—but couldn't afford it. She offered to pay me twenty dollars for it, plus give me a free reading." She pauses like a good storyteller who knows she's got her audience on the hook. "I agreed because the coat looked amazing on her, honestly. She predicted that an old lover would come back to town and ask me for money, and I thought she was full of crap. Then, a month later, out of the blue, my ex shows up here asking if I can loan him a couple grand so he can buy a food truck! I hadn't seen him for about three years before that. Freaky, right?"

"That is pretty weird," I admit.

I turn and look out the window to see that the ambulance is pulling back into the EMS station. I didn't even hear it leave. Could I have been oblivious to the sound of its siren? I've been in the store for at least an hour. The paramedics could have gone on a call and returned already. Or maybe they went out to lunch.

"I think you should go for a reading," Catriona says,

pulling me out of my reverie. "You've got something on your mind, I can tell."

Distracted, I look at her blankly for a moment.

"Oh, yeah, kind of," I say. "Maybe I'll go see her."

A sturdy-looking woman gets out of the driver's side of the ambulance, and someone with dark hair exits the passenger side of the vehicle, but it's hard to see details from where I'm standing. There's a styrofoam take-out cup in the woman's hand and my junior sleuthing skills tell me I was right that they were at lunch.

"She might not seem like the person spirits would talk through," Catriona says, still talking about Isabelle, "but I can tell you one thing, she's accurate."

I pull my attention away from what's happening outside the window. "You don't think she made a lucky guess?"

"No way. She got too many details right. But let me know what happens if you go see her. And enjoy that yellow dress!"

"Thanks." I wave and head toward the door. Instead of opening it, I pause and look through the glass.

"Hey." I look back at Catriona who is folding a silk scarf on the countertop. "Do you know if a guy named Seth works at the EMS station?"

She arches an eyebrow at me in a knowing way. "Hmmm, describe him."

It pains me to be accurate about Seth's looks. "Really tall, broad shouldered, pretty dark hair and eyes. He has a tan dog..."

Catriona laughs. "Yes, he works there. I've known Seth most of my life, and it seems like since he got back from the military, women in this town are thirsty for that boy. I've tried to think of some non-life-threatening emergency that would require me to call a paramedic, but haven't come up with anything yet."

We both laugh, and I want to tell her that he's kind of a dick, but I don't. Let Catriona enjoy the fantasy. Besides, maybe Seth saves his nastiness for me and charms the panties off of everyone else. I study her appearance more closely and see that she's a couple inches taller than me and has the body of a fifties pin-up girl: ample bosom, curvy bottom, shapely legs. She and Seth would make a striking couple. A hot bolt of possessiveness jolts through me, and I douse it immediately. Seth isn't mine, nor will he ever be, and I don't give a crap who he dates.

"How do you know him?" she asks.

"He's a family friend," I say nonchalantly, trying to give her an honest answer that doesn't require a lot of explanation. "I'd like to avoid running into him so if you see me skulking out of here like a criminal..."

I glance out the window again like the chicken shit that I am.

Catriona props an elbow on the counter and rests her chin in the palm of her hand. "Did you two do the chitty chitty bang bang, and now it's totally awkward? Because I'm in that situation with one of the tellers at my bank, and now I can't even go in there to cash a check."

"No!" I yelp the word at such a high decibel that I expect dogs to start barking. "Nothing like that."

"That's too bad." She sighs and goes back to her folding. "I was hoping to live through you vicariously. Why are you avoiding him then?"

"We had a really awkward interaction this morning in the bathroom."

Catriona freezes and looks at me like I might be slightly unhinged. "And why were you in a bathroom together?

More importantly, was he with or without his clothing at the time?"

I put one hand on the door handle. "It's a long story. He was wearing a towel and yes, it was all that you think it was and more. Except we don't get along, and if he sees me here, he's going to make a joke about how I'm stalking him so I'm going to put on my big girl pants and head out now. It was nice meeting you, Catriona."

When I'm fairly certain the coast is clear, I push the door open as Catriona chirps, "Come back soon!"

She must think I'm nutty. Hell, I agree with her, at this point. Eyes straight ahead, I motor down the street gripping my bag of consignment goods in my right hand so that if Seth spots me, I have proof that I've been shopping. The pharmacy bag is in my other hand, for balance, and both palms are slick with sweat within seconds.

By the time I arrive back at the cafe for my well-earned iced latte, a mustache of moisture has formed on my upper lip. I chug down a bottle of water before the coffee so I don't dehydrate and require medical attention. I'd beg whoever found me to let me die on the street rather than call 911, but my throat would be too dry to speak. Seth would arrive in his ambulance, smug, sexy and ready to lecture me before starting an I.V. drip.

My daydreams turn to Isabelle and her tarot cards as I sip my drink inside the cafe. Maybe if I had some clarity about the future, I could relax about the present. My summer school paycheck was deposited into my bank account so I have the cash. Of course, I spent almost seventy bucks on thrift store clothing, but that's beside the point.

Ten minutes later, I'm standing on Isabelle's doorstep, preparing to ring the bell. My finger is still poised in the air when the door swings open. Holy shit, she really is psychic.

She rolls her eyes at my shocked expression. "I saw you coming up the front walk. C'mon in."

I'D HOPED for some eccentricity inside the house of a psychic, maybe some crystal balls, candelabras, beaded curtains or what have you. Nothing major like human skulls with glowing candles inside them, but something for ambiance. The living room she's led me into is disappointingly unadorned and unexceptional in every way. The couch is beige, the piano is ancient and the rug is excrement brown and worn thin. The only artwork on the walls is an ugly oil painting of some flowers and an embroidered Jesus.

I appreciate that she isn't going for showmanship, but it would be nice if her air conditioning were a tad more powerful. The ancient unit she's got perched in one of the windows is working hard, but isn't doing much to cool the room. The cheap white blinds on the other windows are spun shut, presumably to keep out the afternoon sun, which begs the question of how she saw me coming up the front walkway.

"Sorry about the state of the place," she says, glancing around the room. "My grandmother passed and left it to me, but I haven't had time to fix it up to my liking."

"I'm so sorry. When did she pass away?"

"About two years ago."

Apparently, you have to read a lot of tarot cards before you can afford a new couch.

As we set up a card table and two chairs, I decide that her appearance is more "H&M model" than "mystical prognosticator." She has the kind of willowy, small-busted figure that looks great in a thin sundress sans bra. As she moves, I catch a whiff of her jasmine scented perfume.

She does a complicated shuffle with the cards then passes the deck to me.

"Hold the cards in both hands and silently ask them a question," she says. "Don't say it out loud. Just repeat it a few times in your mind."

After asking the cards if Dad will stay here or come back to New York, I pass them to Isabelle. She flips the last card so that all five are now displayed in the shape of a cross. This is the thirty-dollar package. She offered to lay out four more cards, but that would have set me back another twenty bucks. I figure dipping my toe in the psychic pool with the basic reading is a good way to begin.

"Huh, interesting," she says, frowning.

I don't know much about fortune telling, but I'm pretty sure you aren't supposed to make a face that indicates to the client that she's doomed.

"What does it mean?" I pray she isn't about to predict an early and painful death.

"This card on the left." She points toward a fairly benign image of a man looking at a pole he's holding. "It's in the position that represents your past, and it's also upside down. It tells me that you've been coming at this situation from a place of insecurity and immaturity."

My mouth opens, but before I can protest against this claim she pokes the center card with a fingernail that has been chewed to the quick. "See this one in the middle? This is your current situation, and you've got the temperance card here. It means change is coming, and you're going to experience some serious transformation."

"Transformation sounds good, right?" I say, trying to sound hopeful.

"Transformation isn't simply change." Her tone is a warning. "It doesn't mean you're going to get a new job or a different haircut. Transformation," she waves her hands around her head in a sudden, wild motion, "means upheaval, the destruction of the old so that something new can form in its place."

Finally, Isabelle sounds like the new-age guru I was expecting.

She jabs another card. "The one below Temperance is Three of Cups. It's like the ultimate soulmate card. Someone has recently come into your life who will be incredibly important. This is someone you will love more deeply than anyone you've loved before."

Isabelle looks up at me like I'm supposed to reveal that I've already met this person, my spiritual soulmate.

"Recently?" I think of Dan, god forbid. "No, there's no one. Does it have to be a romantic thing?"

"Normally, I'd say no." She tents her fingers, looking pensive. "But in this case, with the cards here, I'm feeling a romantic vibe."

"This has nothing to do with what I asked about."

Isabelle shrugs like she's not concerned. "Sometimes you ask a question, but the cards have other things they want you to know."

"What does this person look like? Do the cards tell you that?" I stare at the guy on the Three of Cups. He has light brown hair and blue eyes just like Dan.

A phone rings in another room, and she looks up in the direction of the sound. My hands grip into fists and press into my legs. She'd better not answer that call before telling me if this cups guy is Dan.

"No, the person on the card doesn't necessarily resemble the person in your life," she says, not moving to answer the ringing phone. "Even when the cards give me a mental image of someone, I never tell my client. I don't want to influence the future. That's not my job. Now look at the card at the top of the spread."

The card she's talking about depicts a heart being stabbed by three swords. Stabbed. By. Swords. There's no way this is going to be good.

"This card tells me that the person who has come into your life, this soul mate, is going to break your heart." Her eyes flicker to mine then back to the cards. "Sorry."

"I'm not even dating anyone." My voice sounds wobblier than I'd like. "Are you sure it's a romantic heartbreak?"

Isabelle looks slightly annoyed, like she just explained this and isn't going to do it again, not for thirty bucks. She studies the table as a cat brushes past my ankles. There are pit stains under my armpits now, and there's nothing I want to do more than leave this claustrophobic little room.

"The good news is this card on the right. You've got The Star in your future position." The card she gestures toward shows a naked woman pouring water out of a vessel while a star shines overhead. "This card represents hope. After the heartbreak, love will come again."

Isabelle continues staring at the cards for another moment, then snaps her head up at me.

"Any questions?"

I think about my dad and Renata having to wait thirty years before reuniting and finding true love again.

"What's the timeline on this 'transformation'?"

She reaches down to pet the cat, and he responds by jumping into her lap. That's when I realize it's not a cat.

My eyes widen. "What the hell is that? A guinea pig?"

Isabelle smiles at my confusion and pets the thing that looks like a combination of rabbit and rodent. "It's a chinchilla. The cards don't give me a timeline. Your guess is as good as mine."

I'd like the spirits to be a little more specific, but apparently they don't give names and dates.

"I guess I could avoid all this by not letting myself fall in love."

"Trick fate?" she says in a Southern drawl. "Bless your heart."

FIVE

I could pretend that when Isabelle said I'd recently met my soul mate, I didn't think of Seth and Michael. That would be a lie. They're the only two romantic prospects I've encountered recently, and I use the word "prospects" loosely. With Michael there's no romantic chemistry. He's sweet, handsome and would make a lovely friend, but I'm sure he'd agree that there's nothing happening down under when we interact. With Seth there's heat—

he has got to feel it, too—but there's also a strong desire to strangle him, and not in a Fifty Shades kind of way. Before I call Hugh, I decide not to tell him about my reading with Isabelle. I don't need him trying to figure out what it all means and freaking me out even more about my impending heartbreak.

"Less shopping information, more farm boy description," Hugh says after I tell him about my thrifting finds that morning.

Based on the sound of television chatter in the background and Hugh's occasional crunching, he's lying in bed watching reality shows and eating snacks. Raymond, who only allows people to eat while sitting at the kitchen table, left for a business trip this morning.

"They're not 'farm boys,'" I say. "They don't work on the farm."

I try to envision Seth and Michael riding tractors, feeding the chickens, milking the goats. In my mind they're shirtless and sweaty during these activities because I'm sure that is how Hugh would like them to be. Okay, I enjoy imagining them that way, too. Maybe I could put together a calendar while I'm down here: shirtless small-town hotties. It would sell like crazy. I could be one of those entrepreneurs who makes a million dollars off one idea and never has to work for the rest of her life. I'm already franchising in my mind. Small-town hotties, a reality TV show: it's *The Simple Life* crossed with *Duck Dynasty*. Small-town hotties cookbook: how to raise a pet cow then slaughter and eat it.

"Please, don't make me beg," Hugh says. "I want to hear about the ex-Marine. Indulge me. Monogamy is brutal."

I sigh. "Brutal? Please. Dating in New York City is brutal. Do you miss getting ghosted by people, STD testing at Planned Parenthood, having randos message you dick pics—"

"Okay, fine, monogamy has some wonderful aspects to it. Excitement, however, is not one of them."

If Hugh wants to know about Seth, I'm going to give him the blunt, unfiltered version.

"Fine. He's got caveman pheromones and an ass you could bounce a quarter on. He's also a self-righteous jerk. He accused me of snooping around the kitchen. Can you believe that?"

"Were you?" he asks.

"Yes, but he didn't know that!"

"What were you hoping to find in the kitchen?

Evidence that reveals Renata's troubled past of shaking down lovelorn retirees?" Hugh laughs at his own joke.

When he puts it that way, I feel completely ridiculous for trying to look through the notebook in the kitchen drawer.

"I'm just saying he didn't know that I was snooping. Maybe I was looking for a paring knife or a zester."

"I'm surprised you know what either of those things are," he says dryly. "So you two have some friction going on. I like it. Hate sex can be fun, but I shouldn't encourage you. You need a healthy relationship for once. Speaking of relationships, have you ruined your father's yet?"

"Very funny. My intention isn't to break them up. I just want to convince them to come live in the city with me."

In fact, I did very little to work toward that goal today. Thrift store shopping and visiting a psychic weren't going to bring Dad home. I needed to focus and get on my game.

"You do realize how evil this is, right?" I hate it when Hugh uses his lecturing tone. "The man is finally happy and in love, and you're putting that in jeopardy because you need to have him living ten minutes away from you."

What he's saying hits dangerously close to the truth. I do want Dad to live near me, and maybe that is selfish. Although, there's more to this than what is at stake for me.

"You know that's not what this is all about. He can't just walk away from his whole life without carefully considering what he's doing. I think if he went back to New York, even for a week, he'd realize that he misses his old life. This is a fun adventure, but it's not who he is. People who make impetuous decisions like this live to regret it."

"And you said the hottie is self-righteous," Hugh says. "Have you considered that Herb isn't like your mother? He doesn't make impulsive decisions. He does copious research and price comparison before he commits to buying a new pair of sneakers. Maybe he came to this decision after thinking it over carefully."

"Right, because becoming a goat farmer is such a logical career move for Dad."

"I don't think it's about a career," Hugh says. "He's thinking about what makes his heart happy, and that's not all bad."

The screen door slams, and my head snaps toward it in surprise. Seth is standing there, and for once his expression isn't inscrutable. He heard me talking about Dad, and he's pissed.

"Gotta run," I tell Hugh. "I love you."

I swipe the screen to end the call, and Seth continues to loom behind me, saying nothing. He's still wearing his work uniform, dark pants and a matching short-sleeved button-down shirt. There's a red and gold patch on his sleeve making him look very official and, goddammit, what is it about a man in a uniform?

"Hey, what are you doing here this late? Did you just get off of work?" I say, casually playing off the fact that I'm mortified.

Thank god I didn't turn on the porch light when I came outside because my cheeks are a lovely shade of scarlet right now. He knows that I want to take Dad back to New York. Still, it could be worse. He could have arrived moments earlier and heard me rhapsodizing about his good looks. That would be unbearable.

"They blew a fuse and needed my help," he says in a flat voice, gesturing toward the house. Then he whistles and calls out, "C'mon, Mutt!"

His dog gallumps across the lawn, all legs and paws, and bounds up the porch steps. Seth opens the screen door to let him inside, and Mutt spots me and makes a beeline for my lady parts. This dog is singularly focused, which is particularly disturbing considering Aunt Flo is in town. This time I'm ready. I intercept his head and scratch behind his ears before he can make contact with my private areas.

"Let's go, Mutt," Seth says darkly.

The dog gives me one last longing look, as if he's having trouble choosing between us so I stop petting him and lean back, my hands clenched on my lap. Once he's been rejected, he gives me a parting lick on the knee and trots to Seth's side. Seth doesn't bother to say goodnight before banging out the screen door and striding off into the darkness with his dog at his heels.

I sit there for another hour, watching the fireflies flicker around the yard and listening to the cicadas drone. The scent of jasmine drifts past me on the night breeze with only the occasional whiff of goat stink to ruin it. It's impossibly romantic and atmospheric here, even to a jaded Yankee like me. The only thing that would improve this fine evening would be a bar of really good dark chocolate, maybe one with sea salt or candied ginger inside it. Also, not being spied on by a judgmental future stepbrother who enjoys giving death stares, that would be good, too. I can't believe I ever considered that Seth could be the person Isabelle mentioned in her reading. That is never going to happen. Never.

This is how Dad became convinced he should stay here. He fell prey to the scenery and the season. It's the classic problem of living in a vacation fantasy world. Like the couple I know who went to Hawaii, soaked in the beauty of the islands, and decided to chuck their lives as corporate wage slaves. They didn't think about natural disasters, housing prices and the size of tropical bugs. Within a year, they were back in Manhattan begging for their old jobs. Unfortunately for Dad, summer nights and the rush of a new love affair won't last forever. This fall the reality of retirement in a hick town will hit him, and he's going to have some serious regrets. Maybe he already does.

For a long time, I rock on the glider, replaying my conversation with Hugh to determine exactly what Seth heard. Eventually, I come to the conclusion that it doesn't matter what he heard or what he thinks about me. He's someone I met a couple of days ago, and someone I won't have to deal with for much longer. The fact that he has some weird effect on my libido is not relevant. It's biological, and I can overcome those urges. That's the advantage of being a human and not a canine like Mutt. We can keep our noses out of inappropriate crotches, so to speak.

EVEN THOUGH I ran this morning, my legs are still restless, the muscles in them twitching like they need to move and release more energy. Before I even get into bed, I know I'll have trouble sleeping. I suppose that's part of the problem. Worrying that I'll have insomnia only makes it more likely that I will. I try to prep myself for a restful night, smoothing so much lavender lotion on my hands that I smell like an old woman's lingerie drawer. After doing a quick ten-minute meditation using an app on my phone, I turn out the light and close my eyes. My mind is unsettled, playing the "what if" game on an endless loop. What if Seth tells Renata what he overheard? What if Isabelle is right, and I'm coming at this situation with Dad from a place of insecurity and immaturity? What if Dan has told Barb about us? What if I lose my job? What if, what if, what if?

As predicted, I have a terrible night, finally falling asleep around one o'clock, then waking up again around three thirty. When it becomes clear I won't be able to go back to sleep, I turn on the light and pull a yellowing copy of *Mrs. Dalloway* off a bookshelf in my bedroom. Even this comfortable mattress and Virginia Woolf's stream of consciousness babble can't ward off insomnia. After reading several chapters, of which I remember nothing, I put the book away and draft three texts to Dan before I realize that what needs to be said can't be captured in this medium. I'm going to have to suck it up and call him. It's almost dawn when I fall into a fitful sleep once again.

When I wake up at ten, I'm groggy and ill-tempered. Everything I was worrying about at bedtime comes flooding back to my mind, like a wave I can't outswim. I'm going to have to deal with my personal issues if I ever want to sleep again.

I sit up in bed and gulp down water from the glass on my night table. There's no point in putting off my talk with Barb. Taking a deep breath, I pick up my phone and find her in my contact list. Barb Wicker. She has both a landline and a cell. I try her home phone first, unsure whether or not I want her to answer. On one hand, it would be nice to get this call over with, and on the other hand, I'd rather get a pelvic exam than talk to her right now.

"Hello?"

"Hey, Barb." I pick nervously at the zit on my chin. "It's Andie Fiarello."

"Andie! How are you? How has your summer been so far?" She sounds genuinely pleased to hear from me, and relief rushes through me. There's no way she would sound this pleasant if she knew Dan and I were sucking each other's faces a few nights ago.

"I'm alright. I'm down in North Carolina visiting my dad right now."

"Fabulous! That sounds like a lot more fun than what I'm doing right now, cleaning out closets and sorting through the things my daughter left here when she moved out. She got married last month."

"That's right," I say, remembering only now that Barb's daughter had a wedding recently. Instead of moving in with her fiancé, she lived with her parents until the wedding, which is incredibly anachronistic by New York standards. Leave it to Barb to have a daughter who didn't want to cohabit until her fiancé officially put a ring on it. "I hope the wedding went well?"

"It was wonderful! We had amazing weather, couldn't have asked for a more beautiful day, and Caroline looked gorgeous. Of course, I'm biased." Barb gives a tinkling little laugh. "But she really did."

"Wonderful! I'm so happy for her!" My anxiety is currently manifesting as over-the-top enthusiasm. "I got your message."

"Yes, yes. We need to discuss next year. We've got a room situation. Have you heard?"

I freeze at the phrase "room situation" and lose all my words, which creates an awkward pause in the conversation. My first thought is that Dan has approached her about switching classrooms to get away from me.

"Andie, are you still there?"

"Yes, I'm still here." I try to sound normal when inside I'm completely wigging. "Sorry, what's the situation with rooms?"

"The school's enrollment has gone up for next year, and they've hired two more teachers for our department. Not that they asked me about it, but that's neither here nor there.

We're stretched for space, and they need teachers to share rooms. I thought since you and Dan are next door to each other, it wouldn't be far for him to move all of his belongings into your space. And you two are good friends already. Would it be a hardship for you if he moved in with you next year?"

I almost laugh out loud at the ridiculousness of this situation. Not only does she have no idea what happened between Dan and me, she's suggesting that we shack up as roomies.

"Have you proposed this to Dan yet?"

"No," she says. "I thought I'd ask you first. I'm fairly certain Dan will be alright with the change. You know how laid back he is about everything."

I'm not sure how to say no without sounding high maintenance and difficult. Then again, there's no way in hell Dan and I can share a room. I have to think quickly if I want to get out of this mess.

"You know what might be a good idea? If I share a room with one of these new teachers. They might appreciate being around someone who knows how the school works."

I peer out the window as we're talking and spot Renata and Seth walking toward the barn. He should be at work right now. Then again paramedics probably have funky schedules like doctors and nurses where they work several long shifts then have a few days off. He's wearing basketball shorts and a t-shirt, and I get another glimpse at his legs. That first night I met him, he was wearing shorts, and I noticed his muscular calves. His legs are paler than the rest of him, most likely because he wears pants at work and probably when he's building the cabin.

"That's an interesting idea," Barb says. "Let me think about that, and we can talk again. You might want to get in touch with Dan and ask his feelings. He may prefer to be with you."

I'm leaning a little too far off the bed to get a better view of Seth and nearly fall on my head when she speculates about Dan's desire to be with me. It's like she's intent on throwing us together. If Barb were less formal and prudish, I'd be tempted to tell her that there's no way Dan and I can room together because there's unresolved sexual tension between us. Scratch that. The tension has been resolved and died an ugly death. Now that I think about it, she's probably the only person in our department who doesn't realize he and I have been flirting. I'm not sure if I'm more ashamed that we've been so obvious or if I let myself be blind to the way we were acting.

"I'll speak with him," I assure her.

"Thanks so much, Andie. I'll check in with you in about a week. Enjoy your time down South!"

"Thanks, Barb. Good luck with the closets, and congratulations to Caroline and..." I realize I don't know her son-in-law's name, "her husband."

Note to self: stop being so self-absorbed and listen to other people.

Barb wants me to contact Dan, and, for my own reasons, I definitely need to talk to him, but I'm still not ready. The room situation actually provides us with a solution to at least part of our mess—one of us will volunteer to move in with a teacher who is on a different hall. That way we can get some physical distance at work. The emotional connection that we need to sever, that's another story. Right now, I need to focus on what's happening with my father though. When I return to New York, I'll deal with Dan. For now, I've got to let him know that I'll be in touch when I get home, otherwise he'll keep texting me. I study the message

I've written him, revising it neurotically at least fourteen times.

Hi Dan. I'm visiting my father in NC. Will call you when I get back in town.

At first I end it with "take care," but that sounds ludicrously casual. I consider adding a random emoji or GIF to lighten the mood, but I don't. Dan and I can't share jokes anymore. From now on, I'll have to act like Barb around him, buttoned up and proper. I decide to leave it at the two-sentence message and hit send. Dan won't like it, but my hope is that with his wife, kids and summer school job, he's too busy to pursue me right now.

WHILE I'M SIPPING my coffee in the sunny kitchen and catching up on the news via my phone, Dad calls me from the cheese room. He's looking for some calculations he scribbled down on a piece of paper in Renata's office. I offer to find them, and it's the first time I've been inside this small room on the main floor. There's a wall lined with bookshelves, a pretty red filing cabinet, and a desk full of papers and mail sorted into piles. On the wall behind the desk is a gallery of family photos. After I give Dad the number he needs, I stay to look at the pictures.

The most prominent one in the center of the wall is a wedding photo of Renata and her late husband. She's fresh and lovely, and he's holding onto her and smiling like he could burst with happiness. Flanking it are Michael and Trey's high school photos, handsome young men who look like their dad and have bright futures ahead of them. Michael got the charming dimple and easy smile, but Trey got the pretty eyes.

Harmony's life is documented from birth, safe in her mother's arms as a baby, smashing her first birthday cake, and racing down a slide as a toddler. There's a more recent picture of her with Michael on a carousel, and some of the light has gone out of his smile in that photo. I know without asking that it was taken after his wife passed away. I can't imagine the pain they both felt, losing a wife and mother way too soon.

There aren't many photos of Seth, and I would bet money that it's because he doesn't like having his picture taken. There is one official looking headshot of him in his dark Marine jacket with brass buttons and a white hat, the black peak of which is pulled down so low it covers his eyebrows. He barely looks like the same person, what with his jug ears revealed by an awful buzz haircut. He was a little baby back then. As I look at the photo, I imagine the fear Renata must have experienced when he joined the military.

"I appreciate your service even if you are an asshole," I say sternly to his picture.

I have the juvenile idea of giving him a loopy mustache with a Sharpie pen, but I don't need to do it. Just the thought is satisfying enough. I smile and trace his top lip with my finger.

Would Renata add a picture of Dad and herself to this wall? The idea is so strange to me, I can't imagine it. A blended family, she said. And that's how strangers become the most important people in your life.

WHEN I COME out of the office, Seth is heading down the hallway wearing his tool belt over his shorts, a tragically dorky look. He stops abruptly when he sees me and stares.

I raise my hands in the air like I'm about to be arrested. "I was told to go into Renata's office to get something for Dad. I wasn't snooping." Instead of responding, he continues looking at me. "What?"

"I heard you on the phone last night," he says. "Obviously."

The best thing to do in these cases is get on the offensive.

"So I'm a terrible person for looking in kitchen drawers, but eavesdropping on people's conversations is fine. Got it."

Seth scowls and sets his hands on his waist. "I wasn't eavesdropping, I was walking out the door. You were sitting on the porch. It's not exactly a private area of the house."

"I'll remember to stay in my room and lock the door when I want to speak on the phone." I mimic his stance by planting my hands on my hips and standing up taller. It's tough to look imposing when you're wearing overall shorts, but I'm fairly sure I'm pulling it off.

"I think you're here to break up Renata and Herb," Seth says. "Am I wrong?"

Mutt's ears perk up in response to our tension.

"Yes, you are. I'm here to make sure Dad isn't jumping into something that's going to get him hurt. Renata is lovely, but he's given up everything to come down here and help her with this place. He gave up his job, his apartment, his friends—"

"What do you think," Seth says, cutting me off, "that she lured your dad here to take care of her? The man can barely change a lightbulb. I was here last night because your dad blew a fuse in the bedroom using his hair dryer and couldn't figure out how to find the fuse box and flip the switch to get it going again. Does this sound like a guy Renata would trap into running the farm while she sits around drinking lemonade?"

Rage. I'm a boiling pot of rage. How dare he make my father out to be incompetent. My mother you can criticize any day of the week, but Dad is my hero.

"Are you saying he's incapable of taking care of someone just because he can't build a cabin in the woods? My mother left when I was twelve, and Dad and I were on our own. He raised me single-handedly on a teacher's salary. He did the cooking, cleaning, child-rearing, clothes shopping, doctor appointments. Everything. Who have you ever taken care of like that in your life?"

His eyes darken, and suddenly I remember that Dad said Seth cared for his sick mother. I'm figuring out how to apologize when he speaks again.

"I've taken care of other people. I also know how to take care of myself, including changing a fuse and knowing enough to clean out the gutters when they're full of debris."

"I thought Renata said you were a feminist?"

Seth eyes me with mistrust. "I am, I guess."

"Then why are you criticizing my dad for not being handy? Maybe Renata can be the one to make home repairs. It's not 1960. Plus, we've lived in apartments our whole lives. He's never had to learn that stuff, but he can, and maybe he will."

"Not if you have a say in it though, right?" Seth shoots back at me. "He's going home with you as soon as you can convince him he made a 'huge mistake.' "

I cringe, hearing my own words spewed at me with such venom. Mutt is looking back and forth between us like a child trapped in the middle of a parental disagreement.

"Even before I overheard that conversation, I knew why

you were here." Seth takes a step toward me. "That first night at dinner it was clear you were lonely and desperate to get him to come home."

My breath catches and it's audible to both of us. How. Dare. He. At least now I know how he's been describing me to other people. Lonely and desperate.

"So what's the bottom line here?" My voice is shaking from anger. "You're going to tell Renata and Dad what I said, aren't you?"

"No, you go ahead and execute your plan. If your dad can be convinced to turn tail and run that easily, he doesn't deserve her."

A low growl escapes my mouth, and I feel myself moving forward, too. There's only about a foot of space between us now, and I'm so close I can hear his breathing. Seth's eyes flicker to my lips for a fraction of a second, and I lick my bottom lip unconsciously in response.

I see what Seth's doing here. If Dad leaves with me, he looks weak-willed. If he stays, I'm alone in New York. Either way, I'm in a losing position. He has miscalculated though. I'm not going to let his opinions of my father stop me from getting him the hell out of here. Sure, I'll need to reflect later on my odd need for other people to esteem my father as highly as I do, but that's why I have a therapist on call in New York. There's no time for psychoanalysis right now.

"I think it's interesting that you're lecturing me on interfering in my dad's life. You, the single guy who built a house on his mother's property."

Seth's nostrils flare, and I know I've hit a tender spot. "What's that supposed to mean?"

I look pointedly at Mutt then back at Seth. "Maybe I'm not the only lonely and desperate person here."

Seth doesn't try to stop me as I stalk away, and the imaginary scoreboard lights up with the points I just made. Having the last word should feel better than this.

The last thing I hear is Mutt's sad whine as he watches me go.

SIX

The farmer's market doesn't open until seven o'clock, but Dad and I are on the road by five. Me: grumpy and bleary eyed. Dad: annoyingly chipper and chatty. It should take us less than a half hour to get there, and I'm not sure why we need an hour and a half to set up a table for the cheese and eggs, but I'm not in charge. Dad is such a super freak about being on time for every event that he arrives ridiculously early. When we go to ball games, we roll into an empty parking lot and watch the grounds crew prepare the field for an hour. Arguing with him about it is useless so I got up today at the butt crack of dawn and pulled on shorts, a tank top and a baseball hat without even bothering to shower. I'm only going to get sweaty in this heat anyway.

The sky is burnished with pinks and golds, and there's no denying the beauty of a morning drive on a country road. The college radio station is playing mellow indie rock, we have thermoses of good coffee, and the air is still cool enough to leave the windows open. It's the perfect morning, or it would be if my life weren't in turmoil.

I look over at Dad's contented expression as he directs

the pickup down a sloping hill and around a bend in the road. Today we'll have a lot of alone time, and it's the perfect opportunity to discuss his future. I have to be careful how I approach it, but I know there's a way to convince him that he and Renata should move back to New York.

When we're a few miles down the road, and I'm awake enough to talk, I ask Dad what he's planning to do about his apartment and all his stuff in it. When he drove down here, he brought one suitcase with him because he was only planning on staying for the summer.

"I'll fly back to New York in a month or two and rent a U-Haul to bring the rest of my stuff down here. I wanted to talk to you about my apartment. I know you like living near the park, but if you took over my place, you'd be paying a quarter of what you do now, and you wouldn't need a roommate."

When Mom left, Dad suddenly had to cover the entire rent by himself. We couldn't afford our Brooklyn Heights apartment anymore, and, to my horror, Dad found us a rent-controlled two-bedroom on a fairly seedy street in Red Hook, Brooklyn. I was motherless and living in what felt like the edge of nowhere, an industrial port full of towering cranes and packing containers.

Over the years, gentrification spread through Brooklyn like a disease, and Red Hook was one of many areas that transformed. Now Dad lives amidst small batch breweries and artisan chocolate stores. It's a shame he didn't invest in property back in the day because the townhouses in Red Hook that were once dirt cheap sell for about three million dollars today. The only downside to it is the lack of subway access in the area.

"It would be a bear trying to get to work every day," I say. "I'd have to take the bus to get to the subway.

I'd be looking at almost an hour commute, if the trains were actually running on time."

"You could buy a car," he says.

"With what money? My credit is good, but car payments would take up all the cash I'd save in rent by living there."

"Maybe you could take my car," he suggests. "I don't really need it down here. We've got the pickup, and I rarely go into town without Renata."

I sense an opening, and my heart rate picks up.

"Maybe you should keep your place for a while. In case things don't work out down here."

I stare out the window at a cornfield that's been stripped clean because I can't meet his eyes. Dad doesn't speak for what's probably a minute, but feels like eternity.

"Things are going to work out with Renata and me," he says, and I'm relived there's no anger in his voice, just conviction.

"Of course." I know not to push it too far. I need to plant seeds, not run a lawnmower over him. "I'm just saying it's wise to keep your apartment for now. In case you guys decide you want to live in the city instead of down here. Or, you know, if the business doesn't pan out like you want it to."

"You like Renata, don't you?" he asks.

"Of course," I say emphatically. "She's great, wonderful, in fact. This relationship is just very new, and living down here is a huge change. I know you guys are really trying to make a go of this goat farm, but I want you to protect yourself a little."

Dad is quiet for the rest of the ride, and I'm hoping that my words have had an effect on him. He's got to see that his decision was rash. If he loses his rent-controlled apartment, it would be impossible for them to find something in New York that they could afford. I'm not being a buzzkill, I'm just being realistic. Those are two very different things, right?

THE FARMER'S market near Chapel Hill is much smaller than the one in Brooklyn and has charm coming out of its mung beans. The vendors' stalls are housed under a gorgeous wooden pavilion made of the warmest pine I've ever seen. On the walk over from the car, we pass a group of elderly people doing tai chi, a middle-aged hula hooper, and a young woman standing in front of a table with a sign that says Everything Free Market. It's the kind of hippie scene you'd expect to find in northern California, and seeing it in the South takes me by surprise. Dad leads me to our table, and I help him spread Renata's pretty blue and white checked cloth across it. He has a system for setting everything up, and I follow his lead.

"We'll cut up cheese samples when it's closer to opening time," he tells me while standing up a small sign that reads *One dozen farm fresh eggs $5.*

"I'm impressed," I say. "You've got this down to a science."

Dad smiles. "It's a lot of fun. I like getting out here and talking to people. We do a decent business, and we're getting our name out there."

He sets up two folding chairs for us to sit on while we wait for the market to open. I'm thankful that he also brought two cushions so my sweaty thighs won't adhere to the metal seat.

"What's the long-term game plan for the farm?" I ask, after taking a seat.

"We're hoping some local chefs will try our cheeses and ask us to supply their restaurants. Then we can start producing in larger batches, but we'd need to own more goats to do that."

"More goats? It seems like you have a lot already."

"Well, they don't produce that much milk. In fact, females only produce milk if they're bred so last winter Renata had to hire a buck to impregnate the herd."

I wrinkle my nose. "One buck for all those females? That seems a little sister wife-ish to me."

Dad smiles. "Very funny. Renata sold the kids that were born last spring. If we have more cheese orders, we could keep the offspring next time, at least the females, and maybe one or two bucks."

Personally, I think there are more direct ways of getting people to taste Joyful Goat Farm cheese than getting up early and sitting in the miserable heat all day, hoping someone will stop by the table and taste the feta, but I don't say so. Over the last few days, I've realized that Renata is so focused on the science end of cheesemaking, she hasn't had time to think about marketing. Clearly, my father with his little farmer's market cheese stand doesn't have a clue, but I've been percolating with ideas. Joyful Goat Farm has zero social media presence, and they need to set up a website and an Instagram account for their business. They could arrange tasting appointments with local chefs, as well as with buyers at local fine foods stores. And then there's the missed opportunity of having events at the farm.

There's only one thing stopping me from making suggestions that could help them build their business: I want my father to come home. If the goat farm becomes a success, there's a good chance Dad will stay here forever.

"What do you enjoy about the goat farm?" I ask. "Other

than being with Renata."

Dad pauses, then says, "It's peaceful. I like the pace of life at the farm. We're busy, for sure, but it's different. There's no need to hurry anywhere, and I don't have to deal with commuter traffic or keep up with which subway line is closed. That got old."

"True."

There's not much I can say in defense of New York's dirty, inefficient subway system.

"It's more than that though," he says. "As a teacher you're always thinking about your students' futures. I spent thirty-three years helping other people launch into the world, and I loved it. But now it's my turn. Renata and I are building something for ourselves, and that feels really great."

A lump forms in my throat. When he puts it that way, I can't bear to think his venture will fail. If I get what I want, it will be because Renata and Dad's dream has died.

Throughout the morning, other vendors smile and say good morning to Dad. When he greets them back, he knows many of their names. This doesn't surprise me. At school, he made sure he knew the name of everyone on the faculty and staff, which isn't easy at a large city high school. Many of his closest friends were from work—the guys he jogged with on the weekends, the women who fixed him up on dates over the years, the people who watched me grow up and saw him transition from married man to single Dad. It was unfathomable to me that Dad cut his ties with these people so abruptly when they were an integral part of his life for over thirty years. There was no retirement celebration for him, not even a goodbye party with his beloved history department members. I still can't wrap my head around how he could jettison his old life when it obviously meant so much to him.

"Have you talked to anyone from back home?" I ask.

"Sure. Mitch called me a few days ago. And I talked to Victor last week."

These are two of Dad's oldest friends who are like uncles to me. Mitch likes to tell people that the first time he met me, I peed on him. Obviously, I loved it when he told that story to my friends when I was in middle and high school.

"What did they have to say about you moving down here permanently?"

Dad takes a sip of his coffee, and I'm jealous he has some left. Mine was gone before we were halfway to the market.

"I think they're a little confused." Dad chuckles like this is silly of them. "You know Vic wouldn't even consider moving to Jersey so my moving down here is—" He makes a gesture with his hands to simulate a brain explosion. "But he said he and Angie will come down and visit me at some point, maybe this fall. Mitch made me promise not to become a Trump supporter. I don't let that kind of closed-minded comment bother me though. They don't know what it's really like here." He greets another vendor with a wave, then says, "I should probably call your mom and tell her what's going on with me."

"Why?" I ask, completely baffled by this statement.

Dad shrugs and waves at the guy across from us who has backed an enormous flatbed truck of corn up to the pavilion.

"I feel like she oughta know where I am and that I'm getting married again."

When he says the word married, my chest squeezes. Even though I'm right here, living with Dad and Renata, I haven't processed the fact that he's really going to marry someone.

"You don't owe her anything," I say.

"I know. But I try to treat her the way I'd like her to treat me."

Dad has always been this considerate of my mother, which is noble, especially since she informed him that she was leaving him for her dermatologist in a thirty second message on his voicemail. After divorcing Phil, she married a financial consultant con artist, but that relationship lasted less than a year. Last I heard, she was dating a retired professional golfer. Mom rarely told Dad about these changes in her marital status, and he only knew because she called me every few months to celebrate her happiness or rail against her misfortune. None of it was ever her fault, of course. Things happened *to* my mother, and she took no responsibility for anything.

"Did Mom know Renata?" I ask.

They all attended the same high school, but Mom was two classes behind them.

"No, but Renata's name came up once or twice over the years. She might remember, but probably not."

We exchange little eye rolls that acknowledge Mom's self-absorbed nature.

A young man with pretty blue eyes and brown hair that the sun has washed blond at the tips approaches our table. He's holding a little green carton full of fruit and has a wide friendly smile that I find myself returning. Nice body, good teeth, confident walk. Check, check, check.

Down girl, I remind myself. The fact that I've been on a sex starvation diet for the past nine months is beginning to show its effects. Lately, I'm thinking about jumping the bones of every cute guy who comes within a ten-foot radius. Hell, I considered getting naked with Seth, which must mean he's right. I am desperate.

"Hey, Herb." The young man's eyes flitter over to me then back to Dad. "I brought you some of our berries, as promised. They're one hundred percent organic and just picked this week."

"Hey, Rhett." Dad reaches out and takes the blackberries, raising the container to his nose to take in their scent. "Wow, these smell amazing." He holds the berries toward me. They smell sweet and earthy, and I can't help popping one in my mouth.

"Delicious," I say.

Rhett looks proud, like he grew and picked these berries himself, and maybe he did. The t-shirt he's wearing says Blue Sage Farm. He's got a deep tan and a wiry, muscular body that suggest he spends his days working outside.

Dad gently wraps an arm around my waist.

"Rhett, this is my little girl, Andie."

I kind of love that he still calls me his little girl. At least someone still sees me as young and innocent.

"She came for a surprise visit from New York," Dad says, "which is so wonderful, I can hardly believe she's here."

Rhett and I shake hands. His grip is warm and firm, and a flicker of lust stirs in me again. I should be glad to know my libido hasn't completely died. It seems like the change of scenery down here has reawakened my sexuality, which is unexpected and not exactly convenient.

"How long are you here?" Rhett asks.

It's a simple question, but I haven't got an answer.

"I'm not sure yet. Probably another week or so."

"I'm afraid she's going to get bored out at the farm, Rhett. Are there fun things for young people to do around here in the evenings?"

Dad is not being subtle, and I'm embarrassed both for Rhett and myself.

"Not much." Rhett doesn't appear phased in the least at my Dad's awkward attempts to fix me up with him. "But there is a local place on Highway 68 called Ricky's. I'll be there Saturday night with some friends. You should come out, Andie."

He sounds earnest, and I find myself considering the invitation.

"Thanks," I say. "Maybe I will."

I could use a night out of the house, and Rhett is easy to look at. I'm not sure how old he is, but I'm guessing a couple years younger than me.

"She's a vegetarian," Dad says. "She's in heaven with all these vegetables around."

I poke Dad with my elbow to let him know he's overselling me.

"Oh, yeah?" Rhett says. "So am I. I'm trying to go vegan, actually. You've got to try the peaches and watermelon we've got right now. They're amazing. And I'll hook you up with some vegetables, too. Come down to our table." He points to the other end of the pavilion. "We've got some great stuff this week."

Dad forces Rhett to take a sample of goat cheese before he lets him leave. Then we wave goodbye, and he heads off to his precious produce stand.

"Rhett wants to have his own farm someday," Dad says. "He's got direction. I like that in a young man."

"Dad, stop," I warn him. "I'm only here for a couple days. You want me to find a boyfriend who lives hundreds of miles away?"

Our conversation is cut short by our first customers of the day. We have a steady stream of people for the first hour, some coming by for cheese tasting and others interested in the eggs. The returning customers have nothing but praise for our chickens. Dad is in his element. He's always been at ease with people, knowing what to say and how long to keep the conversation going. He's just as friendly to the people who only come by for a sample as he is to those who spend twenty dollars on eggs and cheese.

After an hour or so, I need to use the restroom; afterwards, I stop by the Blue Sage Farm table. Rhett keeps his word and hooks me up with the best of what they're selling, but I insist on paying for everything I get. I'm excited about making a salad for dinner—butter lettuce, arugula, cucumbers, radishes, tomatoes and red pepper. I'll top it off with Joyful Goat's soft cheese and a sprinkle of nuts. Even I can't ruin a salad.

Rhett mentions again that I should come by Ricky's on Saturday night. He describes it as an old-school bar and grill, kind of honky tonk, but mostly in an eccentric, self-aware way. I'm not exactly sure what this description means, but I tell him that I'll probably be there. The bottom line is that I have nothing better to do, and Dad is right. If I stay home every night, I will go crazy. Even though the slow pace of life down here is refreshing, I'm used to living in a city where there's a rush of energy and humanity the minute you walk out your door. Dad and Renata have been heading upstairs to bed—where I like to imagine they go to sleep immediately—at about eight thirty. It's understandable, since they get up at dawn, but it makes for some pretty dull evenings at the farm.

I'm tired of sitting behind the Joyful Goat table long before it's time for us to pack up and leave at two o'clock. Dad, on the other hand, seems invigorated by this gig.

"It's not hard for you to live out at the farm?" I ask him on the ride home. "You're such an extrovert. You were loving it at the farmer's market today, interacting with all those people."

Dad takes a moment to think about it and says, "You seem to forget that I've lived alone for a long time. Even though I was in a big city, it was only me in my apartment. It's so nice waking up with someone every day. I forgot how much I liked that."

"That make sense," I say, guilt welling up inside me.

I didn't spend enough time with him when he lived in New York. Maybe if I'd been around more, not so absorbed in my own job and relationships, he wouldn't have been lonely and looking for a change.

"Dad, I understand wanting to be with someone," I say carefully, knowing this is the moment I came here for, and I can't screw it up. "And I was serious when I said I like Renata. I really like her. I just don't understand why you feel the need to change everything in your life. Do you really want to spend your retirement milking goats, dealing with hoof rot and shilling eggs on a folding table?"

The last sentence of what I've said comes out harsher than I intended, but I'm fired up. I need to shake Dad out of this dream world.

He glances over at me, his eyebrows drawn close together. "What are you getting at, Andie? I feel like there's something you want to say, so go ahead and tell me."

Finding the right words has never felt more crucial, like if I say the wrong thing our relationship is going to be damaged permanently. I'm not used to feeling this way. Dad and I have always been able to talk about anything, even hard stuff like how he couldn't stand my high school boyfriend or how I became depressed my junior year of college. Those issues revolved around me and my choices and feelings though. This is the first time I've questioned one of Dad's important life decisions, and it's throwing our dynamic into a tailspin.

"People who have worked as hard as you have are taking river cruises and learning Spanish and volunteering at the museum of art." I take a deep breath and say, "I guess I'm asking if this is really how you want to spend your golden years? Because it looks like an awful lot of work to me."

Dad's silence makes me nervous. We drive up and down a hill and around a bend in the road before he responds.

"First of all, I kind of resent the term 'golden years.' I'm only fifty-five! And this might not be how I imagined spending my retirement, but that's because I never dreamed Renata and I would be together again." Just the mention of her name puts a goofy look on his face. "And I'm enjoying the goat farm adventure. This business is something we can build together, and we've got lots of plans for it. We can run the farm for ten or fifteen years and then retire and take river cruises or whatever."

"It's that easy for you? You can just leave your job, your friends, and me, no problem. It's all about Renata, and you don't miss a single thing about your old life? You can walk away from it all?"

Dad slows the pickup to a stop as a flock of geese waddle across the road, and he turns to face me.

"Honey, I'm not walking away from anything. I'm going toward something." He gestures forward with his hands. "What kind of role model would I be for you if I gave in to fear and didn't make a change like this? Did you know I had an opportunity to spend a year teaching in Europe?"

I cross my arms over my chest. "What are you talking about?"

"I applied to a teacher exchange program that would have taken us to Spain for a year when you were in high school. I got accepted, but then I chickened out. I told myself it would be too difficult, changing your school for a year, getting permission from my principal, subletting our apartment. So I turned it down, and I always regretted it. But it wasn't that logistical stuff that held me back. It was fear, plain and simple."

The geese are safely across the road now, and Dad resumes driving.

"Why didn't you ever tell me about this?"

I imagine myself as an American teenager in Salamanca, sitting on a plaza, drinking espresso and smoking cigarettes while my friends and I discuss Nietzsche and Foucault.

"I guess I didn't want you to be upset with me for chickening out."

"You were being logical and responsible," I say, even though I'm pretty sure teenage Andie would have been incensed that she was being robbed of a European experience.

"I've spent my whole life being logical and responsible," he says with a little smile. "It's time for me to take some risks and jump into the unknown. I hope you can support me in that."

"I guess so." I pick at a chipped fingernail. "I'll try."

"And I want you to know, moving away from you was the hardest part of my decision."

My chest tightens, and I turn toward the window so he won't see the tears forming in my eyes. We drive in silence for several miles. I can't help feeling that there's nothing more to say.

"I should head back in a day or two. I'll look for a flight when we get home."

"No, don't do that," he says. "Stay at least another week

or two. You have time before you have to go back to work."

"I'm in the way. You and Renata need time as a couple."

The lump in my throat is expanding, and I close my eyes and rest my head against the glass.

"We already have Seth coming over all the time to use the shower. And Harmony is coming to stay for Grammy camp. It will be great if you stay longer. We love having all our chickens in the nest, so to speak."

He's using an over-the-top enthusiastic voice like I do when I'm anxious. When he senses I'm about to cry, he always compensates by ramping up the jolly factor.

"Maybe a couple more days." I try to sound happy about spending more time at the farm.

"A week, at least," he says. "Please?"

I agree to another week because I do want to spend a little more time with him before the school year begins. Now that I know he won't be coming with me, every minute feels more precious.

"OH MY GOD, I didn't know there would be a shower scene in this program!" Hugh says when I tell him about walking in on Seth.

I'm lying on my bed talking on the phone because from this point forward I'm going to make sure no one overhears my conversations. We haven't spoken for the last few days because Hugh and Raymond were out of town. We've texted a bunch of times, but I didn't mention seeing Seth in a towel because it seemed like news that he'd want to hear in detail.

"Very funny. This is my life, Hugh, not a telenovela I'm producing for your enjoyment."

"Of course, of course. Still, I'd like to know, does he resemble the lovechild of Keanu Reeves and Adam Driver? Is that an accurate description? Maybe with a little bit of Kit Harrington thrown in?"

He's freakishly on target, and it's not just that Seth and these actors have the same dark, sexy, slightly villainous looks. They also share a hard masculinity combined with a softer sensitive quality—like they'll be ready to go to battle right after they finish pouting and writing their poetry.

"I'll ignore your willful misunderstanding of reproduction and say yes, that's what he looks like."

Hugh makes a contented purring sound. "I need a picture, please."

"Sure, I'll ask him to pose for one right after hell freezes over."

"I still contend you need some sexual healing after your recent Dan disaster. Speaking of which, when I went over to your apartment to get your clothes, your roommate was there."

Hugh overnighted me a care package of clothing, shoes, and loaf of slightly stale sourdough bread before he left on his trip. Honestly, I also wanted him to make sure Marly hadn't turned my entire apartment into a terrarium. At first she'd kept all her plants in her bedroom, but over time they began spilling into the living room and kitchen. Before I left for North Carolina, I noticed the tendrils of a Wandering Jew trailing over my coffee maker, which is a sacred object for me.

"Is the place a disaster?" I ask, dreading the answer.

"Not any more than usual. Marly has a gig writing articles for some horticulture website so we talked about that for a while. She let me know that a guy came over to see you recently. Twice actually."

"Oh god," I whisper.

"Yeah, it was definitely Dan. He asked Marly to tell you he stopped by, and she said she wasn't sure if she should say you were out of town or not."

"I texted him that I was away though. Why would he come by?"

I haven't given him my home address, either. Dan has done a little detective work to find out that information. I pray he hasn't been blabbing to our co-workers. We need to be containing, not spreading, the gossip.

"You know why he stopped by," Hugh says. "He wanted to check that you were telling the truth. He thinks you're avoiding him."

I moan. "I am avoiding him. He just isn't getting the message."

Hugh asks me to hold on for a second while an ambulance races down his block with its siren blaring. For the last few days, I haven't thought about how quiet it is here. I guess I'm getting used to it.

"Sounds like you need to be more direct," Hugh says after the siren fades into the distance. "Tell him to give his attention to his wife and kids and leave you alone. Seriously, this is getting stalkerish."

"I'll handle it. I wonder what would make Dan run for the hills? Playing the 'too clingy' card usually drives men away, but he's already laid that card on the table."

"There's something else I need to tell you about," Hugh says. "I'm not sure it's even going to happen, but I don't want it to come as a shock if it does."

I let out a long breath. "Okay, just hit me with it."

I'm terrified that he's going to tell me he and Raymond are adopting a baby because once your friends become parents, you never see them again. My good friend Cara had a kid nine months ago, and the only way I know she's still alive is that she posts baby pictures on Facebook hourly. When I tried to set up a dinner with her, she said that she'd let me know when the feeding and napping schedule allowed her the free time to get out of the house without the baby and that was the last I heard from her.

"Raymond is up for a huge promotion, and the job is in Chicago. That's where we've been the past three days," Hugh says.

"Hugh! No!" I scream. "That's worse than saying you guys are pregnant!"

"I know, I know. I don't want to move there either. I'll freeze my ass off, and I look absurd in puffer coats. But he's the big salaried accountant, and I'm the freelance writer who can do his work from anywhere so...who knows, maybe he won't get the job."

"Yes, he will," I say miserably.

Raymond is a workaholic math wizard. He probably crunches columns of numbers in his sleep. I've never met someone as passionate about tax deductions. People think that accounting is dull, but honestly, Ray is more stoked about his career than Hugh and I have ever been about ours.

"Yeah, he will totally get it," Hugh says, sounding as depressed about that fact as I feel.

"I can't believe this."

Hugh blows out a breath. "I know. It totally sucks."

I try to think of something positive to say because I want to be supportive, but I feel like the wind has been knocked out of me.

"Let's talk about something else, otherwise I'm going to get completely depressed," Hugh says. "Tell me what's happening with Herb."

"Pretty sure he's here to stay," I say, hating to admit

defeat.

"Damn, are you sure?"

"I think so. We had a big talk today, and he's pretty adamant that they're going to try to make this farm thing work."

"You should just screw around with your future stepbrother then," Hugh says. "I mean, if things are already weird, why not just make it totally fucked up. In a post-*Game of Thrones* world, incest is much more acceptable."

"Sure, great idea." I look out my window toward Seth's cabin. It's not visible from here, except for what I think is a light on his porch. "That plan can't possibly go wrong."

After I hang up with Hugh, I want to cry, but the tears won't come. Instead, I lie on my bed and stare at the wall, wondering what's going on in the universe. Too many things are changing at once. I can't imagine life in New York without my father and my best friend. All of my other friends are getting married and having kids. I don't even want those things, but I seem to be the only person who wants life to stay the same. Who am I going to write down as my emergency contact at work this year? Certainly, not my mother. She'll get the call from the hospital and ask what my chances of survival are to determine whether it's worth the drive from Long Island.

People are always saying change is inevitable, and I'm okay with things moving forward, of course. But the pace of what's happening right now has my head spinning, and it's leading me to make terrible decisions, for example, kissing my married co-worker.

Hugh is wrong. The last thing I need right now is to get involved with a surly caveman who treats me with contempt. The best idea right now is to clean up the messes I've already made and stay out of future trouble.

SEVEN

Dan is following me down the hallway of the bar again. This time I'm wearing a skirt, one that's short and clingy. I know those are his footsteps behind me, and when I turn, his lips are on mine, without a word being exchanged between us. He presses me back against the wall, his body lining up perfectly with mine. His hands trace along the sides of my thighs, stroking upwards while our tongues flicker against each other. This is what I wanted from Dan. Short, flirty kisses that grow in fervor as our excitement increases. I have to show him with my tongue that I want to kiss deeper, wetter, and he responds with a groan and matches my intensity. Then I slow down again, gently biting his lower lip to drive him insane. In response to my teasing, his fingers begin to slide under the soft material of my skirt. I gasp and pull my head back to look at him, but it isn't Dan's blue eyes that I see. These eyes are the color of chocolate and incredibly intense. They're Seth's.

"Do you want me to stop?" he asks in his deep grumbling voice. There's a catch in his throat when he says the word stop, as if he would do it, but it would hurt him so much.

When I answer no, it sounds like a breath not a word. His mouth lowers to kiss my neck as his hands caress higher and higher until they're playing with the edges of my panties. I'm so desperate for his touches to move higher and deeper that I'm silently begging him for it. He can take me right here, in the back hallway of a bar, because I don't think I can wait much longer.

I'm leaning against him, my head tilted backward, eyes half closed. My hands are gripping his shoulders, and he's whispering how much he wants me and has since we first met. His warm hands are under my panties now, his fingertips caressing me. I feel every one of the rough spots on his fingers, and they're stroking all the right places. As a feral sound of pleasure escapes my mouth, I wake up in a panic to see sunlight streaming across my bed. Shit, did I really make that noise out loud? Can he smell my pheromones through the wall?

I'm covered only by a sheet, and its damp from my perspiration. And that's not the only dampness around here. There's no denying that dream. The warm throbbing between my legs is proof of it. Inside the bathroom, there's the rushing sound of a shower being turned on, and I cringe at the thought that Seth might have heard me cry out in my sleep. Of course, he had no way of knowing I was dreaming of him, but still, it's like being seen naked.

Speaking of naked... Seth is in the shower right through that door. Water cascading over his beautiful body. I hate Seth, I really do, but it has been a long time since I've gotten any action. The reason he's in my subconscious brain is the fact that Hugh and I spoke about him before I went to bed, and I'm not going to feel guilty about it. Women fantasize all the time about people they would steer clear of in real life. Jaime Lannister. Loki. Sirius Black. Okay, these are all fictional characters, but still, I feel there's precedence here. I can use Seth as a character in my fantasies to satisfy my sexual needs and still hate him. Right?

Yes, yes, yes. I creep out of bed and unzip the pocket of my overnight bag. I've had the same reliable vibrator for years, but I recently bought myself the travel version. Let's see how this miniature baby works.

I slide my hand underneath the sheets and flick on the switch, hearing it gently hum to life. It's time to create a mental movie about joining Seth in the shower. I'm fairly sure that if I went in there right now, he wouldn't turn me away despite the fact that he loathes me. In fact, sometimes I wonder if he's thinking about me while he runs the soap over his body.

I let that thought turn into a longer fantasy and the vibrator does its work while I enjoy the rush of blood to parts of me that have been unattended for too long. Unlike in my dream, I'm the one telling Seth what I'd like him to do to me, and he's being a very good listener. I imagine his mouth starting on my breasts then moving down to my stomach and inner thighs, kissing and nibbling my body with the attention of a connoisseur, until he gets to the most tender place of all. His work down there is absolutely expert. He's gentle, patient and as turned on as I am by what's happening between us.

I try to finish before he turns off the shower, but even with the dream to get me started, I'm not quite there when the house goes silent. What is it with him and water conservation? He's not even paying the fucking water bill!

As my vibrator buzzes softly, I consider whether it's loud enough for someone to hear on the other side of that door. I'm too close to stop now though. If he hears me, I don't care. I let myself fade into my fantasy again, Seth teasing me with his fingers and tongue, until the pleasure builds to the point where I can no longer contain it inside me. I turn to the side and let the pillow capture my moan as I shudder with release. I'm still breathing heavily, but my body is more relaxed than it has been in ages. This was just what I needed, and now I'm free. My attraction to Seth has been satisfied, and I can go back to loathing him.

IT'S NOT until I shower and come downstairs that I realize it's Saturday, the day Michael is bringing Harmony over to the house to spend the week here. He's had her enrolled in day camps all summer because he needs childcare while he's at work. She's already done camps that involve coding, basketball and something called circus arts. Renata requested a week to have Harmony to herself, and they decided to name it Grammy Camp. She's been talking about it since I arrived at the farm.

I smell the maple syrup and pancakes as I'm coming down the stairs, and my mouth waters. The whole family is in the kitchen with Renata whirling around them as she pours batter into a sizzling pan and directs Michael, who is chopping fruit, and Dad, who is pouring drinks. She does it all with a calm smile on her face.

Yes, everyone is here, including Seth. He and Harmony are setting the table with silverware and pretty yellow napkins with a bold flower print on them. Renata directs Harmony to place a small vase of wildflowers in the center of the table, and I'm impressed, once again, at how she can make even an ordinary day feel special.

I call out good morning, gratefully take the mug that Renata hands me and head to the coffee maker. My heart picks up the pace when Seth and I brush against each other, but I will not let the sight and scent of his freshly showered self throw me off my game. We haven't spoken since he called me desperate and lonely, and insulted my father, and I'm not going to be the one to break the silence.

"Hope you slept well, Andie," Renata sings out, expertly flipping a pancake on her skillet. "Breakfast will be ready in just a few."

I glance over at Seth, but he's turned away, taking a bowl of fruit to the table.

"What can I do?" I ask Renata, as she and Dad plate up the pancakes and bacon they've finished cooking.

"I think we're all set," she says, handing me the platter of golden brown pancakes. "If you could just bring these to the table, that would be great. I've got more in the oven for seconds."

I take the plate from her hands and say, "I'll do the clean up then."

Renata smiles innocently. "Seth has already offered because he got here late, too, so you two can be on KP duty together. Isn't that what they call it in the military, Seth?"

Seth's eyes cut to me, then back to his mother.

"Yeah, but I can handle it on my own."

"I can do my share," I say, placing the platter on the table.

I'm not going to let him do the work and make me look like the lazy one. He's going to have to deal with me, as uncomfortable as that may be for him. The R-rated scene from my dream pops up in my head like a bubble, and I put a pin in it as quickly as possible.

We all take our seats and Renata asks us to take a moment to say a prayer with her. She thanks God for bringing us all together this morning and for giving her this week with her sweet girl, Harmony. My father has his eyes closed during the prayer, and I'm pretty sure he and Renata are holding hands under the table. My heart squeezes, and I'm mortified that what I feel right now is jealousy. Is it because she's the apple of his eye now, or is it that I envy the passion and devotion they share?

"That bacon looks delicious," Michael says, eyeing the plate of meat. "I never make it for myself anymore. Harmony doesn't eat it."

Seth, who is sitting next to Harmony, tugs on one of her braids. "Who doesn't like bacon?"

I want to ask if this pig was his personal pet or just a random victim, but I refrain.

Harmony points her fork at me. "Andie doesn't. And I'm going to be a vegetarian, too. I decided the other day."

Renata gives Michael a surprised look. Grandma apparently didn't know about this development.

"You know how determined she is when she gets an idea in her head," Michael says.

I twist the napkin on my lap. "Sorry about that. I didn't mean to make your life harder, Michael."

Seth's life? Making that more difficult is fun, but I have no interest in inconveniencing a man who lost his wife and is raising a child on his own.

Michael laughs softly and waves me off. "It's fine. I'm glad she has convictions. My wife, Val, was a vegetarian for years before she got pregnant. Then she started craving barbecue and never looked back."

Harmony looks up from the pancake she's devouring. "What was her favorite food of all time?"

Michael thinks that over for a while. "She loved peach cobbler. That was her favorite dessert. But she liked a lot of things: sushi, burritos, blueberry pancakes."

Harmony's face lights up. "I love those things, too! Except sushi. That's nasty."

"What about seaweed?" Michael says. "Your mom loved seaweed salad. I always said she was part mermaid."

Harmony wrinkles up her nose and says to her dad, "Are you serious? She ate seaweed?"

We all laugh, and he nods.

"Yeah, it's true."

I'm amazed at how comfortable they are as they talk about Harmony's mom. The way they're keeping Val alive for her daughter is beautiful and heartbreaking at the same time. After my mom walked out on us, we rarely spoke about her and when we did, it was never without awkwardness and pain. I was afraid that bringing her up would hurt Dad, and now that I'm an adult I can see that he probably felt the same way about me. Of course, my mom was alive, and I could still see her, when she made herself available. The pain of Harmony's situation is hard to fathom.

After breakfast, Michael, Seth and I help Harmony bring her belongings into the house. She's got enough luggage to stay for a month, and Michael explains that two of the three bags are filled with stuffed animals and toys. I carry in her pillow and quilted comforter, remembering how I had a favorite knitted blanket that I had to take on trips with me, too.

"I'm going to miss you, Daddy," she says as we climb the stairs to the bedrooms.

Michael smiles at her over his shoulder. "You'll have so much fun though. And we can talk every day, whenever you want."

"You can Facetime with him," I say. "I can show Pop how to do that on his computer or we can use my phone."

"I know how to use Facetime," Harmony says. "I'll teach Pop and Grammy."

There are five bedrooms in this old house, and Harmony gets to pick the one she wants for the week. She chooses what Renata calls the lilac room, which is decorated in soft lavender and white and has its own private bathroom. Michael stays to help her unpack, and Seth and I head downstairs to clean up the kitchen. Walking behind him provides me with an opportunity to check out his backside, but I force myself not to look. Except then I do.

"I can clean the kitchen by myself," I say.

Seth shakes his head. "Nope, I'll do it."

His tone implies that hanging out with me won't be pleasant, but he's an ex-Marine, and he made a commitment, dammit.

I grit my teeth. "Fine, we'll both do it."

Dad is still cleaning up in the kitchen when we return. He finishes clearing the table while Seth begins scraping, rinsing and stacking the plates on the counter. I take the top plate from his stack and slide it into the dishwasher, but I can feel his eyes boring into me. Not letting that stop me, I put in a few more dishes before I turn to look up at him. Sure enough, Mr. Frowny Face is looming over me.

"What? Am I not doing this right?"

I can tell he's struggling with whether or not to criticize me because he knows it's going to make him sound uptight. His fastidious nature wins the battle over his embarrassment.

"You can fit more in if you put all the plates together in the front." He eyes the disarray of the dishes I've shoved into the machine.

I throw my hands up and step away from the dishwasher.

"Go for it. You load the dishwasher, and I'll do the hand washing."

I'm more amused than annoyed as I watch him go to work. Disorder is clearly his kryptonite.

"Thanks," he mumbles.

Dad picks up a greasy bacon pan and heaves an exhausted sigh. I take it from him and run a hand over his back.

"Dad, you take a break. You helped cook. Seth and I will clean this up."

He sighs deeply again and rubs his hands over his eyes.

"Would that be okay? We trimmed hooves after milking this morning. Maybe I'll just lie down for a little while."

"Go," I say, guiding him gently toward the door.

He walks away, then pivots and says, "Don't forget it's Saturday. That's when Rhett said he'd be at that Ricky's place. You should go out tonight."

Seth, who is bent over loading dishes, straightens to a standing position when Dad says Rhett's name.

"Do you know Ricky's?" Dad asks Seth.

"Yeah, I know it." Seth returns to aligning the plates to his satisfaction.

"Maybe you could drive Andie tonight? She hasn't been there before."

Dad is overstepping again, just like he did with Rhett at the farmer's market. I know it's because he doesn't want me driving to some unknown location at night. Every birthday he gifts me a tiny bottle of pepper spray that attaches to my keychain then gives me a talk on "street smarts."

"I can drive," Seth says, "if she wants me to."

He has moved on to re-organizing the glasses now. He's actually going to fit our huge pile of dishes in there because of his meticulous arranging.

"No thanks," I say immediately. "I like having my own car. That way I can leave when I want. Plus, Seth probably has his own plans tonight."

"I do, but—"

"See? Everyone has their own plans." I wave Dad out of the room. "Go take a nap."

He shuffles away reluctantly, as if he'd love to stay and interfere in our social lives some more, but the pull of his bed is too strong.

For several minutes, Seth and I clean together in silence, and I pretend not to notice the effect his physical presence has on me. The temperature in the kitchen seems to have risen a few degrees, to the extent that I check that the oven has been turned off. I pull at the front of my t-shirt to let a little air breeze up on my chest.

"How do you know Rhett?" Seth asks, as if we've already been having a conversation.

"I don't, really," I admit, filling the bacon pan with water and soap so it can soak. "We met at the farmer's market."

The dishwasher is completely full now, and he gently closes the door then leans back against the counter. He's wearing well-worn Levis and a black t-shirt that makes his eyes look even darker than usual. From the amused turn of his smile, I have the terrible feeling he's going to say something about my orgasmic morning.

"What?" I wipe the counter with gusto to avoid his gaze. "Clearly, you want to say something about Rhett."

"Is he out of college yet?" His tiny smile blossoms into a grin.

I pause my cleaning frenzy. "Are you joking? He looked at least twenty-five."

I immediately regret including the words "at least" in that sentence because it sounds like I'm aware Rhett is young. Maybe too young. Being around Seth always gets me flustered into saying the wrong thing, and he is full-on loving my discomfort at this moment.

"I'm pretty sure he's barely legal," he says. "But maybe that's your thing, younger guys."

His face is the next thing I'm going scrub off with this sponge.

"I'm not hooking up with Rhett," I say defensively, even though I know I'm giving Seth exactly what he wants by showing my irritation. "He invited me to hang out with his friends tonight, that's all. And it's not like I'm some old lady creeping on boys. I'm only twenty-eight so even if he's twenty-two—you know what? Forget it. I don't owe you any kind of explanation about my life."

He crosses one foot over the other like he has all the time in the world to harass me.

"It's interesting that you want to make friends here. I thought you were going to snatch up your father and head north as soon as possible."

It's absolutely broiling in here now. Someone needs to check the thermostat and make sure the air conditioner isn't on the fritz.

"So what are your plans tonight?" I wipe the perspiration off my forehead with the back of my hand.

"I'm hanging out with my friend Jenny and her girlfriend Luisa."

"Oh, so you're third wheeling it with your couple friends." I grimace like he's the saddest thing ever. "That sounds like fun."

Before he can answer, I flick the sponge at him. He catches it right before it hits him in the face. His expression changes from smug to stunned, and I stride out of the kitchen with my head held high. When he thinks I've gone,

I pop back in the room and say, "Better put the soap in the dishwasher and get it started. Otherwise all your anal-retentive work with those dishes will go to waste."

There's nothing quite like getting the last word in a conversation with Seth. It's nearly orgasmic.

I'M close to the end of my evening run when the music coming through my ear buds is replaced by a loud ring tone. I pull the phone out of its holder on my bicep to see the name of the caller, and it's no surprise. Dan. Again. I can let it go to voicemail, but I can't avoid him forever. He called this morning during the family breakfast, but I didn't notice the message until later and haven't returned his call. Considering he's called twice in one day, it's safe to assume he's fed up with waiting.

I slow to a walk and answer breathlessly, "Hey, Dan."

"Andie! You picked up. What's going on? I've been trying to reach you for over a week."

"I texted you." My voice is strained from exertion and frustration. "I told you I'd call when I was back in town."

"You've been gone for over a week! How long did you think I'd wait? When are you coming back, anyway?"

I start explaining that I'm not sure about the timeframe of my stay here, but he cuts me off mid-sentence.

"It doesn't matter. We can talk now. I need to know where things stand with us."

Dan's voice has a desperate quality that worries me. Plus, he seems to think there's an "us."

"Where things stand?" My words come out in puffs as I chug up the last big hill before the entrance to the farm.

"You're acting like that night at the bar never happened. We kissed, remember? You can't deny that it was amazing."

I could argue that the kiss wasn't amazing for me, but there's no point in taking a shot at his ego. The important thing is to end the relationship talk so we can figure out what to do about our work situation.

"You're married, Dan. Did you forget? We made a drunken mistake that we both regret, and to make matters worse, Ronnie saw us." I cringe as I replay that moment in my head. "Barb called me the other day, and I was so scared that she knew."

"Does she?" There's real terror in his voice.

"No, she wants us to share a room next year!"

"Why?" he asks incredulously.

"Something about overcrowding, I don't know. I tried to talk my way out of it, but if she finds out what happened between us, both our jobs are in jeopardy, not to mention your marriage. We seriously fucked up."

I bend to slap the mosquito who's sucking blood from my ankle. They seem to like a slow-moving target so I increase my speed to a jog.

"I think we both knew this was coming," he hisses. "You've been flirting with me all year."

I laugh in disbelief. "Oh, so now this is my fault? You followed me to the bathroom and lunged at me. Have you conveniently forgotten that?"

He can't gaslight me. Our flirtation was mutual, and he was the one who took it to the next level. Plus, he's the one who took marriage vows!

"I'm not saying I didn't want that to happen. Hell, Andie, I can't stop thinking about that kiss. That's why when you get home, we need to get together and figure this out."

My mouth drops open in shock. He doesn't regret what we did.

"No, Dan, that's the exact opposite of what we need to do. You need to get some marriage counseling with your wife and figure your shit out. I'm going to try to salvage my career—" A baby cries in the background, and I gasp in horror. "Are you with your kids right now?"

"They were asleep, but I think the baby just woke up."

I can still hear his child wailing.

"You think?"

His breath quickens, like he's running through his apartment. "Listen, I'm going to change him, then call you back."

I can tell he opened the door to the baby's room because the crying has intensified five-fold. The fact that we are having this conversation while his kids are in the next room makes me feel like a monster.

I run my sentences together so he doesn't have a chance to interrupt and challenge me. "No, do not call me back. You know where I stand on things. Save your marriage and do not call me again."

I end the call with shaking hands and a churning stomach. I know that Dan isn't going to let things be because that kiss had a totally different meaning for him than it did for me. In my mind, it was a sloppy, embarrassing wake-up call, like A-Rod's 2014 suspension for doping. But that doesn't mean my life is over. Look at A-Rod now, hooked up with Jennifer Lopez and living his best life. I'm headed to a random bar with a guy I met at a farmer's market, but hey, you have to start your rehabilitation somewhere.

EIGHT

My GPS politely tells me to make a U-turn because I've missed my turn onto a side road for the second time. I swear colorfully, find somewhere to flip the car around, then reduce my speed to twenty. Finally, I locate the turn for Zebediah Church Road. The turn-off is hidden by a clump of overgrown bushes, and the street sign has fallen down. In the dark, it's nearly impossible to see that there's a road here at all.

It's questionable at this point whether I'll find Ricky's before I run out of fuel. I'm down to less than a quarter tank and haven't passed a single gas station on this godforsaken road to nowhere. If Seth had mentioned that this place was impossible to find, I would have accepted a ride from him. Maybe.

Zebediah Church Road is even less commercial than the two-lane highway I turned off of a moment ago. Other than a few houses and falling-down barns, there's nothing out here. If I run out of gas, I'm spending the night in the car.

I'm starting to question whether Ricky's exists. What do

I really know about Rhett anyway? He could be a serial killer or a survivalist with a stockpile of guns and ammo. Maybe he's a cult leader, and I'm heading straight for his compound. He probably tells people he's an organic produce-loving vegan to throw them off the trail of his crimes.

I'm giving myself five more minutes to find Ricky's, then I'm turning around and heading home.

GPS woman tells me that my destination is in a half mile, which gives me some comfort. I try to remember what Rhett looks like, but all I can come up with is light brown hair and green eyes. He was definitely cute, but tonight is only about getting a drink and socializing with people my age. Is Rhett my age? Seth was probably messing with me when he said Rhett was "barely legal." He's at least twenty-one if he's hanging out at a bar, and that's certainly old enough to engage in consensual sex, not that it matters.

I still don't see the lights of a business or any signage for Ricky's. After I round a hill, a dirt driveway appears on my right and GPS woman calmly indicates that I should turn into it. Just in time, I make a sharp swerve into a large gravel lot that's mostly full of pickups and SUVs. Adjacent to it is a long flat brick building. There's a hand drawn sign—black paint on white wood—announcing that this is indeed Ricky's Bar and Grill. The proprietors helpfully placed a janky old spotlight on the ground below the sign so it can be seen. Stephen King would appreciate the vibe of this place, but me, not so much.

My car tires crunch over rocks as I stare down four rows full of vehicles, with not an empty space to be found. Finally, I locate a slice of dirt between two huge pickups and guide my tiny car inside it. I sit in the car for a few minutes, dwarfed by the vehicles on either side of me, wondering why I'm here. Rhett might not even be here tonight, and even if he is, do I really need to be out flirting with someone who's potentially only a couple years older than my students? I'm still trying to get rid of Dan, my New York mistake. I don't need to make another error in judgment.

The alternative to going inside Ricky's is sitting on the porch glider by myself, attempting to read *Mrs. Dalloway* again, a depressing prospect. An evening at Ricky's is at least good for some stories to take home, and I'll make it clear to Rhett, if he's inside, that we're just going to be friends. I take my lip gloss out of my purse and glide it across my lips, fluff the bottom of my hair and inhale deeply. If it's awful, I'll make another U-turn and head home.

The door to Ricky's is industrial strength, but even before I open it, I can hear the music inside the bar. I'm expecting Rascal Flatts or Blake Shelton, but it's Coldplay's "When I Ruled the World." The room inside is dim, the floor is sticky and the stench reminiscent of other dive bars: stale beer and cheap liquor with undertones of piss and man sweat. Directly to my left is a long wooden bar that runs the length of Ricky's. Most of the stools lined up in front of it are housing the rumps of middle-aged men. Above the bar are neon signs lit up with the names of beer companies, as well as a framed certificate proclaiming the sanitation grade Ricky's has received: 91%. Raymond would be out of here like a shot. Actually, he never would have made it past the parking lot.

The majority of the room is full of pub tables, and, as the parking lot indicates, it's a full house. It's going to be difficult to find Rhett in this crowd so I decide to begin the evening by getting a drink. The head of every dude sitting at the bar swivels to check me out as I approach. Pretty sure every woman who walks toward them receives this treatment.

I'm looking forward to getting a drink, but my limit is set at two. I don't want to get drunk and find myself re-enacting the parking lot scene from *Thelma and Louise* with any of these creeps. As I wait for the bartender to come my way, I check out the crowd. The patrons are pretty much all white, and they range in age from "he must have a fake I.D." to "older than dust." The older crowd has a redneck style: boots, wranglers and beer bellies. The younger contingent varies widely from Southern preppy to crunchy granola to scary biker. Even if I don't find Rhett, people watching here will be interesting.

The bartender has tan, deeply lined skin, and she's missing at least one tooth. Standing here in the light of neon beer signs, she brings to mind the saying "rode hard and put away wet."

"What can I get for you?" She wipes down the counter with a once-white towel and waits patiently for my order.

"What do you have on tap?"

"Miller, Miller Lite, and Rolling Rock." She lists the available beers with the enthusiasm of someone who already recited them four hundred times tonight.

"And in the bottle?" I ask.

"Bud, Bud Light and Corona."

The pickings are slim out here in the boondocks. I could order a gin and tonic, but those go down too easy, and I need to drive home tonight. A beer or two, some conversation with Rhett (assuming I can find him), and I'll call it an evening.

I rummage through my purse for the cash to pay her.

"I'll have a Rolling Rock."

She fills the glass efficiently, barely a head on it, and slides it across the counter to me.

"Three dollars."

As I'm handing her the three dollars plus tip, I feel someone slide up to the bar on my left. A quick assessment tells me it's not Rhett unless he's aged two decades and smells like a distillery. I'm about to grab my drink and walk away, when the guy's finger pokes my shoulder. His touch makes my beer slosh onto the floor, and I'm already annoyed before he speaks.

"Hey, pretty lady, I haven't seen you here before."

Drunk old guy. He always finds me. His eyes are squinty, his breath rank and his hope springs eternal.

"What are you drinking there?" He peers into my glass, like he can't tell it's a beer. "And can I buy you another?"

"Nope, I'm good." I scan the room to locate Rhett before this guy can engage me in a conversation.

He attempts to lean back against the bar and slips a little before he catches himself. I pretend not to notice because any attention I give him, good or bad, will be perceived as interest.

"Your hair is the color of an angel's," he slurs.

The bartender reappears behind him. "Why don't I call you an Uber, Frank?"

I turn around and gape at her. "You have Uber out here?"

"Well, there's just one driver, Karl Whitman in his Chevy, but he's real reliable," she says.

"No need." Frank opens his eyes wider, as if he's going to convince us he's sober. "I'm going to finish this drink before I hit the road. I'll be fine."

His last word is accompanied by a burp that he doesn't

acknowledge. The bartender and I roll our eyes at each other.

Frank addresses my chest like there are eyes on my nipples. "You're so lovely and ripe, like a delicious strawberry."

"I made a pact with an old crone in the forest." I pause to sip my beer, and Frank is hanging on my every word. "She gifted me with great beauty, but I have to bring her the severed heads of men if I want to stay young forever."

Frank squints at me for several seconds then smiles, like he's in on the joke.

"You're funny."

"You stay classy, Frank," I say over my shoulder as I wade into the sea of pub tables.

I don't find Rhett right away, but I do spot three pool tables at the back of the room. Suddenly, I don't hate Ricky's quite so much. A few years ago, my friend Cara made me take pool lessons with her so she could meet guys. I thought it was a stupid idea, but she ended up marrying our instructor, and I got ridiculously good at pool. I finally found a sport that I excelled at, especially after a beer or two.

I cruise around the room with my drink in hand and right when I'm about to give up, I locate Rhett and some of his friends sitting at one of the tall tables. He doesn't see me until I tap him on the shoulder, and a smile of recognition flashes across his face.

"Hey, you made it!"

"I'm kind of amazed I did." He raises his eyebrows, trying to guess my meaning. "This place is a hidden gem. I almost drove right by it."

Rhett and his friends laugh.

"There aren't too many people here who didn't grow up

in this town or somewhere nearby," Rhett says. "Ricky's is an institution. He doesn't even need that sad sign outside."

Rhett introduces me to his friends, two girls and one guy. They all seem friendly and exude the same fresh-faced, youthful spirit as Rhett. Seth was right, he is young. They all are. How young is the question. Not that it matters because I was being honest when I said I didn't intend to hook up with Rhett. Of course, I didn't plan to kiss Dan, either.

"Do you want to play some pool?" he asks. "The tables are full right now, but I can put some coins down."

I follow his eyes to the pool area, which is indeed crowded, and my eyes zoom in on a muscular six-foot-three frame. Seth is bent over, aiming a ball toward the corner pocket. He's concentrating hard, his body still and his eyes fixed. He slides the pool stick firmly between his tented fingers and makes solid contact with the ball. I imagine that I hear the thud from across the room, but it's unlikely with all the voices and music drowning my ears. A slow smile slides over his face as the ball sinks out of sight. Suddenly, my mouth is dustbowl dry, and I need to take a long gulp of my beer.

I know I should look away and pretend I don't see him, but I can't, and when Seth straightens up, our eyes meet. I flush and turn away, wondering what the hell is going on. Seth knew I'd be here, and he made sure he was, too. He's spying on me.

RHETT and his friends carry the conversation, and I do my best to focus on what they're saying about the politics of organic farming. It's not a topic I know or care about though, and my mind keeps wandering back to the pool table area. Even though I can't see him at the moment, Seth's presence looms large in my mind, which is both distracting and irritating.

When Rhett leaves to get another round of beers for the table, I allow myself to twist in my seat and look over at Seth again. He's leaning on his pool stick, watching his friend set up for a shot. He's with a guy I've never seen before, someone slightly shorter and fairer than Seth, and handsome in a more conventional way. There's a woman playing pool with him, too, and I'm pretty sure she's the one I saw getting out of the ambulance the other day.

I stare at Seth's side profile, which allows me to see that his nose is too big, his face is too long and he's not attractive after all. In fact, there's nothing to like about him, not even those broad shoulders and that nice, full bottom lip that's begging to be bitten. I bite my own lip instead as a reminder that I need to repress such thoughts. Down, girl.

He's brooding about something, as usual, although maybe that's just his permanent pensive expression. He lifts his beer bottle to his lips, turns his face to the side, and we make eye contact again. I suck in my breath and force myself not to look away. There's no reason to be embarrassed. He's the one who came here tonight, knowing I'd be here with Rhett.

Before I think it through, I'm on my feet, crossing the room toward the pool tables, my eyes still connected to his. My legs feel shaky and numb after sitting on that high barstool for so long or maybe it's the intensity of his gaze that's causing this reaction. He's got one hand in his pocket and the other on the pool cue, watching me with a completely unreadable expression.

"Wow, funny seeing you here." I force my face to relax

because I'm fairly sure my eyeballs are popping out and my mouth is snarling. I am coming unhinged. I'm glad I wore sandals with a heel because it puts me closer to his eye level, although he still has about five inches on me.

"Not especially," he says. "There are only a few bars in this town. And I already told you I was meeting up with friends here."

"No, you didn't say you would be at Ricky's. Do you hang out here frequently or just when you know I'm going to be here?"

I sound ridiculous—he did say he had plans tonight—but I can't stop myself. In the immortal words of Ozzy Osborne, I'm going off the rails on a crazy train.

Seth narrows his eyes. "You think I came here tonight because I knew you'd be here?"

"Obviously."

He turns to his female friend who is watching Eli take a shot.

"Jenny, when do we meet here to play pool?"

She leans on her pool stick and looks back and forth between us, like she isn't sure what answer he wants her to give.

"Pretty much every Saturday night."

"Seth knew I'd be here tonight," I tell her. "And it's funny he didn't mention he would be here, too. Especially when my dad asked him to give me a ride over here."

"And you turned down that ride," Seth reminds me.

The guy playing pool with them tells Jenny it's her turn at the table, then sticks his hand out to me.

"I'm Eli."

Eli has dirty blond hair, green eyes and a charming smile.

"Hey, I'm Andie. Seth's future stepsister."

Eli gives Seth a confused look, then turns back to me. "Nice to meet you, Andie."

Seth shakes his head. "We're not related."

I lean back on the pool table and attempt to look at him in a casual way. "But we will be when Renata and Dad get married."

"Not really," Seth says. "Because Renata isn't my biological mother, but whatever."

Jenny rejoins us after taking her shot and nods at the table. "You wanna play pool with us?"

Seth glances at her with surprise, like he can't believe she issued me an invitation. Clearly, he just wants to glower at me from afar. I smile slowly, relishing this opportunity to kick his ass.

"Sure, I'd love to. As long as I'm not on Seth's team. We don't play nicely together."

Jenny and Eli laugh, but Seth doesn't. He's the only one who knows I'm dead serious.

"You and I can be a team," Jenny says. "If you don't mind having me as a partner. I'm not good."

"Shouldn't you get back to your date though?" Seth says through gritted teeth.

His frustration isn't about the fact that I'm ditching Rhett. I get under his skin, and it's delightful to know that I'm capable of ruffling the calm demeanor he projects to the world. I want to fluster and provoke him until he can't take anymore. My thoughts turn to Seth in a bath towel again, but I drop those images into a mental lockbox that can only be opened when he's not in my presence.

"As you're already aware, he's not my date." I wave to Rhett anyway, to be polite and possibly to piss off Seth.

I'm glad when Rhett smiles and gives me a two fingered wave before returning to the conversation at his table. Points to him for not being threatened by a woman who does her own thing.

I walk over to the pool sticks and inspect the tips, selecting the one that's in the best shape. Then I roll the stick on the pool table to make sure it doesn't wobble. Finally, I swipe chalk across the tip, then tap the other end of the stick on the ground to loosen any excess powder. When I finish this process, the three of them are staring at me.

"Okay, now I'm scared," Eli says.

I laugh lightly and shake my head. "Don't be silly."

We're going to crush these boys.

Seth suggests we play eight ball, and we all agree. They chalk their sticks, and Eli racks the balls. He does it incorrectly, but I'm not going to be a dick about it. Okay, I am. I reach into the triangle and put the eight ball where it's supposed to be in the middle of the third row of balls. Eli, who's taking a sip of beer, doesn't even notice, but Seth is watching my every move.

"Should we flip a coin to see who breaks?" I ask.

Seth slips a quarter out of his pocket and says, "Call it."

As he flips the coin in the air, I call out, "Heads."

It's tails.

I love breaking, but I'm also curious to see what Seth can do. The minute he gets in his stance, I can see he knows how to play or at least he knows how to look like he does. He strikes the cue ball with confidence, sending the other balls spinning to the rails to begin the game. The cue ball isn't set up for an easy second shot though, and when he misses, I'm up. Because I've played a lot of pool, I see a way to get the four ball in the corner if I can tap it perfectly with the side of the cue ball. I love that pool is a game of angles and points, like a math puzzle that can be solved. People sometimes say "lucky shot," but there's less luck involved when you get to a certain level of play.

When the cue ball hits the four, I know what will happen, even before the ball sinks into the pocket.

"Wow," Jenny says. "That was awesome."

"Thanks," I say modestly. "I took some lessons a few years ago."

I don't add that after those lessons I spent many evenings shooting pool at the dive bar on my block. I hang out there so often, in fact, that the bartender knows what kind of beer to pour me when I walk in the door. One slow night at the bar, I taught her how to play pool, too. Now she beats a lot of the older men who hang out there.

I sink two more shots before I miss. Seth is sipping his beer while watching me, and there's no telling what he thinks about my skills. Not that I care. Eli takes his turn and, to his chagrin, accidentally pockets the cue ball. Jenny is up next.

"Any suggestions?" she asks me, tapping her pool stick on the floor.

My eyes study the table, assessing her best chances to make a shot while setting herself up for the next one. I sidle up next to her and point to the six ball.

"If you tap it with enough force, I think you can make that shot. You just have to line it up properly. That will leave the cue ball in a good position for you."

We lean over the table, and I show her the angle I'm seeing.

"Any other tips?" she asks.

I love teaching women how to play pool because they're always willing to listen to advice. Guys, not so much.

"Let me see how you hold the stick."

Jenny leans over the table, getting into position to strike the ball, and I watch her technique.

"You've got good form with your arm. Just don't slow down on your follow through. Push through the ball, don't stop." I lift my stick and show her what I mean.

She nods. "Got it. Thanks."

She takes the shot I suggested and the ball heads toward the pocket. When it drops in, she turns and grins at me. "Yes!"

I give her a high five and Eli groans.

"We're gonna get slaughtered, Seth. I'm going to get another drink."

Instead of responding to Eli, Seth sips his beer. Jenny makes a good attempt on her next shot, but her angle is slightly off and she misses. Seth is up next.

He studies the table, looking for a shot while absent-mindedly running a hand through his thick, dark hair. I feel a clenching in my stomach and realize that I'm imagining it's my hand brushing the hair away from his cheekbone. I don't realize that my mouth has dropped open an inch, until his eyes catch mine. I quickly snap my lips shut and form them into a hard line.

Seth sets up for his shot, and I'm careful to keep my eyes off any areas of him that might show my interest in anything other than his pool skills. It seems safe to focus on his fore-arm, until I feel my gaze wandering up to the corded muscle in the bicep peeking out of his shirt sleeve as he stretches over the table. Clearly, there's nowhere safe on his body for my horny eyes, so I turn to Jenny instead.

"How do you know Seth?"

"We work together," she says, confirming my guess. "I'm pretty much his work wife. We're usually on shift together, although sometimes they change the schedule, and I'm with Ernie or Lou."

There's the solid clunk of two balls connecting with each other, and Seth makes his shot. As he sets up for his next one, I can tell he's watching us out of the corner of his eye.

"Is he a good work husband?" I ask her.

"Seth? He's awesome. He doesn't talk all the time, always has my back, and doesn't complain all day like Lou. Plus he ate arepas for lunch for a whole year for the sake of my love life."

"Ooh, tell me that story."

Seth sinks another shot and smiles to himself. He's a decent player, although his elbow drops a little during his stroke and that's going to hurt his game.

"Seth and I used to go to the food truck Luisa owns," Jenny says. "She makes these amazing arepas with fish, meat, veggies—anyway, we started going often, like two or three times a week, because I had a crush on Luisa, but I was too shy to do anything about it. My idea of flirting is ordering extra plantains and tipping really well. Seth finally took matters into his own hands and gave her my phone number, without my permission, of course."

She says that last part loudly so Seth can hear her. He's moved around to our side of the table, and I know he's listening to us even though his eyes are assessing the balls on the table.

"She was clearly into you, otherwise I wouldn't have done it," he says.

"I was so pissed at him, but after she called me, I forgave him and the rest is history, as they say. You probably wouldn't think Seth is a romantic, right? But he totally is."

Seth leans over to take his next shot. "I was just tired of eating arepas all the time."

I dust the tip of my pool stick with chalk while I watch him intently. I'm not surprised when he misses the pocket. That elbow drop messed him up. He also nearly pocketed the cue ball, and he doesn't look pleased.

Rhett and a couple of his friends walk over to the table to watch our game. I smile at him before taking my turn and manage to sink the rest of our balls, then put away the eight ball for the win. Jenny and Rhett clap when I make my last shot, and I'm pretty psyched. This was one of the best games I've ever played.

Seth gives me a steady look. "Nice game."

"Thanks," I say, sticking out my hand.

He closes his hand around mine and squeezes gently, and it's like everything else in the room suddenly goes silent. It's just the two of us, his warm hand in mine and our eyes connected. Then the world breaks in again, and I pull my hand away. My face is warm, and I carry my pool stick to the stand so no one will see my red cheeks.

"Hey, Rhett," Seth says.

Rhett lifts his beer in greeting. "Hey, Seth. How's the cabin? Ashley told me you're building a place out there at the goat farm."

"It's coming along," Seth says. "How's school?"

"I graduated in May," Rhett says with pride.

I take a sip of my beer so I don't have to acknowledge Seth, who I know is enjoying this moment. I draw back my shoulders and refuse to look at him because so what if Rhett is six years younger than me? Dudes date younger women all the time. Plus, I'm not even on a date—we're just friends hanging out at a honky tonk (which I think is a noun, but it might be an adjective).

"You two know each other?" I direct my question to Rhett.

"Seth graduated from school with my oldest sister, Ashley."

"How many sisters do you have?" I ask him.

"Three. I'm the baby of the family and the only boy. So I pretty much got away with everything."

Speaking of babies, a redhead who looks younger than Rhett saunters over and puts a hand on Seth's arm.

"My friend and I want to challenge you and your partner to a game," she says, standing so close to him that their hips are almost touching.

Her friend is lurking nearby, watching Eli with hungry eyes. The denim shorts these girls are wearing are so tiny and tight that I'm pretty sure they'll be getting yeast infections.

Seth steps slightly away from her and nods his chin at me.

"Andie and Jenny won so it's their table. Y'all should play them."

"That's okay," I say sweetly. "I'm done playing for now. You guys go ahead."

When I get back to Rhett's table, I'm sure to face the opposite direction from the pool tables so I won't know what Seth is doing with the redhead. Obviously, he can do whatever he wants, and it's no concern to me. I'm just glad I got to beat him at a game of pool.

Rhett and his friends are lovely, but talk mainly revolves around the farms they work at and the people they know, and I don't have much to contribute to the conversation. After a while, Rhett and I start talking by ourselves, and he explains that he lives at the farm in sort of a barracks for the young people who are interning there, training to be farmers. It sounds fairly rudimentary, like summer camp but with manual labor instead of volleyball and sailing lessons, and there's little privacy. There are eight people living in his cabin and eight more in the cabin next door, with a bathroom joining the two. He sleeps in a bunkbed above a guy who snores incessantly. His plan is to spend a year or two there, then travel a bit, working on organic farms in Europe.

"I wish I'd done something like that after college," I say. "Not that a farm would have been my thing, but I didn't take any time off to be adventurous or consider what I wanted to do next."

"Why not?"

"I didn't have any money and college loans needed to be paid. And maybe I wasn't as brave as you are."

Rhett looks at me with the naïveté of someone who has never paid for health insurance. "It's not too late. You could have your big adventure now."

I laugh and run my finger around the rim of my beer glass. "No, I think that ship has sailed. I'm still paying my college loans, and honestly, sharing a bathroom with fifteen strangers doesn't sound that appealing at this point."

"What would your big adventure be, if you could take one?" he asks.

I think about it for a minute, then say, "I don't know. I've always wanted to see Ankor Wat and the Taj Mahal. Traveling around Asia would probably be the thing I'd do, if I had the time and money."

"You should save up and go," he says. "Life is too short."

"Hopefully we still have sixty or seventy more years left."

Rhett's smile has a tinge of sadness to it. "Yeah, but you never know what life will bring. A friend of mine was killed in a car wreck last year. It really made me think about how I need to live my life for today and not do things that don't make me happy. He thought he had another seventy years, too, you know?"

Rhett is young, but he's much more mature than a lot of people I know. There aren't any romantic sparks, but I enjoy being with him. For a little while, I even forget about Seth being on the other side of the room. Our talk goes on for another half hour before I find myself yawning and needing to get on the road.

When I tell him I'm heading out, Rhett offers to walk me to my car. It's a kind gesture, but I've got pepper spray on my keychain. Then he asks for my number, and it's the first time I sense that he's interested in stimulating more than my brain. If we were back home, I would probably give him a soft rejection so he didn't get the wrong idea, but it's awkward being that direct, and I'm pretty sure I won't be here much longer anyway. I take his phone and enter my contact information for him. When I'm done, he gives me a warm hug goodbye, and his shirt smells lightly of patchouli. There's still no zing of attraction between us, which is neither a disappointment nor a relief. It just is.

On my way to the door, I pass by Seth who is at the bar listening to some older guy tell a story, and I'm reminded what it feels like to get that little flicker of excitement in your stomach when you're attracted to someone. My feelings for Seth are so baffling. I want to pinch him as I walk by, but I'm not sure if it's because I need to touch him or I want to hurt him. Maybe it's both.

He turns and sees me, and I give him a little wave. He chin nods in reply, and I catch his glance over at Rhett. He's checking to see whether I'm leaving alone. There's a moment, just a second or two, when I think he's going to speak to me. He puts his hand on the bar and turns toward me slightly, our eyes catching hold of each other. And I pause, waiting. His mouth opens, but the man speaks to him again, and he turns away from me.

What am I feeling? Irritation, disappointment, regret? All in all, it was a good night, and what did I expect to happen? There's no reason to feel like the evening ended badly.

I open my window as I drive, letting the night air rush into the car. The cool wind is exhilarating after another hot day, but it's not dissipating this heavy feeling in my chest. I don't want to acknowledge it for what it is, a deep well of loneliness that has opened up inside me. Hugh's news about Chicago has shaken me to my core. I know I depend on him too much. Dad, too. But they've been the most important people in my life for so many years. Is it wrong to want them near me? I feel like someone is rending the threads from the pattern of my old life, and somehow I'm supposed to sew myself back together again. That must be why I'm still thinking about Seth, and the way he was looking at me tonight when I left the bar.

NINE

Dad and I are at the goat barn preparing for the evening milking when my phone dings with a message from Rhett. *Are you coming back to the farmer's market this week? We've got an amazing crop of melons, zucchinis and tomatoes. Hope to see you there!* He includes an artful photo of the aforementioned produce.

"Rhett wants to know if I'll be at the farmer's market tomorrow." Dad looks up from sterilizing a goat's teat, and I hold up the picture on my phone. "He wants to show me his zucchini."

Dad tries to hide a smile. "You're terrible."

"I guess this is an organic farmer's idea of a dick pic."

"Stop!"

"Maybe they can rehabilitate Anthony Weiner at Blue Sage Farm after he's released from prison."

Dad shakes his head and laughs. "I think you should go to the market with me again. I loved having you there, and you said you had fun with Rhett the other night. Don't you want to see him again?"

Dad moves alongside the final goat on the milking

stand, sprays her teats with cleaning solution then wipes them with a cloth.

I wrinkle my nose. "Geez, I feel like I should give you guys some privacy."

"Ha ha. I don't even think about what I'm doing anymore. It's just routine. And stop using humor to deflect my questions."

I tap my fingers against the side of the bucket I'm perched on. "Rhett is a good guy." Dad shoots me a hopeful look. "But he's too young, lives too far away, and isn't my type. The best part of the night at Ricky's was beating Seth at pool."

Dad stands up and puts away his sterilization supplies. "I'm still annoyed he didn't give you a ride."

"He offered. I wanted to drive myself."

"Still, he knew that place was really difficult to find. You could have gotten lost out there."

"Please don't say anything to him about it."

Seth already thinks I'm a daddy's girl, and that idea doesn't need any reinforcement.

"Fine, I won't say anything." He gestures to the goats. "Time to fill their buckets with food. Eating keeps them occupied during the milking process."

"Got it."

I pick up the bucket of goat food next to me and fill the containers in front of the goats while Dad messes with the milking apparatus.

"Sometimes you have to give things a chance," he says. "I didn't fall for your mom right away. It wasn't until we'd been dating for a few months that I really started to see a future for us."

"How about with Renata? Did you know right away?"

Dad smiles. "Pretty much."

He attaches tubes to the goats' teats and flips on the power switch. The machine hums to life. What's happening in front of me looks eerily similar to when I walked in on a co-worker pumping breast milk in the faculty bathroom.

"With Renata, it was infatuation at first sight. She was in my chemistry class, and the minute I saw her walk in the door on that first day of school, it was like kapow!" He grabs his heart like he's been struck by Cupid's arrow. "I know it sounds silly, but I was drawn to her right away. Of course, I didn't know her yet, and once I did, my feelings grew. She was the smartest girl in the class—an A on every test—and the prettiest, too. Prettiest girl in the whole school."

"Wow, you had it bad."

Dad sighs like a lovesick schoolboy, then laughs at himself. "First love. There's nothing like it."

First love. I always thought of Mom as Dad's great love and biggest heartbreak. What he's telling me changes everything I believed about my parents' relationship. Renata was always the one for him.

Dad stares at the milk pouring into the containers, but I know he's seeing forty years into the past.

"I asked her to go out with me at least three times, and she kept saying no. Finally, I stopped and focused on becoming her friend. I wanted to be around her, and if being friends was the only way, so be it. But after a few months, she asked me why I wasn't asking her out on dates anymore. She was ready to say yes. Of course, she knew better than I did what would happen if she started dating a white boy."

"But it was the late seventies. I would have thought things were different by then."

Dad shakes his head. "Honey, things aren't that different now. Some people are still unhappy to see us together. Back then, it was much worse. Kids at my school didn't date across the color line."

I try to imagine the two of them, my father, the wiry track runner with a head of shaggy hair, and Renata, the straight-A beauty. They were young, like my students, a combination of innocence and raging hormones, flirting with each other over Bunsen burners and test tubes.

"So what happened?" I ask.

"She lied to her parents, and I lied to mine. We'd meet up at the movies. I took her to Coney Island—that was a great day. We'd go on long walks in the park. I was just happy to hold her hand and talk to her. We talked for hours about everything. She had plans for nursing school, and she helped me think about what I wanted for my future. We were living in a dream, thinking we could actually be together after graduation. Eventually, word about us got back to her folks and mine. And they were not happy."

"Her parents were opposed to it, too?"

He shrugs. "They agreed to meet me, and I think they liked me, but they knew our life would be very hard. They feared I'd take her away from her community, that she'd try to fit into my world and never be welcome. Maybe they were right. My parents weren't exactly open to the idea."

"And by that you mean..."

"Oh, they were furious. They told me I was breaking their hearts, ruining their lives, the whole thing. They refused to meet Renata and told me never to see her again."

I love my father's parents, but they aren't progressive people. It's hard to label people you love as racist, but in this case, the label fits. Because not all racists are burning crosses in people's yards. Some of them just refuse to allow their son to date a black woman.

"We broke up then got back together again because I

convinced her to give our relationship a chance. It ended when she took a boy from her church to our prom. Her parents forbid her from going with me, and she wouldn't defy them. I didn't even go to prom. I couldn't stand to see them together."

"Dad, this is the saddest story. I can't believe you never told me all this before."

He checks the pump on one of the goats. "I guess I thought I did."

"And that was the end of everything between you, before you reconnected last year?"

"We spoke once after prom. At graduation, she told me she'd accepted a scholarship to a nursing program in North Carolina. I was devastated, but there was nothing I could do. A few years later, I heard she'd gotten engaged. That was it. I knew it was really over then."

He looks as devastated, as if it were happening right now.

"But you found each other again. You got your happy ending."

"Yeah, but I think of all the years we lost," he says. "Of course, if we'd stayed together she wouldn't have had her boys, and I wouldn't have had you. So it all worked out the way it was supposed to."

"Sometimes you have to let fate take its course," I say, thinking about Isabelle's predictions.

"True," he says. "But I still think that there's also a time to fight for something that feels right. If you find someone you think is your true love, don't let him go."

I LEAVE Dad at the barn to finish up the milking process

and head back to the house to change into my running clothes. All this talk about love and heartbreak is giving me anxiety, and I need to run it out if I'm going to sleep tonight. I'm getting sick of running the same route along the road and decide that I'm going to head for the woods, ticks and mosquitos be damned.

On my warm-up walk down the driveway, I pass by Seth in his truck heading up to the house. Mutt's head sticks out of the passenger side window, his tongue lolling from his mouth. I scoot over to the side of the road and lift a hand in greeting, expecting they'll cruise right by me. Instead, the truck stops.

Seth rolls down his window and leans his arm on the ledge. "Hey."

He's in his paramedic uniform, probably getting off a long shift at work.

"Hey, Seth."

I pause in case he has something profound to share.

"There's a storm rolling through here in a little while."

I glance up at a clear blue sky then back at him. "Okay."

He pauses, like he's waiting for me to say something more. When I don't, he continues, "You might not want to go running right now."

"Actually, I do want to go running right now. I'll be back before it rains, and if I'm not..." I start jogging down the road as I finish saying, "I won't melt!"

I know he's supremely irritated that I didn't take his advice, just like I'm annoyed about getting the advice. Seth loves telling me what to do, but he's not in control of me. I'm a grown-ass woman who can handle running through a little bit of rain.

I'm also a grown-ass woman who is lost in the woods thirty minutes later, unable to figure out where I came in and how I can get back out. I assumed that the trails in the woods would loop around at some point and return me to where I started. When that doesn't happen, I decide to turn around and head back the same way I came; however, it soon becomes clear that I've veered onto a different trail because there's a fallen tree in my path that was definitely not there the first time. I spend the next hour backtracking and bushwhacking through thorns and branches in an effort to find the road or any other sign of civilization. My ankles are scraped up, I've acquired a dozen new mosquito bites, and my pride is in tatters.

Unfortunately, I decided not to bring a phone with me tonight because I wanted to unplug and enjoy the noises of nature. Now the light is fading, and I'm definitely not going to get my bearings in the dark. What if I have to spend the night huddled under a tree? How many mosquito bites can a person survive? Can you really drink your own urine to stay alive and at what point is that a necessity? As the reality of my situation sets in, I hear the rumble of a car engine, and I'm able to follow that sound to the road.

My feet hit pavement, and I consider dropping to my knees to kiss the ground. Due to the preponderance of animal droppings I've seen today, I opt for a little leap of joy instead. I actually succeed in clicking my heels together like some kind of demented Dorothy on her way to Oz. The next problem to face is which direction to turn. The way the road slopes upward to the right looks familiar, and I'm inclined to head in that direction, although I'm not completely sure, and there aren't any landmarks to guide me. A tree is a tree is a tree.

As I jog up that hill, which is steeper than it looked from fifty feet away, a cooling breeze caresses my arms and face. It feels wonderful, but I know it's not a good sign. A storm must be brewing. The swirling clouds above me and a clap of thunder in the distance confirm my fears. Even if I'm headed in the right direction, I'm going to get wet.

The first raindrop hits my arm, and it's not long before there's a steady shower. I shiver in my damp t-shirt and try to pick up my pace, but my body is shaky from the effort I've spent up to this point. Thunder resounds again, louder than last time, and I count the seconds until I see a lightning bolt strike in the sky. Twelve seconds. I urge my legs not to quit, and when I reach the hill's apex, I'm thrilled to look across a field and see the old barn that sits on the back end of Renata's property.

Another clap of thunder and ten seconds before the lightning this time. I send up a prayer to the universe that I will be in the barn before things get really scary. I don't mind a little rain, but I'd rather not become a "death by lightning" statistic. I can see the local headline now, "Fool Yankee Struck Dead by Lightning in Open Field."

The run to the barn is somewhere around a third of a mile, and my legs are rubbery from exhaustion and fear. The sky is the color of charcoal, and the wind whips the trees into a frenzy, spiraling leaves to the ground. As I run toward the shed, I spy a figure moving perpendicular to me across the pasture. Shit. It's Seth.

He begins waving, then points to the sky as another rumble of thunder echoes around us, followed by lightning. Without counting, I know that this strike is closer. The timing makes Seth look like Zeus, pointing his scepter toward the sky, a comparison I will never share with him because he already thinks he's the almighty with his dishwasher loading skills and storm warnings. Apparently, he also thinks I can't hear or see the storm and need him to point it out to me.

He reaches me when I'm about twenty feet away from the barn, and I don't say a word or even look at him. I'm sure he's gloating right now, and I don't care to witness it. To my shock, the rain suddenly turns solid, and when I extend my palm, I'm pelted with hail about the size of a marble. Fantastic. I'm being shot with nature's ice bullets.

"Hail," Seth shouts unhelpfully.

He really does think I'm an idiot.

I yelp as a piece as big as a chicken nugget strikes my shoulder, and Seth shoots me a concerned look.

"I'm fine." My raspy breathing and wild-eyed appearance betray my words.

We race alongside the barn, past a row of mowers and a small tractor that are parked beneath an overhang. Seth arrives at the barn door a moment before I do, but he holds it open for me, allowing me to enter first. I find his chivalry anachronistic and annoying as hell, and I mutter something to that effect. Either he ignores me or can't hear me over the sound of the storm.

He pauses, taking one more look at the sky before he slams the door behind us. We're enveloped in darkness until he flicks on the overhead lights. They flicker for a moment as they struggle to life, casting a dim glow in the room. There's no way my legs are going to keep me upright anymore, and I attempt to sit down gracefully instead of flopping on the dirt floor. My success is limited at best.

Seth paces through the barn, which is empty except for some rusty farm equipment and old hay bales. His t-shirt is soaked through to his skin and clinging to the outline of the muscles in his chest and back. His basketball shorts are clinging to him, too, water droplets trickling over his knees and calves. I allow my eyes and my mind to wander all over his body, admiring the skin I can see beneath the wet fabric.

Appreciating his body is acceptable. It has nothing to do with liking Seth. When he catches me looking, I pretend to be stretching my legs.

"Where the hell were you all this time?" he asks. "I've been looking for you for thirty minutes."

He's standing still now, hands on his waist, sounding more annoyed than concerned. When his eyes flicker down to my breasts, I follow them and see that my nipples are erect from the cold rain and the chafing of my workout bra.

"I don't remember asking you to come searching for me," I say, crossing my arms across my chest and rising to stand on newborn calf legs. No matter how tired I am, I can't stomach the feeling of him looming over me, especially when I'm getting a scolding.

Seth scowls. "I told you earlier about the storm coming in. Do you not listen to anyone or is it just my warnings you willfully ignore?"

New energy surges though me and suddenly I'm no longer weak and tired. Indignation will do that to a woman.

"I thought I'd be back earlier, but I lost track of time. Do you give unsolicited advice to everyone or am I the only lucky person?"

I'm positively sneering, and I can't hold myself back. He's partially correct. If someone else warned me about the storm, I probably would have been more willing to postpone my run. His superior attitude makes it impossible for me to admit I'm wrong.

"It's a little rain," I say. "We're fine."

Seth takes a step toward me. "A little rain? It's thunder, lightning, hail and potentially a tornado." He might as well have added the "you moron," since it was implied by his tone.

My body is thrumming with outrage and mortification.

In hindsight, I shouldn't have run through the woods on paths I didn't know, especially with my crappy sense of direction. Thank god he doesn't know I was lost. The last thing I need is to be chastised for that. I move closer until we're only a few inches apart.

"You wouldn't mind if I died in a tornado so it's unclear why you ran out here to rescue me. Oh, wait, it was probably so you could tell me how stupid I am to run in a storm!"

"Now that you mention it, you are stupid to run in a storm!"

Thunder claps again, shaking the ground outside, but our stand-off continues, neither one of us flinching. I can smell his spicy scent so clearly that I can almost taste it. There are water droplets on his forehead and cheekbones, a mixture of sweat and rain that I'd like to lick off of him. Wait, what? No, no, no. My brain is fried and thinking crazy thoughts without my permission.

Seth stalks away and lets out a primal growl of frustration, shaking his fists at his side like a fighter warming up for the next round. I'm surprised and scared by the fact that I want to hit him—and not in a girly pummel of fists to the chest kind of way. I'd actually like the claw off some of his skin. This man is turning me into a sadist!

He circles back, standing even closer than before.

"You know, I'm generally a laid-back guy." His voice is trembling with all the effort it's taking to tame his temper. "But you really get under my skin. Why is that?"

It's not clear whether he's asking me this question or himself. I wish he hadn't used the word skin though because I'm trying to ignore his damp, clingy clothing and the hard body underneath, which is difficult to do when he's this close to me.

"Maybe you can't handle strong women," I say between

clenched teeth. The muscles in my neck and shoulders are so tight, I'm afraid they'll snap from the tension.

"Maybe I was concerned." His voice crackles with frustration. "Maybe I came out here in a storm because I was worried about you."

His words are a strange kind of revelation, like I'm looking at someone new. He's saying he genuinely cares about me, which runs counter to everything I'd previously considered. Then again, maybe he just wants to be a hero.

"I didn't ask you to worry about me."

I'm not willing to give up my anger so easily. It's the only thing keeping me from rending his clothing from his body.

"That makes no sense!" He throws up his hands. "Sometimes people worry about you whether you ask them to or not. Get over it."

I can't hold myself back now. I step toward him, closing up the last bit of space between us. My hands find the bottom edge of his t-shirt. Yanking him toward me, I make a sound that comes out like a snarl, a groan and a growl rolled into one.

"You. Are. Awful."

His hands grasp my shoulders, and he pulls us even closer together. Our lips meet in a clash that isn't soft or hard, it's simply inevitable. We're opposing magnets that got too close and can't resist the attraction.

There's nothing laid back about Seth's kisses. They're possessive and greedy, like he can't get enough of me, and I'm responding like a sin eater—yes, please, give me more of these lips, tongue and teeth. I've waited far too long. He's teasing me and hungry for me at the same time, and I'm both relieved and even more ramped up now that it's happening.

I couldn't do this if I wasn't completely sure that he is as lost in me as I am in him, and I have no doubt of that. Both of us are out of our minds. Hands are roaming bodies, and I finally get to stroke the golden skin and muscles I've been admiring from afar. They don't disappoint.

Just as I'm abandoning myself to the moment, there's a voice in my head that asks, "What the hell are you doing, Andie?" It's a low hum in my ears, reminding me that hooking up with Seth is a not a good idea for a variety of reasons, but his lips have moved down my neck and are devouring it for dinner so fuck you, voice of reason! The shivers he's sending down to my lady parts, igniting a fire down there, are enough reason to continue. His hands slide down my sides to rest on my hips, which he tugs up against him as the parade of kisses heads down to my throat.

"Oh, my god," I whisper as his lips find my clavicle.

For some reason, I find that I'm on my tiptoes, my hamstrings quivering both from exhaustion and nervous excitement. My desperate legs aren't going to hold me up much longer, not if he continues this onslaught. I've dropped my head toward my shoulder to make sure he has enough space to devour me, and without meaning to, I let out a whimper of pleasure. I can feel him smile against my skin, and I don't care anymore. I don't care that he's getting the best of me, as long as he doesn't stop.

When his strong hands slide up under my shirt, I'm eager to get rid of our clothing altogether. His skin needs to be on mine, and we need to move this party to the barn floor before I collapse. From the hard bulge in his shorts, I'm pretty sure he'll be good with that suggestion.

Suddenly there's a vibration near my waist, and my hot take on this is that my vagina is sounding the alarm because I'm in serious danger of having sex right here, right now. Of course, it's not. My vagina has never been that sensible. The phone in his pocket is buzzing. He swears and steps back to retrieve it, and as he fumbles to swipe the screen, I reel with the loss of his warmth and his touch. But his distance also has a positive effect on my reasoning. Holy hell, what am I doing? And, more importantly, why is he stopping to answer a call?

It's obvious that whoever is on the other end of the line has been worried about me.

"She's right here, and we're both fine. We took shelter in the barn. I'm sorry I didn't call. I got..." He looks over at me and runs his fingers through his hair, "...distracted."

My legs are truly useless at this point, and I sink down onto what was probably once a nice firm bale of hay but is now a scratchy lump. Seth talks endlessly about the storm as I consider more important things, like why that kiss felt destined to happen. The word "destined" makes me think of Isabelle's prediction, but I refuse to entertain the idea that Seth is the great love of my life.

When he ends the call, he explains that it was Dad on the other end of the line. Apparently, he's been frantic since he heard the tornado alert sound on his phone and couldn't find me in the house. The one time I run without my phone is the night we have tornadoes raging nearby, of course.

"He called me to say you were missing, and I offered to look for you."

I correct him gently but firmly. "I wasn't missing. I was running."

His voice sharpens slightly. "In the dark for over an hour?"

I look down at my leg and scratch an inflamed area. I'm beginning to look diseased from all the red welts on my skin.

"I took the scenic route."

"Wait, were you *lost*?" I can practically see the lightbulb go on above his head.

I pretend to retie my shoe as I think of a way to bend the truth.

"I wouldn't say lost, exactly. I tried running in the woods for the first time, and the loop I went on was a little longer than expected."

Seth narrows his eyes. "None of those trails loop back."

"Well, now you see my conundrum." I look up, into the rafters, as if the barn ceiling is endlessly fascinating.

There's a two-second delay before he guffaws loudly. I can't help but smile, too, because I have to admit that my adventures tonight have been kind of ridiculous. I've never heard Seth's laugh before, not this kind of unguarded belly laugh. He's actually bent over at the waist, hands on his hips, gasping for air.

When he finally stands upright again, I see something that I'm not going to forget easily, even though I'm going to try like hell.

Seth has a wickedly cute grin.

TEN

Seth is still laughing at me when his phone rings again. It's Renata this time, calling to make sure we know the storm is letting up already. The risk of a tornado has passed and so has the thunder, lightning and hail. There's only light rain falling now, nothing to keep us shacked up any longer. I hadn't noticed the quiet outside because of all the activity going on in the barn.

He hangs up the phone and slips it into his pocket, reminding me how we were pressed against each other so closely that I felt the phone vibrate.

I jump to my feet and brush hay from the seat of my shorts. "I'm glad I could provide you with some entertainment for the evening."

The air in the barn is thick with humidity, and I pluck my damp shirt away from my chest. What I need most right now, besides my dignity, is a shower.

"Andie..."

There's a gentleness in Seth's eyes that's as new to me as his smile, and I'm thrown by it. If I let this door open with Seth, I'm giving up on bringing my father back to New

York. My focus will be on a relationship that can't go anywhere, not on keeping my family intact. How can I maintain that this is the wrong place for Dad when I'm running around having flings and good times?

I try to keep my voice light and breezy. "Let's agree that we will never speak of this again."

"What are we not speaking of, the fact that you got lost or..." Seth lets his voice trail off, but I know exactly what he means.

"Both," I say, assuming this is what he wants. "Let's pretend none of this ever happened."

He processes what I've said, and I'm surprised to catch a flicker of disappointment on his face. He quickly covers it with his usual mask of imperturbability.

"Fine by me." He strides to the barn door and throws it open. "After you."

I head toward him. "Perfect."

He holds the door for me, and I swear I can feel the heat emanating from his chest as I slide by him. It takes all my resolve not to burrow my nose into his torso and inhale deeply like some kind of demented addict.

After taking a few steps into the mist, I look behind me to see that Seth is already headed off in the direction of his cabin. I did the right thing, telling him to forget about the kiss. I can't lie, it was a panty-melting make-out session, the hottest one I've ever experienced. But what good could come from us discussing it? We're too different, we don't like each other and we live hundreds of miles apart.

I continue watching him, wondering if he'll turn around and look at me, but he doesn't. I run my fingers over my neck where he kissed me, the delicious shock and surprise of it still present on my skin.

EVEN THOUGH I told Seth to pretend the kiss never happened, it's all I can think about the following morning. I find distraction in helping Renata entertain Harmony. After we paint shells, turn them into bracelets, and cook up a pan of muffins, Harmony starts using the couch cushions to construct a fort.

The effort of caring for her granddaughter full time is finally starting to show on Renata's face. "I thought it would be relaxing to spend a day at home, but I'm running out of activities, and it's not even lunchtime yet. I wish it wasn't so hot, otherwise we could do something outside."

"What about setting up a sprinkler for her to run through?" I suggest.

Harmony loves this idea, and I agree to get in my bathing suit and play with her. It seems I've also run out of things to do with my time. There's only so much reading and internet surfing one can do in a day. If I ruminate any more about Dad's impending marriage, Hugh's potential move and Dan's obsession with me, I'll lose my mind. Not to mention the number of times I've replayed what happened last night with Seth. Jumping around with a six-year-old sounds like a great way to forget my worries and obsessions for a little while.

Dad sets up the sprinkler in the grassy area behind the house while we change into our suits. I brought my favorite black bikini with me, and this is my first chance all summer to wear it. I also smear on sunscreen because instead of getting my Italian father's olive complexion, I got my Scandinavian mother's pale skin. If I'm in the yard in full sun without protection, I'll be roasted within thirty minutes.

"I don't need to put this on," Harmony complains when

Renata insists she wear sunscreen, too. "My skin is brown, not white like hers. I'm not going to get burned."

"Everyone gets sunburns." Renata rubs the lotion onto Harmony's squirming body. "It doesn't matter what color you are."

When we're suited and sun-screened up, Harmony and I run through the back porch and out of the door, racing to be the first one in the water. She beats me out and leaps gracefully over the sprinkler, screaming when the cold spray hits her body. I follow behind her, leaping much more awkwardly and screaming even louder. The cold water feels amazing in this ninety-eight degree weather, and I don't try very hard to avoid the sprinkler as it rotates around the yard. Being with Harmony turns me into a kid again, and I recognize that she's one of the great parts of being joined with this new family.

Dad brings out some old balloons he finds in the house and we fill them with water from the hose. This leads to a water balloon fight, of course, and within minutes Harmony and I are both drenched. I love that she can take a hit from a water balloon without whining and has good enough aim to give back what she gets.

When there are only four balloons left, we declare a truce and decide that we'll save some ammunition for later. As we dry ourselves with towels, I spot Seth and Mutt walking across the lawn toward their cabin. Harmony sees them, too, and we look at each other and smile maliciously. Without a word, we grab two balloons each and prepare to launch them. When Seth and Mutt are within about thirty feet, it's on like Donkey Kong.

Being aware that Seth was in the military, I don't want to traumatize him completely, so right before we launch our attack, I yell, "Hey, Seth!"

He turns to look at us and begins to wave. Two seconds later, our missiles rain down around him, one hitting him square on the shoulder. We hear him shout something and watch Mutt sprint away from the water that's released when the other balloons hit the ground. Then Harmony and I run into the house, giggling all the way.

"I think I heard Uncle Seth say a bad word!" Harmony says, when we're safely inside and breathing hard from our getaway.

"What's going on?" Dad asks.

He's standing at the counter, cutting up apples and carrots for our snack.

"We bombed Seth with water balloons," I say casually.

Dad laughs and shakes his head. "I would have loved to see that."

A few seconds later, the screen door on the porch creaks open, and I know exactly who is coming inside the house. Seth enters the kitchen a second later, the right side of his light blue t-shirt soaked with water. Suddenly, I'm very aware that I'm wearing only a bikini.

"I'm looking for the people responsible for an assault by water balloon." His voice is deep and menacing.

Harmony scurries over and hides behind me, as if her giggling won't give her away.

"We don't know what you're talking about," I say innocently. "We don't have any water balloons. You can search us."

At my suggestion, Seth's eyes roam over my nearly naked body. I notice that he pauses at several significant places, and when our eyes meet again, he blushes at being caught.

He clears his throat and says, "I think there's enough

evidence on the grass that water balloons were thrown, and you two were the only ones in the vicinity."

Harmony peeks out from behind me. "You can't prove those balloons were ours. Any fingerprints would be washed away by the water!"

"She makes a good point." I grab a carrot stick and snap it in half with my teeth.

Seth grumbles and looks to my father for support, but Dad knows better.

"I'm staying out of it," he says. "I didn't see a thing."

"I guess I'll let it go this time," Seth tells us. "But you guys better be careful. I'm out for revenge now."

I put a hand on my hip. "We'll be ready."

Seth's eyes travel down to that hand, then quickly up again, as if he knows he shouldn't be ogling me, especially in front of my father. Fortunately, Dad is so busy spooning hummus into a bowl that he doesn't have a clue about the sexual tension humming in the room.

Harmony breaks the spell by stepping out from behind me and planting her hands on her skinny little hips.

"You'll never catch us," she says defiantly.

"We'll see." Seth stretches out his arms, pretending to take a step toward her.

Harmony squeals with delight and races around the island, hiding behind my dad.

"Hmmm, I'll go for now," Seth says, "but you two better watch out."

He trains those beautiful brown eyes on me, and my face isn't the only part of me that's heating up. I give him my best scowl and make a motion to shoo him out the door. I'm not going to let those Neanderthal pheromones get to me.

After Seth leaves, we eat everything Dad has set out for us, and I realize that I'm sublimating, replacing sex with food. Last night's kiss combined with today's interaction with Seth has me horny as a teenager. I spend the rest of the afternoon trying to forget that look in his eyes as he checked out my body in this bikini. It's the same look he had in the barn right before he kissed me. There's nothing I want to do more than provoke him to give me that look again, but I know it's entirely the wrong thing to do so I break into the stash of chocolate in my room, instead.

FRIDAY IS the final day of Grammy Camp, and Renata goes full tilt, taking Harmony to the Chapel Hill planetarium, the town swimming pool and the nail salon for a mani-pedi. In her attempt to wear out Harmony, Renata ends up exhausted. Harmony, on the other hand, arrives home fresh as a daisy and ready for more entertainment. Seth is called in to help this time, and he agrees to let Harmony sleep over at his place. She has been dying to sleep up in the loft area he built in his cabin so she's thrilled with the arrangement.

With Harmony gone for the evening, the house is quiet again, and I take up residence in my usual spot on the porch glider. I'm reading *The Color Purple,* having finally given up on *Mrs. Dalloway,* but after a few chapters, I admit to myself that I can't concentrate on my book. My mind keeps flashing back to kissing Seth in the barn, the feel of our wet clothing pressed against each other, his strong, warm hands running down my sides. When our lips met, it was like someone dropped a match in gasoline. I've never been so caught up in a moment in my life. From what was happening with his body, I know he felt the same.

I set my book aside and decide the best way to focus on someone other than Seth is to accept Rhett's invitation to join him on Saturday night. Maybe I can convince him to go somewhere other than Ricky's so we don't run into Seth again. Right as I'm texting him, Renata appears on the porch holding Harmony's favorite stuffed animal, a brown and white dog whose fur has been loved smooth.

"She forgot Patcher." Renata slips on a pair of flip flops. "Seth asked me to bring him over."

"Can't he come get it?" I ask.

She quirks her mouth. "They're...in the middle of something." Her voice sounds tired, but also slightly amused. She's already in her pajamas and her hair is in a silk wrap. "I'll be right back."

I click off my phone and set it down on the glider. "I'll take it."

Renata hesitates for a second. "Are you sure?"

"Of course." I reach out and take Patcher from her. "I'm not going to bed for a while."

She smiles warmly. "I appreciate it. Seth will be annoyed that I sent you, but he'll get over it. Here take this with you."

She pulls a small flashlight out of her pants pocket and hands it to me. I hear her chuckle as she goes back inside the house and wonder why Seth will be annoyed to see me. Maybe Renata isn't aware that he and I are on better, or at least more neutral, terms now, if you can call the terms "neutral" after sharing a steamy kiss.

The crickets are singing as I cross the field to Seth's cabin, and I hear what I think is a frog join their chorus. It's funny how I've gotten used to the noises here in the country, and I almost like them now. The yard gets darker with every step I take away from the lights of the main house, and I flick on the flashlight Renata gave me to guide my way. Seth's cabin isn't far, probably an eighth of a mile, but it's hidden behind a grouping of trees that give it some privacy.

The air has finally cooled, and the sky is clear tonight. The stars are on full display, and I marvel at how many there are. It feels strange that they're always there, even when I'm in New York City where I can barely see them at all. I haven't seen a night sky like this since my college friends dragged me to a meditation retreat in rural Mexico. Five excruciating days of sitting on stone hard cushions and a bout of traveler's diarrhea, but the night skies were beautiful.

I find myself thinking that I need to set up a hammock in the yard to enjoy stargazing, then remind myself that I'll be leaving soon. A hammock wouldn't be a waste of money if Harmony would use it after I'm gone. Sadness creeps up on me, but I nudge it away. There are so many things waiting for me back home. My bed. My friends. Decent bagels. I don't want to think about how my job is looming there, too, with the ongoing problem of Dan's presence, or about the possibility of Hugh leaving New York. I know in my bones that Raymond will get the job. The angst I feel about it tells me I rely on Hugh too much. Friends have hinted at it for years. When my friend Cara found out Hugh was moving out of our apartment to live with Raymond, her response was, "It's like you guys are getting a divorce." And it definitely felt that way.

I have to admit that having Hugh in my life did lessen my need for a romantic partner. He was my best friend, my soul mate, really. I dated other guys to fulfill my physical needs, but Hugh and I shared our histories, our problems and our secrets. Even when he moved out, we still talked every day on the phone and spent a lot of time together. It suited Hugh, too, since Raymond worked long hours. I suspect Raymond felt less guilty about working so much, knowing that Hugh had someone to keep him company. Now Hugh won't be a subway ride away, he'll be living halfway across the country.

I literally stop in my tracks because it dawns on me that this is what Isabelle meant: Hugh is the soulmate who will break my heart. There's some comfort in having figured out the real meaning of her prophecy. At least I don't have to worry about yet another heartbreak coming my way.

The lights are all still on in the cabin, and I hear music coming from inside as I walk up the steps of his porch. I admire the two friendly rocking chairs and the wrought iron table between them, then knock loudly on the door so that they'll hear me.

Seth is the one to fling open the door, and now I understand Renata's amusement. He and Harmony certainly have been busy. His hair is done up in tiny braids and bows. Those feminine touches juxtaposed with his powerful frame and facial scruff, make him look completely ridiculous. Something that sounds like "Pfft!" escapes my mouth.

"Thanks," he says, reaching out for Patcher.

I pull the stuffed animal away and make a closer inspection of his head. This is retribution for laughing at me in the barn, and I'm going to enjoy it.

"This is a good look for you. Can I see the back?"

Seth growls and grabs the toy from me. I want to pull out my phone and snap a picture, but he'd never let me. I'll have to delight in the fact that this shared memory will live on in our minds.

A Taylor Swift song is playing in the background, and Harmony calls out, "I can do your hair next, Andie!"

"Oh, sorry, Harmony, I'm going to bed now, but maybe you should do Seth's makeup, too. He'd love that."

I wink at him, bubbles of laughter rising up in my throat.

Seth glowers and says, "Add this to the list of things that we will never speak of again."

"Gender identity is just a construct!" I yell as he shuts the door in my face.

I gallop like a drunken horse all the way home, singing that Taylor Swift song at the top of my lungs and feeling happier than I have in weeks.

THE GOOD MOOD I'm in on Friday night evaporates the next morning when Dan texts to tell me he spent the previous night coming clean to his wife. He says that she knows about our relationship. I'm not sure how our flirty friendship and one kiss became a "relationship." My ex Kirk never once called me his girlfriend in the whole year we dated, but Dan and I were in a relationship. Okay, sure. Men are a nightmare.

Right before dinner, Hugh calls to tell me that Raymond did get the job in Chicago. They won't leave until September because Raymond has to complete a major project in the New York office first, but it's happening. I congratulate Raymond and assure Hugh, who is freaking out, that he'll be alright. I'm not sure if I'll be okay, but I play the part of supportive friend and reserve my meltdown for when I get off the phone. I'm too upset to even cry so I scream into the pillow on my bed then punch it repeatedly until feathers fly from it.

My bedroom is too small to contain my emotional spiral, and what I'd really like to do is throw something, which I'm sure Renata wouldn't appreciate. As an alternative to violence, I strap on my sneakers and flee the house, leaving Dad to call after me that they'll keep my plate of food warm for me. Heading for the road with Janelle Monae blasting in my headphones, I run at a pace I can't possibly sustain. By the second hill, I'm panting and the tears finally come. Once I start crying, I can't stop. I've got sweat, snot and tears running down my face as I hobble down the road on one of the hottest days of the summer. It's not my best look. I finally give up on getting home and stumble to the side of the road. After flopping down on my bottom, I sob into my tank top, feeling pathetic, small and totally dysfunctional. I should be able to handle what's happening in my life. I'm a grown-up, and things could be so much worse. My friends are dealing with cancer, aging parents, and children with disabilities, and I'm overwhelmed by much less traumatic events, some of which are my own doing.

I remember what my therapist once told me about not comparing my troubles to those of other people. They may not seem big in relation to other people's worries, but it's okay to admit you're struggling with the load you're carrying. And I'm definitely struggling right now. I want to forget about everything for a little while, even for one night. That's when I make a decision, right on the side of the road as the mosquitos feast on my blood: I'm getting fucking lit tonight.

DAD AND RENATA are already in bed by the time I'm showered and dressed in a black tank dress, fresh as a peach and ready to consume multiple gin and tonics. For some reason, cell service is patchy on the screened porch so I walk into the yard and open the Uber app. As I'm entering my destination, Seth walks by on the way to his cabin. Renata said he was working a long shift today, nine to nine, and he's still got on his work clothing. I'm surprised that I find his navy blue paramedic uniform incredibly sexy. Maybe it's because it fits him so well or perhaps there really is something about a man in uniform. Mutt, who's running beside him, turns and makes a beeline in my direction. I nearly drop my phone, trying to maneuver and block.

"You'd think this dog was starved for attention," I say, rubbing Mutt's ears.

"Don't let him fool you. He's been spoiled today. The lady who owns the hair salon brought some leftover steak for him. All the ladies love Mutt."

I'm pretty sure all the ladies love Seth, including the one at the hair salon.

"You should exploit it, use him as a way to meet women. Guys with babies do it all the time."

Seth looks genuinely perplexed. "Why would a guy with a baby be meeting women?"

"Not everyone shares your morals," I say bitterly.

Mutt wants to waggle through my legs so I'll scratch his butt. I've seen him make this particular move before, but I'm not interested in participating while I'm wearing a dress.

"C'mere Mutt." Seth drags his dog away by the collar. He takes a better look at me, and I feel as naked as I did in the bikini. "You look nice. Are you going out tonight?"

"I was about to call a ride." I lift my phone. "I'm going to Ricky's to meet Rhett and his friends. Planning on having a few drinks so I don't want to drive."

Seth strokes Mutt's head. "You're hanging out with Rhett again?"

There's nothing confrontational in his voice, but I'm in a pissy mood and take offense anyway.

"What, I can't make friends while I'm here?"

Seth gives me a tired look, as if he isn't up for a fight tonight, and runs a hand through his hair. He must know that move gets to me.

"Hey, you can do whatever you want. In fact, I'll give you a ride to Ricky's. I could use a beer after today."

"You don't have to do that." I brush dog hair off the jersey fabric of my dress.

"It's not a big deal. My friends will probably be there, too. I won't bother you when we get there. Let me get a shower, and I'll take you."

When Seth says the word shower, my mind gets dirty. Then soapy. Then... no, no, no. Tonight is not about men. It's men who are screwing up my entire world. Tonight is about drinking away my sorrows.

Seth walks toward his cabin, and Mutt trots beside him.

"Why are you walking that way?" I point to the farmhouse. "The shower is in there."

Do not picture the towel falling to the floor as Seth gets into the shower. Seriously.

He keeps walking and shouts back at me, "I finished tiling my bathroom. Shower is up and running."

No more naked Seth on the other side of the door. Today is seriously one big loss.

ELEVEN

Seth comes back twenty minutes later—speed shower in effect—and finds me waiting for him on the screened porch.

He opens the door and leans inside. "Ready to go?"

I hop to my feet. "Born ready."

He holds the door open for me, and as I pass by him, I surreptitiously drink in his freshly showered smell. He's wearing gray shorts and a white t-shirt, his dark hair still damp and curling a little at the ends.

We walk in silence to his truck, and when we get to it, he beats me to the passenger side and opens the door for me. It's a gesture that's both antiquated and chivalrous, and definitely something you'd do on a date.

I adjust my skirt for the climb into the cab of his truck. "Thanks, but you don't have to do that."

"It's the way my mom taught me. It's just good manners. I know you can open the door yourself."

Getting into a tall pickup truck when you're wearing a tight tank dress isn't the easiest maneuver in the world. I move slowly, keeping my knees pressed tightly together to avoid giving him a crotch shot. I must look absurd, but I do prevent him from seeing my underwear, so overall it's a win.

After I'm carefully settled into my seat, he closes the door and walks around to his side. I get a nervous flutter in my stomach as I wait for him to return, then pinch myself hard on the arm to remind myself to cut that shit out. This is ridiculous. He's my designated driver tonight, my neighbor who is giving me a ride to a bar. He's not trying to win my affection.

I wait until we're off the farm's property before starting a conversation. This will be a long ride if I don't say something and, if I know Seth, he'll be content to sit in silence the whole way.

"So you had a bad day, too?" I say, remembering what he mentioned earlier about needing a beer.

"We had some rough calls. A little girl who was in anaphylaxis. She wasn't in good shape when we dropped her at the hospital, but I heard she made it. Later we got called for a drug overdose, and it was too late when we arrived. Kid was only nineteen."

He's quiet then, and I know he's far away, replaying the events of the day in his mind.

"I could never do what you do." I shift in my seat as I imagine the intensity of what he experiences on a regular basis. "I'm not good under that kind of pressure."

"Unfortunately, I thrive on it."

"Is every day at work this hard?"

Seth thinks for a moment. "Sometimes it's boring, you don't get a call for a while, and the day seems long. Then you're suddenly thrown into a situation that can be life or death, and every decision you make is crucial. It's a lot like being in the military, in some ways, which is why I enjoy it, I guess."

"It sounds stressful."

"We also get calls that aren't emergencies. Miss Vivian, who's about ninety-five, called our dispatcher today when she heard a noise coming from her closet."

I smile, secretly studying his profile in the darkness of the car. "Did you go over there and check it out?"

"Yeah, and it's a good thing we did. One of her cats got into a box of gift wrapping and couldn't get out. Pretty sure we saved his life."

We both laugh, and it's nice to feel like we've let our guards down.

"To me, teaching high school would be hard," he says. "I wouldn't have the patience for dealing with teenagers all day. I was such an asshole to my teachers."

"I haven't thrown any chairs in my classroom yet, but then again I've never taught you."

"I was truly awful."

I remember the picture in Renata's office of young Seth, an awkward boy who hadn't grown into his good looks yet.

"I can't imagine you were that bad. You were probably really quiet with a perma-frown, am I right?"

Seth laughs. "I was quiet and completely lazy when it came to doing the work. If I was interested in the subject, I'd listen and ace the test. If I wasn't interested, I'd put my head down and fall asleep or zone out. Not the best student."

"School is challenging for some kids. Your teachers probably knew you were smart and were frustrated they couldn't get you to do the work."

Seth smiles. "Not sure they thought I was smart, but I'm sure they found me frustrating. I know my mother did. I passed my classes to please her, but after she died, that motivation was gone. I barely squeaked through and graduated."

I have to stop myself from reaching out and touching his face.

"She'd be proud of you now."

"I hope so."

We fall into a comfortable silence, and some of my stress from the day melts away. If we were on a date, I'd move closer and put my hand in his, but we're not, so I don't.

"I bet the boys in your classes have a crush on you," he says quietly.

I look over at him, his face outlined by streetlights shining through his window.

"Maybe some do. I don't dress like this at work for that very reason."

His eyes wander over to me, and we stare at each other for a second before he looks back at the road. I clench my thighs together, trying to make the aching sensation down there go away.

"Lord, I should hope not."

His voice is gruff, and I look out the window so he won't see my face. My attraction to him must be written all over it. Part of me wishes he'd take one hand off the wheel and place it on my thigh. It would be a bold move, and we'd probably end up wrecking the car because it would lead to me climbing onto his lap. I'm grateful when he speaks again, because it breaks me out of my R-rated reverie.

"I'm actually going back to school this fall. Are you too warm?" He taps a button on the dash and cool air gusts through the vents.

"I'm fine," I assure him, although the longer I'm alone with Seth, the warmer I get. "What are you going back for?"

"I'm getting my nursing degree." He looks over at me again. "I want to work in the I.C.U. eventually, but that requires experience and even more training. That's why I haven't been up to New York lately or traveled much at all. As former military, I don't have to worry about tuition, but I want to go part-time at work to focus on classes. I need to save up money to do that. I haven't even told Renata yet."

"That's amazing," I say. "I'm thinking about a career change, too, actually. But I don't know what I want to do."

"You don't like teaching anymore?"

"I need a change." I grip my purse tightly and look away.

Memories of Dan come flooding through my head, souring the good mood that's been building during the ride. Dan and I flirting. Dan and I kissing. Dan texting me that he's trashed his marriage. Suddenly, I'm ready for that drink again.

RICKY'S IS PACKED, maybe more so than last week.

"College kids are home for the summer," Seth explains. "It always gets crazy in here this time of year."

Seth and I approach the bar together and order drinks.

"Gin and tonic," I tell the bartender. "No, wait, make that a shot of tequila and a Bud."

She lifts her eyebrows, but doesn't say a word. Seth on the other hand lets out a low whistle.

"That's a serious order. I'll just have a Bud."

When she leaves, I lay down my purse and casually drum my fingers on the bar.

"Are you trying to get wasted?" he asks. "If so, I'd say you're off to a good start."

I fix him with a stony look. "It would appear so, yes."

"This should be interesting," Seth says under his breath.

The bartender sets down our drinks, and we both pull out our wallets.

"I'm buying your drink," I say, pushing his hand away. "You gave me a ride here, it's the least I can do."

"Thanks," he says, slipping his wallet into his back pocket.

I gulp down my shot and slam the empty glass on the counter. Then I pick up my beer and clink it with his.

"Cin cin," I say, before taking a hearty sip.

Seth watches me carefully. "I hope that means 'I won't vomit in your truck later.' "

I make claws and hiss softly at him like a cat before draining a third of my beer.

"There's Rhett." He gestures with his bottle to a group of people across the room.

I follow his gaze and see it is indeed Rhett with some of the same people he was with last week. The problem is that I want to stay over here and keep bantering with Seth. If I'm completely truthful, I want to go home with him, throw off all my clothes and jump into his bed.

Or maybe that's the tequila hitting my system.

Since I told Seth my plan was to hang with Rhett tonight, it will look weird if I don't. The only other option is to be honest about the fact that I'd rather spend time with him. As I'm considering whether I want to save face or get laid, a pretty girl with colorfully bold tattoo sleeves on her arms approaches Seth and gives him a warm hug. That's the cue I needed. Before they disengage, I'm headed across the room to Rhett and company.

For the next hour plus some, I endure conversations about sustainable foodscapes, soil microbes, and biochar fertilizers. The only way to survive is to order another round of tequila and beer. I know the old adage "beer then liquor, never sicker," but I've got a stomach of steel so down the hatch it goes.

When I get up from the pub table we've been sitting at, I have to pause and recalibrate. I'm happily buzzed, nothing to worry about yet. Memories of my real life are hazy around the edges, just like I wanted them to be. Unfortunately, the liquor hasn't dimmed my interest in Seth, and I decide to look around the bar for him because he's my ride home. At least that's the reason I'm giving if anyone asks why I'm searching for him. If I were being honest, that reason isn't at the top of my list for finding my brawny paramedic friend.

I must be drunk if I'm calling Seth my friend.

Seth is at the bar, and the tatted-up girl is still with him. She's been joined by another girl who's also edgy and attractive, if you're into medieval looking nose rings. There's no way I'm interrupting that conversation so I head to the other end of the bar to order myself another beer. While I'm trying to catch the bartender's attention, I feel a hand on my shoulder.

"Are you ready to go home?"

I turn to face Seth who's standing behind me.

"Not quite yet." As I say each word, I tap his chest with my finger. "One more beer and then I'm good to go."

"Do you really need one more beer?"

I roll my eyes like a bratty teenager, and turn back to the bar.

"Seriously," he says, trying to turn me around again by gently pulling my shoulder. "Let's get out of here."

Instead of answering, I place my order with the bartender. Then I turn around to face him.

"Seth, I do need another beer because my plan is to get shitfaced tonight. And you do not need to wait to drive me home."

I have no idea why I'm doing or saying any of this. I

don't really want another beer, and I totally want Seth to drive me home. Unfortunately, I just can't admit it.

"How are you gonna get home then?"

I point to Rhett. "I'm sure he can drive me home or I can call that Uber guy. You aren't responsible for me so if you want to take one of those girls home," I wave in the direction of his friends who are still at the bar, "that's cool. Do what you want."

Seth closes his eyes and bites his lower lip, like he's trying really hard not to say what's on his mind right now.

"I want—" He shakes his head. "You know what? Forget it. I'll see you tomorrow."

I barely taste what I tell myself is my last beer of the night and sit down on a stool so I can have a pity party. In my mind, I was testing Seth to see if he'd really leave or wait for me. But why did I need to test him? He said he wanted to drive me home. I'm such a jerk, and now I'm alone at a bar in a strange town and drunk off my ass.

A few minutes later, I spot Jenny and an attractive woman I presume is Luisa. Luisa is paying for their beers, and Jenny is rubbing her back. They're stinking adorable.

I wave and raise my voice to get her attention. "Hey, Jenny!"

Her face lights up with a sincere smile when she sees me, and she whispers something to the woman with her before they move over to stand next to me.

"Hey, Andie. What's going on?"

"Not much." I nod my chin over at Rhett and his friends. "Just learning the ins and outs of organic farming. Hi, you must be Luisa."

Luisa transfers her drink to her left hand, then extends her right hand to shake mine.

"Nice to meet you."

Her lovely accent suggests that Spanish is her first language.

"Where's Seth?" Jenny asks, scanning the room and not finding him anywhere.

The crowd hasn't thinned yet, since it's only a little past eleven-thirty.

"He left a while ago."

I take a swig of my drink only to find it's empty. I'm bloated and burpy and full of regret for drinking beer instead of gin. Judging by the swirling sensation in my head, the tequila was also a bad idea.

"I thought you guys came together?" she says looking confused.

I'm not sure how she knows this, but maybe Seth texted her or she saw us walk in earlier.

"He was ready to leave, and I wanted to stay. I'll get a ride home with someone else, it's fine."

Luisa leans over Jenny and looks me directly in the eye. "What's going on with you two?"

"Luisa..." Jenny says with a warning tone.

It's clear they know Seth and I kissed, or at least they know something happened between us.

"Nothing is going on," I say innocently and receive two hard stares for trying to bullshit them. I sigh, not having enough willpower at this point to hide the truth. "I think we found out there's a thin line between lust and hate."

Jenny laughs, but Luisa looks concerned.

"We don't want to see him get hurt," she says.

I shake my head in confusion. Maybe it's the alcohol I've consumed or the noise in here, but I can't possibly have heard her correctly.

"I think you have the wrong idea about what's going on."

"It's none of our business anyway." Jenny looks over my shoulder at something. "I think Rhett is looking for you."

Rhett walks toward me from the other end of the bar with a beer in each of his hands.

"Hey, I got this for you, but then I couldn't find you," he says, extending one of the bottles toward me.

I guess this beer will be my last one of the evening. I thank him and set the bottle on the bar, and the four of us strike up a conversation that I'm fairly sure I won't remember tomorrow.

I HALF-LISTEN TO LUISA, Jenny and Rhett, but mostly I'm ruminating about Seth's departure. Having sex with him when I'm drunk is the worst idea ever so it's a relief that the temptation is gone. Still, I can't stop thinking about him and, at one particularly desperate point, consider knocking on his cabin door when I get home. A drunken booty call, really? I can't possibly have sunk that low.

After I play the longest and worst pool game of my life with Rhett, he offers to take me home. I don't plan on drinking anything else, and it's close to closing time, but something stops me from accepting his offer: I don't want Seth to hear that Rhett and I left the bar together. It's ridiculous, but what Luisa said got to me. If there's a chance that leaving with Rhett will hurt Seth, I don't want to do it, and no one is more surprised by this turn of events than I am. Annoying Seth should delight and entertain me. But it doesn't.

Because I've told Rhett that I want to stay and have one more beer, I have to make good on that lie. I wave goodbye to him and attempt to climb on an empty barstool that feels much taller and wobblier than it did a few hours ago. After several attempts, I'm finally on my perch. The drunk middle-aged guy who hit on me last time I was at Ricky's is slouched on the stool next to mine.

"Let me buy you a drink, little lady." His eyes float from my face down to my chest.

I narrow my eyes at him and scowl. "Your name is Frank, right? Frank, I'm going to be totally honest here. You don't have a shot with me and neither one of us needs anything else to drink. Now please be quiet while I order a beer and pay for it myself."

As I flag down the bartender, Frank gives a low whistle.

"Sounds like you've had a bad night. Want to talk about it?"

"Not particularly."

Then I forget all about my (third) last drink of the night and begin railing about men, love, the New York City public school system and anything else that comes to my mind. Frank is an enthusiastic audience, and although he takes up for the male sex from time to time, he's generally sympathetic.

I don't even notice the bartender ringing the bell for last call so it's a surprise when she announces to Frank and me that it's time to close up. Her exact words are that he and I need to vacate the premises immediately.

I look around and see that Frank and I have indeed shut down the place. Before the bartender can object, I scurry to the bathroom for one last pee and now the world is tilting at an uncomfortable rate, and I have to hold onto the toilet seat like I'm riding a mechanical bull.

When I return to the bar, Frank is getting up from his stool, and I pull out my phone and open the Uber app, planning to offer Frank a ride home. A second later, the door to

Ricky's opens and a police officer walks in. This guy is the dictionary definition of tall, dark and handsome, and that's what I tell Frank. Loudly.

"Thanks for coming, Officer Vega," Shirley says, slipping her purse onto her shoulder.

"Evening, Shirley."

I smile at Officer Hottie, but his mouth remains a tight little line as he assesses me.

"These the two who need to get home?" he asks Shirley.

I shake my phone at her. "I'm getting an Uber. You didn't need to call the police."

"Karl isn't picking you two up. Frank has puked in his backseat one too many times. He's done with drunks. Officer Vega here is going to see you home."

Drunks? Did she just call me a drunk? I'm drunk as in the verb, but not the noun, certainly. Shirley looks determined and definitely a little fed up, and so does Vega, so I decide to keep my outrage to myself.

Internally, I direct my indignation toward Seth. He was supposed to be my ride home, and he ditched me. Okay, I ditched him. Whatever.

Officer Vega's squad car is parked right outside the front door of Ricky's, and Frank slides into the backseat like it's routine for him, which it apparently is. I follow him inside and press myself against the door, praying Frank isn't going to hurl. He's already snoring before we even leave the parking lot, which seems like a good sign. Without realizing it, I start humming the theme to the television show "Cops." Then I add the words.

"Bad boys, bad boys, what you gonna do—"

"Stop," Vega says from the front seat. "Please, I beg you. Stop singing."

I stick my tongue out at him, but comply. It's also

possible I fall asleep on the ride home because the next thing I know Officer Vega is shaking me awake. That last things I remember are leaving the bar, getting into the police cruiser and eating blueberry pancakes with Idris Elba...on second thought, that last part might have been a dream.

Dizziness has fully set in now, and I have to concentrate on putting one foot in front of the other as I walk to the house. Officer Vega stands outside his vehicle, watching me from the farm's parking lot. I stumble over a hole in the lawn, but remain on my feet.

"I got this," I tell myself aloud, as if the task of walking is something that I'm struggling to master. Because I am.

I concentrate hard on walking up the front porch steps. One foot touches each step, not two. That would be wrong. Only toddlers need to go up stairs that way.

Unfortunately, it takes me a long time to locate my keys in my bag, and when I find them I squeal and hold them up like treasure. When I turn, I see that Officer Vega is still watching me, and I know I should be embarrassed, but that feels like something there's plenty of time for in the morning.

BIRDS HAVE no respect for hangovers. My headache is compounded by every squawk from outside my window. I would sell my soul for noise canceling headphones or a sound machine. The sun's deadly rays are also a problem, but at least I can cover my eyes with a quilt. There's nothing I can do about my ears.

I need water. I need coffee. I need someone to pronounce me dead so I never have to leave this bed. Every time I roll my head to one side, there's a sloshing sensation like someone has put my brain inside a magic eight ball. Will I survive this hangover? Answer remains cloudy, try again later.

Staying in this bed forever is not a terrible plan. That way I won't have to deal with Dan and the fact that I shat where I ate. This is a nice mattress. I've had better pillows, but these will suffice. Sure, I'll atrophy eventually, but I can figure out some exercises that require very little head movement.

I doze in and out of sleep, various parts of the previous night's adventures floating through my consciousness. Did I ask Officer Vega to give me a ride home or did he arrest me? Neither one seems to be the correct answer. I definitely made a suggestive comment about his handcuffs that I now regret. Running into him again is going to be humiliating to say the least—another reason to never leave this bed. My saving grace is that I didn't vomit in the squad car, at least not that I recall.

My mouth is like sun-dried adobe at this point, and there's no choice but to seek hydration. Plus, I have to pee. I didn't take these things into consideration when I planned on remaining in bed for eternity. I'm sure I look ridiculous, standing myself up with as little head movement as possible. I need to pause after I swing my legs over the side because a wave of nausea hits me in the gut. I never throw up from drinking. Never. It's an achievement I wear like a badge of honor. Only this seems to be the point at which I give up my badge...

The wave of nausea passes, and I'm alright again, although whoever is rocking this bed side to side needs to stop. I feel like I'm on a raft at sea.

Everything is going to be fine. There's a tap in the bathroom that will bring forth delicious running water, if only my legs will take me there. Thank god Seth finished tiling his bathroom. I seriously could not deal with him seeing me like this.

There's no cup in the bathroom so I hang my head over the sink and drink straight from the tap. Sweet relief. When I look up in the mirror, I realize that somehow I managed to take off my dress last night. I'm naked except for my underwear. My mascara and eyeliner have streamed down my cheeks, and I make a valiant effort to swipe my face with a washcloth. It's not an improvement. With my makeup gone, I resemble a body in the morgue.

The effort I've spent drinking water and turning myself into a corpse has taken up most of my remaining energy, and I still need to pee and get back in bed, where someone will find my remains. Good-bye, sweet world.

Once I'm on the toilet, I locate my dress. It's wadded up in a ball on the floor with my purse tucked against it. Good to know I made it in here clothed and still have my wallet and phone. I check my messages, and I'm relived to see Dan hasn't contacted me again. Not yet, anyway.

Once I'm back in bed, rehydrated and exhausted, I close my eyes and fall into a deep sleep. When my phone rings, I grab it and punch the answer button, just to make the noise stop. I don't even consider who's on the other line, which is a horrible idea because it's the last person I want to speak with right now, my mother.

"Hey, Miranda!" she chirps.

Mom is the only person who uses my given name because everyone else cares that I hate it. According to her, when you take a nickname, it's a personal affront to the person who chose your original name.

"Hey," I groan.

"Are you all right? You sound like I woke you up, but that's impossible, since it's past ten in the morning."

"I'm not working right now," I say, running my tongue over my teeth, which are wearing tiny little sweaters. "I can sleep as late as I want."

"You're not a teenager anymore, honey, but whatever," she says, like she doesn't agree, but she'll just passive aggressively fight me on this one. "I called because I have a favor to ask you."

My mother's favors always involve inconvenience, money or both. The fact that she hasn't mentioned Dad makes me think he never called her about leaving New York and getting engaged. I'm sure as hell not going to be the one to bring it up. Even though she left Dad, I'm pretty sure she won't be gracious about him finding love again.

"I have a fantastic opportunity to get a new car," she says, excitement humming in her voice.

As far as I know, she still has the luxury car she got in the divorce settlement with her second husband. I always thought she should sell it and buy something more practical. Every time that thing needs repairs, she goes deeper into credit card debt. Maybe she has finally seen the light.

"You're getting rid of the BMW?"

"Yes, I'm so over that car. It needs a new transmission or something now, and I swear, it's a fortune to fix it. Robert's friend owns an Audi dealership, and can get me an amazing deal on a sedan—"

"Wait," I interrupt, "a used Audi or a new one?"

She clicks her tongue, like I'm nuts to think she'd buy used. I should have known. My mother has never bought anything pre-owned in her life, except her second and third husbands.

"It's new, of course. But you don't understand, he's going

to give it to me for way under asking price. It's a steal, really."

I shove my head under the pillow, remove the phone from my ear, and squeal my frustration into the mattress. A full-on scream isn't possible when my head hurts this badly. When I return to the conversation, Mom is rambling on about all the extras the salesman is throwing in: leather interior, GPS, heated seats. I'm pretty sure most of these things are standard, but there's no use arguing with her.

"This is fascinating news, Mom. What's the favor?"

I already know what it will be.

"You know my credit isn't good." Before I can say a word, she adds, "It's not my fault I was married to a con man so don't even start with me."

Mom's third husband was involved in a Ponzi scheme, smaller than Madoff, but big enough to get him arrested. They declared bankruptcy before they divorced, and I do think Mom should take a little of the blame for marrying a guy who was a crook. The first time I met him, I knew he was a complete douchebag. And let's be real, even if Mom had known he was a criminal, she would have overlooked it in exchange for vacations in the Caymans and a full-time housekeeper.

"I need you to co-sign my loan," she says sweetly. "It won't cost you a thing. Can you come out to the island tomorrow? Robert says I really need to close this deal."

The sharp laugh I let out cuts through my skull like a knife.

"You have got to be kidding me."

Mom is quiet, and I can picture her trying to decide what tactic to use next. Should she guilt me or bully me?

"Miranda, this is not a big ask," she says, casual as can

be. "I'll pay for your train, if you want me to, but I really need you to come out here."

I'm weirdly proud of my FICA score. Unlike many people my age, I never miss my student loan payments. I only have one credit card, and it gets paid off each month. Growing up without a lot of money has taught me to be very careful with what I have. If I ever do get engaged, I'm going to be running a credit check on my fiancé before the wedding takes place. That's why the answer to her question is simple.

"I'm sure you want this new car, but I'm not co-signing any loans. Sorry. I've worked too hard on my credit score to screw it up now."

"After all I've done for you, I think you could do this one thing for me."

As if this is the first request she's ever made of me. If my brain weren't pickled in tequila, I'd remind her that I paid for her root canal six months ago.

I can only summon the energy to issue a stern, "No."

As soon as I hear her hang up, I chuck the phone on the floor and dive under the covers. I'm never getting out of bed again.

TWELVE

"Dad?" I croak. After clearing my throat, I try again. "Dad!"

Unless I dreamed it, a metallic banging noise woke me from my nap. I wait for a response from my father or for the sound to occur again, but there's silence now. The clock says it's seven at night, which means I've been asleep for several hours. My head feels much better, but I've got cottonmouth again, and I'm hungry, which is a good sign. All I've eaten today is some toast around three o'clock, during my first foray into the world.

I'm headed for the shower when the clanging noise reoccurs. Suddenly, my headache is back. Someone knows about my hangover and wants to kill me, obviously.

"What the hell," I mutter, opening my bedroom door to find the source of this evil.

I peek into the bedroom attached to mine, but it's empty. Dad and Renata's room is down the hall, and when I get to their door, I hear a stream of swear words that would make Amy Shumer blush.

"Dad?" I say, as I enter their room. "Where are you?"

There's a grunt and more swear words, followed by, "I'm in the bathroom."

I peek my head in the door and see Dad crouching next to the toilet. Water is slowly but steadily streaming out of the valve near the floor, flooding the bathroom. There's a wrench in Dad's hand and a panicked expression on his face.

"This toilet has been leaking a little, and I tried to fix it, but I think I broke the valve and now..." He gestures to the leak and the floor, which is the only explanation necessary. "I wanted to do this while Renata was out and surprise her, but I'm such a screw-up. I called Seth for help, but he didn't answer. I'm not sure what to do."

"There has to be a place to shut off the water for the house," I say. "Right?"

"Shit. That's a good idea. I feel like such an idiot. I don't want her to come home and find this."

"I'll Google it," I say. "Maybe we can find out where it would be."

"There's no time," he says. "We need to call a plumber. Can you look one up? I'll get towels for the floor."

Dad heads to the linen closet while I research plumbers on my phone. Perfect Pipes LLC answers on the first ring, but the receptionist tells me they can't send anyone for at least an hour. I ask her if there's another plumber in the area who might get here faster, and she explains that most companies won't send anyone out after five o'clock. Fortunately, Perfect Pipes offers an emergency after-hours service, which I'm sure will cost us a fortune.

She asks whether we have well water or city water, and I call out the question to Dad. When I tell her he thinks it's well water, she explains how to find the main shut-off valve. Dad is in full-on crisis mode now. He's on his hands and knees mopping up water, and his pants are getting soaked. I tell him to try calling Seth again, but he shakes his head.

"I left a message," he says, rising to stand. "He'll come over when he gets it."

We stand at the bathroom door watching the water slowly soak into the blue towels. I don't want Seth to come and find this mess. He already thinks Dad is useless.

"Of course, we'll be submerged by then," he says.

"Don't give up. Let's see if we can find the shut-off valve."

He blinks rapidly, like I've woken him from a nightmare.

"Okay, let's do it. Where did she say to look?"

We locate what looks like a hot water heater and another tank that could be the pressure pump in a closet next to the laundry room, but there are several valves and nothing is labeled.

"Should we just try turning them all off?" he asks.

"She said to locate the pipes coming into the house and follow the one that leads to the water pressure pump."

I get down on my knees and inspect the area.

"This looks like a hot water heater," he says, pointing to the white tank. "So maybe the blue one is the pump for the well?"

Sure enough, there are four pipes running along the base of the wall, and I follow the two that lead to the blue tank.

"Let's try this green one." I tighten it all the way to the right, and Dad runs back upstairs to see if it worked.

About ten seconds later, I hear him scream, "Yes, yes, yeeeees!"

It's like the Yankees won game seven of the World Series.

I sigh with relief and roll backwards onto my butt. We got the water shut off and Perfect Pipes will be on their way soon. Crisis mostly averted.

I hear Dad pound down the stairs before he jogs back into the kitchen.

"You did it, honey! Thank you so much."

"We did it," I say. "Team work."

I stand up and Dad high fives me, and then he does his little happy dance, which is a cross between the Hora and a Leprechaun's jig. Right in the middle of our celebration, Dad frowns.

"Oh crap, I forgot that I have to get the chickens in for the night. I told Renata I'd take care of that, but I've got to wait for the plumber."

"What do you mean?" I ask.

Dad explains that the chickens have the run of their fenced-in area during the day, but at night they're put away inside the hen house for safety. Otherwise, they'd become some nocturnal animal's supper. I'm on a high from our plumbing success, but even so, dealing with chickens sounds like more than I can handle. A leaky toilet is one thing. Birds are another.

"I can wait for the plumber," I say.

Dad hesitates. "I know you don't like the chickens, but I feel like I should stay here in case Renata comes home. I don't want her to find this mess and think I've left you here to deal with it. Plus, the plumber can show me what I did wrong. Maybe I can learn something."

I would refuse, except Dad's face is totally pathetic. He's saved me many times over the years, and I owe him this one.

"Okay, fine, I'll do it."

WHEN I GET to the chicken enclosure, they're strutting around happily, pretending to be completely harmless. I'm not going to be lulled into complacency though. I know these peckers would love to stab my eyes out if they had the chance. They're just too short to do it. I can't blame them. If I were locked up in a pen all day with people tossing dried worms at me and groping around under my rump for eggs, I'd be pissed off, too. They don't look upset, I have to admit. It's possible I'm anthropomorphizing them a tad too much.

I'm still wearing the cotton pajama pants and vintage Bowie t-shirt I put on earlier today, and there are no pockets in my outfit. I have to stretch my shirt out at the bottom and make a little hammock to fill with mealworms, which I don't look at too closely because doing so will induce my gag reflex. I already regret that I agreed to help, but I need to at least make an attempt before going back to the house.

When I enter the chicken run, a few of the birds dash for the gate, and I have to slam it closed behind me to prevent an escape. Then I realize they're not trying to bolt, they're coming for the treats, the little gluttons. I toss some of their food away from me so they'll disperse while I formulate a plan.

The coop is located in the center of the run, and I have to get eighteen chickens inside it. Since they seem to love these delicious mealworms, that's my first approach. I dribble a little trail of treats leading to the ramp, then sprinkle more on the ramp itself and chuck some inside the coop. Then, I wait.

The chickens start devouring the food, bringing them closer to the house, and for a moment, I feel brilliant. Farm life must come naturally to me, I guess. I'm probably one of those naturalist savants, and let's not forget the fact I found that shut-off valve in the house. I literally pat myself on the back as my little friends continue to feast, and I imagine them walking the plank right into the coop. I begin planning what I'll eat when I get home, now that my appetite is back with a vengeance.

That's where my plan falls apart. They eat the food on the ground and the ramp, but they're not moving into the coop. It's like they don't realize it's their home. I toss more mealworms into the coop itself, and the white chicken closest to the door wanders inside. I slam the door behind her and do a little dance in my flip flops. A small victory. One down and seventeen to go. As a result of my dancing, I lose a shoe and have to hop around the pen to retrieve it. Who knows what diseases I could get in here if I walk barefoot.

I assess my next victim, a chicken with pretty brown and white feathers who seems interested in the food on the ramp. Once she's at the door, I open it and try to encourage her inside, without actually touching her, of course. Instead of her going in, chicken number one comes, jetting down the ramp like she's yelling, "Sayounara, Muthfucka!"

"Noooo!" I try in vain to block her escape with my outstretched hands.

I'm not sure she pecks me on purpose, but there's definitely beak to hand contact. After I take that hit, she dodges the barrier I'm forming with my legs, and just like that I'm back down to zero chickens captured.

After letting loose a stream of choice words for my feathered friends, I take a deep breath and regroup. This feels like an impossible task. It's like those games where you stand in a glass box, and they blow cash in the air around you. There's no way you can catch all those freaking bills, and every time you catch one, you drop another. If this were a reality show game, they would call it Chicken Round-up and recruit accomplished urban women to play, just to humiliate us. I look around the pen, like I'm going to find someone filming me with a camera.

If you asked me to get ten drunk friends onto the A train at three in the morning, I'd simply pretend I saw Tom Hiddleston (or Jennifer Lawrence, depending on their preferences) boarding whatever subway car I wanted them to get into. They'd happily stumble inside, one after the other, no problem. But this situation with the chickens is not in my wheelhouse. I don't have celebrity poultry to lure these birds anywhere, and the mealworms aren't enticing enough to convince them to board the train.

If I hadn't promised Dad I'd get the chickens into the coop I would run out of here and never look back. He looked so desperate earlier though. Night is settling in, and I need to move on these beasts if I'm going to finish before it's completely dark. The last thing I want to be doing is chasing birds that I can barely see.

"This is a nightmare," I mumble to myself, slapping at a mosquito and dropping about three-quarters of the food left in my pouch.

I stare down a grayish chicken with a red comb who is pecking the ground near my feet. Maybe I can hold food under her nose and lead her all the way to the coop, the way we used treats to lead our cat Norman to his cat carrier.

I hold the remaining mealworms under gray bird's beak and shimmy backwards toward the coop, but she doesn't seem to understand the plan here. She only follows for a few inches, then gets distracted by something under a clump of weeds. Great, I picked the bird with attention issues. I dump the rest of the food on the dirt and watch with futility as a couple of the chickens zoom in to eat it.

These birds are stubborn, but I'm a "never give up, never surrender" type of woman. They aren't going to take me down. Would the Marines give up if their mission was to house these chickens before nightfall? No, sir.

The chickens weigh, what, maybe five to ten pounds? I can't believe I'm even considering this, but I could pick them up one by one and place them in the coop. Close up, their feathers aren't as nasty as I'd imagined. Some of them are quite beautifully patterned. I assess the situation and decide that, yes, this is the only remaining course of action, if I can psych myself up to do it.

I select one of the birds who is already close to the coop; it's the white one I nearly captured earlier. I remember Harmony saying she was a nice chicken, one of her favorites. I approach slowly from behind, like a creepy chicken stalker. Then I gently bend at the knees, stick out my arms like a forklift and scoop her into my arms. She doesn't make a sound or struggle very much. Trying not to think about the feel of the feathers against my skin, I project her into the coop and swing shut the door. Success! I only have to do that seventeen more times...

I find my next chicken and attempt the same maneuver. Bend, scoop, lift. Unfortunately, this bird is more resistant to my plan. When I get my arms around her, she squawks and flaps her wings wildly. Certain I'm going to be murdered by her wings of death, I release her to the ground and jump away. Then I hop up and down, screeching like I've been attacked by a knife-wielding killer. For a good minute, I jump around the pen, screaming to no one in particular about feathers and flapping and how I really hate chickens.

When I slow down, I realize that I do have a scratch on my arm where her talons ripped into me. I double over, breathing hard. It's time to face facts, these birds have got me on the ropes.

"What are you doing to that poor chicken?"

I turn, wild-eyed, to see Seth and Mutt peering into the chicken run. He's got an armload of lumber and an amused smile on his face. When he registers my panic, his expression turns serious.

"You need some help?"

"Dad said I have to get all these chickens into the house thing." I flail one of my useless arms at the chicken condo. "But they're not responding to food bribes so I tried picking them up—"

I cut myself off mid-sentence because there's a hiccup in my throat and if I let it out, I'm going to start sobbing. I had no idea how upset I was about the disobedience of these damn chickens until Seth arrived. Or maybe it's just the general tenor of the day that's got me so emotional. Phone calls from my mother have a history of roiling me. She has the opposite effect of my father. He's my rock, she's the jackhammer.

Seth is looking at me with such concern that it's got me unhinged. When he releases the wood to the ground and walks toward the pen door, I'm flooded with relief. The Marine has arrived, chickens. Your asses are grass.

"Did you turn on the light?" he asks, opening the gate to come inside.

"What light?"

Seth walks up the ramp and into the coop, ducking his head as he enters. He snaps on a little light that hangs from the ceiling and comes outside again.

"They like the light. Give them a few minutes, and they'll tuck themselves into bed."

Did Dad mention the light? I don't remember it, but in my bird-phobic state, maybe I blocked it out. It takes a couple of minutes before the first chicken migrates up the ramp and into the coop. I have no doubt that the rest will eventually follow, and they'll all soon be snug in the house for the night.

"You can go," Seth says. "I'll come by here in a little bit and close the door to the coop."

"No," I say firmly, "I've come this far, I'm finishing the job."

Seth chuckles as we watch another chicken waddle up the ramp. "I wish I could have seen more of you chasing those chickens around because what I did see was priceless."

I scowl, but it's difficult to keep a straight face. I'm too grateful for the rescue, and I have to admit, I did look ridiculous.

"You don't even know about my fear of birds. What I did was heroic. In middle school, my science teacher let his pet pigeon out in our classroom, and I dove under a lab table and refused to come out for the rest of the period. I was traumatized for life."

"You don't have a pet and you hate birds. Tell me again why you're a vegetarian?" he asks.

This time around, I get that he's teasing me, not criticizing my life choices.

"Just because I don't want to hang out with them doesn't mean I think people should kill and eat them."

Now that I'm no longer in a hot panic, I notice how Seth looks in his worn jeans, black t-shirt and work boots. My mind flashes back to the way his damp shirt was clinging to his abs on the day of the storm, and I flush from my neck up to my cheeks. I'd like to grab that black t-shirt with both of my hands and raise it up over his head—

"Are you sure you're okay?" he asks, breaking me from my dirty daydream. "You look like you might have heat exhaustion. It's really hot out here today, and if you don't drink enough water, it can be dangerous."

I'm getting warm again, but it has nothing to do with the weather.

When we first met, I thought Seth was a patronizing jerk, but now I'm realizing that he's sincere in his concern. Seth worries about other people. He's a bit of a caretaker, actually.

"I'll drink some water when we get back," I say, placing my palms on my burning cheeks. Thank god he isn't a mind reader.

"You have scratches." He gently pinches my arm at the elbow and inspects some of my chicken war wounds. I wonder if he feels me shiver at his touch. "I'm sorry. If I knew you got scratched like that, I wouldn't have laughed."

"Who knew chickens were so lethal?" I say lightly, even though we both know I was terrified.

"Chickens aside, this place is growing on you, right?" His dark eyes study my face.

Mutt is watching us from outside the chicken run, his pink tongue rolled out of his mouth like a carpet. He's happy now that Mommy and Daddy are using kind words. Poor dog. What is he going to do when he finds out Mommy is heading back to the big city? He'll have to find another crotch to bury his head inside.

"What do you mean?" I ask warily.

"Maybe now you can see how your dad might be happy here."

"He was happy in his old life, too," I say, but I lack the same fiery conviction I had in our previous arguments.

"Was he?" Seth asks. "Because he told me he was lonely before he met Renata. How did he describe it? Tidy apartment, neat little life, no surprises. She rocked his world, in a good way."

I'm gutted, thinking about Dad that way. Was he that unhappy? If so, I never suspected. Sure, I wondered if he got lonely for female companionship, but he always brushed off any queries about his love life, as if that ship had sailed long ago. He adored his job, exercised every day, played poker twice a month with his buddies. It was all very...dull. And I'd never seen it for what it was because I was too busy relying on him to be there for me, to listen to my issues, to give me advice and support.

Seth is looking at me expectantly. He's waiting for me to disagree with him and poke holes in his logic.

"That's probably true," I admit. "Sometimes people need their worlds rocked, I guess."

I don't know if he's thinking about our kiss in the barn, but I am. It was a world-rocking kiss.

Slowly, but surely, all the chickens head into the coop. Seth shuts the door, and I give a little cheer. He walks me back to the house for some unknown reason, and Mutt trots along between us.

"I'm sorry I didn't accept your offer to drive me home last night," I say when we're almost to the porch. "I was drunk, but that's no excuse for being an asshole to you."

Seth stops walking and looks down at the ground, digging at the mud with the toe of his boot. When he looks up at me again, I can tell we're going to get honest here, and my pulse quickens in response.

"It's probably better that you got a ride from someone else."

"Why?" I ask, afraid of what he's going to say.

"I wanted to kiss you, but you were too drunk. It wouldn't have been a good idea."

I bite my bottom lip and imagine that kiss we didn't have last night. He's right. Hooking up when I was that drunk would have been a disaster. We both would have been uncomfortable the next day, not knowing what it meant or why it happened. That's the last thing I need right now.

"You weren't worried about Rhett driving me home though? He's pretty cute, you know."

I'm leading him to think Rhett drove me home, but not saying so directly. It's not technically a lie. There's no way I'm offering up the information that I came home in a squad car.

"He's a good person," Seth says. "He wouldn't put the moves on a drunk girl."

I think about Dan and what it means to be a good person. Is Dan a garbage person for kissing me when I was drunk, and he was married?

"No, I don't think he would either, but no one is all good or bad," I say. "People make mistakes."

Seth looks at me closely. "There's a line though, right? Good people don't cross that line when the time comes."

I have a feeling we're talking about different situations from our own lives, not completely understanding each other. But if I went with Seth's definition, I'm a bad person for crossing the line with Dan. I know that isn't the whole truth though. I'm flawed, just like everyone else, but I can find redemption. I need to go home and set things right with Dan. He needs for me to tell him in person that that this thing between us isn't going anywhere. I'll encourage him to save his marriage.

"You look so serious. I think you missed the part where I said I'd like to kiss you again," Seth says.

"Is that what you said?" I start walking. "I wasn't sure I heard you right."

Seth gives me a lazy smile as he walks beside me. We're close enough that our hands bump up against each other, sending a zing down my back.

"Yeah, I still want to kiss you, even after seeing that ridiculous chicken dance."

We're at the porch steps now, and I take one step closer to him, trying not to smile like an idiot. Then I pull lightly at the bottom of his t-shirt as I lean in and say, "Good to know."

Even though my face is bare, my hair is flat, and I'm wearing pants with printed hearts all over them, he's looking at me like I'm beautiful. I have that feeling you get when you're flirting with someone who isn't only physically attracted to you, but genuinely likes you, too. I can't believe I'm having these feeling with Seth, but the chemistry we have is undeniable.

Seth tips his head slightly, and I get ready for another amazing kiss when the outside light snaps on above us.

"Hey, did you get the chickens in?" Dad calls out the door, oblivious to what he's interrupting.

Seth and I break apart like two teenagers caught making out in the family basement.

"Yeah, they're snug in bed," I say.

"Aw, great!" Dad pokes his head further outside the door. "The plumber showed up. Things are all set in here. Come check it out."

Seth shakes his head, and I'm sure we're thinking the same thing. My dad is becoming a real cock blocker.

I sashay up the steps in my pajama pants like I'm a supermodel and call out over my shoulder, "Thanks again for helping me with the chickens!"

"Sure," he says dryly. "No problem."

While I'm drinking a cold glass of water at the sink, I watch Seth and Mutt lope across the lawn together, presumably to retrieve that lumber he dropped near the chicken coop. As far as boyfriends are concerned, I've never dated a guy who would literally drop everything to assist me. I once asked my ex Kirk to help me put together a dresser from IKEA. He was too busy looking at records at a flea market.

I will not fall for Seth. I will not fall for Seth. I will not fall for Seth.

He glances back over his shoulder toward the house and runs a hand through his dark hair. Now that I've been close enough to kiss him, I know that his hair is closer to black than brown, like that shade of mascara I like named Nearly Noir. Goddammit. I can't give my heart to this man who lives hundreds of miles away and seems to see past my bullshit and swagger. If I did, I'd have to tell him all my secrets, even the terrible ones.

Sip the water, slow the breath.

I need to get my head on straight. In a few weeks, I'll be home and back to my normal routine. I'm not Dad. I don't need a romance that's going to shake me to my core.

DAD STRAPS a band-aid over the Neosporin he's put on my arm and gently smooths down the tape. I'm reminded of sitting on the edge of our bathtub while he washed off my scraped knees and elbows before bandaging them.

"Remember when you decided to take up skateboarding?" he says, clearly experiencing the same walk down memory lane.

"It was that damn kid Jaylon who lived upstairs. I wanted to be cool like him."

Jaylon had blue hair and could jump off ramps, while I barely mastered stopping.

Dad shivers. "I was so relieved when you gave up that thing."

"I wasn't the most coordinated child."

Dad hugs my shoulder and plants a kiss on my head.

"I'm so sorry I gave you chicken detail. I didn't want Renata to come home and think I'd abandoned you to deal with the plumbing issue. I feel like such a failure."

"Let's face it, we both needed a rescue today," I say, giggling as I picture Seth watching me wrangle chickens.

"I was bested by a toilet, and you were mauled by birds," he says.

Laughter bubbles up from my chest and suddenly I'm cackling so hard I nearly fall off the bed. My stomach hurts, but I can't stop. Dad is cracking up, too, tears streaming down his cheeks. I can't remember the last time I laughed this hard. At least I can thank the chickens for that.

Eventually, Dad wipes his eyes and gets quiet.

"Seriously, Andie, tell me the truth. Did I make a mistake coming down here?"

My chest tightens. This is it. The opportunity I've been waiting for since I got here. One little snip of his confidence, and I can slice him away from this place.

"You know I trust your opinion," he continues. "You're not just my daughter anymore. You're my friend, too, and you know me better than anyone. Am I a fool for thinking this could work out?"

He's not going to ask me again. If I want him to come back with me, this is the time to do the deed.

I hedge, saying, "Both of us struggled today. Farm life ain't easy."

Dad sighs. "Yes, but this will be my life now. You're going home soon, back to the city."

Something weird is going on with me because my heart sinks a bit at the idea of getting in my car to drive home. It's stunning to think I'll have any regrets about leaving this place. Besides my father, what's to miss? Honky tonk bars, blood-draining mosquitos, stinky goats.

"I'm here permanently," he says. "Can I do this?"

I think of what Seth said about Dad being lonely before he rekindled his relationship with Renata. If I encourage him to leave the farm, I doubt she'll come with him. This place is her home, and she's determined to make a go if it. He'll be back in the city, but heartbroken and single again.

"The decision to move all the way down here after so little time with Renata was definitely hasty." I watch him deflate, shoulders slumping, and his pain is unbearable. "I was worried until I got here and saw that you were completely smitten with one of the most wonderful women I've ever met. You should stay and make this work."

The words rush out of me, as if I might lose my nerve if I go slowly. Dad's smile is my reward. It could illuminate an entire city.

"Really?" he says.

"Yeah, and you'll get the hang of all this house and farm stuff. You guys have Seth around, too. He seems kind of handy."

Dad laughs. "Yeah, he can probably fix a thing or two. Or build us a new house when I destroy this one."

"You have many amazing qualities, Dad. You're doing the bookkeeping for the business, and you'll be a great host when you start having events here. Plus, you're a loving, supportive partner. That's not nothing."

"Thanks, sweetie. I guess I needed a little reassurance today."

The real shock is that I'm the one who gave it to him.

THIRTEEN

I knock on the office door, even though it's open, and wait for Renata to invite me inside. She's sitting cross-legged on the floor going through the contents of a cardboard box. Photos are scattered around her, and it appears that she's sorting them into piles. So this is where she's been holed up all morning. The house is quiet, and I expect to find my father with her, but he isn't there.

"Hey," I say. "I'm looking for Dad."

Renata sets down the picture in her hand. "He went to the general store to buy food for the animals, and then he's getting his hair cut. Can I help you with anything?"

"I just wanted to let him know I've decided to leave on Friday."

Renata frowns and picks up another photo. "We'll miss you, but I'm sure you've got things to do back home. At least we get you for a couple more days."

"Yeah...I think I'm quitting my job. If I do it now, they'll have time to find a replacement before school starts."

When I say it out loud, it feels like I've already made the decision, and I guess I have. There's no explanation for why

I tell Renata before Dad except that I feel the need to get it off my chest. Last night I lay in bed for hours trying to come up with a good reason to stay in my current position. The list of pros came down to stability and not much else. The cons were so large in number that I wondered why I'd stayed in the job this long. Instead of being scared at the prospect of finding a new career, I'm filled with relief and excitement, which seems like a sign that I'm making the right choice.

"Wow," she says. "What brought this on?"

I enter the room, careful not to step on any pictures, and sit down on the floor across from her. "Something Dad said made me realize I need a change. I'm not exactly sure what I'm going to do next, but I have some ideas. I'll be okay."

Renata smiles and leans over to pat my leg. "I have no doubt you will. Life is too short to do a job that doesn't make you happy, that's for sure." She gestures to the piles around her. "Look at this mess. I need to clean things out now that your dad is here—these old houses have the tiniest closets. People back then didn't have all the crap we have today. I've got all these boxes of old photos that I need to go through and either throw away or organize somehow. I'm thinking about making albums for each of the boys."

"You need to give your closets the KonMarie treatment."

Renata gives me a confused look. "The what?"

"A Japanese woman wrote a book about radically paring down what you own, and people went nuts for it. I'll send you a link to it."

"Thanks. It does feel good to clean things out and live a little more lightly," she says. "But it's totally overwhelming."

I pick up a photo of a bride and groom from one of the piles. It's a wedding picture. Seth's wedding picture. Michael is standing to his left and on his right is his bride and another woman who appears to be her maid of honor. Seth's hair is different—longer than in his military photo but shorter than it is now—and he looks at least several years younger. I can tell someone told him to smile because that's not his real one. He's wearing a dark suit, and his wife is in a simple white strapless dress with her brown hair cascading over her shoulders. She's lifting her hemline just enough so that you can see the red cowboy boots on her feet. She reminds me of a beautiful singer whose name I can't remember, someone who fronts an alt country band and croons songs about whiskey and heartbreak.

"I don't know what to do with Seth's wedding photos," Renata says, her voice tinged with sadness. "I'm sure he doesn't want them, but it feels strange to throw them out. It is part of his history."

I study his face some more, trying to guess what he felt in that moment.

"I didn't know he was married."

"Not for long. They divorced after a year or so. It was a while ago."

"So this is his type?" I hold the picture up so she can see it.

Renata takes the photo from me and sets it aside. "He's dated all kinds of girls. Different races, different personalities. I don't think he has a type. Besides, if you looked at your dad's first wife, you'd think I wasn't his type, right? And here we are."

"True. Maybe some people don't have a type."

"Do you?" she asks.

I consider my past before answering. "Non-committal. That's how I've historically liked my men."

Renata laughs. "Interesting. Don't get involved with Seth then. He's the commitment type."

First Luisa, now Renata. I'm not sure why everyone seems to think I'm considering a relationship with Seth. I'm leaving in a few days and, besides, we're like oil and water. Or we were. Now I'm not sure anymore.

"What was she like?" I ask. "His ex."

"McAllister? She was like a candle, and he was a moth. I'd never seen him like that with a woman before, so wrapped up he couldn't see a single flaw in her. Truth? I never liked her that much. Sticking with the candle metaphor, I knew he'd get burned eventually. Don't you dare ever tell him that though."

It's petty, but I'm glad Renata didn't like her.

"Why did they break up?"

"I'll leave that for Seth to tell you someday." She pauses and looks up at me. "You know I love your dad, don't you? I'm in this for the long haul. I'm not just trying him on to see if he fits."

"Honestly? I came down here because I thought he was making a terrible mistake." Renata's eyes widen, and I quickly say, "I really liked you. I thought you were kind and smart, but giving up his job, his apartment, his friends, everything back home—I was really concerned, especially since it happened so quickly."

"I can understand that," she says, nodding her head. "My boys were worried, too, at first."

"But since I've been here, I can see how much you two love each other, and that you're really good together. You make him so happy, and he loves your family."

My chest hurts when I say the word *family*, and Renata must sense it because she reaches out and takes my hand.

"You're part of this family, too," she says. "No one wants to push you out. I've been feeling terrible because I can see that's how you feel. It's not what any of us want."

I didn't know I was waiting for someone to say these words until I heard them. The tears that fall aren't from sadness. I'm relieved that someone finally understands me.

"Thanks," I say, sniffling and reaching up to the desk for a tissue.

"You know you're welcome here any time. That room can be yours. You can leave whatever you want in there, make it your own."

I blow my nose and regain some composure. "I thought you might turn this place into a B&B. It's got enough rooms and so much charm."

"We talked about it, but I don't think I could handle having strangers traipsing in and out of my house."

"Have you thought about having weddings here at least?" I ask. "It's so beautiful at sunset. I can totally picture the tent in the open part of the lawn and the chairs set up under the big oak tree for the ceremony. You could even have Seth build a gazebo for picture taking. He might have time for it now that his cabin is almost finished."

She smiles. "I thought about having my wedding here. But as far as renting the place out for weddings, I'm not sure I could handle it right now. The cheese business alone is keeping me so busy. It's one thing making the cheese, but then there's the packaging, the branding, the website, the sales. The marketing alone feels like a full-time job."

I lean back on the heels of my hands. "You should really get on Instagram and Twitter. You could have an account for one of the goats and post things from her perspective. It would be hilarious."

Renata sighs. "See, that's a great idea. I don't know much about social media and neither does your dad."

"You need someone to take care of marketing for you." I

straighten one of the piles of pictures. "Maybe a college student would do it for free, just for the experience."

"Or maybe I should hire someone to do marketing and event planning here, like weddings and other parties," she says thoughtfully.

"That would be a fun job." Renata gives me a meaningful look. "For someone else, I mean. I live in New York."

"So did your dad," she says with a sly smile. "And you said you're thinking about quitting your job and looking for something new..."

I laugh and shake my head. "I'm not ready to give up city life just yet. You should have your wedding here though," I say. "It would be beautiful."

AFTERNOON SLIDES INTO EVENING, and I'm a party of one, sitting on the porch in the sweltering heat like a fool, hoping Seth will pass by. Dad and Renata left for a Mudcats baseball game a little while ago. They invited me to go with them, but I felt like they deserved a date night without a tag-along. I also secretly thought Seth might show up at the house to continue what we started yesterday. He did say he wanted to kiss me again, and although it isn't a good idea to get involved with him when I'm leaving, it's all I can think about.

Dinnertime comes, and there's still no sign of him. Hunger and disappointment lead me to pick through the refrigerator for salad fixings when Seth bangs through the door from the screened porch. There's blood on his t-shirt and shorts, and he's got gauze wrapped around his right hand, which he's holding in the air.

"What happened? Did you hurt yourself?" I ask, stating the obvious as I shove the lettuce back into the crisper.

"I cut my hand with the saw. It was a stupid, lazy mistake, but I think I need stitches."

"Jesus." I move toward him. "Can I see it?"

"You don't want to," he says, taking a step backwards. "Can you drive me to the E.R.? If I drive, I'm going to bleed all over my truck."

"Of course." I gather up my phone and keys. "Just let me get my purse from upstairs." I pause before leaving the room. "Is there a finger we need to pack in ice or anything?"

He lowers himself into a kitchen chair. "No, it's still hanging on."

I shiver and run out of the room before he can give me any more gory details. Within a minute, we're climbing into my rental car. Another evening storm stirs the trees, and there's thunder in the distance. As I slide the keys into the ignition, my fingers shake slightly, which I realize is absurd. He's not hurt that badly, but every time I look at the blood on his shirt, I feel woozy.

When my central nervous systems gets overwhelmed this way, I hyper focus on what I can control. Right now, I'm checking points in the car like an airline pilot. Motor running. Headlights ignited. Emergency brake released.

"I'm going to be fine," Seth says, noticing my anxiety.

"Right, of course." I reach for the pink case in the console, open it and slide my eyeglasses on my face. Seth is staring at me. "What? I need glasses for driving."

He rests his head back and says, "Adorkable."

I slide the gearshift into drive and step on the gas a little too hard. The car lurches backwards before I correct my mistake.

"Gee, thanks." If he's trying to relax me with insults, it's not working.

He's already closed his eyes, but he opens them again and looks over at me.

"No, seriously, you have that sexy librarian thing going on."

I touch the little bun I pulled together on the top of my head and give a smile that probably looks more like a snarl. When I dare to look at him again, his head is leaned back on the headrest, his skin marshmallow pale, and, once again, I'm worried.

"Are you okay?" I ask.

"No," he says, "I'm bleeding out."

"Ha ha. I'm serious."

I don't wait for his answer before speeding down the driveway to the road. If he passes out on me, I'm going to have to use the map on my phone to find the hospital.

"Don't worry. It would take more than that to mortally wound me."

"How much exactly?" I say. "Asking for a friend."

He lets out a hearty, deep laugh, then swears. "Ow, even laughing hurts my hand."

I cringe, returning to a state of concern and guilt. "I'm sorry. I shouldn't joke around when your finger is falling off."

"It's fine. I'm lucky actually. It could have been a lot worse."

I don't want to imagine "worse." It would definitely involve the retrieval of his finger off the floor, and I'm not made of strong enough stuff for that.

We stop at a red light, and I study him, trying to assess how bad he really feels. He opens his eyes and rolls his head to face me, like he knows I'm staring at him. I should look away, but I don't. As a result, we're locked in another one of our stare downs, but not our usual hate-filled one. Instead there's this other intensity to it, and I'm afraid to admit what it might be. Something has shifted between us these last few days, and my feelings for him are rapidly changing.

I don't even register the horn honking behind us until he smiles slowly and says, "Green light."

I tighten my grip on the wheel and take a deep breath. I cannot have these feelings for Seth. Number one, I have enough issues to deal with in my personal life right now. Number two, we live hundreds of miles apart. Number three, he's so different from me in every way: carnivore, Southerner, soldier.

"Why are you more freaked out about this than I am?" Seth asks.

"Freaked out about what?" My voice sounds more high pitched than normal. Has Seth just read my mind? It's like he knows I was thinking about our relationship. If so, he's more prescient than Isabelle.

"About my injury," he says. "What else would I be talking about? Turn onto the highway at the next light."

"Right, that's what I thought you meant," I say. "I told you, I'm just not good with blood. You're used to seeing people's guts and bones and—" I flap my tongue around, unable to say anything else.

"I'm sorry I had to ask you to do this," Seth says. "If Renata and Herb were home—"

"No, it's fine. Now we're even. You saved me from the chickens, and I'm bringing you to the E.R."

I follow Seth's directions and swing the car onto the ramp to the interstate, picking up speed.

"I saved you from getting swept away in a storm," he says. "So I think you still owe me one. I'll call that in later."

There's teasing in his voice, and I'm not sure what he means by "call it in later," but I really want to find out.

"You didn't save me from the storm," I remind him. "I made it to the barn just fine without your help."

My tone is light, not salty like it would have been a few days ago.

"Are we still not talking about what happened in the barn?" he asks.

"What happens in the barn, stays in the barn," I say, using my best mob boss accent.

"Huh. That's disappointing. I have thoughts about what happened there. A lot of thoughts."

Dirty thoughts, obviously. My toes curl inside my sandals at the thought of his lips and hands on me.

"Care to share some of those thoughts?"

"I'm sorry," he says with a sigh. "Not allowed to discuss it here. Those are your rules. We'll have to meet up in the barn if you want to find out."

He. Is. Impossible.

THE HOSPITAL WAITING room is packed, which Seth says is unusual for a random Tuesday evening. He checks in at the registration desk while I scope out two empty chairs for us. There's a secretary and a security officer behind the desk, and Seth has a brief conversation with them before the woman hands him a clipboard, and he joins me in the waiting area.

"Do you know them?" I ask when he sits down next to me.

"Yeah, I pretty much know everyone in the E.R. That's the problem. I'm never going to live this down."

I gesture toward the clipboard he's holding. "How are you going to fill out forms in your condition?"

"I'll manage," he says stubbornly.

It's clear from his grim expression that he's in pain, even though he won't admit it.

"Let me do it." Without waiting for his permission, I take the paperwork from him. "Name please?"

Seth rolls his eyes and says, "Seth Lewis Conrad."

"It asks for a nickname/likes to be called. I'm going with Schmoops, is that okay?"

"Andie..." he says in a warning tone.

I tap the clipboard with the pen like I'm a very busy person. "Address?"

Seth groans and makes a grab for the clipboard with his one good hand.

"You know where I live, and I can write with one hand."

"Although I'm sure you're very good with one hand—" I waggle my eyebrows suggestively "—I just saw you wince when you reached over here. Let me help you. This is a great 'get to know you' activity anyway. Now let's see, next question: do you have both testicles?"

"What the hell?" He lunges to take the form from me.

"Okay, maybe that question isn't on there," I admit, holding the clipboard out of his reach. "I was just curious about that one. I'll be good now. Promise."

I follow the form exactly as written, and Seth grudgingly gives me the relevant information. I insist on writing myself down as his emergency contact in case something happens while we're here. A nurse calls Seth back a few minutes later to get his vital signs, then sends him back out to wait until a doctor is available to suture him. He has a proper bandage over his hand now instead of the bloody gauze, which is a relief.

"So what did you learn about me from filling out that form?" Seth asks.

"Well, I still don't know how many testicles you have." I give him a disappointed pout. "But I do know that you're not pregnant or menstruating so that's good."

"I didn't know you were so curious about my genitals," he says, checking the tape on his bandage.

I shudder then frown at him. "Please never use the word genitals again. I seriously hate that word."

"Okay, I'll only use it when I'm mad at you then," he says. "Like, Andie, you're really getting on my genitals."

We start cracking up like two obnoxious middle schoolers, and a woman across the room gives us a disapproving look.

I pinch his arm, noting that it's all muscle. "Shhh, behave yourself."

His totally unexpected response is, "You look cute with your hair up."

Because I need to hide the fact that I'm blushing, I grab a women's magazine off a side table and flip through it.

"You must have lost a lot of blood to be giving me compliments," I tell him. "And it's very cheeky of you to be checking out my bun in public."

We both pause to listen as they call someone's name, but it isn't Seth's.

An elderly man in our row of chairs stands up slowly and maneuvers his wife's wheelchair past us. Seth moves his long legs aside and the man thanks him before pausing to pull up the blanket that has slipped off his wife's legs. Then he gently places her hands on top of it. The compassion implicit in his movements brings tears to my eyes. Seth is watching them, too, and I wonder what he's thinking.

He waits a few minutes, then asks me, "How come we haven't talked about the fact that we kissed?"

There's no teasing in his voice now. He's staring up at a television set that's bolted high up on the wall in front of us. *Jeopardy* is playing with the sound off, which seems rather pointless.

"I don't know." I close the magazine and lay it on my lap. "What is there to say? I'm leaving in two days."

"So that's it then," he says grimly.

"I guess so. What's the point of starting something that can't go anywhere?"

I'm holding my breath, waiting for an answer because I really want there to be one, even though it's an impossible ask.

"What if we had one great night while you're here?" he says. "I could take you out tomorrow, repay you for spending this evening with me in the E.R."

"Sadly?" I say. "Tonight would be the best first date I've had all year, if it were a date, which I realize it isn't."

Something about this feels weirdly like a first date though. It's the getting to know each other conversation, the flirtatious banter. I'm struck by how scared I am about the feelings I'm having for him. My former opinion that Seth is an asshat has been replaced over the last few days with the terrifying notion that I might be falling for him.

"That is sad," he says. "But I haven't gone on a date in a long time either."

"What about tattooed girl from the bar?" I ask. "She sure gave you a big squeeze."

"Piper? We're just friends, and she's a hugger. We dated in high school, but that was a long time ago."

"Pretty sure she still has the hots for you," I say.

Seth openly grins at me, loving this. "You sound a little jealous."

"Like you were of Rhett," I say in my defense.

"I'm not jealous of Rhett. He's just a boy. You don't need a boy."

Our eyes connect, and the wind is knocked out of me.

"I don't?" I say breathlessly. "What do I need?"

Right when the sexual tension is at a crescendo, the nurse calls Seth's name.

He gently taps me on the shoulder as he rises from his chair. "C'mon, since you insisted on being my emergency contact, you can come back there with me and hold my hand."

FOURTEEN

The physician's assistant working on stitching Seth's hand back together is a short, stout, middle-aged woman named Lynn. Everything about her is rough, including the way she's cleaning out his wound with anti-septic. Personally, I think she could be a little more gentle with her technique, but Seth, as always, is being stoic.

"Geez, you're tall," she says, putting her fists on her hips and sizing Seth up. "I'm gonna need a stool. No, I'm just kidding. Let's lower this bed."

Seth leans over and presses the button to lower the bed down so that Lynn can comfortably work on him. Now instead of being eye level with her, he's boob level, and Lynn's rack is quite formidable, like the rest of her. She preps a needle of lidocaine then injects it into Seth's hand.

"Your chart says you rejected pain medication earlier," she says. "You want something now? That looks like it hurts."

"I'm good," Seth says.

She looks over at me, raising her eyebrows like no one

has ever turned down pain meds before. "What is he, a masochist?"

"Yes," I say in a somber tone. "He asked me to cut off his finger, which is how we ended up here."

I can tell that Seth is struggling to keep a straight face. Lynn squints at me, trying to figure out if I'm serious.

"It was a masochism joke," I explain, not wanting her to call security on me. "I didn't actually injure him. Although I've thought about it."

She shakes her head and continues her task.

"You two are a pair," she mumbles.

"I don't need narcotics," Seth says. "Just stitch me up, please."

Lynn makes an irritated grunt. "Suit yourself, sweetheart."

When she begins stitching his hand, I'm surprised to find that I can't look away. It's disgusting and fascinating at the same time.

And then I remember why I'm there.

"Aren't I supposed to be holding your hand?" I ask him. "The good one, I mean."

Seth gives a little smile and continues watching Lynn sew.

"You're a paramedic here, right?" Lynn asks, pulling the thread through his skin.

"Yep." Seth's mouth barely moves when he answers.

He probably doesn't want to distract her and end up with two fingers stitched together or something. It's like when my hairdresser got too fired up telling me about her car accident and cut off two extra inches.

"That explains a lot," Lynn says. "Paramedics are a different breed."

She pulls the needle through his skin again, and I'm amazed by how simple this process is. I probably could have done this myself, if Seth and I were trapped in the Andes after a plane crash. I would have had to use dental floss and a safety pin though. I'm not saying I'd be his first choice.

"There's a P.A. here who's madly in love with you," Lynn tells him. "Stephanie. Do you know her? At least I think it's you she's in love with. She calls you the hot paramedic."

"Okay." Seth's tone suggests that he'd like her to stop talking.

"You fit the description—tall, dark and handsome and sort of unfriendly."

I snort. "That sounds about right." When I realize I've confirmed his brooding good looks, I add, "Especially the unfriendly part."

Seth grimaces, and I know it's not from the pain of the needle. He can't stand being the subject of our conversation.

After appraising my Liberated Woman t-shirt and smirking knowingly, Lynn says, "Are you his girlfriend?"

I've now officially decided that Lynn's bedside manner sucks. In addition to being pushy and judgmental, she's a busybody. I'm sure Stephanie, the lovesick physician's assistant, would agree with me. Anyone who outs her co-worker's crush is a traitor.

"No, I'm just his emergency contact," I say, winking at her like there's some kind of double meaning to it.

She looks at me for a second, waiting for clarification that I'm not going to provide. Then she gives up and completes her stitching job. After she's finished, she admires her work before giving Seth his hand back.

An attractive young doctor enters our curtained area

with a brisk manner and an air of authority that contrasts with her petite stature. She introduces herself as Dr. Chu, then allows Lynn to explain Seth's injury and how she repaired it. Dr. Chu inspects his finger closely, then sets his hand back on the table.

"Looks good." She gives Seth a smile that doesn't reach her eyes. It's not a fake smile, just detached and professional. Lynn could learn a thing or two from her. "I hope you feel better soon, Mr. Conrad."

She turns on her heel to leave, but Lynn stops her by saying, "Don't you recognize Seth here? He's one of our paramedics."

Dr. Chu looks more closely at Seth, and her face softens with recognition. She blushes slightly, but otherwise remains composed.

"Right, of course. I'm sorry, I didn't recognize you at first."

"It's fine," Seth says, giving Lynn an irritated glance. "Thanks, Dr. Chu."

"Certainly. Take care of that hand."

There's an awkward pause before she exits our curtained area. I'd take Dr. Chu's social fumbling over Lynn's bullishness any day.

"We're almost done here," Lynn says. "I'll bring your discharge papers and let Stephanie know you're single."

"Please, don't," he says in a pained voice. "I don't date anyone where I work."

Apparently someone heeds the "don't shiteeth where you eateeth" advice.

IT'S ironic that in a place called "Emergency Room," things can move at such a glacial pace. By the time we get back to the farm, it's ten o'clock, and I feel like days have passed since we left for the hospital. I'm not sure what Seth and I are anymore, but it's definitely not enemies.

We're both starving and exhausted, and Seth insists that he can make us something to eat, even though he has a bum finger on one hand. I agree to his offer and text Dad and Renata to let them know where we've been. They're just getting home from the baseball game and are shocked to hear about our eventful evening. They're probably even more shocked to hear that I'll be at Seth's house eating a late dinner.

The ride home was quiet, maybe because we're both tired, but there's also an undercurrent of awkward excitement running between us. Seth and I are going to be alone at his place. I don't think I've ever wanted to kiss someone this badly, especially since it's not even the first kiss. Every time I look at him, my eyes drift to his lips, and I'm seized with the desire to pounce on him. If he suggests watching a movie, I'm not going to make it through the opening scene.

On the walk from the driveway to his cabin, I can smell the jasmine more intensely than ever. We must be walking right past it. I need to capture every sensory detail of this place and this night because I feel like it's going to be important later. All of our arguing and joking and lusting has led us to this point.

There are lights on in the cabin, and I'm reminded he left in a hurry. He's reassured me that the saw with the blood on it is in the barn so I don't have anything to fear, which is fortunate because even the thought of that horror scene makes me feel faint.

"Come in," he says, turning the key and entering the cabin.

Mutt bolts toward us and wiggles through his dog door on the porch. He isn't interested in me for once. The poor dog has been locked up for hours and needs to relieve himself immediately.

I peer inside the cabin, instead of following Seth in the door. Why does crossing this threshold feel so difficult? Maybe because if I step inside, there's no going back to how things are now. If I go inside, there's going to be a new version of Seth and Andie, and I don't know what it will be or what it will mean.

I realize that I've paused for too long when he misreads my anxious expression as disgust.

"What? Come in. It's not some freaky man cave. I don't have lamps made out of deer hooves, if that's what you're worried about."

I attempt a cheerful smile, to convince him I'm not a basket case when it comes to relationships, but I must look like a serial killer because I can't seem to get my lips to slide over my teeth. Dry mouth. I might be having a panic attack.

In the year that we dated, my ex-boyfriend Kirk had me over to his place twice. Once would have been more than enough. He had three permanent roommates and a rotating cast of couch surfing friends from out of town. His place smelled like weed, fast food and unwashed laundry. If you wanted to get high and play video games, his apartment was the place to be. Otherwise, not so much.

Seth's house is the opposite. You can tell that a grown man lives here. He has real furniture that doesn't look like he found it dumpster diving, and there are framed pictures hung on the walls. The floor plan is open concept with a spacious living area separated from the kitchen by an island with bar stools. The hardwood floors have been stained a honey color, and the walls are painted a soft white. There are large windows on every wall, giving the place an airy feeling and providing views of the outdoors.

I was never concerned that his place was going to be awful. He's too anal retentive to have a slovenly living space, but this is even lovelier than I imagined. I'm worried that I'll never want to leave. It's going to be a Goldilocks situation where I try out every dish, every chair, every...bed. But tonight's visit to this cabin might lead to heartbreak, and that's the last thing I can handle, what with Dad and Hugh both moving away.

"At first when I heard you had a cabin, I thought this place would be built out of logs," I say, running my hand along the wall as I walk inside.

Seth laughs, sounding slightly nervous. "That's dry wall."

He's watching me closely as I walk around the room, taking everything in for the first time. I realize that he's putting himself on the line here, showing me something he built himself. It's more personal than most people's homes. Half the time when I visit my friends' apartments, they complain about everything their shitty landlords won't change or fix. Seth can't do that here. This place is his creation.

"I built the cabinets myself," he says, referring to the pine cabinets in the kitchen and the bookshelves built in around the fireplace. "Did the floor, too. I had a lot of help with the fireplace though. That was something I'd never attempt on my own."

"I thought there was nothing you couldn't do," I say. "I half expected you to suture yourself today."

Seth smiles, and it changes his whole face. I want to

make him do that again. This could be my job now, saying things that are funny enough to make Seth smile.

"It's beautiful," I say. "I love it all."

To prove my point, I flop onto the couch and tuck myself into a little ball in the corner.

"You stay there," he says. "I'll make some food."

"Seriously, Seth, do not cook anything. At this point, I'm happy with a bowl of cereal."

"Really?" His shoulders drop an inch. "I am tired, but I'm happy to make you a meal, if you want."

I shake my head. "Cereal or toast or whatever is fine. Do not cook."

Cooking and kitchen cleaning time would mean delaying the kissing, and I am not down with that.

"I have half of a pan of leftover lasagna," he says uncertainly.

"Perfect! Heat that up, and we're golden," I say. "Wait, it's vegetarian, right?"

"As far as you know, yes," he says, an evil glimmer in his eyes.

"I'll just be going through your underwear drawer and reading your diary while you're in the kitchen." I wave him away. "Now, go."

He gives me a look like he's not sure whether or not I'm serious before he retreats into the kitchen area. While he's getting food for us, I walk around the main room, inspecting the weight of every door, sliding my hand along the fire-place mantle, taking in every detail. The whole place is a miracle to me. After all, I did grow up with a dad who could barely change a lightbulb.

Seth comes back a few minutes later with a tray in his hands. He sets two plates of lasagna, silverware, and glasses of water on the dining table. I'm kind of relieved when he pulls out paper napkins.

"Cloth napkins might have been overselling it a bit," I say out loud, and Seth gives me a confused look. "I mean I'm already so freaking impressed you live this way. It's making me feel bad about my own life."

"Stop." He sits down at the table. "It's not that big a deal."

I point to the ladder leading up to a loft. "Do you sleep up there?"

"No," he says. "Mutt can't climb the ladder, and he's used to sleeping in the room with me. There's a bedroom back there."

He gestures to a door off of the living area that I haven't opened yet, and I feel myself gulp air. Seth's bedroom, where the magic happens.

Seriously, Andie, get a grip.

AFTER WE EAT, Seth and I clean up together. I know not to interfere as he places dishes and silverware in his perfectly organized dishwasher. It doesn't annoy me anymore though. In fact, I find it kind of adorable. Mutt is snoring up a storm on the couch, and it's close to eleven o'clock now.

"So do you want to hang out and watch a movie or something?" he says as he rinses a plate in the sink.

I run the sponge slowly over the countertop. "Do you want to watch a movie?"

Seth stops and meets my gaze. "God, no."

Our eyes lock, and it's the moment I've been waiting for all night. He takes a step toward me, and I put a hand on his chest to stop him.

"No," I say, watching his expression turn into a frown. "I need to brush my teeth before I kiss you. I probably have spinach stuck in my incisors."

Seth laughs and shakes his head. "This seems like a weird moment for dental hygiene, but then I never know what you're going to say to me next, which is part of your charm. I have some toothbrushes in the closet."

"Yay!" I say. "And where would that be?"

"In my bedroom."

There's more intense staring, and I have no idea I'm going to say the words until they're out of my mouth.

"So what do you think about me sleeping over tonight?"

Seth's jaw actually drops about an inch, and he's at a total loss for words. Something like uhhh comes out of his mouth. He's not the only one who never knows what I'm going to say.

"I don't mean a naked sleepover, I'm not suggesting that we go there. It would just be nice to have time with you and talk all night. And I can sleep in the loft or whatever. Or not. I can go home." I inch toward the door because he's still not responding. "Cause this is weird now. I just made it really weird..."

"No." He comes after me and grabs my hand. "Yes, stay. That would be great. I want you to stay."

"Okay," I say quietly.

"And," he says, squeezing my hand. "We should go brush our teeth because I don't think I can wait much longer before I kiss you."

HIS BEDROOM IS PAINTED a serene gray and the furniture is solid pine. There's a wood chair in the corner, which I bet he built. It looks sturdy and comfortable. On the night table is a blue lamp and a neat pile of paperback books. Seth is taking his turn in the bathroom after letting me freshen up, and I feel awkward sprawling out on the bed while I wait for him so I stand and flip through the books instead.

When he returns, he sees what I'm doing and grimaces. "My books are being judged by an English teacher."

"I'm not judging," I say. "Just curious."

The Things They Carried. When Breath Becomes Air. Timber Frame Joinery and Design.

"You have good taste," I say, re-stacking them.

He raises his eyebrows. "I thought you weren't judging?"

"I wouldn't have run out screaming if you had a pile of James Patterson over here, but I'm not going to lie, I'm glad you don't."

"Are you surprised I read?" he says.

"No, I figured you were literate," I say sarcastically, then pause. "But I guess I'm a little surprised at the range. Not everyone reads that widely."

Seth plugs his cell phone into the charger and takes his wallet out of his back pocket, setting it on the dresser. I'm getting a ridiculous amount of pleasure watching him go through what looks like his nightly routine. The fact that we still haven't kissed yet is making me ache inside, but in a good "delayed gratification" kind of way.

"There isn't much to do in the evenings out here besides read. I guess I could watch Netflix, but I've been enjoying the quiet of summer nights on the porch." He looks around the room like he's going to find a mess I've made. "Did I miss the part where you rifled through my underwear drawer?"

"Yes, and I was surprised about all the thongs." I'd love

to do some actual snooping now that he's here to watch me. "Let's look around some more, shall we?"

I wander over to a huge armoire and run my hands over the wood. It's over six feet tall and about five feet wide. The wood is stained a pretty walnut color, and the design is simple and classic.

"I wish I could make things," I say, gripping the handles on the armoire. They look antique, like he found them in the dusty back room of a hardware store and polished them to a shine.

"This was my first major project in the woodworking class I took years ago." He comes to stand beside me. "It's not perfect, but it has sentimental value to me now."

I pull on the handles and the doors to the armoire swing open. I have the slightly hysterical feeling that I might find something frightening inside it, and I do.

"Wow, you really want the full tour," he says nervously.

There's a hanging rod across the inside, and arranged on it are about thirty tops. They're separated into categories—button down dress shirts, casual flannels, and t-shirts—and then arranged in color-coded order. Each section is its own perfect rainbow, except the plaid flannels, of course.

"Whoa," I say. "This is serious."

"You can take a man out of the Marines..."

"They did this to you?" I ask. "You weren't this freakishly organized before the military?"

"Hell, no," he says. "I slept late, left dirty dishes in the sink, threw my clothing on the floor. But they don't tolerate that in the military. Plus, I like it this way now. I like knowing where things are and coming home to a clean space."

Above the hanging clothing is a shelf of neatly folded wool sweaters and hoodies. I stop myself from pressing my face to them to see what they smell like. Then I say to hell with it, and do it anyway: fresh air and cedar. It hits me like a punch to the stomach: I won't be here to see him in his winter clothing. Not unless I come back down here for the holidays. By then, he might have a girlfriend, which is an even more troubling thought. A guy like Seth won't stay single forever.

"Is my neatness that distressing to you?" he asks. "And why are you smelling my sweaters?"

"What?" I ask, coming back to the present moment.

"You look sad all of the sudden."

I force myself to smile mischievously, reaching out to caress the sleeve of a blue flannel shirt.

"What if I just moved a few things around when you weren't looking?"

"You wouldn't," he says in a mock horrified voice.

I slide my hand toward the hanger, and he grabs me by the waist and attempts to hoist me over his shoulder, forgetting about his stitched-up finger.

"Ow! Dammit!" he says, cringing in pain.

"Are you okay?"

"Yeah." He looks at me with chagrin. "Picking you up with this bum hand was overly ambitious."

"We'll just pretend you did." I charge toward the bed and shake my fists in the air. "Put me down! I will destroy you and your organizational madness, you man-beast!"

I leap onto the bed dramatically then roll onto my side and pat the empty space next to me.

"Those theatrics seemed unnecessary," he says, carefully rolling onto the bed with me as he holds his bandaged hand in the air.

"We got to the bed," I say. "That's the important thing."

His eyes darken with concern as he looks down at me.

"Tell me why you looked sad just now."

He'll think I'm even loopier if I tell him the real reason. I'll sound like I've got a pathetic crush on him, like Stephanie the P.A. I try to look relaxed, although I'm not feeling that way with Seth so close that I can feel the heat from his body.

"I was just thinking about what a mess my apartment will be when I get home. My roommate is growing a jungle that's taken over the entire place, apparently."

"You mean she's a slob?" he asks.

"No, I mean a literal jungle. She's a plant junkie. Seriously, there's a fern living in my shower now. Apparently, it needs the humidity."

"I'd be annoying, too," he says, "As a roommate, I mean."

"Yeah, you'd probably iron my underwear and label everything in my closet," I say with a sigh.

"I'd yell at you for eating in bed," he adds. "I hate sleeping in crumbs."

"Oh, so we'd be roommates who share a bed?" I ask slyly. "Is that what roommates do?"

"In our case, maybe. After what happened in the barn, I'm just guessing that's where we'd end up."

The barn. The most passionate kiss of my life, if I'm being honest. No one has ever kissed me like that before.

My voice comes out a bit strangled when I say, "Probably a good guess."

His eyes are sliding over me, my lips, my neck, my breasts. He places one hand on my stomach and the heat from it nearly burns me through my clothing. As he leans down toward me, I don't close my eyes. I don't want to miss a second of this.

"I don't want to be your roommate," he whispers, and kisses me gently on the lips.

"No?" I whisper back.

"I want to be more than that."

His hand slips under my shirt, and glides across the skin of my torso.

"More?" I say. "Show me."

Seth responds to my challenge by shifting onto his back and rolling me on top of him, a move that's complicated by his injured hand. I love how sturdy and strong he feels underneath me.

"I'm not going to crush you?" I ask, letting my full weight release on top of him.

"Not possible," he says, sounding delighted.

He traces one hand up the side of my thigh, over my backside and under my t-shirt. As his fingers draw lazy circles on my bare skin, I break out in goose bumps. God help me if we're ever completely naked, skin on skin. I'm pretty sure I'll fall to pieces.

I bend my head down and give him a few gentle kisses on the mouth, my lips opening slightly with the promise of more. Then I pull away because I like teasing him. His head comes up off the pillow just an inch when I move away from him, like he wasn't ready to part with my mouth.

"The other day when you were wearing that black biki-ni," he says, his voice sounding pained. "That was unfair."

"You liked that?" I kiss his neck and his scruffy chin tickles my cheeks. "Or you hated it?"

I continue kissing his neck, then move to his jawline. When I get close to his mouth, I feel him smile.

"I hated that I liked it so much."

I pull up the bottom of his t-shirt, lifting it over his stomach and letting my hands explore his skin. He's warm and tightly muscled, and so much more solid than any of the men I've been with in the past. They seem like boys in comparison. I keep tugging his shirt until he gets the hint and rips it over his head and tosses it onto the floor. My hands slide over his pecs and down to his ribs, and I learn by touch what I saw that day he was wearing a towel.

"Are you keeping your shirt on?" he asks, a little breathlessly. "I don't know the sleepover rules."

"The rules of conduct state that shirts are optional for all participants," I say, trying to sound official, but I'm too breathless to be convincing.

It's impossible to get my shirt off when I'm lying on top of him so I sit up, and he follows suit, scooting his back against the headboard. Then he repositions me so that I'm straddling his lap and together we pull my t-shirt over my head. The standard black racerback bra I have on is nothing special because who the hell knew I'd end up here tonight? Seth seems to find it enticing nonetheless.

He runs the fingers of his right hand under my bra strap, from my shoulder down to the cup. Then he traces along the edges of the fabric and dips his fingers inside.

"I really wish I had both hands working right now."

I want to tell him he's doing just fine with one, but I have no words. When he starts stroking my nipple with his thumb, I close my eyes, not wanting him to see how far gone I am already. There's a pulsing heat building between my thighs, and I can't believe how turned on I am when we're only getting started. When I open my eyes, he's watching me with a half-smile, like he enjoys driving me crazy, but can barely hold himself back from devouring me.

Our lips find each other again, and this time there is nothing slow or tender about our kisses. We are consuming each other, like we did in the barn, and the flame is turned up to high. The reasoning regions of my brain go dark while the animalistic areas light up. My pelvis grinds against his as if I can't get enough of his skin, his mouth, his everything. I can feel him growing hard against me, and this only thrills me more.

However I imagined it would be with Seth, it's better. He tastes as good as he smells, he feels even better than he looks. We go on like this for what might be minutes or hours, perfecting the rhythm of our kisses and pushing each other toward what will be a spectacular finish, if we let it go all the way.

Without a rational thought in my head, I feel my fingers reaching for the button on his jeans. In response, he groans and his hands begin pulling at the top of my shorts.

"Wait," I say, suddenly cognizant of what we're about to do.

"What's wrong?" He immediately pulls his hands away from my body.

I climb off of his lap and sit down beside him on the bed. My breathing is ragged, and I take a moment to regroup. If things go any further, we're going to be naked and looking for a condom, and I'm not sure I'm ready for that.

"We're getting really carried away here," I say. "Maybe we should slow down a little."

My bare skin is chilly now that's he's not under me, keeping me warm. I consider grabbing my shirt, but it appears to be somewhere across the room.

He takes a couple deep breaths before saying, "Okay."

I try to convince my thinking brain to turn on again.

"It's not that I don't want to, but..."

He nods and sits up higher on the bed, and I move next to him. My bra is still on, and my skin is flushed pink. All of the sudden, I feel more exposed than I did a second ago when he had his hands all over me.

"I understand," he says softly.

My heart bangs inside my chest, and I sling one of my legs over his.

"This is happening really quickly."

We both know that I don't mean the speed of what's happening in this bed. It's the way our feelings have turned and sprinted in a new direction.

"I know." He runs his hand down my thigh and over my knee.

The effect his hands have on me is beyond reason. Immediately, I want to reverse my "no sex tonight" vote.

"Then again, I'm leaving soon so maybe we should just go for it."

"No," he says, continuing to rub my leg like he has no idea that it's driving me wild. "We should wait."

"It sucks that I'm leaving so soon. We wasted so much time hating each other."

"Let's not talk about you leaving. Let's talk about our date instead."

"Okay." I twine my fingers through his because if I let his caresses continue, I'm going to rip his pants off. "Where do you want to go?"

"I know a cool local place that has live music. Eli's band is playing there tomorrow night. I'd like to take you there."

"So you're planning this date?"

I can't remember the last time someone asked me out on a real date. I've been propositioned many times at the bar where I play pool, and a guy I met at the laundromat a few months ago invited me out for coffee. He took me to a cafe where he gets free drinks because his ex-girlfriend is a barista there, but I had to pay for my own scone.

"Yeah, if it's okay with you, I'll make the plans. I can come get you at the house around six-thirty."

"You're coming to get me at six-thirty." I sound bewildered, like I was raised in the forest by wolves.

"Isn't this how dates usually work? And I just want to say in advance that I'm paying for everything because this is our first date, and I'm the one inviting you. I'm not trying to be a sexist asshole or anything. I just want to take you out."

"Okay," I whisper. "Is this an episode of *Black Mirror*? Are you going to turn into an alien now?"

"You're just not used to dating nice guys," he says, bringing my hand to his mouth and kissing my knuckles.

I give an unladylike snort. "When I first met you, the last word I would have described you with was 'nice.' "

"But you did say my ass is—what was it—so firm you could bounce a quarter off of it?"

I pull my hand from his in horror, then grab a pillow to hide my face. I garble something from underneath it about him being an eavesdropper before he pulls the pillow off my face and tosses it to the side of the bed.

"You should learn to whisper if you're going to objectify people like that," he says, pretending to be hurt.

"Ass aside, I kind of hated you."

"The feeling was mutual," he says. "You have a beautiful ass."

"When did you start liking me?" I sound like I'm digging for a compliment, which is probably true.

He pretends to think deeply. "I'd have to say things turned around about the time of the chicken dance. That sealed it for me."

I find another pillow and whack him with it.

"Is this the pillow fight portion of the sleep over?" he asks, protecting himself. "Because I have a hurt hand."

I put down the pillow and roll my eyes at him. "Pulling the hurt hand card, okay. This is actually the part where we get in our pajamas, turn out the lights and tell ghost stories. I'll do your hair in those braids you love."

Seth stretches out on the bed and carefully puts his hands behind his head.

"Great. That sounds so much better than sex. Do you want to borrow a t-shirt?"

"Yes, please." I pull back the quilt and climb under the sheets.

His bed is insanely cozy. The mattress is not too firm and not too soft. Goldilocks says it's just right.

"Wait," he says, standing up in a hurry. " I should change the sheets, since you're staying the night."

I wave my hand like he's being silly and burrow under the covers.

"Not necessary," I say. "I know you're worried you've got your man juices on these sheets, but it's no worse than those hotel duvet covers. God knows what's on those things."

Seth continues to look worried and hover over the bed.

"It's just that I usually change the sheets on Wednesday, which is tomorrow. I don't mind changing them for you."

"You change your sheets on the same day every week?" I ask incredulously.

He crosses his arms over his chest. "Of course, doesn't everyone?"

"No, no they don't. I'm not even going to tell you how often I wash my bras because you'd be horrified."

"I'd like to talk some more about your bras. Go on." He walks over to his dresser and opens a drawer.

He pulls out a Metallica t-shirt that has faded from black to gray from repeated washings and throws it at me. It's worn in and soft and about three sizes too big for me. He's never getting this shirt back. I snap off my bra and toss it to him, hiding my naked chest with the sheets. He catches it and stares at it for a second before looking over at me with lustful eyes.

"You're trying to kill me, aren't you?" he says.

I cackle and pull the shirt over my head, letting him have one glimpse of my fabulous breasts.

FIFTEEN

When I wake up the next morning, Seth isn't in bed. For a second, I entertain the thought that he's in the shower, and my fantasy of getting under the water with him can come true. Forget about waiting to have sex. After a night of kissing, talking and touching, I'm ready now.

The noises I hear are coming from the kitchen though. I brush my teeth with my new red toothbrush, pull his comb through my hair and wash my face before padding out into the living area wearing only the huge Metallica t-shirt and underwear. The shirt is long enough to cover everything that needs to be covered and leaves a lot of my legs to be appreciated. Seth is standing at the stove, and Mutt is at his feet, waiting for something to drop.

"Hey," Seth says, turning to greet me. "You look good in that shirt. There's coffee if you want some."

"Umm, yes, please." I yawn, still bleary-eyed from sleep.

He gives me a famous Seth half-smile and goes back to cooking. As I pass him on my way to the French press, I run my fingernails across his broad back. He's wearing only a pair of basketball shorts, and he doesn't look nearly as sleep-deprived as I feel.

"I'm making scrambled eggs," he says. "I hope that's okay."

On the countertop, there's a cutting board with chopped vegetables on it and a bowl of whisked eggs. My vegetables would be random sizes and shapes; his are nearly identical cubes.

"How long have you been up?" I ask.

"I'm on military time, remember?" he says, evading my question.

I squint at him suspiciously. "Have you been watching me sleep for hours, you creeper?"

"No, Mutt and I went for a walk this morning. Then I did a little reading on the porch. I thought if I made some food, you'd smell it and get out of bed, lazybones."

I'm not much of a morning talker so I sit down on a counter stool and watch him cook, delighting in the precise way he moves, not leaving any countertop messes. Even with his bandaged finger, he's a neater cook than I am. Mutt doesn't get any droppings, but Seth throws him a carrot and the dog happily disappears into the bedroom with his treasure.

I'm amazed at how normal this all feels. A week ago, we were sworn enemies. Now I'm sitting around in my underwear and a t-shirt while he makes me breakfast. Life is strange.

When my meal is ready, Seth walks around to my side of the counter and slides it in front of me. The plate is full of fluffy eggs dotted with colorful vegetables and a side of buttered toast. My mouth begins to water at the smell of it.

"How can I ever repay you?" I say in the voice of a Southern Belle, reaching out for him.

He slips his arms around me and kisses me gently on the lips. My fingertips play over the muscles and bones of his shoulders, wanting to explore every part of him. What starts out as a slow, playful kiss, quickly turns into something more, and in seconds, my legs are wrapped around his waist.

"Damn," he says, leaving my arms too quickly. "You are irresistible."

"So don't resist me," I suggest.

"You eat your breakfast." He gives me one last kiss on the neck. "Because if we keep this up, I'm going to strip your clothes off right here and all that good food will be wasted."

"Ooh, what would you do with me?" I ask, cutting my eggs with my fork.

"I'd sit you right on that countertop and take my time with you," he says, returning to the stove to fix his plate of food. "Head to toe."

I take a bite, but have trouble swallowing. Just watching him cook is erotic. Add the sex talk, and I'm about to slide right off this stool onto the floor. I have no idea how I'm going to wait until the end of tonight's date to jump this man's bones.

I SPEND the afternoon washing and ironing my new yellow dress like it's my job. When I bought it a few weeks ago, I never thought I'd be wearing it on a date night with Seth. I should be tired from staying up until all hours of the night with him, but instead I'm fizzing with anticipation.

After my dress is ready and waiting on its hanger, I get into the shower, taking extra time to deep condition my hair and shave my legs. Normally, I approach a first date with a heap of cynicism topped off with a sprinkle of existential dread. Tonight is completely different, and it's throwing me off kilter. I know exactly why I'm nervous, and it isn't because I fear that my date will confirm everything that is wrong with modern relationships. I'm nervous because I already really like him. A lot. In fact, I've never experienced this trifecta of happiness with anyone: sexual chemistry, playful banter and meaningful conversation. I have the sinking feeling I'll find a way to fuck it up.

Once I'm out and toweled dry, it's time to moisturize my entire body then blow-dry and loosely curl my hair. For my make-up application, I want a fresh-faced, pink-cheeked look with this sweet dress. Even if I can't be an innocent little 1950s virgin—and who really wants to—I'm going to look like one, dammit. I slip the dress over my head, making sure not to get makeup on the collar, and when I look in the mirror, I'm delighted to see that I've achieved Sandra Dee status on the outside. Inside, I'm still all Rizzo. As I'm putting a sheer rose tint on my lips, my phone buzzes with a message from Dan.

Nicky and I saw a counselor today. She suggested that you come to our next session. When you are coming back to New York?

I throw the phone on the bed like it's on fire. He's gone batshit mad if he thinks I'm accompanying him and his wife to therapy. They seriously want me to sit on a couch and listen to their marital issues? Worse, they might want me to talk about my relationship with Dan and how it led to our hook-up. No way. I'm not putting myself through that kind of torture. Maybe the therapist can play the part of Andie in this drama, but the real Andie will not be in the building.

I'm furious at Dan for even asking me to do this, especially when I'm going on my special date night with Seth. Clearly, Dan didn't hear me during our previous conversation. I need to talk to him in person and set him straight on where I stand. No more texts and phone calls, and certainly no group therapy sessions. We need to cut the cord and move on with our lives.

There isn't time to think about Dan anymore. It's almost six-thirty, and I'm positive Seth will be on time. I fill my clutch purse with everything I might need tonight: money, ID, lip gloss, tissues. I come across some condoms I keep in my travel kit and shove a few in my purse. It's never a bad thing to be prepared.

What will I do if Dan texts or calls me tonight while I'm out with Seth? The last thing I want to do is lie to Seth right at the beginning of our relationship. Everything that's happening with him feels pure and new. He already knows that I came here with the intention of getting Dad to leave, and he forgave me for that, but I'm not sure how he would feel about me kissing a married man. Seth is such a stand-up guy, I know he won't brush off what I've done. On the other hand, I wasn't the married person, and I was the one to stop things when they went too far. That must count for something.

I glance out my window and see that I was right about Seth being on time. He's walking across the yard toward the house at this very moment. I grab my purse and head downstairs to meet him, passing my father in the hallway.

He lets out a low whistle. "Wow, you're pretty dressed up for your evening out with Seth."

He's teasing me, but I also hear the hint of concern in his tone. We didn't discuss the fact that I spent last night at Seth's house, but it seems impossible that he didn't notice.

"It's a good excuse to wear my new dress. What do you think?"

He appraises me and smiles. "Beautiful."

My eyes choose that moment to get misty, and I lean forward and give him a peck on the cheek so he can't tell. "See you later, Dad."

"Have fun!" he calls to me as I move past him and head down the stairs.

The kitchen clock says it's six thirty on the dot, and Seth is leaning against the counter, waiting for me. A smile spreads across his face as I enter the room.

"You look amazing," he says, extending a bouquet of flowers towards me.

He's more dressed up than I've ever seen him, in khakis and a collared short-sleeved shirt. He hands me a bouquet of wildflowers of various colors and types—red zinnias, black eyed susans, white daisies and purple irises—like the arrangement I admired at the farmer's market

"You brought me flowers."

"The normal response is thank you," he says.

That's when I realize he's still holding the flowers in front of me, and I haven't taken them yet. He's right, I'm not a normal girl. My heart is racing. It's the fight-or-flight response kicking in, telling me to run, run, run as fast as I can. Bouquets of flowers, a collared shirt, dinner reservations. I'm breaking out in a sweat simply because he's made an effort to take me out tonight.

He sets the flowers on the counter and gently grips my arms, which are folded across my body, then leans his forehead down so it's touching mine.

"Hey, what's going on in there?" he says quietly.

I scoot toward him and wrap my arms around his waist, laying my head on his strong chest. I can feel his steady breath, in and out, in and out. We stand like that for at least a full minute, until I've synced my breathing with his and no longer feel like I'm going to pass out.

"I'm fine now," I say, pulling myself away from the heat and comfort of his body, which is no easy task. "And thank you for the flowers."

"You're very weird, but you can hug on me any time you want," he says. "If the flowers are freaking you out, wait until you find out I washed my truck and vacuumed out Mutt's hair."

I love that he understands my mind well enough to know that it's the flowers that sent me in a tailspin. I'm glad that I don't have to explain why seeing a guy holding flowers felt like a sign of the apocalypse.

He sighs and opens up a cabinet door. "I'll look for something you can put them in so you can go breath into a paper bag."

While I focus on calming down, he pulls out a Mason jar and fills it with water before taking the flowers from me.

"I'm a New Yorker, Seth," I say breathlessly. He wasn't wrong about needing the bag. I fill my lungs with air and try to keep my tone lighthearted. "I'm not used to being wooed this way. You're going to have to take it easy on me."

"No one has ever given you flowers?" He carefully slides the stems into the jar.

I wrack my brain, remembering the roses I got for Valentine's Day from an old boyfriend.

"Not since high school."

"Oh no." He comes over and hugs me into his arms again. "And I bet I know what happened to that poor bastard. He got dumped for being too nice."

Immediately, I relax into the warmth of his chest and inhale his scent. Tonight he smells like citrus with undertones of cedar. He's so delicious, I wish I were a vampire so I could drink his blood. I probably shouldn't voice that thought aloud.

"Don't worry." I give his shoulder a gentle bite. "You're not as nice as he was."

I feel him shaking with laughter, his breath on my hair.

"No doubt," he says. "I can be awful."

"True."

"I'm way too judgmental and overprotective."

"You're just a worrier," I say. "You like to make sure everyone you care about is okay."

I look over at the pretty arrangement in the mason jar. The fact that he got wildflowers instead of a dozen red roses makes me feel like he knows me. They're exactly what I would have picked out for myself.

"I love them," I say earnestly. "Thank you."

He runs his hands down my arms, and I get goose bumps from my shoulders to my fingertips.

"Now, was that so scary?" he asks.

He has no idea.

FOR DINNER, we're headed to yet another small town in the area where some of Seth's friends recently opened a restaurant. Apparently, there are endless rural enclaves around here that are being revived under the local food movement. This one a twenty-minute drive from the goat farm. On the way there, Seth plugs in his phone to play music, and I feel myself start to relax to melodic alt-country guitar rhythms and melancholy male voices.

Typically, I feel the need to fill silences when I'm hanging out with quiet people, but with Seth I'm comfortable being together and having my own thoughts. Most of what I'm thinking is about him though. His shirt is ironed to perfection, and he would have done a better job on the bodice of this dress than I did. He taps his fingers on the steering wheel in time to the music as he drives. I remember how those fingertips felt running over my lips and holding my hands above my head. In one night, I feel like I know his body so much better than I did before, yet there's a world more of him that I want to know.

I lean over and kiss his stubbly cheek, feeling so full of affection for him that it almost hurts. He turns to me, surprise and pleasure lighting up his face, then reaches out with his right hand and places it over mine. I know in that moment that Seth is someone I'll always have intense feelings about, no matter what those feelings might be. Hate. Anger. Lust. Maybe even love, someday. The sensation in my stomach is a version of what I feel at the top of a rollercoaster.

The Blue Sage Cafe is an old white farmhouse that has been converted into a restaurant. The original beadboard ceiling and heart pine floors have been restored to pristine condition, and they've knocked down walls to make the inside feel open and expansive. The name strikes a familiar chord with me even before I see a sign that says the cafe is affiliated with Blue Sage Farm, where Rhett works. Rhett is even in a photo that hangs in the restaurant's foyer, where Seth and I wait for our table. The group of young people in the picture all look to be under age thirty, and they're standing in a field of ripe strawberries.

"An old friend of mine owns this place," Seth explains. "Andrew and I go way back, to our 4-H days."

The teenage hostess who is about to seat us overhears him. "Andrew isn't here tonight. Marietta had a baby a few days ago so he's taking some time off."

"No problem," Seth says. "I heard they were expecting again."

"Savannah is in the kitchen though," she says, picking up two menus.

Seth nods. "Thanks. You don't need to bother her on my account."

She smiles politely and leads us to a table, while I wonder about Savannah and where she fits into Seth's past. He has a history in this town, and I can't turn into a green monster every time someone mentions a woman he knows. If there's one thing I never want to be, it's the jealous girlfriend.

Our hostess seats us next to a window that overlooks the fields behind the restaurant. A family of deer wander in to graze in the grass. With the setting sun as their backdrop, it's almost too picturesque.

I point to the deer. "Paid actors?"

He laughs. "Yeah, I threw a bunch of corn out there earlier to attract them. I pulled out all the stops tonight."

We decide to order several small plates and salads that we can share, and Seth orders himself a steak that he will be eating alone.

A statuesque woman with a head of wild blond curls approaches our table, and Seth rises from his seat to greet her. She's wearing a white chef's jacket over a pair of worn jeans.

"Seth! It's so good to see you," she says, enveloping him in a hug.

She's wearing shoe boots that raise her to at least six feet, and she carries her height proudly. When they embrace, I'm not getting a flirtatious vibe, just two old friends seeing each other again.

Seth remains standing, hands in his pockets. "I heard you moved back to Foster's Creek, but I didn't believe it."

She grins and shrugs her shoulders. "Andrew and Marietta opened this place and needed a pastry chef. It was good timing for me to come back."

Seth gestures toward me. "This is Andie Fiarello. Her father is marrying Renata."

Savannah's eyes widen in surprise. "Wow, that's great news! So nice to meet you, Andie."

She takes my hand in her warm grip.

"Likewise," I say.

"Andrew is going to be bummed he missed you," she tells Seth. "I guess you heard about baby number three?"

"I did," Seth says. "Every time I turn around, they've got another one."

Savannah laughs. "It does seem that way."

Our waiter arrives with our tray of food, and Savannah steps aside.

"Let me get out of the way so y'all can enjoy your meal. I'll send out some desserts later."

I give her a grateful wave, hoping she plans to send something chocolatey. "Thanks so much."

Seth says goodbye to her and takes his seat again. "Savannah and Andrew's wife Marietta are twins. Completely different women though."

"How so?"

"Marietta couldn't wait to settle down, and Savannah ran out of Foster's Creek as fast as she could. Moved to Paris for a while, then San Francisco. Never thought she'd come back."

"She seems nice."

"She is. And she's funny, kind of quirky like you. I think you two would be good friends."

"If I were staying here."

Seth puts his napkin on his lap and doesn't respond to the reminder that I'm leaving soon.

My first bite of peaches on a bed of freshly picked greens topped with a sprinkle of goat cheese and crushed pistachios tells me that this is going to be a meal to remember.

"I can't believe food like this is being served next door to a gas station where you can buy fishing bait," I say, after I've devoured my salad and a slice of fried green tomato with garlic aioli. "You should talk to your friends about buying cheese from Renata."

Seth gently bumps my knee with his under the table. "Great idea. I'll get in touch with Andrew about it."

Even that small touch sends my pulse racing. We're having a lovely evening, but I'm already mentally fast-forwarding to the end of the night when I get to see him naked.

Conversation at dinner has been easy, as we talk about our friends and our pasts. He laughs about fact that I ran for class president my senior year, just to depose the popular girl who was the incumbent. I find out he was ROTC, which comes as no surprise.

"Did you always want to be in the military?" I ask.

"Not really," he says. "When I graduated, Renata and James had one son in college and another one other headed there. I knew they couldn't afford to help me with tuition, and I had no idea what I wanted to do with my life anyway. The military seemed like a good way to earn money for school while I figured out what I wanted to do. My mom wouldn't have wanted me to join the military, but I didn't have many other options."

"Why would she have opposed it?" I ask.

"My dad died in the Gulf War when I was a baby. I don't have any memory of him at all."

I reach across the table reflexively.

"I didn't know that was how you lost your dad." I squeeze his hand in mine. "You lost both your parents so young."

"I think that's part of why I liked the military. Our unit was sort of like a family," he says. "Everyone takes care of each other. You get close to other people when you're depending on them like that, doing something that feels like it matters. It's probably like teaching that way."

His brown eyes gaze into mine, and I tense up at the mention of my career. It is a job that feels important, and that's one reason why it's hard to walk away. Being a teacher has become a part of my identity, and I've been proud of doing something that's meaningful and noble.

"Teaching is definitely rewarding in a lot of ways," I say, deliberately being vague.

The waitress interrupts us to take away our empty plates.

"I have dessert for you, compliments of Savannah," she says.

We're both stuffed, but when we see the chocolate torte and slice of pecan pie, we can't resist having a taste.

"I have a food baby," I declare, patting my round stomach.

Seth looks at me curiously. "Do you want kids someday?"

His blunt questions don't even faze me anymore.

"Maybe? But I've been told I'm not maternal so..."

"Who told you that?"

My face heats with embarrassment. "Ironically, my mother."

His expression hardens, like this answer displeases him. "Do you think she's a good judge of character?"

"Not really."

"Then I wouldn't put any stock in what she thinks."

"Thanks," I say quietly. "Good advice."

After Seth pays for the meal, as promised, we head to a music venue nearby. Eli's band is performing blue grass, and I'm skeptical about whether or not I'll enjoy it, but it hardly matters. I have less than thirty-six hours left in North Carolina, and I want to spend all of them with Seth.

I could change my plans and stay a few more days, but that would put me in a bind. I need to give notice at my current job and clean my belongings out of my classroom. Then I can start working for LaTonya and pay my bills. I texted her yesterday to see if she needed me, and she responded with the word yes followed by about ten exclamation points. I wish I could share my career plans with Seth, but telling him about my job change seems like it would lead to a discussion of Dan, and I'm not ready to go there.

The band turns out to be excellent, and it's fun to see Eli up on stage, in his element. He's pretty fierce on the fiddle, and I can tell he's got quite a few female fans. Seth offers to buy me a beer, but it's still too soon after my last encounter with that particular beverage to want another one. The wine I had with dinner will be it for me this evening. He buys us both bottles of water, and we stand in the darkness of the theater soaking up the music together. The place is crowded, and Seth stands behind me so we have enough space. He's so tall that it's easy for him to see the stage over my head. When I lean back against him, he wraps his arms around my waist and every nerve ending in my body sparks at the places our bodies are touching. He's warm and strong and nothing that I ever thought I needed in my life, but as I rest against him, I can't help thinking that he fits me perfectly.

During the show's intermission, Seth and I wander outside, into the cool night air. There's a cement path that leads around the music venue to shops and restaurants. He takes my hand in his, and I move close enough so that our clothes touch as we walk.

We find a nice bench and sit down, enjoying the quiet after the noise of the music hall. I wouldn't mind going back inside and catching the rest of the show, but I'm just as happy out here, under the starry sky.

"When do you have to go back to work?" Seth asks, slipping an arm around me.

I rest my head on his shoulder for a few seconds before raising it and answering him.

"I'm not sure I'm going back to my teaching job," I say, smoothing out the skirt of my dress. I take a deep breath because it's time to put on my big girl panties and tell him the truth. Better that he hear it from me than Dad or Renata. "In fact, I'm definitely not going back to it. I'm quitting."

"You're quitting your job?" He pivots his body to look at me with a baffled expression.

"I'm going to work at my friend's catering company," I say, not wanting him to think I'm quitting my job so I can do something crazy like move down here to be with him. "I can run events for her and make enough money to live on for a while, until I figure out my next move."

"Why?" he asks.

It's a reasonable question, and one that has many answers. I start with the easiest one.

"I think I went into teaching because I didn't know what else to do. My dad was a teacher, and he always loved his job. Then it turned out I was good at it, so I thought it was the right career for me. I didn't realize it wasn't making me happy until Dad confronted me about it recently. He's afraid I'll become one of those teachers who only stays in it for the great pension, and he's right. I don't want to spend my life counting the days until retirement."

Saying this out loud feels good, like I've spoken a truth that I've felt for a long time, but been afraid to express out loud. It's okay for me to be good at teaching and still leave the profession. And if for some reason I find out it was a mistake, I can always go back to it later.

"Sounds like you've thought it through," he says, settling back next to me and placing his arm over my shoulders again.

And then my phone rings. And rings. And rings. If it's Dan, he has terrible fucking timing.

"Are you going to get that?" he asks, staring at my purse. "It could be your dad."

"Right." I move slowly enough so that the phone finishes ringing by the time I get to it.

There's one missed call, and it's from Hugh. I blow out a breath of relief that it isn't my married stalker and put the phone back in my purse.

"It was my friend Hugh," I say. "I'll call him back later."

"Why did you look panicked when your phone rang?" Seth asks suspiciously.

"I didn't," I say, avoiding his eyes.

Seth stands up and walks down the sidewalk a few feet, then turns and paces back to me.

"Maybe I'm being crazy, but if there's something you're not telling me..." He takes a breath, then says, "Do you have a boyfriend back in New York?"

I look up and see the hurt in his expression.

"No." I answer quickly, wanting to dispel that idea immediately. "It's nothing like that."

Seth sits back down next to me. "Then what is it? You can tell me. I know something is wrong. Is it the same reason you were hell bent on getting drunk the other night?"

I stare at my hands on my lap, trying to find the right words, but there's no way to sugarcoat what I have to tell him.

"Right before I came down here, I kissed a co-worker and someone saw us. We were drunk, and it was a huge mistake. I thought that was him calling me. He keeps calling and texting me, even though I told him to stop."

Seth closes his eyes for a few seconds before responding, and I know he's already guessed the rest.

"Why was it a huge mistake?"

"He's married," I say quietly.

The worst is when you tell someone something that you've been scared to say out loud, and they're silent. I wait a long time for Seth to speak, knowing that when he finds the words, they won't be what I want to hear.

"How could you do something like that?" he asks.

"It wasn't something I planned. It's something that happened—"

"This was a choice," he argues, standing up and pacing again. "It's not something that happened to you. Don't make excuses."

I'm self-aware enough to know that one of my worst character traits is my inability to admit when I'm wrong. When backed into a corner, I want to fight my way out rather than confess or apologize. If I do that with Seth, I'm definitely going to lose him.

"I understand what I did was wrong," I say, sounding calm even though my pulse is racing double time. "I feel totally sick about it, I do. And I ended it immediately. He's the one calling me, wanting me to go to therapy with him and his wife."

Seth's expression is fury and disgust.

"I don't want to hear this," he says, rubbing his face with his hands.

I stand up and face him. "So it would have been better if I'd lied to you?"

"It would have been better if you hadn't screwed around with a married man."

I throw my hands up in the air and say, "It was one kiss! Jesus, paint a scarlet letter on my shirt and put me in the stockades!"

Seth shakes his head and looks at me like he doesn't know who I am anymore. "How could I ever trust you after what you just told me."

I grab hold of his arms. "Seth, you can trust me exactly because I told you. I didn't want to lie to you about what was going on in my life."

Seth shakes my hands away and steps back from me. "Well, thanks for letting me know."

His posture and his voice tell me this conversation is over and so is our date.

SIXTEEN

My first two days back in New York are spent in bed. Other than the delivery people who bring my take-out meals, I don't see or speak to anyone. Dad and Renata know that something went terribly wrong on my date with Seth—something bad enough for me to leave a day early—but I haven't had the energy to explain everything to them yet. I even put off Hugh, telling him I'll call in a few days when I'm feeling better.

On day three, I force myself to get out of bed, shower and make an appointment with my principal. I arrive at his office looking like hell and resign from my job. After that, I call Barb and let her know, too. She's sympathetic at first, but when she realizes I'm not leaving because I have a terminal illness or a job in another state, she gets a little snippy. I understand it won't be a picnic finding someone to replace me a few weeks before the opening day of school, but there is no way I can make myself walk back into the classroom when I feel certain it's not where I'm supposed to be anymore.

I should feel elated after quitting, but, thanks to Seth,

my goddamn heart is broken, and I can't enjoy this new world of freedom and opportunity. This is what Isabelle was talking about when she predicted I was headed for a heartbreak that would rock my world. When I went to see her, I couldn't imagine that Seth would work his way far enough into my life to decimate me so completely.

After Seth and I got home from our ruined romantic evening, he walked me to the house without saying a word because apparently even when he's furious at someone, he's still a gentleman. The next morning, I got in my car and drove home, and it has been complete silence from him since then. Absolutely no contact. Leaving things on such a sour note has literally made me sick. I've had a headache, queasy stomach and little appetite for three days straight. I'm not contacting him, since there's nothing left for me to say. I'm not going to grovel when I haven't done anything wrong, at least nothing that directly affects him.

I want to settle things with Dan, too, but after resigning I need another day to hole up in my apartment before tackling that beast. Hugh refuses to be put off any longer and shows up at my door with a pint of chocolate ice cream.

"I know you're up there," he says into the speaker. "Time to come out of your cave."

He enters my apartment and appraises my dirty pajamas and the litter of take-out boxes surrounding me. His eyes darken. "What did this guy do to you?"

At the sight of him I begin crying, and we end up talking for three hours about my dad, Seth and the future of my career. He unloads about Raymond and the move to Chicago, which makes both of us so sad that we order and eat an entire pizza, as well as the ice cream, while watching my favorite movie, *Amelie*. That movie always makes me emotional, but I don't usually need an entire box of tissues to get through it. I tell myself it's cathartic crying. I'm letting go of all my feelings for Seth, purging them so they can't hurt me anymore.

I know it won't be that simple though. The feelings I have for him aren't going away any time soon. We were starting something that felt so right, and it crashed and burned just as quickly as it began. I can't imagine feeling this way about anyone else. Hell, I can't imagine dating, period. The relationship hiatus is back in session.

FOR MY MEETING WITH DAN, I choose a coffee shop near my place so there's no danger of running into one of his neighbors or friends. When he arrives, I'm already there waiting for him. We have that awkward moment where I don't want to get up to hug him, but shaking hands is too weirdly formal. In the end, I stay seated and give him a little wave. He orders a coffee at the counter then takes the seat across from me, and I note that he has showered and dressed in fresh clothing, which makes me nervous. I purposely didn't wash my hair or wear mascara, and here he is in a J-Crew outfit that his wife probably bought for him.

"How was your vacation?" he asks.

I can't bear to do the small talk thing so I launch right into my big news.

"I quit my job." I fully expect the stunned look that I receive. "Not because of you. I realized that I want to do something other than teach. I'm going to find a new career that's a better fit."

"You expect me to believe that?" he says, leaning across the table towards me.

His quirky choice of glasses and close-cropped salt and

pepper hair totally did it for me at one time, but now I feel nothing when I look at him. At first I can't understand how my libido changed its mind in a few weeks time, and then I realize I'm comparing him to Seth. That's why I find him lacking now. There's nothing wrong with Dan—he hasn't changed, but I have. I went and fell in love with a broad-shouldered, pigheaded Southern boy who broke my heart.

"I don't care if you believe it or not, it's the truth," I say. "And it's best for you, too, so you should be thanking me. This way you can tell your wife I won't be anywhere in your orbit, and you guys can continue working things out."

Dan frowns and grips his coffee mug with two hands. "I don't think Nicky and I are going to make it as a couple."

My heart lurches. "I thought you were going to counseling?"

He takes a sip of his coffee before answering, and fear rises in me. I'm not only concerned for Dan and Nicky; I'm worried about me, too. I don't want the demise of their relationship on my conscience for the rest of my life.

"We are, once a week. It's not helping much though. Mostly Nicky talks about how angry she is at me for the whole hour, and I'm not allowed to respond. Then we get homework like, stare into each other's eyes for eight minutes every night." He uses a goofy voice when he's explaining the assignment to suggest he thinks it's bunk. "I'm pretty sure the whole time Nicky is looking into my eyes she's thinking I'm a total asshole who has wrecked our marriage."

"You should hang in there though, maybe try a new therapist," I say, thinking how this is the crackpot counselor who suggested I come to their therapy session.

"I miss you, Andie," Dan says fervently, looking at my hand on the table like he wants to grab it, but knows he shouldn't.

I pull my hands onto my lap and link them together. I've prepared a few words for Dan, and it's time to deliver them.

"I get it, you want someone new so you can see lacy underwear again, not the stained, worn-out granny panties your wife probably wears during her period. News flash: we all have that underwear. You just won't see it until we're in a committed relationship with you. You've never had to buy me tampons or see me clip my toenails, that's why the fantasy of me is so enticing."

"That's not true."

"It is! You're obsessing about me because you're bored with real life. Guess what? I'm real, too, and if you were with me, you'd find that out eventually."

Dan covers his face with both hands. When he takes them away, he looks like he has aged five years.

"My wife doesn't even take her clothes off during sex anymore. She's so tired, it's just, 'let's get this over with as fast as possible so I can go to sleep.' There's nothing there. We're just co-parents who happen to share a bed at this point."

"I think that's monogamy, Dan, and parenting, from what people tell me. It gets boring. You're both exhausted. You have to actually make an effort. What have you done to get her excited for sexy times?" I hold up my hand to stop him, realizing we've wandered into inappropriate territory again. "Wait, don't tell me. I don't want to know. All I'm going to say is that I hope you and your wife can work things out."

"Come on," he says, "you can't deny we have amazing chemistry."

I did think that about Dan at one time. Compared to the guys I met in bars, he seemed fantastic. He was cute, funny and grounded, and I remember wishing I'd met him when he was single. All those feelings seem like a lifetime ago.

"I'm sure you and your wife had great chemistry when you first met," I say. "You can work on getting that back. This thing with me? It isn't going to happen."

Even though everything I've said has pointed in this direction, Dan looks shocked when I get up from the table.

"You're seriously going? This is it?"

"This is it, my friend. I wish you the very best, but please do not contact me again."

Dan stands up then, too, seeming shaken. "Can I at least give you a hug?"

"I think a handshake is more appropriate."

I extend my hand, and he takes it in his. Dan's hand is so much smaller and softer than Seth's, and there's a pain in my chest at the thought of never touching Seth again. I have to expunge that thought from my mind before I start crying. I don't want Dan to think all these feelings are for him.

"Goodbye, Dan." I force a cheery smile.

I squeeze his hand then pull away, hoping this is the last time we'll speak, but knowing that I'm totally going to have to block him on my phone.

PROSPECT PARK IS one of the best things about living in Brooklyn. Just like on any September Saturday, there are plenty of Brooklynites here, soaking up the last pleasant weather of the year before gray, bitter winter blows in. Today is particularly beautiful, and I'm a little sad that I have to go to work in a couple of hours.

Weekends are busy for caterers, and LaTonya has put me in charge of the wedding we're doing tonight. She was thrilled when I said I wanted to work for her full time, since her business has expanded exponentially. Now she can play more of an admin role and send me out to manage some of the events instead of overseeing every one of them herself. When I told her I wanted to start my own events business down at the goat farm, she said she'd mentor me so that I'd be ready to go out on my own whenever the time is right. The fact that Seth lives at the farm complicates my business plans, but I'm not going to let him stand in the way of my dreams.

It's still strange to sleep in on weekdays and work late into the night on weekends, but I'm enjoying the change. In my off hours, there's no grading, no planning, no meetings, and no parent contacts to make. My free time is really my own. Being busy on weekend nights leaves little time for dating or socializing in general, but that's fine for now. I'm focused on my career, and I'm saving more money than ever before. I still get in the occasional pool game on a weeknight, and Hugh's schedule is flexible so I see him much more frequently than I did when I was teaching. We're meeting today for a walk in the park and maybe a movie afterwards.

I walk through the grass, past frisbee games, soccer matches, and blankets full of people eating salads out of Tupperware containers. Hugh lives on the other side of the park from me in a brownstone where he and Raymond own the bottom floor. They're planning to sublet it when they move to Chicago in a few days. We've discovered a spot in the park that's about equidistant from both of our places, and we made it our meeting spot.

I know Hugh by his gait before I can see his face clearly. He kind of bounces slightly up and down on the balls of his feet which I find endearing. When we're about fifty yards apart, I throw my arms wide like Fraulein Maria on the mountaintop and gallop toward him. He mirrors me, and we meet in middle in the most gloriously goofy hug. I want to squeeze the life out of him, or at least his will to get in a car and drive to Chicago. They won't fly because Hugh is afraid of what the changes in air pressure will do to Norman the cat.

"Hey, sweetie," he says, crushing me in his arms.

Hugh is a champion hugger. It's one of the things I love about him. I'm the kind of hugger who bends to the will of the other person—if they give a tight squeeze I reciprocate in kind. If it's a tentative stiff-armed embrace with a little back patting at the end, I can do that, too. Whatever you give, you'll get. But not Hugh. He commits to the hug every time, with everybody.

"Wanna walk a bit?" I ask.

"Sure," he says. "Let's take a stroll around the park. Maybe we'll see the guy who sells lemon ices."

Hugh and I walk to the paved street that circles all of Prospect Park and link arms as we walk, leaving the inside lane to the runners, bikers and roller bladers whizzing past us. It's like old times, as if Dad weren't gone and Hugh weren't leaving. For a minute, I want to pretend that life is as it always was, not that it was perfect, but it was good. Then again, I'm excited for the new life ahead of me, the one that I'm carefully planning piece by piece. Being excited for the future feels like an accomplishment in itself.

"Are you ready for the big move?" I ask, determined to be happy for them.

I've done enough to prevent the people I love from moving on with their lives. This time I'm going to try being supportive instead. It can't end worse than my trip to North Carolina did. Four weeks I've been home, and still no word from Seth. Although I was tempted to have a rebound fling with someone random, I decided that wasn't what I needed. I'd only be comparing him to Seth anyway. I need time to forget his voice, his hands, his lips. It made me spitefully happy to hear from Dad that Seth seems—how did he put it?—kind of lost. Me, I've got laser focus on what I want, like I never have before. Let him be the sad puppy. I've moved on with my life.

"Yes and no," Hugh says in answer to my question. "It will be interesting to explore a new city, but I'm going to miss you terribly, and you know how I feel about New York."

"You're a diehard New Yorker," I say. "This won't be easy, but it might be fun. And you can always come back if it's awful."

Hugh puckers up his face. "I can come back, but will Raymond come with me? His job is his life."

I pat his arm. "You're his life, too. He'll want you to be happy."

Hugh sighs, and we both silently reflect for a moment.

"I was thinking that maybe we should give you Norman."

"Why?" I ask in surprise.

Hugh gives me a guilty smile. "I feel bad about taking him when I moved out. I didn't really give you a choice in the matter back then. Do you want to keep him for a while?"

Pain hits my chest with the force of bricks as it does any time something reminds me of Seth. He teased me for not having a pet, and now Hugh is presenting me with a chance to have one again. I slam the door on my memories of Seth. He's not going to ruin the little time I have left with Hugh.

"I think you should take him," I say. "You might be lonely at first. He's good company."

Hugh steers both of us around the spit wad a passing jogger has just hocked onto the ground in front of us. I love New York, but sometimes it's a minefield.

"Besides," I tell him, "I'll be moving eventually, too. Norman would be just as stressed out then."

Hugh looks over at me doubtfully. "Do you really think you'll move to North Carolina? You could always start your events company here in the city. Lord knows there's enough money floating around this town to keep every good caterer busy."

"I'm excited about my plan," I say. "I'll be like Ina Garten when she ventured out to the Hamptons to run a gourmet food store. She had zero experience running a small business and turned that one gourmet food store into an empire, so why not me?"

Hugh points out the lemon ice seller, and we stop to order two. In a few minutes, our mouths will be puckered and our tongues numb. We start walking again to the sound of a group of drummers in the park. It's hard not to fall into the rhythm of their beats.

"Believe me," Hugh says, picking up the thread of our conversation, "I have total confidence that you can become the event planning diva of central North Carolina. And you're one hundred percent right that the farm is the perfect venue for weddings."

"It is, right?"

When I told LaTonya about the farm, she had the same positive reaction. She also hooked me up with a friend of hers who runs an event space on Long Island so I could get more information on how to handle things like insurance and taxes.

"I'm just worried about your proximity to the lumberjack," Hugh says, refusing as he always does to use Seth's real name. I think it's his way of punishing Seth for hurting me. "You can say it's all good, and you don't care anymore, but I saw you a few days after you got home. You were..."

"A mess, I know."

I can't help but harbor resentment toward Seth for creating that kind of emotional turmoil inside me. He had no right to judge me so harshly, like he's never made a mistake in his life. At least I told him the truth, a fact I refuse to regret.

"I don't want you to get down there and be miserable living so close to him."

"I'm over him. Completely." I work hard to sound convincing. "He and I don't even have to interact that much, and when we do, it will be fine. I'm going to be so involved with my new business that I won't even have time for him."

Dad and Renata are completely supportive of my event planning business, but they initially expressed concern about the tension between Seth and me. I gave them the same speech I delivered to Hugh, about being completely over Seth. Every time I say it, I come closer to believing it.

Hugh suggests we stop and sit on a bench to finish our ices. The minute we're seated, three pigeons land at our feet and start strutting and bobbing. One of them takes an interest in something near my shoe, and I pick my feet up and tuck them under me, not wanting to be in contact with his nastiness. Scenes from the chicken coop incident flood my brain, and I'm about to tell Hugh the story before I remember that it ends with Seth saving me.

"I think I'm also being selfish," Hugh says. "If you leave New York, you won't be here when we come back to visit friends and family. I guess I can come down South."

The wince that follows this statement reveals his true feelings about that idea.

"It's not as backwards as you make it sound," I say, surprised that I'm feeling a little defensive. "I told you about Jenny and Luisa. There is an LGBTQ community south of the Mason Dixon line."

"I'll keep an open mind," he says, and he sounds determined to try.

"Besides, I'm not leaving right now. I need to save money first."

"And we can meet up in New York, once we're both settled in other places."

Deep sadness fills me at knowing that Hugh and I might never live in the same city again. I'm determined that we'll stay close, but it won't ever be quite the same. It's the end of an Andie-and-Hugh era.

"We'll come for a weekend and fill our bellies with tacos, pho and bagels," I say.

"We'll go for a walk in the park, then head to the baths to have a good sweat."

I set down my ice and reach over to take his hand in mine, like we're an old married couple on this bench with all the time to watch the world go by. I'm glad I'm moving toward something new and exciting. If I were staying here in the same old life without Hugh and Dad, it would be so much harder.

I look over at my very dearest friend in the world, and tears fill my eyes.

"I love you, Hugh."

He squeezes my hand tightly. "Love you, too, baby."

SEVENTEEN

In Brooklyn, not too many friends drop by unannounced and ring my doorbell. City dwellers also don't deal with many solicitors so when someone buzzes my apartment on a random Thursday afternoon, I assume Marly has forgotten her keys. Not wanting to let a rapist into the building, I press the intercom and ask who it is, just in case it's not her.

A rich, low voice says, "Hey, it's me, Seth."

I stare at the intercom for a few seconds like I've heard the voice of a creature from another planet. Seth is here in New York, standing in the tiny entrance space of my building. I've thought about what I'd do when we met again, but I pictured it happening at the farm. I was going to look amazing and possibly take a Xanax first.

"What do you want?" I ask, stalling for time as I glance over my shoulder. My front door is at the end of a long hallway, and I can't get a good look at my living room from here. Since I got back from the farm, I've been trying to keep the place neater, meaning there aren't dirty dishes on the couch or socks on the floor. It doesn't look like a former Marine's living quarters, but it's clean. There's nothing I can do about the fact that the plants make it look like the set of Little Shop of Horrors.

"I'd like to see you," he says, reminding me that he's still there, waiting for me to unlock the door.

His tone suggests that he isn't sure I'm going to let him come up here, and I'm thrilled that he's the one feeling vulnerable. Taking the stance of a runner on the blocks, I buzz him in and sprint down the hall toward the bathroom. I have less than a minute to brush my teeth and improve my hair before he arrives at my door. I'm still spitting toothpaste when he knocks. He can wait while I run a comb through my hair and apply lip color. I'm wearing my favorite Madewell sundress because I was planning to hit the flea market in Williamsburg later. I'm also having a terrific hair day. I make a steely-eyed assessment of myself in the mirror and whisper, "Eat your heart out, my little carnivore."

First, I open the door with the chain still hooked on it and peer out, as if I'm checking whether it's really him. Our eyes meet and the wind is knocked out of me. He's standing on the other side of my door, all delicious six foot three of him. I re-close the door gently, leaning my body against it and allowing myself to experience the full pleasure and pain of having him so close to me again. Then I pause, draw a deep breath and straighten my shoulders before unchaining the door and opening it all the way.

"Come in," I say, as formally as the Queen of England.

He enters and sets his backpack down on the floor, and I motion for him to walk down the dimly lit hallway, past the bedrooms and bathroom, to the main living area of the apartment.

There's nothing more awkward than this, Seth and I standing in my living room, staring at each other. He looks so out of place here in my apartment. It really is like an alien has landed in Brooklyn.

"You weren't kidding about the plants," he says, taking in the vegetation surrounding us.

"I know, it's crazy."

And then the conversation dies an ugly death. The silence stretches between us, and I wait for him to tell me why he's here.

"Have a seat," I say, finally. "Can I get you a drink?"

"A glass of water would be great."

He folds himself onto our low couch, nervously rubbing the knees of his jeans. He's wearing Levis and a white t-shirt with the blue Joyful Goat logo. Instead of his usual work boots, he has on Pumas I've never seen before.

My hand is trembling as I take the glass out of the kitchen cabinet and fill it with water. I clutch it tightly so that when I give it to him, my hand looks steady, or at least I hope it does.

"I'm sorry to barge in like this without telling you I was coming," he says, stopping to take a sip of water before placing the glass on the table.

His hand looks a bit shaky, too. I'm still standing, hovering near him, trying to decide whether to sit across the room in a chair or take a seat with him on the couch. I decide on the chair, since maximum distance from his body seems safest at this point.

"Why didn't you text me?" I ask, curling my legs under me.

Seth runs a hand through his dark hair. "I didn't know what to say. I guess I was also worried you'd tell me not to come."

"It's fine that you're here." I try to sound nonchalant, even though the mere act of looking him in the eyes is making my hands sweat. "But it would have been nice to be prepared."

As if I could ever be prepared to see Seth. I imagine that I can feel his heat from across the room, hear the heart beating inside his chest. My own heartbeat feels out of rhythm, like it might just bounce itself out of my body and soar across the room to find his to recalibrate itself. No one has ever had this kind of visceral effect on me, and it's more than a little frightening.

"So why are you here?" I ask.

He stops rubbing his knees and gazes at me intently. "To apologize."

"Okay," I say, crossing my arms over my chest. "Go for it."

He takes a deep breath before speaking.

"For the first two days after you left, I marinated in my self-righteous bullshit. I was so angry at you. Then by day three I started hearing what you said to me that night."

"It took three days?"

Seth grimaces. "My brain works slowly, but I eventually realized you were right. You were trying to tell me the truth so we could start with a clean slate. You were being brave, and I shouldn't have shut you down like that. I'm really sorry."

I start to speak, but first I have to clear away the lump that is now lodged in my throat.

"Thank you, I appreciate that."

I'm not sure if he's here to get closure or to create an opening for us, and for that reason, my walls aren't coming down any time soon.

Seth looks down at his hands. "Did anyone tell you that I'm divorced?"

"Renata mentioned it," I say, remembering his wedding

picture, and the way he looked so uncomfortable posing for the camera.

"My ex-wife, McAllister, wanted me to quit the military because she didn't like me being away so much. What I didn't know was that she was filling her time while I was away by cheating on me. So I quit the Marines, which I loved, and came home to her, and we were divorced within a year."

Even though I'm still pissed at him, I don't like hearing the sadness in his voice as he tells his story. What he went through in his marriage really sucked. Then again, I understand why he's telling me this now. He's equating me with his cheating wife. My hands are trembling from the emotions flooding through me.

"As I said before, I never would have cheated on you. Ever. So please don't compare me to your ex-wife. That's not fair."

"I know," he says. "I'm just trying to explain why I reacted the way I did. It wasn't about you and that married guy, not really. It was about me. What you told me set off a bunch of old anger, and I'm sorry for taking that out on you."

"I met with him when I got home," I say. Seth looks up at me, his eyes locking with mine. "I told him that he could never contact me again. That situation wasn't really about me either. He's in a bad place in his marriage and was using me as an excuse to run away from it."

"Has he gotten in touch with you since then?" he asks.

I shake my head. "No, but I also blocked his number on my phone, just in case he tried."

Seth leans back on the couch and sighs, and I can see how hard it was for him to tell me everything he did. It's been weighing on him these last six weeks in a way that it hasn't been on me. I thought things were completely done with us, but he was still trying to find a way to make them right.

"I talked to Renata about what happened between us," he says. It's mortifying, knowing that Renata has heard all the sordid details of my life, but I guess he had a right to tell her. She is his adopted mother, after all. "She said you'd talked to her about starting an events business at the farm."

"Eventually," I say, still keeping my cards close to my chest.

"I knew that if I waited until you came back to the farm, you might be completely over me, and it would be too late. So I decided to come up here now and ask you..." He pauses before saying, "Is it too late?"

The emotions rushing through me are so strong, it's like being caught in a riptide. Yes, I want to be with Seth, of course I do. It would be easy in some ways to let my feelings carry me back to him. But something in me is resisting that pull, and I know why. I don't want to risk being broken again.

"I'd like to say we can try this, but I'm not sure," I say. "You really hurt me."

He rubs his forehead with his hands, pain etched on his face, and I know that by breaking my heart, he hurt himself, too. It gives me a little comfort that I won't be the only one taking a risk if we get back together.

He inches forward to the edge of the couch. "Maybe I should go."

Misery seizes me at the thought of him walking out the door. "No, don't go."

Seth's face lights up with hope. "Can I stay for a few days so we can try to work this out?"

"A few days?" I say in disbelief. "You don't have to go back home for work?"

He finishes the rest of his water in one long gulp, like he's spent the earlier part of the day crossing Death Valley.

"I took some time off," he explains. "I had a lot of vacation time banked."

Knowing Seth's work ethic, he hasn't taken a vacation day in years. And then I remember something else.

"I thought you were saving up for money for when you go back to school? Did you spend that money to come up here?"

Seth brushes aside this concern with a wave of his hand. "Don't worry about that. I got a good deal on a plane ticket."

He spent part of his savings to come see me. This is all so surreal. In a minute, my alarm clock is going to ring and wake me from this dream.

"And I can sleep on the floor," he says firmly. "Or go stay with Trey. I need to spend some time with him while I'm here."

I look at him sitting there, all flawed and vulnerable and sexy. No one is perfect. Isn't that what I've been telling him? No one is perfect, but maybe two people can be perfect for each other.

I rise from the chair and cross the room, feeling Seth's eyes following me as I stride down the long hallway. Once I'm at the front door, I lift his backpack, which is quite heavy, and carry it to him. I set it at his feet with a thud.

"You're staying with me. Welcome to Brooklyn."

SETH SAYS he doesn't want me to change any of my plans for him so we spend the afternoon at the Williamsburg flea market and have a late lunch/early dinner at a little Peruvian restaurant that I love. Then we come home to wash the city sweat and grime off of us before going out again for the evening. I'm taking him to my local haunt so we can drink a beer, and I can beat him at pool again.

Seth disappears into the bathroom for his shower, and after a minute I hear the faucet turn on, just like old times. Once again, I'm picturing what's going on in there, with the soap and the water and Seth's body, but this time it's even more intimate. This is *my* bathroom in the privacy of my apartment. Dad and Renata aren't down the hall. There's not much to stop me from joining him and doing the work of his wash cloth except the fact that we still haven't resolved what's going on between us.

There's a jingle of keys at the door, and Marly scurries in, carrying a tiny plastic pot with undoubtedly some kind of seedling inside it. She doesn't greet me, but that's not unusual. Marly is much more adept at socializing with plant life than with humans.

She works nine to five at the Brooklyn Botanic Gardens, and now that I'm catering, we keep very different hours. If I'm lucky, I can go days without seeing her.

"Hey, Marly," I say, setting down the New Yorker magazine I haven't been reading while I listen to Seth shower. "I need to talk to you for a minute."

"Okay." She rearranges the pots on the sill so she can squeeze this one into the line-up.

I want to shout that there's no room left, but yelling at Marly is like shouting in a foreign language at a child. It would only frighten and confuse her, but wouldn't have the desired effect of stopping her from bringing more plants into the house.

"I have a friend visiting from out of town. He's going to stay for a few days."

She looks up at me briefly through her thick framed glasses, then nods briskly.

"No problem."

She presses a finger into the soil of every plant on the sill to test their moisture levels. Apparently satisfied, she forgoes the watering can and walks to the kitchen to retrieve the spray bottle. She's misting a hanging plant when Seth emerges from the bathroom in my striped towel holding a stick of men's deodorant. Crap. I'm busted.

"Seth," I say quickly, "This is my roommate, Marly."

"Oh, sorry, I didn't know anyone else was here," he says, taking a step backwards. "Hey, Marly."

When Seth emerges from a shower with a bare chest and wet slicked back hair, it's seriously like Poseidon has entered the room. Water is still glistening on his shoulders and the towel is low enough to see the delicate trail of hair leading into it. My first reaction is to wrap myself around him like a koala on a tree, which I refrain from doing, but Marly looks positively petrified. Her chin drops as she takes in every inch of him, her pale cheeks flushing with pink spots. She mumbles something unintelligible, then disappears into her bedroom, taking the spray bottle with her.

"Did I scare her?" he whispers, looking concerned.

"It's fine. She's just shy."

"Is this mine?" Seth asks, holding up the deodorant.

Now it's my turn to blush. When I was packing up my belongings at the farm, I realized Seth had left his deodorant in our shared bathroom. On impulse, I stuffed it into my makeup bag and brought it home with me. The spicy smell reminded me of him, and, in those first few pathetic days, I may have huffed it a few times like an addict. In my defense, I hadn't opened it in weeks, not since I got my shit together and started planning my future career. It was part of my Forget Seth project. Step one, only smell the stick once a day. Step two, only smell it once a week. Step three, stop smelling it altogether. Step four, throw it away. I'd only made it to step three, unfortunately.

I make my face as innocent as a Girl Scout's. "I accidentally put that in my makeup bag when I was packing to leave the farm."

Seth is watching me with raised eyebrows and an amused look on his face, the deodorant stick still raised in the air. I'm the worst liar.

"Okay, I took it on purpose. I'm a freak, I know."

He laughs and finally drops the arm holding the deodorant.

"The t-shirt you left at my place has been sitting on a chair in my bedroom." His smile straightens. "It's been torture looking at it every day, but I couldn't bring myself to mail it back to you."

"Well, that makes me feel like less of a loser. Thanks," I say, thinking about how I have his Metallica shirt folded under my pillow. I will need to move it before he sees it tonight because, please bitch, there is no way Seth is sleeping on my couch. Torturing him that way would also mean torturing myself, and I've suffered enough.

"Do you want to keep this?" he asks, waggling the deodorant in his hand.

"No," I say. "I think I'm good now. And I'd like my t-shirt back."

He smiles and walks past me to the bedroom. "I brought it with me. I washed and ironed it, of course."

His towel is so close that it brushes the couch as he passes me. He's lucky—or maybe unlucky—that I have the willpower not to whisk it right off his bottom.

SETH and I spend the evening shooting pool and hanging out at my favorite dive bar. We play three games, and I consider letting him beat me once, but decide against it. He's the kind of guy who can handle losing to a girl. I tell him winner buys our meal and treat him to tacos from the food truck on my block.

It's eleven o'clock by the time we walk home, but the heat of the day hasn't worn off completely. The weather isn't the reason I have goose bumps on my bare arms. I'm a ball of nervous excitement about what will happen when we get home.

Seth puts an arm around me. "Are you cold? It's still about eighty degrees out."

I lean into him, enjoying the snuggle. "No, I'm good."

We stop at a crosswalk and he turns to me and brushes my hair away from my cheek. I'm aching for him to kiss me, and when he leans down, I think this is the moment, but his lips only caress my forehead.

"I had a great time tonight," he says, gazing into my eyes.

"Me, too."

I know he's playing a waiting game. He wants to make sure I've forgiven him before he makes any real moves. Or maybe he just wants to see what happens when I lose my mind from sexual frustration.

This evening was even better than the special date we had in North Carolina—I mean the part before we got into a huge argument—because we're both completely relaxed and relieved just to be together again. And there's nothing standing between us now, no secrets or hidden agendas. I even told him about Officer Vega taking me home from

Ricky's. I thought he might piss his pants from laughing so hard.

When we get to the front door of my building, he stands behind me as I unlock the door, gently rubbing my shoulders.

"You ready to get cozy on that couch?" I tease him. "I'm not sure you can even stretch out full length on that thing. It's going to be a long night."

"It's fine," he says, as we enter the tiny foyer of my building where I'll need to use my key again to open the second door.

He's serious. Seth will scrunch his giant self onto that couch without even trying to finagle his way into my bed, which makes me want to kiss him even more. It's proof that he cares about me and hasn't come all this way just to get a piece of ass. He's here for me. All of me. I turn around to face him, and our chests are almost touching in this tiny cube of space that's filled with all our emotions and longing.

"I guess you could sleep in my bed with me," I say.

"Can I?" His strong hand slides over my cheekbone.

My breath catches in my throat, and I lean into his palm. I've enjoyed the build-up to this moment, but I can't wait any longer. My answer is a kiss, mouth slightly open, lips pressed gently against his. And I'm saying more than yes to the bed. I'm saying yes to us, yes to trying again. Yes, yes, yes.

Seth's lips are as soft and full as I remembered them to be, and he tastes like cinnamon sugar from the churro we shared after dinner. I wrap my arms around his neck and pull him closer, letting my tongue slide into his mouth. His response is something like a low growl, and he takes my hips in his huge mitts, cinching our bodies together as our kisses deepen. Tongues are tasting, teeth are nibbling, and hands are roaming. It's a ridiculous place for a make-out session, this little alcove with mailboxes on the wall and take-out flyers littering the floor, but neither of us seems to notice.

His hands run down my spine, creating shivers as they go, and then settle firmly on my backside. He pulls me even closer to him, and I arch my body toward his, letting him know that this is exactly what I want. What started out as a relatively chaste kiss quickly gets downright hot and dirty. We're in a slow grind, and, I've had all I can take without tearing his clothing off under these hideous fluorescent lights.

I push my hands against his chest and press away from him. "Upstairs. Now."

We gallop up the three flights to my apartment, and while I fumble to get my keys into the lock, he rests his hands on my hips and presses his mouth to my neck. His warm breath and soft lips have a detrimental effect on my motor skills, and my keys clatter to the floor. I can't help but lean my body back against his, his warmth spreading through me. His kisses become love bites as they travel down my neck, and instead of picking up my keys, I spin around and capture his lips with mine. We slide back into deep kisses, but all too soon, he pulls away.

"I wasn't done with that neck."

Picking up where he left off, he focuses on the nape of my neck then moves down to my clavicle. Right when I think I can't get any more stirred up, his mouth finds the little bit of cleavage at the top of my dress. I make a little tortured chirp in my throat and tell my legs to stop quavering.

His hands move up to cup my breasts and stroke my nipples over the thin material of my dress, and my back arches to encourage him. My own hands travel to where I imagine I'll find the button to his shorts, and that's when I realize we need to take things inside.

"Wait," I say in a wheezy voice. His hands freeze. "Get inside, now, before my neighbors see the very indecent things I'm going to do to you."

I squat down to retrieve the keys, unlock the door and fling it open.

"Yes, m'am." Seth strides through the open door first, for once forgoing his gentlemanly ways.

I slam the door behind us, and our hands and lips find each other again in the darkness of my apartment. There's a sliver of yellow light coming from my bedroom, beckoning us toward it. I tug him in that direction by the waistband, as we continue our furtive kissing. Even though my bedroom is only a few feet from the front door, he doesn't make it there without losing his shirt, which is the victim of my shaking, but determined hands.

I run my fingertips greedily across his thick shoulders and down his arms, feeling him shudder under my touch. As we kiss, I lean up against the doorjamb to my room, like I'm too lust drunk to stand up, and Seth fumbles with the bow on the outside of my mini-skirted wrap dress, letting it fall open. He whispers a swear word when he realizes there's another closure holding it in place, and slips his fingers inside the dress to undo it. I tremble with anticipation as he works, feeling like one of those ears of corn having its silks stripped away. He slides the dress off me completely, letting it fall to the floor in a puddle at my feet, then reaches to undo the front clasp on my bra. It snaps open, and I shake the lacy fabric from my shoulders, letting it spin to the floor. His eyes darken as he drinks me in.

"You are so sexy."

Instead of feeling shy or self-conscious, I feel emboldened by his appreciation of my body.

"So are you." I pivot, place my palms on his bare chest and push him through my bedroom doorway.

We careen into my room as we resume kissing, my hands groping for his remaining clothing. I hear him take in a sharp breath as I fumble to unbutton and unzip his shorts, pulling them to the floor, followed by his boxer briefs.

I take a moment to admire the parts of his body I've never seen, and I'm nearly speechless. The word "wow" comes out more like a breath.

Seth laughs. "Well, thanks, I think."

"It was a compliment," I assure him, trying to take another peek.

It's nearly impossible to see anything down below because his hands are in the way, sliding my panties down my legs. As soon as they're off, I'm in his arms and we tumble onto the bed, me on my back and him resting above me on his elbows. Suddenly, he slows down and gazes at me, a grin on his face. There's something both tender and wolfish in his eyes, and I try to pull him toward me. I want him inside me so badly that it's a need rather than a want at this point. I need that connection to him, to be one with him after all this time apart.

"Wait," he says, pulling back. "I want to make you feel amazing."

"Everything you're already doing is amazing," I say, running my hands over his chest.

He kisses my breasts softly, giving each one its turn, then flicks my nipples with his tongue. My hands fist into his hair, and I'm fairly sure my eyes are rolling back in my head with pleasure. When he begins biting me gently, I start begging, please, please, please, although I'm so out of my mind that I'm unable to explain what I need. It should be obvious from the fact that my lower half won't stop writhing on the bed.

My gyrations must clarify things for him because he trails his kisses down my abdomen, taking his time as he travels south. He skips over the obvious pleasure zone and moves down to my thighs, gently easing my legs apart as he kisses them. I never realized that my inner thighs were so sensitive to touch until Seth's mouth is on them. Every little kiss sets a fire.

Then he moves between my legs and finds my sweet spot, and his tongue strokes me gently as a satisfied murmur hums in his throat. He moves slowly, like he has all the time in the world to lap me up like a bowl of milk. Apparently, he wants me to die from prolonged arousal.

After spreading me wider, he slides his fingers inside me, and my body bucks in response.

I grab at the sheets, my words sounding like a moan. "Seth...yes..."

"This feels good?"

"Do. Not. Stop."

He touches me with one hand first, tenderly exploring to see what gets a response—a quickening of the breath, a gasp of pleasure. Just when I think it cannot get any better than this, he uses both of his hands, reaching places that I don't have names for. I let the delicious feelings he's creating build and build, until my legs are quivering and I'm calling out his name. I'm at the top of the wave, teetering on the crest and one more touch will push me over...

When release comes, I turn and curl into his chest, pulsing with waves of pleasure. He doesn't pull his hand away though. His fingers slide against my clit, and I have another climax and another. Finally, when I can't receive any more joy without pain, I push his hand away.

I keep my eyes closed for a few seconds, feeling the blood pumping through my body, all of my nerve endings on the surface of my skin. I'm warm and sated, and my brain, which typically spins like a hamster in a wheel, is completely calm. When I open my eyes, Seth is smiling down at me like it's his birthday, and he got the exact gift he wanted.

"You look so proud," I say with a giggle.

"Should I be?" he asks, although I'm pretty certain he knows the answer from my reactions.

"Oh my god." I squirrel my legs around on the bed. "Where did you learn to do that?"

"It's all the carpentry," he says. "I've gotten good with my hands."

"You certainly did," I say. "Holy cannoli. And even after that carpentry injury."

He's lying on his side, watching me, and I pick up his left hand and find the small white scar the saw left behind. I kiss it gently and then twine our hands together. I'm surprised he doesn't look more smug, but maybe he doesn't fully comprehend the miracles he can perform with those fingers. I've had orgasms before, but never like that, never multiple times or with such intensity. Seth took me to a place where I'd like to return as soon as possible.

He's in the perfect position for me to reciprocate now, and I let my hands run the length of him, eager to please. As I cup and stroke him, his head leans back slightly, and his eyes close.

"Oh my god," he says. "I've been dying for you to touch me. You have no idea."

He's hard and swollen already, but I want to bring him

to that same point of oblivion where he's taken me. I move slowly and deliberately, taking my cues from him as I learn his body and what he likes. He likes to play with my breasts as I touch him, and he definitely likes the feel of my tongue. He tastes salty and wet, and my excitement grows as I feel him losing control.

"I want to be inside you," he says in a tortured voice as I run my tongue along his shaft. "Andie, please..."

I like that he's the one begging now.

"Condom," I say, rolling over and reaching inside the drawer of my bedside table.

He's already on his back so I straddle his body, rip open the foil and roll the condom down, nice and slow. He pulses in my hand, and I can't help but smile. I like being in control of his pleasure. I glide him inside me and begin rocking as he reaches up to grasp my hips.

"You feel incredible," he tells me, his movements syncing with mine.

His body fits mine perfectly, just like I knew it would, and part of me wants to laugh and part wants to cry because I'm so happy and turned on and terrified that I'm falling in love with him. When I know he's close to climaxing, I move faster, increasing the friction between our two bodies.

Seth thrusts into me with more force and then comes, with a moan and a shudder. I lower myself onto his chest and wrap myself in his arms, sticky and naked and warm. I'm so relieved that he didn't hold back for too long, waiting for the mythical simultaneous orgasm to occur.

"That felt incredible," I say, wanting him to know that even when I'm not experiencing the big O, I'm enjoying every minute of his body moving with mine.

We lie there in each other's arms for a long time, not needing to say anything. He kisses my head and pulls me close to him, and I know I should be scared of the feelings surging through me. But I decide that joy is going to push fear into the gutter, at least for tonight while I lie in his arms.

"Long eyelashes are wasted on men," I say, examining every inch of his eyes, the amber flecks in the chocolate colored irises. Those long lashes and ungroomed brows. The little freckle next to his right eyelid. I'm going to need a long time to memorize all of him before he leaves. I'll tackle it like a mapping project. This is going to be the stuff I dredge up when I'm missing him. I'll lie in this bed, staring at the ceiling, trying to remember his eyes.

"I need to take a picture of you," he says, reading my mind. "I don't have any."

He runs his index finger over my lips like he's going to memorize me by touch.

"We took pictures today," I say. "At the flea market."

I got a great profile shot of him when he wasn't looking. I've already made sure it's the picture that will pop up on my phone when he texts or calls me.

"But I need one where I can really see your beautiful face." He cups my chin gently and brings his lips to mine. Then he skims my cheek with his fingers. "Your skin is so soft. How are you so soft?"

"Lack of hard work and exercise."

He laughs, and I try to memorize the sound. I could use the voice recorder on my phone to record his laughter, but that gets into creeper territory again.

"My hands are so rough," he says. "I feel bad touching you with them."

"No, I love your hands! Your hands do amazing work. If I could cut them off and keep them here, I would."

He knits his eyebrows together and rolls away from me. "Wow, thanks, that's not disturbing at all."

I pull him back towards me and bury my head in the nook of his arm.

"I'm sorry I have to work tomorrow evening."

He's on vacation, but my job can't be avoided entirely. I have catering gigs Friday and Saturday night, which means this was our only date night before he leaves. If I could get out of work, I would, but I don't want to leave LaTonya in the lurch.

"It's fine. Marly and I can hang and discuss the magical healing power of aloe plants," he says.

Seth's hot masculinity combined with plant talk? Marly definitely can't handle it.

"I think she would orgasm during that conversation." I'm only half kidding.

"I'll get together with Trey tomorrow night," Seth says. "I wish you could meet him."

"Maybe another time you're here," I say, not wanting to ruin the moment with too much serious talk about the future.

Why rock the bed when things are going so well?

"So I'm invited back?" he asks.

I pretend to mull it over. "Are you up for showering together in the morning?"

Seth goes very still for a moment. "Um, yes, definitely."

"Okay then," I say. "You're welcome back any time.

EIGHTEEN

"Brunch with my friends is a rite of passage," I tell Seth on Saturday morning as we lie in bed together.

He rubs his chin. "You're making me nervous."

We're having brunch with Hugh and Raymond in a little while, and Seth doesn't want to be late. He's been up for an hour and has already showered, but he came back to bed to wake me. My head is resting on his chest, feeling it rise and fall with his breaths.

"You'll eat lox and bagels for the first time," I say. "It will be great."

"What makes you think I've never had lox and bagels before?"

My mouth twists into an obnoxious smirk. "Just like I'd never had grits, my friend. It's regional cuisine. You may think you've eaten bagels before, but you haven't."

Seth reaches over and grabs his phone from my bedside table.

"You have to get up now. It's nearly eleven."

Instead of getting out of bed, I burrow more deeply into his chest. With the arm he has around me, he reaches down to pinch my bottom. It's a playful move, but it wakes up my libido.

"Come on, Andie. We're gonna be late."

"There's time for you to join me in the shower, if we hurry." I sling a leg over his body.

I've been dreaming of getting Seth into the shower with me for months, and Hugh can wait on us a little while. I'll send an apologetic text.

I can tell Seth is conflicted. He wants to fool around, but he's chafing at being late. I let my hand wander down his chest, below his waistline, and begin convincing him that I'm right. My hand slides inside his boxers and strokes him gently but firmly, and when I have him right where I want him, I take my hand away and get out of bed.

"What? Where are you going?" he protests.

"Don't think, just follow me."

I give him an alluring smile as I saunter out of the bedroom. To seal the deal, I pull my tank top over my head and toss it behind me.

"That's not fair!" he shouts, but I hear his feet hit the floor as he jumps out of bed.

And, yes, it's as hot, soapy and delicious as I'd imagined.

THE RESTAURANT HUGH and I chose for today is one of our favorites. Their pumpkin pancakes make my belly happy, and I have a feeling Seth will love their steak and egg on a bagel. They also serve the best bloody marys in Brooklyn.

Seth isn't the only one anxious about today's brunch. I really want Hugh to like Seth. I've never been this invested in him liking one of my boyfriends before, and I know he's concerned about Seth showing up out of the blue. He heard all about our argument last summer, but he didn't get to hear Seth's apology.

Hugh and Raymond stand when we get to the table and give me hugs, then shake hands with Seth. Ray's smile is genuine, but Hugh looks constipated.

"Nice to meet you," Seth says to Hugh. "I've heard a lot about you."

"All good, I hope," Hugh says.

Oh lord, his nostrils are already flaring.

"Definitely," Seth says.

"I've heard a lot about you, too." Hugh takes a seat at the table. "Not all good, unfortunately."

Yikes.

Seth doesn't flinch at Hugh's rudeness, but I'm mortified and mouth the word "stop" at him. I know Hugh is protective of me, but I had no idea he was going to come at Seth this way.

The waiter tells us the specials, and Seth and I both order a cup of coffee and a bloody mary. Hugh is already sipping a mimosa and eating the complimentary biscuits, and Raymond is nursing a giant cup of tea. After the waiter leaves, we peruse the brunch menu and fall into what could be considered a comfortable silence if I didn't sense Hugh seething across the table from us and feel Seth bouncing his knee.

I set down my menu. "I'm going to have the pancakes. How about you guys?"

Everyone shares his order and then there's more silence. I give Raymond a desperate look.

"Seth, is this your first time in New York?" Raymond asks.

"Yes, it is," Seth says.

Hugh mutters something under his breath that sounds like "Took you long enough to get here," but I can't be sure.

"Excuse me?" Seth says.

Hugh pulls a face and unrolls his napkin. "Nothing."

"I'm a direct person." Seth's voice is both patient and firm. "If there's something you need to say to me, let's get it out in the open."

"Fine." Hugh shakes out his napkin with a snap and places it on his lap. "This woman right here is someone special. She's the most loyal, generous, loving person you could ever have in your life. When you're down, she will lift you up. When you're being a dick, she will let you know. In short, she's fabulous. And I hope you realize how lucky you are to be with her. Because if you don't treasure her? If you hurt her again? You're going to have to answer to me. And I know I'm not built like a...a..."

"A lumberjack?" Seth offers.

There's a second of silence before Raymond and I bust out laughing. Hugh turns red, his mouth hanging open with no words coming out. Then he gives me the stink eye for revealing the nickname he uses for Seth.

Raymond pokes Hugh's arm. "You've been busted, sweetie."

"Sorry," Seth says, keeping a straight face, "go on."

"Right, well," Hugh says. "I might not be built like a lumberjack, but if you hurt her again, I will find a way to make your life hell."

Seth lifts his chin in acceptance. "Fair enough. But I promise that I don't have any intention of hurting Andie."

Hugh raises his eyebrows. "No intention of hurting her? That isn't exactly reassuring."

Seth looks a bit exasperated by Hugh at this point. "I want to make her happy. That's my intention."

I thump my hand on the table to get their attention. "What kind of patriarchal bullshit is this?" I look back and forth between Hugh and Seth. "There's only one person in charge of my happiness, and that's me. And I choose to be happy with Seth. And as much as I appreciate your concern, Hugh, you don't have to protect me. Seth didn't mean to hurt me, and don't forget that I hurt him, too. We've made up and we're moving on, the past is in the past. Okay?"

"Fine," Hugh says, picking up his champagne flute.

"I understand though," Seth tells him. "And I appreciate that you're looking out for your friend."

"My best friend," Hugh says. "At least she was until she told you about the lumberjack thing."

"Sorry." I try to hold back a smile.

The waiter delivers our bloody marys, and Raymond lifts his tea mug. "I think we should toast to new relationships and new adventures."

We all repeat his toast and clink glasses, and Hugh half-smiles at Seth. He's definitely thawing.

With the tension broken, we're able to order our food and move on to normal conversation. Seth charms them by answering their endless questions about saving lives as a paramedic and what it's like to be in the Marines. They goggle over the fact he built his own house (even though Hugh knew this fact) and lived for a month without a working shower.

"Don't let him brag about how rugged he is," I say. "He showered at Renata's place every morning I was there."

"Only after you came to stay," he says.

I blink at him, not comprehending. "What did you do before I got there? Stink?"

"No." He smiles sheepishly. "I have an outdoor shower.

It's just a little five-gallon solar bag that hangs from a tree outside the house. The sun heats the water during the day and then in the evening, you've got a shower."

"That sounds like my worst nightmare," Raymond says with a shudder. "No offense. I enjoy indoor plumbing."

"So why did you start using my bathroom to shower?" I ask.

Seth shrugs. "I enjoy showers with actual water pressure. Plus, I was curious about the Yankees fan with the smart mouth and the pretty legs."

"Oh, were you?" I say smugly.

We begin a staring contest that only ends when Hugh clears his throat loudly.

"You two need to get a room," he says. "Otherwise, Andie is going to leg hump you in this restaurant, and I'll never be able to show my face here again."

When Seth goes to the bathroom, Hugh and I take the opportunity to discuss him, of course, while Raymond finishes his egg white omelet in silence. Raymond may not shine like Hugh—he allows Hugh to take center stage, which is why they work as a couple—but he's a great judge of character and I value his well-reasoned opinions.

"So, Ray, what do you think of Seth?" I lean forward in my seat, anxious to hear his response.

Raymond wipes the corners of his already clean mouth before saying, "He's the opposite of the type of guy I thought you'd end up with, so that's a relief."

I feign anger and toss my napkin at him. "What do you mean by that?"

Raymond dodges my torpedo and smiles. "You know, he seems emotionally available and genuinely cares about you. And he wants to get to know us. These are not things we've seen before in the guys you bring around. Your last boyfriend re-introduced himself to me every time we met because he never remembered me. It was exhausting."

"Okay, I get it," I say.

"And before that guy there was the impotent poet," Hugh chimes in. "He was a winner."

"Enough!" I shush them as Seth approaches the table.

He slides beside me in the booth and kisses me lightly on the temple. I can feel Hugh and Raymond swoon from across the table. I'm that person in the happy couple, and it's a bizarre sensation, like I'm in a movie playing the part of "happy girlfriend in diner." The problem is that the movie ends when Seth goes home tomorrow.

When we leave the restaurant, Hugh pulls me aside near the hostess stand and hisses in my ear, "He's actually pretty awesome. Do not screw this one up."

"Thanks," I whisper back. "I appreciate your confidence in me."

"Also," he says sheepishly, "can he come by later and fix our bathroom sink?"

I snort, but consider it. Watching Seth slide under the sink, his hands gripping the countertop above him, ab muscles rippling with the effort, would be a delight. Everyone has their kink. I get off on watching Seth repair things.

WORK RUNS late on Saturday night, and it's almost two in the morning by the time I get home. I try not to wake Seth up, but I desperately need a shower. At the end of a long night of catering, I smell like sweat, cooked food and booze.

After drying my hair and getting into my pajamas, I

tiptoe into the bedroom. Despite my efforts to be silent, Seth hears me as I climb into bed, and he slips an arm around me. He pulls me against his warm chest, and I experience another first: falling asleep in someone's arms.

Seth and I agree on Sunday morning that the best way to use our time before he leaves for the airport is to relax in my apartment. In other words, we will spend most of the day in bed, with breaks for food and water. We'll go sightseeing next time he's in town.

Around one o'clock, Seth makes us a pile of french toast, the only thing he can whip up with the ingredients in my kitchen. I pretend not to notice that we only have a little more than an hour left together before he calls a car to take him to the airport. Time seems to be moving at double speed today. Every time I look at the clock, I think it can't possibly be that late.

Seth is only wearing shorts, and I'm in my underwear and the Metallica shirt, which he knows he isn't getting back. There's no point in pretending I'm a normal person who doesn't steal his stuff. That train has left the station.

"Do you have apple sauce?" he asks, rifling through my cupboards.

"Why? Do you put that in french toast?"

Seth pauses in his search and looks at me like I'm insane. "No, you put it on top of french toast."

I look at him quizzically. "Who does that?"

"My mom did." He pulls an unopened bottle of syrup off the shelf. "But it looks like this will have to do."

The syrup belongs to Marly, like the eggs he just used, but I'll replace it all later today. Between what I eat at work and the meals I eat out with Hugh and my other friends, I cook at home even less than I did when I was teaching.

I set out forks and napkins for us on the place mats I've

put down on the table. I dug the place mats out of my closet yesterday to be classy like Renata. This week I'm going to buy myself a set of cloth napkins so I can really feel like a grown-up.

"Was your mom a good cook?" I ask.

The butter hisses as Seth slides it into the pan and expertly coats the surface by tilting his wrist from side to side. Then he places the battered bread on top of it.

"She made simple things, comfort food. All the stuff kids like to eat: french toast, grilled cheese, chicken and dumplings."

"What was she like?"

Seth watches the toast cooking for a few seconds before he answers. I imagine that he wants to get this answer just right. It's probably an impossible task, summing up the essence of someone who was that important to you.

"She was a strong person. Very opinionated, but also openminded, if that makes sense. She was honest, almost brutally so when it came to me. She didn't let me get away with anything."

He flips each slice of toast, carefully tucking them into the only frying pan I own, which is pathetically small and warped on the bottom.

"Is it okay, me asking questions about her?"

"Yeah, of course, " he says. "She was my favorite person in the world so I love talking about her. I wish you could have met her. She would have loved you."

I squeeze past him in the tiny kitchen so I can get us glasses of water. It's tempting to kiss his neck, but I know we'd end up having sex here against the counter, and the toast would burn in the pan. And if we have any more sex without eating first, I'm pretty sure I'll slip into unconsciousness.

A minute later, he shuts off the gas burner and announces that our food is ready. I bring the water glasses to the table and sit down to wait for him, trying to record this moment like all the others we've shared over the last few days. I'm building a repository of Seth memories that will sustain me for months. They have to.

"This is my specialty," he says, sliding two pieces of golden brown toast onto my plate.

I cut both slices of bread with my fork, salivating at the delicious smell.

"That's what guys usually say when they can only cook one thing well."

"I can cook other things." He sets the syrup down in front of me. "Lasagna, chili, meatloaf. I'll have to start working on turning those into vegetarian specialties."

"I'm starving," I say between bites. "I feel like I could chase this with a stack of waffles and still be hungry."

Seth fills his own plate and joins me at the kitchen table.

"We burned a lot of calories this morning," he says with a grin.

I swallow a huge mouthful of toast before saying, "It was much more fun than running."

"I thought you liked running?"

I nod and consider whether that's true. "I like that it burns my excess energy and helps me fall asleep at night, but I'm not sure I love doing it."

"I'm happy to help you burn as much energy as you need," he says before taking a huge bite of toast.

The food that tasted so good a moment ago feels heavy in my stomach.

"Right, but you'll be gone in an hour. So it's back to running tomorrow."

I strive to sound lighthearted, but the words don't come

out that way. Seth keeps eating, but his expression darkens. I'm dying to know what he's thinking because I'm fearing the worst. Instead of waiting for him to say it, I do it myself.

"I just want you to know that I don't expect a big commitment," I say with all the feigned nonchalance of a terrible liar. "The last few days have been amazing, but long-distance monogamy is probably unrealistic, right?"

"What?" Seth's fork stops halfway to his mouth. "You're okay with me sleeping with other people?"

I imagine him with another woman, like his friend Piper or Stephanie the P.A, and my reaction is visceral. My face contorts, and there's a gagging sensation in my throat. It's excruciating to think about him putting his hands on someone else. Some other woman getting the best sex of her life.

"No, that's horrifying."

"Exactly. That's how I feel about you seeing someone else."

"So what do we do?"

He watches me intently as I squirm into a cross-legged position on my chair. I've never felt more naked than I do right now.

"You're scared," he says.

"What am I scared of?" I ask in a quiet voice while I poke at my food.

"You're scared to fall in love with me because you think you might get hurt."

It's suddenly so quiet in my apartment that we can hear the conversation between two people outside on the street. Granted, they're New Yorkers so they're shouting.

"Aren't you scared?" I ask.

"Yes, of course. I'm scared shitless, but I'm not going to let it stop me from loving you."

Seth loves me. It's not just some fantasy I created in my weird little mind. He. Loves. Me. Wait, did he say he loved me or he wouldn't stop himself from falling in love with me? There's no way to ask now. There's also no way to stop my inner monologue.

"But what if we aren't happy?" I ask, doing my best devil's advocate routine. "Sometimes love ends in terrible heartbreak."

He picks up my hand and rubs his thumb in circles on my palm. The movement has some kind of hypnotic effect on me. I'm completely susceptible to whatever he says next.

"Yeah, sometimes it ends badly, like my marriage and your parents' marriage. But sometimes people find each other, like Herb and Renata did, and it's worth everything you've been through because now you've found your person, the one who feels like home."

"You've been listening to too many country songs."

He laughs and drops my hand. "Stop making jokes when I'm trying to be romantic. You'll bruise my fragile male ego."

His ego is anything but fragile, and it's one of the things I love about him. He knows who he is and what he wants. And he wants me.

"After we eat, you need to shower," I say. "You can't get on the plane smelling like sex. The ovulating women on that flight are going to smell your pheromones and go wild. It will be chaos, and you'll accidentally impregnate someone."

Seth's eyes lock with mine, and I can't look away. He's not going to let me joke my way out of this situation, and I know it.

"I only want you," he says. "If you don't want to do this though, if your heart isn't in it, please say so now."

Everything Isabelle predicted has come to pass: upheaval, heartbreak, transformation. Seth and I aren't the people we were at the beginning of last summer. She promised that after the pain, love would come again, and here it is, daring me to take a chance. I'd be a fool to let it go.

I scoot my chair over to his, take his hand in mine and press it to my heart. The warmth of his touch blossoms inside me.

"This thing?" I say, and we both listen with our hands to the beating sensation under my ribcage that always increases when I'm near him. "It's already yours."

EPILOGUE

As far as all the guests at this wedding know, everything is going according to plan. They aren't aware that two hours ago, Seth and I were chasing goats around the woods after Rapunzel decided to spring her friends from their fenced-in grazing area. She pried the lock open with her teeth, a trick that she's performed several times this year, and set everyone free. I wasn't happy that she chose today for a break-out, but I've learned in the three months I've been living down here that goats aren't rule followers. We captured all of the runaways, except for one. Princess Kate is still loose somewhere on the property and, according to Renata, will come home when she gets hungry enough.

I appraise the wedding venue from the viewpoint of a guest and like what I see. The white tent is set up for dinner and dancing, and chairs have been placed in neat rows under the oak tree for the ceremony. Renata asked the florist to decorate using ivory hydrangeas, blush chrysanthemums and pink alstroemerias, and the displays look stunning. There are servers handing out appetizers and mint juleps, and we have a separate table where a bartender is serving water, sweet tea, wine and beer. I take a moment and bask in the beauty of this day that I've helped plan and deliver as a gift to my dad and his lovely bride.

At the moment, even the weather is cooperating during what has been a temperamental North Carolina spring. The temperature hovered near eighty earlier today, and I worried that the late afternoon sun would be unpleasantly strong. Fortunately, a few puffy clouds rolled in and we've got the perfect blue sky and dappled sunlight for the ceremony.

My father walks over to where I'm standing and hands me a mint julep. "You can relax now. Everything looks amazing. And have you tried the food? The shrimp is incredible."

Hearing his words, I sigh with relief. "I'm so glad."

I take a tiny sip of my drink, enjoying the freshness of the mint combined with the bite of the bourbon.

I'll be nursing this one for a while, since the wedding planner needs to stay sober.

"I've never seen that dress before," Dad says. "You look great."

I'm wearing my favorite vintage dress tonight, a cream-colored lace sheath that reaches just above my knees. The color is acceptable, since the bride, who happens to be my new stepmother, has decided not to wear white. She's a vision in emerald green silk, and no one will be upstaging her tonight.

"You look pretty good yourself," I say, admiring the new suit Renata helped him select.

"How can we thank you enough for planning all of this?"

I smile and kiss his cheek. "You did me a favor. I needed the experience. Now go and have fun."

Dad's friends Victor and Mitch, who are standing

with Renata, wave him over. Undoubtedly, they're telling her some embarrassing story from his past, since she's laughing so hard that she's wiping away tears. I watch as he joins their group and slips his arm around her shoulder.

Seth appears at my side with a glass of ice water that I accept with gratitude, trading him my mint julep.

"It's strong," I say, "and I have an empty stomach right now. You can drink it."

He takes a sip and blinks in surprise. "Dang, this is gonna be a fun wedding."

"Not that fun, I hope. I don't want to become known as the wedding planner who gets everyone trashed at her events."

"We'll have to call Officer Vega to drive people home," he says, giving me a wink.

"Shhh," I warn him. "No one knows about that except you."

"And Frank and Shirley. And probably half the other people in town."

I shut my eyes in horror. "Please don't say that. I like living in my fantasy world."

"Have you eaten anything today?" he asks, gently brushing my hair away from my face. "They're passing around mushrooms and some other vegetarian pastry thing. You're going to get low blood sugar soon."

"Okay, Nurse Seth," I tease him. "I'll get something in a minute."

He puts his finger on my neck like he's checking my pulse, and as always his touch makes it race faster.

"I'll give you a full exam later," he says, running his eyes down my body. "Right now, let's get you some food."

Seth and I pluck appetizers from the tray of a server

who passes by, and right as we eat them, the photographer takes a candid shot of us.

"Great," Seth mumbles through the cheese in his mouth. "That's one for the photo album."

"We should get started with the ceremony soon," I say after we finish eating. "I'll tell Herb and Renata, if you want to tell the minister."

I start to walk away, but Seth guides me back to him, taking my face in his hands.

"You did a great job. It's a beautiful party."

He kisses me softly, and I feel the stress ebbing out of my shoulders. We haven't even been together a year yet, but I know that it won't be too long before I'm planning our wedding here at the farm. It's amazing that this thought doesn't terrify me. In fact, I can't wait to put a ring on that hand and call him mine.

We gather the wedding party and ask them to get in their places while the guests take their seats. Renata has chosen to have her friend sing an acoustic version of Alicia Keys' "No One" as she walks down the aisle. Eli will be accompanying her on fiddle. Seth and I will be first in the procession, followed by Harmony and Michael, then Renata and Trey. We don't have official roles, but she and Dad wanted all of us to stand up with them.

When the music begins, emotion wells in my chest. She's made such an appropriate song choice. For Dad, there is no one but Renata. It's been a long and winding road to this point, and they're finally joining their lives—all of our lives—together forever.

I hold onto Seth's arm as we walk past friends and family, catching Hugh's eye as we pass by him and Raymond. We take our places near the minister and my father. Dad beams at us with tears in his eyes that threaten to spill onto his cheeks. Michael and Harmony join us next. She looks like a little princess today in her lilac dress with a sparkly tulle skirt. Then Trey escorts his mother down the aisle. If anyone can radiate warmth and joy, it's Renata. She's incandescent. Dad's tears are now flowing, and he's not the only one. I'm barely holding it together myself.

As a family, we surround the happy couple with our love, and it's all I can do not to bawl my eyes out as they exchange the vows they've written. Seth squeezes my hand from time to time, letting me know that he's there, feeling it, too. Just as Dad slips the ring onto Renata's finger, there's a commotion among the guests, and I turn to see Princess Kate casually traipsing down the aisle. Renata and I gasp as she pauses to gnaw on a floral arrangement.

Hoots of laughter ring out as Harmony races toward the goat, who has a hydrangea hanging out of her mouth. When she's within inches, Princess Kate sprints off in the opposite direction. Harmony is fast though, and after a bit of chasing and some help from a few of Renata's nephews, she's able to grab the goat's collar.

Tears of laughter stream down Dad and Renata's faces as they watch the events playing out before them.

"I got her!" Harmony yells proudly, the goat tight in her hands.

"Perfect," Renata says.

"Can I pronounce you husband and wife now?" the minister asks.

Dad and Renata give him an enthusiastic yes, and the minister makes it official and indicates that it's an appropriate time for them to kiss. Applause and shouts of joy fill the air when Dad plants a smooch on Renata's lips. I'm smiling so hard my face hurts.

We walk back down the aisle, this time bouncing along to Dad's song selection, Queen's "You're My Best Friend."

THE RECEPTION RUNS MORE SMOOTHLY than the ceremony, and is just as fun. The food is plentiful and delicious, the music is just cheesy enough to get everyone on the dance floor, and Michael's toast makes me cry again. I couldn't have asked for a more perfect day for Renata and Dad. When Seth asks me for a slow dance, I melt into his arms with exhaustion and relief.

"I'm glad you can laugh about Kate crashing the ceremony," he whispers into my ear as we sway together.

I shrug and tuck my head against his shoulder. "What kind of wedding at a goat farm doesn't include goats?"

"Hopefully ours."

I tip my head up and look at him. "I'm okay with a goat attending, but absolutely no chickens."

"Got it," he says. "No chickens. And I think we should make it official."

I blink at him. "What?"

He takes my elbow and pulls me to the side of the tent, a few steps away from our family.

"I can't wait anymore. I know it's probably too soon, but it feels right."

He pulls a small velvet box out of his pocket and opens it. Inside is a beautiful antique platinum ring with a delicate diamond in the center.

"This belonged to my mother and her grandmother before her. It's not much, but I always thought it was pretty. And if you prefer we can get the diamond reset into a band you like better. The point is—" He clears his throat. "This ring is a part of who I am, and I've never offered it to anyone before. And I know you want to focus on your business right now, and I just started school. But I want us to plan our lives together because I am completely, now and forever, in love with you. So, Andie Fiarello, will you marry me?"

And it's the simplest, clearest decision I've ever made in my life. I make him wait for it though, until after I kiss those soft lips.

"Yes. One hundred percent, yes."

BONUS CONTENT

I created a chapter of *Homewrecker* from Seth's point of view and would love to share it with you. Please visit my website jillwestwood.com to join my newsletter and receive chapter 15.5, told from Seth's perspective during the time he and Andie were apart.

ACKNOWLEDGMENTS

There are many people who helped me through the writing and publishing of this book:

Sue (also known as Suzy-Q and Q-ster), in seventh grade you became the very first reader of my romantic stories. They were written on notebook paper and passed from hand to hand. Somehow these stories convinced you that someday I would write a novel. Your belief in me gave me the first seeds of belief in myself.

Nicole, my soul sister, critique partner, and life support system, there's no way I could have written this book without your editorial guidance and wisdom, not to mention your friendship and faith in me. Even oceans can't keep us apart! I am so glad we are on this writing journey together.

Christine, big sister and lifelong bestie, thank you for reading this book in its infancy and telling me that you loved it. Your belief in this book is one reason I had the confidence to share it with the world.

I have the best friends a woman could ever ask for: Anna, Steph, Cindy and Allison: thank you for supporting my dreams! It's so comforting to know that you have my back, and I've got yours.

Michelle, your honest feedback and insights helped me to take a scalpel and sometimes an axe to this manuscript. Thank you so much for sharing your skills with me and for telling me to push forward when I was losing steam.

Mom, you made me a reader and a writer. Many of my early memories involve our public library and staying up at night to read under the covers with a flashlight. Thank you so much for helping with childcare duties so I could write this book.

James at Goonwrite.com, I love my beautiful book cover and appreciate your talent and patience. I can't wait to see what you come up with for the next Nasty Woman.

Finally, to Richard, my amazing husband, I cannot thank you enough for supporting and encouraging me throughout the writing of this book. Fictional men cannot compete with you. You're my real-life "happily ever after."

ABOUT THE AUTHOR

Jill is a native New Yorker who now lives in North Carolina with her family. She has been writing stories both in her head and on paper for her entire life. After forty-seven years and several completed manuscripts, she finally published one. Her Nasty Woman series was born from a desire to create contemporary love stories that empower women sexually, are body positive, include mutual consent and celebrate diversity. She's proud to call herself an author of romantic feminist fiction. She loves to hear from fans. You can visit her website at jillwestwood.com.

Made in the USA
Coppell, TX
07 November 2021